RAIN CITY
LIGHTS

AUTHOR'S NOTE

Rain City Lights portrays subjects that may be sensitive to some readers. These subjects include addiction and sexual violence, and I have attempted to write about these issues in a way that is not gratuitous, but with honesty and understanding.

RAIN CITY LIGHTS

a novel

MARISSA HARRISON

PINE CITY PRESS

The song "Wayfaring Stranger" has been reimagined to further plot development, and was published in Cabin and Plantation Songs - Third Edition, 1900.

The song "In the Pines" has been reimagined to further plot development. The song originated from two folk songs, "In the Pines" and "The Longest Train," authorship unknown. One of the earliest recordings was by Dock Walsh in 1926, and the song has since been recorded by hundreds of talented artists.

First Pine City Press paperback edition February 2021

Cover design by Chris Jordan, Shipwreck Design

Manufactured in the United States of America

ISBN 978-1-7344357-1-9
ISBN 978-1-7344357-2-6 (ebook)
ISBN 978-1-7344357-0-2 (hardcover)

For my mother

PROLOGUE

Christmas Eve, 1972

THE RAIN PELT so hard it sprang up from the porch like bullets. The detective removed his hat, water dripping down his face, hiding tears but for his red-rimmed eyes. He couldn't help crying, after what he had seen and for the scene before him. The Christmas tree lit with multi-colored lights and draped with silver tinsel. The cookies on the mantle. Frank Sinatra crooning "Jingle Bells" from the record player. And a small boy wearing red pajamas. These were the reasons the detective wiped his nose like a baby, and steeled himself to bear the bad news.

MIKAEL SASHA COEN already knew why the detective had come. Someone once said he could smile with only his big, blue eyes. He tried this by focusing his eyes hard into the sadness that seemed to hunch the detective's shoulders. He curved the corners of his mouth upward just a little. It was enough to make the detective smile back.

"He should leave the room," the detective said.

Daan shook his head. "The sooner he gets used to hearing bad news, the better."

The detective scratched his sideburn.

"Mr. Coen, I'm so sorry to say this, tonight of all nights. But there's been an accident. Your wife's car went over the Ballard Bridge. She didn't make it."

Daan Coen keeled over and keened, a sound more piercing than nails dragged against a chalkboard. The detective described what happened. The grates were slick. His wife had been speeding to beat the drawbridge, raised to let a party yacht into the Fremont canal. She skidded and lost control. Daan sobbed and asked the Lord why. But Mikael thought he knew that, too.

After a moment, Daan asked,

"But wouldn't she have seen the warning lights? Wouldn't the gate have dropped? I don't understand how this could happen."

The detective pursed his lips. He spoke in the way adults sometimes did that made Mikael feel as if he'd been naughty.

"Not here," the detective said.

Mikael watched from the porch as Daan left to identify the body. He'd promised to stay with one of the neighbors that lived in the apartment units of The Bridgewater. As Mikael turned, he heard a chattering sound, and it drew his attention to the stoop next door. A young girl sat with her head pushed between her knees, her body rocking back and forth and her arms enclosing her shivering shins.

"What're you doing? It's raining," he said.

"No shit," she muttered. "I'm locked out."

"Why?" He bit his lip. "Also, you shouldn't talk like that. My dad says bad words send people to hell."

The girl didn't answer. When she looked up, he saw the gray eyes of a feral cat ready to scram into the city gutters.

Mikael walked inside and turned up the music. He took the

cookies from the mantle and went back to the porch, holding them in the rain, in view of the girl.

"Want a cookie?"

"I'm fine. My mom is coming soon."

"You want to help me open my presents?"

The girl shrugged and stared at her knees.

Mikael sighed and stomped back to the Christmas tree. He moved the gifts from beneath the tree, one by one, into his bedroom. He knew the girl would come out of the rain soon. No kid could resist Christmas presents. On each trip to the tree he passed a photo of his mother. It was the kind with two faces, one of the smiling front and the other a profile. The two-faced photo was ghoulish, and each time he passed it became harder to look at because of the goosebumps that tickled his arm. He didn't want to open presents in front of the ghost that had once been his mother.

Mikael waited on his bedroom floor. The music blared from the living room, but over the smooth, velvet voice of Sinatra came the soft pattering of uncertain footsteps.

"I'm in here," Mikael called.

The girl appeared in the open doorway of his bedroom.

"Hi," Mikael said.

Her eyes were glued to the presents.

"Where are your parents?" she asked.

"My mom is dead. My dad went to see her."

"What happened?"

"A car accident."

He sniffled and pushed the presents towards her.

"Here. You can have them all."

He handed her a football wrapped in gold paper, something he never wanted. Mikael's father wanted it for him, in the same way Daan wanted other things. Be a good, Christian man. Don't cry. Stand up straight. Don't tell lies.

The girl tore the paper from the gift, filling the silence with the sound of shredding paper. Her eyes sparkled. She tossed the football in her hands as if it was something she was made to do.

3

"My name is Montgomery. But you should call me Monti. I'm seven."

"My name is Mikael." He paused, thinking of his Norwegian grandfather for whom he was named, a strict Lutheran who built the walls that enclosed them now. It was a name his father wanted for him.

"But you should call me Sasha. I'm seven and a half."

Monti shoved an entire cookie into her mouth. She smiled, showing the crumbs stuck between the gap in her front teeth.

"Why aren't you sad?"

"I was sad yesterday," he said. "My mom said goodbye yesterday."

She took another cookie and ogled the rest of the gifts.

"I can't take your presents."

"Yes you can. I don't want them."

She sputtered cookie crumbs from her mouth.

"Why the hell not! I'd kill for this many toys."

"They're from my dad. And he's the reason my mom's gone." He picked another gift and laid it in her lap. "Also, you shouldn't swear."

She nodded, as though everything he'd said made perfect sense. He felt very brave next to her, so he whispered through clenched teeth,

"I hate my dad."

He watched her pick a scab from her knuckle.

"Why were you locked out?" he asked.

She shrugged. "My moms got stuff to do."

"She's not home right now? Will she be back in time for Christmas?"

And then she smiled, sending dimples to her cheeks and sunlight to the rippled, gray eyes. It was a smile that meant they'd be friends forever.

"That's right! She went to the midnight service at Mt. Calvary. I had to use the bathroom and she forgot me. That's why I was locked out."

"How could she forget you? And why didn't she come back?"

Monti's eyes narrowed. "I don't tell lies, Sasha."

He swallowed. She'd been nice enough to use the name he wanted. Her eyes turned red and wet. Sasha decided it was okay if she didn't want to tell the truth about why she'd been locked out.

They sat in silence while she opened the rest of his gifts, his mood lifting in tandem with her joy. He liked making her happy. He was the captive audience and she the ringmaster, and surrounding them was a circus of domestic tragedy.

After some time, when the world grew quiet and everyone awaited the coming magic of Christmas spirits, she said something he would never forget.

"I'm sorry your mom died. If my mom died, I don't think I'd cry either."

PART I

1981

CHAPTER ONE

TODAY NOTHING CHANGES.

Ever since he could remember, Sasha Coen had a gift. His mother said it was because an old soul had been trapped inside his young body. He was inherently sensitive, and she called it *intuition*. Being a trusting boy he took her word for it, that he was special. That his intense bouts of sadness were actually an attribute.

"The ability to love is one of God's greatest gifts," she'd told him. "And sometimes all that loving brings great sorrow."

When he came home from school with bruises and scrapes, sad from another day of teasing and a recess spent in solitary, she would say he was not boring, just observant. He was not weird, only thoughtful. And when kids called him "retard" because he'd rather watch the birds fly than play war with GI Joe's, she told him he was simply unique. She said these things because she loved him. But then she died, and so went every occasion for this unconditional praise.

Today nothing changes.

As a crow barked outside his window, bathing in the subtle warmth of a June sun, and he wiped the dried sleep that had caked around his eye, these words wove through his consciousness, and he was glad.

A portentous tide surged towards Seattle, despite the beginning of a bright summer. Two bodies had been found in the Duwamish River, a murky snake of water that connected Seattle's industrial ports to Elliot Bay. The victims were young and black. Teenage girls from the Central District that had been missing for over a week, though no one knew it. And some of the patrons at Mt. Calvary Baptist felt no one really cared. Because the dead girls were prostitutes. Addicts. And their skin darker than a brown paper bag. A small clip in the crime section of the *Seattle Post* described the horrid details. They had been raped, and when the perpetrator finished, had their skulls bashed in. They didn't even make the evening news.

On the first Sunday after the discovery of the bodies, Pastor Pritchard bowed his head before a silent congregation and prayed for the dead girls. Sasha did not however, unsure of his belief in God, and watched as light poured through stained glass windows, turning the cotton-like hair of Pritchard's humble crown a mixture of pink and gold.

"Almighty Father,

We ask you to welcome the souls of Shandra and Kameel into your heaven and grace, for we know that you love and accept all your children and show mercy on the innocent."

After more words about trust and faith, Pritchard motioned the choir to stand, and Sasha felt a wave of nausea overtake his trembling body.

He pulled at the polyester collar of his purple robe and wiped his sweaty palms down the front. He scanned the crowd as the choir began a hymn. His gaze settled on her face. It was his first time singing for anyone on his own. Not even his best friend knew what he could do. Just one of the many secrets he kept from her, always for her own sake. Monti stuck out her tongue and crossed her eyes, then resumed biting her fingernails.

The choir finished the first verse. Sasha made his way in front of the pulpit and accepted an electric guitar from Arnie, the leader of the church's band. He made a bargain with a god he barely trusted, swearing to tell the truth if he could only sound the way he knew how. His voice broke, and he looked into her eyes which served as his lifeline in a raging storm of nerves.

I am a poor, wayfaring stranger
Wondering through this world of woe
But there is no sickness, toil or danger
On that bright plain to which I go

He sang from his gut, pulling his voice through his cracking vocal chords, strained from puberty and smoking so much pot. He took a deep breath while members of the congregation shouted *Yayesssss!* and *Amen!*, clapping and stomping their feet. He opened his throat and let his hands bend the notes so they sounded like mourning, ignoring the burn from the strings as they dug into the pads of his fingertips. He caught a glimpse of Monti's gaping mouth, her gapped teeth on full display.

I'm going there to see my momma
She said she'd meet me when I come
So I'm just going, over Jordan
I'm just going, over home

Applause erupted, causing an involuntary upturn of his mouth. He felt his blood thrash against his veins, but gave his audience only a subtle smirk. Monti did not smile back, she did not clap, and her jaw hung open. Sasha ducked his head and worked the toe of his sneaker against the carpet, brushing away the praise, but not before kneading it through his mind like dough.

"When did you learn to sing like that?" she asked as everyone spilled into the churchyard for the post-service barbecue. "Why didn't I know you could play the guitar?" He heard the accusation in her voice.

He shrugged, "It never came up."

They were almost to the door when he took her hand, a single truth burning his tongue like hot sauce. But a friendly voice stopped them.

"Hi Sasha! Are you volunteering for the food drive next week?"

Treesha Jensen approached them, flipping her black braids over

11

one shoulder. Her yellow sundress landed just above her dark, knobby knees. She stopped with a hand on her hip, smiling sweetly and batting her bald eyelids.

Treesha kissed him once, after choir practice while they retrieved abandoned sheet music from beneath the pews.

I wanted to know how a white boy does it.

She'd grabbed his hand and pressed it to the place the Pastor had warned against, into the soft skin between her legs. The visceral touch and pungency made it so he tasted her in his mouth, but he didn't feel what he knew was supposed to happen. He assumed it was because her breath had smelled like sour cabbage.

"I dunno. Maybe," Sasha told her.

She looked at Monti and grinned. Sasha suspected it wasn't meant to be friendly from the way Treesha's eyes roved over Monti's battered shoes and second-hand overalls.

"I'll help you put some cans aside. Don't want to leave nobody out. What you like Monti? Spaghettios?"

Sasha had seen the kids from the Central District give Monti a hard time, slinging insults like *Casper, Bisquick Bitch,* and *you make ashy look like a disease.* Monti looked like an ill-defined, Mediterranean wanderer, her black skin the color of toasted cappuccino-foam. And he'd heard, on more than one occasion, a portion of the church donations set aside for the needy ended up in her mother's pocket.

"You should shove them up your twat, only way your cherry'll get popped," Monti said, turning up her nose.

"You'd know wouldn't you? Girls with no daddy be lookin' for it everywhere," Treesha said, stepping closer.

"At least I don't look like Gary Coleman with braids. Your momma should get got for spreading the ugly gene." Monti's nose nearly touched Treesha's. Sasha tried to pull her back, but she swatted his hand away.

"At least my momma won't end up in no river like them other whores."

Treesha's nose bled the second the words left her mouth. The red ran down her dark face and turned purple with melanin. It pooled between the pads of her thick lips. Sasha didn't see the first punch because it happened so fast, but Monti was now on top of her, pummeling her fists into Treesha's ribs. He used his whole body to pull her off, like an anchor to a ship caught in a wayward drift.

"She just hit me!" Treesha cried, but Monti was running through the churchyard towards the parking lot, dodging the picnickers and maple trees. Treesha reached for Sasha's hand, but he ignored it and chased after his friend.

He found her by his '77 Chevy Suburban, bought used with the money earned the previous summer doing landscaping for his grandparents. She turned away, and he pretended not to see the tears welling in the bottom lids of her eyes. Her shoulders trembled, and he noticed how the sun put toffee streaks in her black, crimpy hair. He wanted to hold her, but she would only push him away. So he unlocked the truck instead.

He started the ignition and rolled down the window, letting in the smell of spicy chicken and grilled hotlinks. It made his stomach churn, though he wasn't hungry.

"We should stay for the picnic."

"No," she said.

"I know you're hungry."

"You don't know anything," she said, jutting out her jaw.

"Banana pudding is your favorite. You really gonna deny yourself the pleasure?"

"I won't enjoy it with that dumb bitch hovering over you the whole time."

Sasha chuckled. "Yeah. Treesha's pretty into me, huh?"

Monti rolled her eyes.

"Do you want me to stop at Dick's on the way home?" he asked. "I'll buy you a milkshake."

"No thanks," she mumbled, her forehead pressed against the window.

They'd reached downtown before she spoke again.

"Why didn't I know you could sing like that?"

"It's not something I feel comfortable doing, I guess."

"You should. I've never heard anything like that before."

"Thanks," he said, turning the dial of the stereo so the blare from his Black Flag cassette might distract her. "Do you want to stop at McDonald's? Tommy works there. He gets free fries and sometimes sandwiches if they've been sitting long enough."

She scoffed and turned off the music.

"I don't want to go begging for food like I'm homeless. Especially from some dropout that sells drugs. I don't know why you hang out with that guy. And listen to this trash." She motioned to the tape deck. "Ever heard of Michael Jackson?"

"Ever heard of Iggy Pop?" he countered.

They were almost to The Bridgewater when she spoke again.

"I'm not going back to Mt. Calvary. I don't belong."

"I'm a Norwegian Lutheran singing in a gospel choir," Sasha said. "Who cares about belonging?"

Her silence sealed the end of the discussion.

He pulled into the shared parking lot of The Bridgewater, a simple, covered port on Seventeenth Avenue and adjacent to the north side of the building.

"Monti, I have something to tell you."

She looked at him, but the scowl did not soften.

"Well don't be a pansy. Spit it out."

Just as he began to unravel his making, the words from that morning came back to haunt him.

Today nothing changes. But nothing will be the same.

He froze. She grabbed him by the neck and pushed his head beneath her armpit. The musk of her skin was both familiar and foreign, and while used to her roughhousing, he shook her off. She was water, pure and clean, and he was the stank of wet dog.

He wanted to believe the truth wouldn't change their friendship. But that look on her face when he sang - while the rest of the church sat in awe and admiration, her face stood out. She wore the look of the betrayed. *Don't be a pansy* said the girl who beat him in arm wrestling and talking shit, though they might be more evenly matched these days. But match or not, a negative reaction would crush his resolve, and might end their friendship forever. So he turned off the truck, tucked his keys in his pocket and convinced himself his cowardice was for the best.

§&

MONTI SLAMMED THE PASSENGER DOOR. She couldn't believe her best friend would keep something from her. When he stood at that pulpit he transformed from a comfortable companion into a stranger, his beautiful voice a mockery of her mediocrity. A black woman sharing the pew had dropped her head and sounded a quiet, *mmm mmm hmm.* Monti knew then that Sasha had something special. Was someone special, and suddenly she suspected she'd been patronized the past nine years. He was simply too cool to be her friend.

Sasha grabbed her hand, stopping her in the center of the courtyard. The blooms on the rhododendron bushes had turned brown, as though they'd been neglected.

"Have dinner with me tonight," Sasha said.

"Maybe. It's my mom's night off, so we might do something. She promised to get takeout."

"Okay, sure. But if for some reason you don't, or if she's like, not home, come over. I'll leave my window open. We can watch *Over the Edge* or something."

Warmth spread into her stomach and she almost forgot the hunger. He swatted a bee away from her elbow, and his arm brushed against hers. She thought of its sinewy muscles as he'd played those haunting notes on the guitar, and how her toes had curled in her muddy sneakers. She wanted to say thank you, express how much he meant to her always, and especially in that moment.

"Yeah, maybe," she said.

Monti glanced at Sasha's house. As much time as she'd spent in it, she never felt truly welcome.

The Bridgewater looked like a vintage, English settlement and was located in the heartland of commercial Ballard. Sasha's grandfather had built it shortly after he immigrated from Norway. The U-shaped complex was made of seven, Tudor-styled row-houses. The combination of brick, timber framing, prominent cross-gables and thick hedges gave it a dated and haunted look. Sasha's house was at the crux of the U-shape. It had a large front porch and was the only house that hadn't been split into single-story apartment units.

The front door opened and Monti heard it slam against the wall inside. Daan Coen came onto the porch. He crossed his arms and looked down his nose until it made her want to cry again. He nodded his head towards her apartment.

There lay Monti's mother, her back against the front door and her legs spread-eagle, spilling down the concrete steps and baking in the sun. Her black mini-skirt looked soiled and bunched around her waist. A bra strap fell away from her orange tank top and rested at her elbow. She was out cold.

Sasha reached for Monti's hand and squeezed. She looked at his face - the light in his eyes seemed to wither as he stared back. He might've been an angel, or a Norse god. In the sun his long, blonde hair looked molten and his pink mouth held her transfixed.

"What can I do?" he asked.

She tried to answer, but all that came from her mouth was stuttering and nonsense.

"I can help you carry her inside," he said.

Even when he spoke, his voice sang. He drawled out his vowels, letting them drop into his deepest octave like a jazzy slide, turning single syllable words into two. He over-pronounced his R's so the ear became drenched by his slow, Northwestern cadence. It was as if his voice kept a secret and he hadn't decided if the world could be trusted.

"Monti, please say something."

But what could she say? Something was different. Something had changed. When she wasn't looking he went from a sweet, shy boy with a bowl-cut to a lanky, mysterious rocker. They once bathed together, shared candy and traded secrets when life was just a game. She'd fight away the bullies and he'd lend her his toys. And now she wanted more.

Monti looked at her mother. A tattered, crimson line of lace flashed from between Birdie's thighs. Faces peeked from behind the curtains of her neighbors' windows. She felt emotion break out on her face like a pubescent bout of acne. Fear. Anger. And when Daan clicked his teeth and said *time to come in son* - Shame.

She let go of his hand and grinned so wide she thought her cheeks would strain.

"What are you talking about? She worked a double at the bar last night and had to close. She must've fell asleep, or maybe she forgot her keys. Either way, it's no big deal."

He reached for her again but she turned away, desperate to get her mother inside.

"I'll see you later, Sasha!"

CHAPTER TWO

THE FOURTH of July was once Richard Adamson's favorite holiday because it represented freedom. As he grilled burgers on the wraparound deck of his three-story beach house, a breeze sent white magnolia blossoms fluttering to the scenic road, and made the bay ripple and sparkle in the sunlight like a fireworks display. A yellow convertible cruised past his driveway, and Richard waved to be neighborly. He lived apart from the city, on a hill called Magnolia that sat above all of Seattle, above the port and boatyards, above the train tracks that rattled in Interbay, a swath of industrial land between Queen Anne and his house. He lived beyond the grime. He was on top. Yet, in this moment, in the prime of his life, he felt he was anything but free.

"Hey Dad, come watch me throw! I've got a perfect spiral."

His son Clarke stood beside him, his second coming in both looks and ability. They both had red hair that seemed to catch fire in the light. They both had mossy green eyes. Both were muscular and athletic, and had the inherent, self-serving disposition of a streetwise alley cat. The only difference between them was that Richard had to claw for everything he had in life, working nights to put himself through law school. And Clarke was a spoiled, sniveling, teenaged brat who expected the world be handed to him.

"In a minute, son. I don't want these burgers to burn," Richard said. "Your mother would never forgive me for it."

"I don't care about the burgers! We should've ordered pizza. Come on, watch me throw, you'll be like, amazed I swear!"

It was just like his son to suggest pizza at a family barbecue. To want the opposite of what an occasion called for, not caring that his colleagues would be in attendance, judging his home and family.

He handed Clarke an ivory platter of expertly charred meat. He'd had it butchered and ground fresh from sirloin specifically for the occasion.

"Please take these inside to your mother."

"I bet I can balance these on one hand."

No surprise, Clarke would believe he could waiter though his whole life he'd only been waited on.

"Stop horsing around and take the food to your mother."

"No, seriously look!"

Clarke put the heavy platter in the flat of his palm and walked inside. Richard watched as his foot caught in the thick, cream carpet of the dining room. The platter leaped from Clarke's hand and smacked against the cherrywood table, leaving a small dent in the polished wood. The meat he'd had butchered fell to the floor, its greasy fond staining the carpet a coffee brown.

Richard didn't get angry. He'd stopped feeling anger years ago. It was nothing less than what he expected. He walked past his son and avoided eye contact.

"Call Pizza Hut," he said.

He squeezed his eyes shut when Clarke replied,

"But I want Little Caesar's!"

§◆

"Hand me that perfume there, baby."

Monti handed Birdie the bottle from the cedar dresser. She caught her reflection in the cloudy mirror, stained over the years with cheap window cleaner, dust and smoke. She looked so plain next to her mother, her hair a frizzy, kinky mop, her skin caught somewhere between white and redbone and her teeth an unfinished afterthought.

Birdie sprinkled the drugstore perfume on her wrists and rubbed them together, filling the room with the smell of rose-scented alcohol.

"Want to go to Gasworks Park, Momma? We could get hot dogs and watch the fireworks."

Birdie smiled, her gold tooth glinting in the sunlight that streamed through the window and illuminated the dust particles floating through the air like tiny ghosts.

"Can't, baby. Momma's got to work."

Birdie ran a tube of fuchsia lipstick across her bottom lip, then pressed both together. She filled in her eyebrows with a sepia pencil and swiped purple shadow over her eyelids. She pulled at her lashes with a mascara wand until they batted each time she blinked. Birdie's golden skin seemed to come alive right in front of Monti's eyes.

"You look beautiful," Monti said.

"Thanks, baby."

Birdie covered her ample breasts in a primary-blue blouse, allowing them to spill over the frill of her neckline. She let her hair down, freed the sea of braids from the checkered scarf she wore to prevent frizz. Monti gasped as they cascaded down her back. Her mother turned heads, everywhere she went, and Monti could only hope to have a fraction of that beauty.

"You should see what your little friend is up to," Birdie said, shimmying her thick thighs into fitted, flared jeans and strapping on a pair of platform sandals. She whipped her braids over one shoulder and checked herself in the mirror.

Monti sighed and leaned against the dresser, ignoring the acid that burned in her stomach. "Can't. He's in Edmonds visiting his grandparents."

"Alright then, I got to jet. I'll see you later tonight."

"Momma?" Monti said, hovering in the living room as Birdie opened the front door.

"Yes, baby?"

"The fridge is empty. Will you get some groceries on the way home?"

"Of course baby, you know I will. Now where did I put my..."

Birdie dug through her purse in the doorway, standing just inches from where Monti found her sleeping days before.

"Momma?"

"Hmm?"

"Why don't we ever have money?" Monti asked.

Birdie froze.

"There you go, being ungrateful again. Know what I was doing at your age? Nursing that greedy little mouth of yours and wiping your spit-up from my chest."

"I was just asking."

"'Why don't we have money,' girl you done lost your mind."

"Will you be home early?"

"Why you asking?"

"Mr. Coen was pretty angry about you sleeping on the porch the other day."

"Man, that cracker can mind his business. Can't a working mother be tired from standing on her feet all night serving fools like him? And you know I be gettin' sick."

"But Momma—"

"Baby girl, I got to get down to the Wanderlust. You quit all that frettin' now."

Birdie kissed Monti's forehead. Her mother's face was full of warmth and love. "It's all gravy," she whispered.

Monti smiled until the image of her mother half-exposed on their stoop stopped hurting. She kissed Birdie goodbye.

Summers were always the hardest, when Birdie worked the most and there were no school lunches. But Monti knew everything would be fine. *It's all gravy.* And Birdie was right every time. Things worked out in the end.

21

Certain things made the summers bearable. Sneaking into the movies with Sasha, hiking Seattle's urban hills or pounding on her drums until the sticks began to splinter; these things made time stop, giving pause to the ever growing hunger that hollowed her belly.

Monti had barely eaten in two days, and the pit of her stomach roiled with hunger. She left The Bridgewater and walked across the Ballard Locks, watching as yachts passed from the Puget Sound into Lake Union, blue herons flying overhead and the gardens lush with flowers. She relished the burn in her strong quads as she moved up the hills of Magnolia, looking into the windows of the beautiful homes that smelled of beauty bark and fertilizer, summer wreaths on the front doors and birdhouses hung above the patios, hoping to catch a glimpse of a life well-lived. She found a shaded patch of grass at a park on the bluffs and watched boats float idly in the middle of the bay. She picked unripened blackberries from the wild bushes that grew along the bluff, and they were enough to ease her craving. There was much to be grateful for. Some years it rained so hard that fireworks and barbecues were deemed unseasonable, the red, white and blue banners made into soggy, purple towels. But this year the sky was clear. When the sun set, this spot on the bluffs would be the best place to watch the fireworks, the small plumes bursting from the waterfront houses on the opposite shore, like blooming, bay flowers that lived and died in a single, perfect, fire-filled moment. As she sat, the hunger baited her, called to her like a devil in heat. But she didn't worry and didn't heed its call. She would eat soon. She always found a way. Because everything was gravy.

RICHARD SAT on the back deck and admired his yard. The grass was lush and catalogue-green. Blue hydrangeas grew along the fence, and a stone pathway led from the deck to a recessed pool in the center of the yard, surrounded by white, stone tiles. In the corner of the yard and behind a grove of rhododendron bushes the size of trees was a pool house, which mostly went unused. Over the years his wife Cassandra had grown to love the fuchsia and lilac-colored blossoms, and so what started as well-tended bushes had grown into an unkempt floral thicket. Sometimes Richard forgot the pool house existed at all.

Cassandra played croquet with three attorneys, men he'd known since law school. Tim Atkins and Jon Maim had gone into private litigation, and Lance Dell, like Richard, was a state prosecutor. He hoped they were enjoying themselves - it cost $300 a month to keep his yard immaculate for such occasions.

Richard sipped his whiskey, eyeing Lance as he, rather indiscreetly, rested his hand on the small of Cassandra's back.

"Adamson, where did you find such a stunning wife?" Lance asked.

"Would you believe she stalked me?" Richard said.

Lance spun on his heels, slack-jawed.

"I wouldn't. She's too far out of your league."

"That's what I thought, too," Richard said. "Cassandra Cummings, daughter of real estate mogul Armand Cummings, walked into a frat party of all places."

"Oh don't tell this story," Cassandra said. She pointed her mallet at him as if she was shooting at a target.

Richard continued.

"And at that party she said to me, 'you forgot to zip your fly.'"

"So how did you win her?" Lance asked.

Richard set down his drink and leaned forward.

"I shrugged and said, 'thank you for noticing.'"

"Then what happened?" Lance said.

"The next weekend she was sitting at my bar twirling a cherry stem between her lips. To this day she won't tell me how she found out where I worked."

Lance looked at Cassandra.

"You tigress," he said.

Cassandra looked at Richard.

"Sometimes a woman has to take matters into her own hands, exhausting as it is."

She dropped her mallet and walked to the pool. Her blonde, feathered curls bounced as she flounced into the cabana, her goddess silhouette reflected in the water. She sipped her white wine with a raised pinkie, and looked as though she hadn't a care in the world.

There was a time it would've made him jealous, possessive even, to see his colleagues moon over his wife. But beauty couldn't expunge loneliness, and what many thought was love had actually been youthful lust, dripping and hot before the inevitable congealment once the heat dissipated, much like the pizzas that cooled beside him on the patio table.

"Hey Dad, watch this!"

Clarke tossed the football back and forth with Lance. His son wasn't good, but was the best Ballard had. Once Richard gave his attention Clarke chucked an ugly spiral that seemed to skip in the air towards Lance. Fortunately Lance was a former lacrosse player who moved well, and his sandy brown hair bounced with enthusiasm as he stretched out to catch the wayward ball before it ripped through the hydrangeas.

"Don't throw so hard, someone will get hurt. If you want to play like that, call up your teammates and go to the park."

Clarke skulked towards the house. When he was close enough for Richard to hear, he muttered under his breath, "Why don't you grow a pair?"

Richard stood up and clamped his hand on Clarke's shoulder. He leaned in so close his lips almost grazed Clarke's ear.

"Don't. Embarrass. Me."

Clarke didn't turn around. Richard could see his ears turning red. He flicked Richard's hand away and walked inside.

Cassandra took a seat on the deck, Lance following close on her heels.

"Really honey, you should throw these pizzas away. No one is going to eat them." His wife had insisted on dragging the butcher away from his family to cut more meat for the burgers. Refined principles prohibited her from serving food in a cardboard box.

Richard clenched his jaw. "I'll do it later. Someone might get a second wind."

Lance sat closest to Richard, eyeballing Cassandra as she wiped her chest with a moist toilette. It wouldn't be a surprise if he discovered they were sleeping together. They always found a way to be near each other at work functions, and his wife had lived her thirty-six years without hearing the word "no."

But worse was the fact that he didn't care, and might be relieved by the idea of his wife taking a lover. It would make his desire to pack a bag and disappear into the forests of the Pacific Northwest easier to swallow, without that lump of guilt.

Tim and Jon stopped playing croquet and joined the party on the deck.

"Did you guys hear about the body they just found under the Ballard Bridge? Time of death makes her the first victim in what the cops are calling the 'Headbanger Murders'," Lance said.

"That's three in one month," Tim said. "But how do they know the murders are related?"

"All were black prostitutes. The papers say the killer bludgeoned them so violently their faces weren't recognizable."

"Cool. Did the paper show any pictures?" Clarke asked, appearing from behind Richard's chair, his eyes wide.

Lance, Tim and Jon stared at Clarke. Cassandra looked at Richard, rolled her eyes and smiled.

Richard felt a chill slither down his spine. "This is an adult conversation," he said to Clarke. "You should leave the table."

Clarke pouted, then made a considerable show of removing his shirt and jumping into the pool, though Richard wasn't sure who his son was trying to impress. Certainly his own mother didn't care how fit his body was?

"Have they identified the body yet?" Richard asked.

"Yes, her name was Evie Tucker," Cassandra said triumphantly, no doubt happy to have something to add to a topic Lance found interesting.

Lance raised his eyebrows at her, and she shrugged.

"I read the paper every morning," she said.

The blood drained from Richard's face. He took a sip from his drink, and then choked as a piece of ice caught in his throat. Cassandra stared at him, her beautiful mouth pursed.

"So who do you think is doing it?" Lance asked, popping an olive from his martini into his mouth.

Richard cleared his throat and relaxed his shoulders down his back, "Probably some lonely guy with mother issues."

Lance shook his head. "I bet it's a Boeing's worker who's just been laid off. Maybe a janitor. And definitely a black man." He threw his hands in the air in a way that might've suggested he'd been directly affected. "First the recession, and now this. They put Ted Bundy away just two years ago. Pretty soon Seattle will be known as the serial killer capital of the world."

Richard swirled the whiskey in his glass.

"Why do you think the killer is black?"

"Because he obviously prefers black women. So he can't be white."

Richard shook his head. "Unbelievable."

"Chin up," Jon said, pouring a glass of water and wiping the sweat from his forehead into his slick, black hair. "It's people like this Headbanger Hunter who keep men like us in business."

"I personally don't see what the big deal is. Seems to me this Headbanger is doing what you lawmen haven't been able to," Cassandra said.

"What do you mean by that, sweetheart?" Lance asked.

"Downtown is disgusting. Drug dealers and prostitutes conduct their business out in the open. You can't go to the Market without getting hustled or whistled at," Cassandra said. She flipped her hair and simpered for what seemed like Lance's benefit.

Richard finished his whiskey in one gulp, letting his hand fall so the glass cracked against the table. Everyone jumped.

"No one deserves to die like that," he said.

His wife shrugged and smiled, became preoccupied with her manicure, and his fingers curled around his empty drink as if he might choke the last drops of whiskey from the glass.

Jon smirked and shrugged at Tim, and they shared the look of two parents appeasing a tantrum.

Lance cleared his throat. "I think what Cassandra meant is that, though tragic, criminal behavior breeds violent consequences. And maybe this Headbanger Hunter will give incentive to the prostitutes and pimps to close up shop."

Lance tapped the table with his forefinger and raised his eyebrows at Richard. Who was he trying to impress? Why was it that every cocksure male was looking for his approval today?

"That was cute, Lance. Really. But I don't think my wife has the ability to reason so eloquently. Street people are icky and she'd rather see them dead. Isn't that right, honey?"

Cassandra bored into him with her ignited, hazel eyes. It was a terrible game of foreplay. He was the poor, foster boy from the wrong side of town from whom she'd lost favor. And she desperately tried to regain his affection. Not for love of course. For some women, rejection was just a challenge to prove their self-worth.

She crossed one of her bare legs over a knee, and let her white, silk dress slide up her lean, tanned thigh.

"If you say so," she said. "Though you've always been sympathetic to the less fortunate." She turned to Lance. "You wouldn't know it by looking at him now, but when he was young Richard was quite the—"

Richard kicked her shin beneath the table, hard enough to bruise her perfect, porcelain skin. She gritted her teeth but didn't cry out. And though her nostrils flared he saw the dusky attraction in the wilt of her eyelashes. He pictured the threat of her nails cutting into his hard back. Maybe he would fuck her later, a punishing act that slammed her against the chestnut headboard and made her feel fleetingly desired. But then again, maybe he wouldn't.

· · ·

27

THE SUN SUNK below the clouds, turning them into polarized, neon tufts in orange and purple. Clarke had taken the Mustang to find his friends, their guests had gone home, and Cassandra was in bed complaining of a headache. Richard sat at the island in the kitchen, his backside sore from the wooden stool. The setting sun shone through the sliding glass door so he could see his reflection in the floor's white, marble tiles. The cabinets and appliances were yellow and bubbly, just like Cassandra, and there were white lilies in a crystal vase in the center of the counter island.

It was a perfect moment in a perfect life.

He gathered up the pizza boxes from the counter, muttering to himself about waste. He walked outside and to the side of the house where the garbage cans were kept. He didn't see the figure rifling through the trash. They nearly collided.

"What are you doing? This is private property and you're trespassing."

He dropped the pizza into the trash, but stopped his tirade when he saw the girl's scowl. She looked to be his son's age, and wore a baggy, moth-eaten t-shirt that drowned her cut-off jean shorts. Her hair was black and shoulder-length, coiled into frizzy spirals that gave it a mane-like quality. She was tall, the crown of her head reaching the height of his nose, and Richard guessed she was just shy of six feet. But the most outstanding feature was her gray eyes, dark and stormy and hooded like Seattle's sky during a rainstorm.

"Rich people got the cleanest trash," she said.

Richard looked at the pizza, uneaten and discarded though it was perfectly edible. He felt ashamed. Because when he looked into her eyes he saw the boy he'd once been.

Most kids grew up believing in magic, that if they wished or prayed or asked of their loved ones, their dreams would come true. But growing up in foster care taught Richard one thing: he would have to create his own magic, by any means necessary. He suspected this girl was looking to do the same, because in her blank expression he recognized the neglect he knew all too well as a child.

She ran before he could say another word, and something compelled him to follow. He stood in his front yard and she on the other end of the street, florets of fireworks popping around her like rainbow fireflies. She looked like a fallen angel, with gravel streaks on her face and broken teeth, and he knew it was his calling to save her. Because it was the only way to save himself. He waved; 'we are kindred' he tried to convey. But in response she flipped him the bird and walked calmly away, disappearing over the bluffs.

CHAPTER THREE

I⊤ WAS the day after America's birthday, and Sasha was jonesing hard. He hadn't been able to touch his guitar for the two days the store was closed, fearing his father would hear him play. Though it felt sacrilegious to walk into an establishment named *Holy Mountain Books & Worship,* his father's store was the only option for work that summer. Most businesses were not keen to hire a sixteen-year-old boy who painted his nails black and thought wearing a spiked dog-collar, with the words *I'M A GOOD BOY,* was amusingly ironic.

Holy Mountain was located in the heart of downtown Ballard, nestled between a Bavarian meat shop and a diner. Ballard had been settled in the late 1800's, and was a beacon for Scandinavian immigrants. It was a place of opportunity, with its maritime and logging industries and direct access to the Puget Sound, and in 1907 became annexed into the city of Seattle. Sasha called it Caucasia. Even June Cleaver would've said it wasn't diverse enough. Everyone was either too old or too young, and so incredibly white and conservative that the DJs working the school dances played "The Hokey Pokey" for the last song of the night. Neighbors waved to one another as they swept the pathways to their craftsman houses. They shopped for dinner at the Scandinavian Shoppe, complaining to the owner about the deer that assaulted their vegetable garden. Most last names ended in "son" or "sen," and substitute teachers struggled with morning roll call as they stumbled over names like "Bjornstad."

But beneath the layers of the blue collar and middle class, intermingled with the single families living on their expansive green lots with old barns in their backyards, were the people that skirted beneath the awareness of every American community. Single mothers raising their kids in small apartments. Fishermen who drank away their sea-given sorrows after a hazardous crabbing season. And the dope fiends who frequented the motels dotting the corridor from Fifteenth Avenue and east to Highway 99. And somewhere, amidst the high-living and disparity, Sasha found himself caught between his easy life and the apathy he felt towards it.

Sasha stared mindlessly at the droning television, which was mounted above a shelf holding cheesy, teen books like the *Elizabeth Gail Wind Rider* series. He blew the hair from his face and drummed his fingers on the counter, playing air guitar in his mind.

The door opened, sounding the welcome bell, and Ms. Jenkins wobbled into the store. Her cane made pockmark sounds on the hard, gray carpet and Sasha smelled her perfume though she was a good yard away. Ballard was a small community, but he didn't involve himself in the conservative gossip, and knew only that Ms. Jenkins was old and had never been married. He thought it was sad, for someone to be so devout and also a spinster. She was probably a seventy-year-old virgin. And the most exciting thing to happen to her body was the desperation-induced phenomena of speaking in tongues. Women like Ms. Jenkins only made love to God.

Sasha was also a virgin, but knew he wouldn't be waiting by the law of God. He planned to have sex, lots of it. But not in the cliche way he heard boys talk about in the locker room before gym class. As with music, he felt sex should be a form of fervent craftsmanship. Something made between two people to release the energy of tangential love so the vagabonds of the universe wouldn't starve.

And though he had yet to define the nature of his future partner, he was certain it would not happen with just anyone.

"Good afternoon, ma'am. Is there something I can help you with?"

Ms. Jenkins placed her cane on the counter, forcing Sasha to sit up straight.

"Yes, sonny, sure can. You can help me by cutting that hair. You look like a little girl. I know your father has asked you on more than one occasion." She winked, drawing the wrinkled skin around her eyes together like an accordion. "I come here every week to get a new story, so we get to chatting, him and I."

"Would you believe that I'm the second coming of Samson? My strength is in this hair. I can't cut it."

She reached across the counter and pinched his chin.

"Such a pretty, sad boy. I'll forgive you for being a smart-ass."

"I can't believe you just said 'ass' Ms. Jenkins."

"How now, so did you. Do you have *Once Upon a Summer* by Janet Oke? I'd look myself, but my hip hurts."

Sasha went to the shelf of new releases and found the book, but he stopped short as Daan took his place behind the counter. His father was only in his forties, but had the stooped stance of an older man, a man who'd lost his fight but still struggled against the tide. His once blonde hair was turning white, and the limp he acquired during a short stint in Vietnam had become more pronounced.

"Make sure the cover's not bent, Mikael." Daan turned a friendly smile on Ms. Jenkins. "Only the best for my favorite customer."

Sasha cringed at his father's address of his given name. He'd given up years ago, because Daan could not understand a son with his own identity, a son who insisted on naming himself. According to Daan, "Mikael" was a strong name, with a Norwegian spelling and special meaning. In the Bible, Michael was the archangel who defended God's people, and it was Daan's hope that his only child would live up to the title. But Sasha was no angel, no defender of God. The best way to save people was to get them high off acid and make them listen to *Bad Religion*.

"Sure thing, Daan," Sasha said through clenched teeth.

He handed Ms. Jenkins the book, but her attention was on the television. Daan turned the volume up, and even Sasha was intrigued by the breaking news.

A curious disease has reared itself in the cities of New York and San Francisco. A rare and often rapidly fatal cancer has been diagnosed in forty-one cases, and eight of the patients died within twenty-four months after the discovery of the disease. But what makes this disease even more curious? It affects only gay men between the ages of twenty-six and fifty-one.

The report cut to an emaciated man in a hospital gown, reddish-purple spots seared into the pale skin of his back. His skin looked stretched, the rough bumps of his spine nearly piercing the surface. Like a leopard, once beautiful but now ravaged by disease.

Sasha felt his stomach clench, a flock of butterflies stirring up his breakfast. The newscaster called the disease Karposi Sarcoma, but before he could find out more, Daan switched to a Christian channel.

"Hey!" Sasha said. "I want to know what's happening."

"I'll tell you what's happening. That's God smiting the wretched. Serves them right, damn faggots."

"It's a shame, really. These poor men, they could help themselves if only they'd denounce Satan. If we could get them to church, I'd bet they'd find their way," Ms. Jenkins said.

"I don't want queers at my Sunday service," Daan said.

"Now that's not very Christian-like. Everyone can be saved," Ms. Jenkins said, tapping her cane on the floor.

Sasha looked up and found them staring at him, as if he was a stray dog that had just wandered in.

"I think you need to stop hanging out with that girl. She's a bad influence on you," Daan said. "Maybe a dyke, too."

"You don't know what you're talking about."

"I know something changed in you, ever since you started going to that nigger church. Wearing makeup and your hair long. You look like a faggot."

Ms. Jenkins politely excused herself, leaving a five dollar bill on the counter.

"That mother of hers exposed herself in broad daylight. I want you to stop seeing her. She's no good. That family is touched by the Devil. And I forbid you from going to that church."

Sasha considered his options. He knew he would never leave Monti. She'd been the only friend he'd had since his mother's death. But since she'd already decided against attending Mt. Calvary, he smiled sweetly and said,

"Yessir. I will not go to Mt. Calvary anymore."

What he did not say was that he had no intention of attending Daan's church either, with all the posers who preached purity and forgiveness, yet spit hate and judgement from their mouths just as easily. Or that he would never cut his hair - it didn't bother him if people thought he looked queer. He had to pick his battles in the war against his freedom. He had to be strategic until he graduated, or risked losing that freedom forever.

THE LOWERING sun hid behind a blanket of clouds as the workday drew to a close. Daan had retired to the stock room to finish his order for the coming week. The bell chimed once again, but this time Sasha was excited to see the visitor.

"Hey."

Tommy Pearson stood at the entrance, wearing all black in spite of the heat. His hair was also black, and combined with his lanky frame, it gave him the simple and unassuming look of a Bic pen. He lifted a single finger in greeting as he blew a dank cloud from his mouth.

"You can't smoke pot in here, man. My dad will flip."

Tommy licked his fingertips and extinguished the joint with a crisp hiss, half-grinning.

"Rough day?" he asked, making Sasha tuck his face into one of his knobby shoulders.

"You shouldn't be here."

"Why not?"

Sasha considered the answer, pulling his chin length hair away from his face. There was a rumor Tommy had been locked in a broom closet with the school janitor, that he was both a delinquent and a fag. And everyone in the neighborhood had heard about the Pearson boy, including his father.

"My dad would kick your ass, if he knew we were friends."

Tommy laughed. "Is that what we are?"

Sasha shrugged, tracing the counter.

"What are you doing here?"

"Brought some more stuff over. A whole backpack full. Walked my ass all the way from downtown so I wouldn't get robbed on the bus. So be grateful. I put it in your truck."

"The truck was locked," Sasha said.

Tommy winked. "Not for me."

Daan coughed loudly from the backroom, causing Sasha to jump.

"Wow, you're all wound up. I've got something for that." Tommy leaned against the counter, so close Sasha smelled his shampoo.

"Let's get out of here. I just got the Sex Pistols on vinyl. That and some of my finest pot oughta mellow you out."

Sasha looked over his shoulder at the back room.

"Alright," he said. "Let's go."

THE TROUBLE with boys is they think they know everything. Daan had been a boy once, hopped up on confidence and nicotine. He'd joined the army and left his wife at home with their new baby. By the time he'd returned, with part of his knee cap blown away and shrapnel caught in his hip, his son was three years old. And his wife could no longer recognize him.

The trouble with boys is they think no one knows anything. Its why Sasha believed he hadn't been caught with the Pearson boy, why he believed Daan was doing inventory when in fact he was sitting idle in a stockroom, surrounded by the words of Jesus, rubbing the faded spots on the photo of his wife with his thumb, a photo warped by his tears.

"Daan." It meant "Judged by God." And if, as a young boy enlisting in the war of Vietnam, Daan had known anything, he'd have realized how true this was. Because he watched as villages, surrounded by the lush, green jungles of a foreign Eden, burned down to char and coal, taking the lives of babies and grandmothers and everything between.

Innocence. Helplessness.

One moment, the golden fingers of a teenage boy plucked rice from the fields. In an instant, those same fingers curled against the marrow of his broken wrists.

Ash and bone.

One moment, a mother clutched her child to her breast, cooing comforts in a foreign dialect, only to have their skulls shattered by the bullets he'd loaded into the rifle he carried. The rifle he'd named, "Savior."

He'd seen the horrors of men, the evil that lurked inside them, inside himself, waiting to be unleashed. Hell was not a place to avoid, buried beneath the earth, but a cage from which mankind needed to escape. And so there had to be a God. There had to be one, and that's what kept Daan living. Otherwise, everyone was doomed.

Daan knew it was too late for him. And though he tried, it soon became too late for Daphne as well. And maybe that was his punishment for being the worse kind of sinner. The kind that licked the blood from his lip, left in the wake of his crimes, as though it were sweet jam.

But he would keep Mikael from the horrors of the world.

The liars. The leeches. The fags. The niggers.

The sinners.

Even if it meant his son would despise him.

CHAPTER FOUR

NEARLY FOUR WEEKS WENT BY, and then Birdie got sick. Monti returned home from summer school, sweaty after the three mile walk. A large box stamped with the the words "Mt. Calvary Baptist" waited on her stoop. She went inside and found her mother sobbing on the red pleather couch. She put the box in the kitchen and, distracted by Birdie's mewling, forgot it instantly. The kitchen walls were wallpapered in olive green patterns, and she hated how they clashed with the orange stove and gold laminate flooring. So she pretended to be in a high-class gallery that featured fresh, state-of-the-art appliances. Like silver pans that hung from rafters over-head. Everything white, from the counter tops to the cabinets to the gardenia's that sat on a center island topped with varnished pine. The type of kitchen in the kind of house featured in *People Magazine*. Still dreaming, Monti ran a dishtowel under the faucet. She returned to her mother and mopped the sweat from Birdie's forehead.

"Oh baby, I hurt so bad," Birdie said. "The pain is everywhere."

"Ssh. I know, Momma. It'll be alright. I'll make you something to eat."

Monti opened the refrigerator. Inside was an old container of yogurt, a loaf of stale Wonderbread and a bottle of ketchup.

"The fridge is empty," Monti said from the kitchen.

Birdie groaned.

Monti bit her lip.

"I could, uh, go to the store real quick. That sound good?" Her palms were clammy and her throat had gone dry.

"Girl, what you say?" Birdie asked.

Monti grabbed the bread from the refrigerator and poured ketchup on a slice, then pressed another hard piece on top. They were no strangers to ketchup sandwiches.

"Eat this," Monti said.

Birdie took a bite and then spit it in Monti's face. Sandwich crumbs scattered and disappeared into the matted, shag carpet.

"Tastes like shit. Girl you know I don't eat them shit sand-wiches! Git! Just get on outta here, you're making me feel worse. And I need to get well."

Monti chewed her bottom lip until she could taste blood and picked at the padding that leaked from the ripped couch cushions.

"I said I could go to the store, if—"

Birdie raised an open palm, but her swing was weak enough to miss.

"You so stupid," she said.

Monti's shoulders slumped.

"Alright, I'll wait until you feel better, okay? We both know how you act when you get like this."

"Maybe if you'd help me I wouldn't have to act this way."

"Well what you got Momma? A cold? The flu? How can I help you when I don't know why you're sick?"

"I done told you it's my bad immune system. This is adult busi-ness, don't you be asking me my business."

Monti grabbed the sandwich for her own grumbling belly.

"I'm going to find Sasha," she said, though Birdie did not appear to be listening.

She opened the door to a visitor, and the sight of him quelled her appetite. A tall, lanky man bearing the shadow of a beard removed his brown fedora and gave Monti a cursory look.

"Where your momma at?" Reggie said in a gravelly voice, pushing past her.

Birdie sat up, clasped her hands together and said,

"What you got for me?"

Reggie sat beside her. "I've got everything for you, baby girl. Not a thought short of what you deserve."

He held up a greasy bag of fast food. Normally Monti would salivate but instead she had an icy feeling in her gut. She wouldn't take her last breath from that man.

They fondled each other, Reggie's long, tawny fingers grabbing her mother's beautiful skin, his thin lips staining her neck with his kisses.

"I'll be home later," Monti said, though no one seemed to hear. Reggie's presence made her a ghost, even in a small, two bedroom apartment where privacy was hard to come by. She shut the door on their reunion without another word.

Monti walked aimlessly. Away from The Bridgewater and through Ballard's industrial core, where the neighborhood's fishermen toiled for their daily bread. She felt the sun's last rays on the back of her neck as it cast purple shadows in the darkening sky. She smelled Salmon Bay behind her, the salt in the air making her mouth water. She walked past a row of cement trucks, kicked rocks at the fences bearing "KEEP OUT" signs in angry, red letters, signs that reminded her of the "KEEP OUT" looks Tommy threw her way when he wanted Sasha's attention, and listened to the unruly sounds that spilled from a nearby pub. She wondered if the dead girl Evie, whose body had been found beneath the Ballard Bridge, had walked this same path. She wondered if Evie felt as out of place as Monti did at that moment.

"It's all gravy," she told herself, but in the pit of her consciousness, where she told no lies and let perspicacity reign, she knew it wasn't true. Reggie brought destruction wherever he went, and no matter how much pain he caused, Birdie always went back to him.

From the little information Monti scraped together, she knew that Birdie had moved from Montgomery, Alabama to be with him.

He'd moved from the same town months before to find success in Seattle's music scene. She'd found old clippings in the apartment. They were from the *Seattle Post*, reviews about her beautiful mother singing at a club in Chinatown. In the photos, Reggie played his saxophone behind her. The strain was noticeable, in his cheeks and glistening forehead. But his eyes were calm and focused on the back of Birdie's neck.

"Birdie James Sings The Jailbird Club Into Stunned Silence," the headline read.

She'd felt proud, reading about her mother and how she turned a rowdy juke joint into a quiet, classy establishment with "one of the best performances of 1967." Monti did the math, and realized she had been a baby at that time. It was in that article she learned Reggie shared the same last name, Jackson. And she had yet to find the courage to ask her mother what that meant.

Because Birdie was a fool to love Reggie, and the makeup she used to cover the bruises fooled no one. Brand name makeup wasn't made with tones for people like them, only varied shades of white. And in the small, white community of Ballard it was the only option at the drugstore after Reggie beat his lover for "talkin' shit." The influx of hang-up calls, when there was enough money to pay the phone bill, were no mystery either. Birdie thought they were Monti's friends making pranks, but Monti had no friends beside Sasha, and he would never taunt her that way.

She had observed Reggie come in and out of their lives since her first memory, and began to intuit that he was a man with no compass. And a man with no compass kept many fools on deck. Monti knew better than to love a man she couldn't trust.

It was dark by the time she reached Tommy's house, a brick rambler built during the Boeing boom in the 1960's and nestled between a substation and Phinney Ridge. She'd been there once before, when she and Tommy were assigned a make-up project after he butchered their frog in Biology class. Before it had been anesthetized.

The deepened tenor of Sasha's voice leaked through the heavy door, and she let herself into the basement without knocking.

Sasha and Tommy jumped apart, startled expressions on their faces. They were both shirtless, and Sasha's lean torso was covered in sweat. A moment passed before she realized she was staring. She looked away, at the record player spinning out the loud voice of some guy who couldn't sing, at the coffee table covered in beer cans, magazines and canned ravioli, at the posters of rock bands that graffitied the cement walls. Anything to avoid seeing Sasha half-naked and Tommy's condemning glare. Sasha glanced in her direction before clearing the contents off the coffee table. He walked an armload of canned food and instant noodles to a room at the back of the basement, and returned carrying his guitar. He sat on the green couch and lit a cigarette. While he smoked he rubbed his chin and stared into space, signs that something was bothering him.

"You should knock first, you know?" Sasha said after a moment.

Monti huffed. She was shamed and hurt. He may as well have said *KEEP OUT.*

"Never had to before. Do punks need more privacy? Can't imagine why."

"Whatever," Sasha said.

His indifference sounded breathy. Sexy.

Monti sniffed the air, flaring her nostrils.

"Your dad will kill you if he finds out you're selling pot."

Tommy rolled his eyes.

"You should take a pill, anyone ever tell you that? Just chill, you're not his girlfriend or anything."

"Neither are you," she said. "Not too smart either. I can see your plants back there." She pointed at the door Sasha had left open. She could see half of the dryer machine and marijuana leaves creeping from behind the doorframe. She'd heard a rumor at school that Tommy grew marijuana in his basement, and what he didn't smoke himself he sold downtown.

"You'll just get him in trouble," she said. "He's not waste like you are."

"Man you're a drag. No wonder he started hanging out with me."

"Can you guys, like, stop talking like I'm not here?" Sasha said.

Tommy ignored him.

"And don't worry about him getting in trouble, sis. People know better than to rat on me. And they know better than to come barging into my basement without knocking. So scram, Sasquatch."

Monti crossed her arms.

"Make me," she said.

Tommy stared her down. He nodded slowly and frowned, as though he played at taking her seriously. But everyone in the room knew Tommy couldn't make her do anything. Kids at school didn't call her "Sasquatch" for no reason.

"What are you guys doing?" she asked finally.

"Well if you must know," Tommy began, but Sasha cut him off.

"We started a band. Needed to practice."

Tommy glanced at Sasha. Sasha gave only the slightest shake of his head, turning his body as if he hoped Monti wouldn't see. But she noticed, and bristled at the idea that Tommy knew something she didn't.

"You weren't playing anything," she said.

"We were working on our moves. You know, head banging, hair flinging. Crap like that."

Monti crossed her arms.

"What's your band's name?"

"Section Rejects," he said.

Sasha smiled and patted the seat beside him. She took it gratefully, instantly forgetting her suspicion. She let her shoulder rest against his, and relished the sulky look of jealousy in Tommy's downturned mouth.

Sasha turned on the television, flicked through some channels, then stopped on one she'd never seen before. The promo called it MTV, which was short for Music Television. The first music video came on the screen, "In The Air Tonight" by Phil Collins. Monti saw a light go on in Sasha's eyes. Bright and focused, like a lighthouse beam finding a lost vessel.

"This is fucking awesome," he said.

Tommy leaned forward on the couch, forcing Monti to edge closer to Sasha.

"Hell yeah," Tommy said.

Monti stayed silent, her attention focused on her knee and how it pressed into the hardness of Sasha's slender thigh. She felt the energy pulsating from Tommy. She saw in his stolen glances, as Sasha remained transfixed by the television screen, that he wanted to be where she sat. She felt his wanting, but only because she wanted it too. There it was, in the night air that seeped through the cement walls, the skunked up smell of their teenage yearning.

"I want to be in the band," she said quietly.

Tommy scoffed.

"We're into, like, hardcore punk. Definitely not your scene. And besides, Sasha's gonna be the lead singer."

"Who said I wanted to sing?" she asked.

"Yeah, Monti is completely tone deaf dude. But she's always welcome. I'm sure we could find you a tambourine. Something like that."

He laughed and chucked her on the shoulder. Tommy snickered.

"No. I want to play the drums."

"What? But you're a girl. You won't be able to play fast enough. Or hit hard," Tommy said.

Monti looked at her knees, her shoulders sinking down her back. She blinked hard to keep her eyes from smarting, and then looked at Sasha. His face looked different, as if he was angry somehow. His steely eyes were no longer warm, no longer friendly, and she worried that maybe she'd overstepped. As if she'd asked to be a part of something he didn't want to share. But then he surprised her.

"You don't know Monti if that's what you think." He touched her wrist. "You still have that kit?"

43

He was referring to the drum kit stored in their garage from Birdie's performing days.

"Yeah."

"And you still play?"

"Sometimes."

Tommy threw his hands in the air.

"Chicks aren't hardcore man!"

"Wrong. A band fronted by all dudes is typical. A band fronted by dudes, but with a female drummer?" Sasha winked at her. "So punk."

Later that night, Tommy had tried to convince Sasha to sleep over.

"My mom is making pancakes in the morning," he said.

But Sasha had chosen Monti, and her heart soared until he followed with,

"I should drive her home. That Headbanger guy is still out there."

Now they sat on a bench in the courtyard. Sasha smoked a cigarette, ruminating in silence while Monti fidgeted beside him. Though Monti thought smoking was a disgusting habit, and never hesitated to tell him so, she found comfort in Sasha's sooty smell. He once told her that he rolled his own cigarettes because *name brands suck and you can't trust capitalism.* His had the smell of burnt dandelions, an earthy, sweet aroma that reminded her of their summers together as children, playing in Ballard's abandoned, weedy lots.

"Tell me something new about you," he said.

"But you already know everything."

He rolled his eyes and gave her this look that seemed to say, *bullshit.* She once found it annoying. Now it made her knees quiver.

"We both know that isn't true," he said.

"Well. A package came today."

He kept his gaze on the stars overhead, but she detected a shift in his voice.

"Really? What was it?"

"Don't know. Didn't open it. The mailman probably made a mistake, there was no name on it. I'm gonna take it to the post office."

"Or you could open it," he said. After a moment, he followed with,

"That was weak. What else?"

She thought about what to say, about how honest she could be. *I'm afraid of who you're becoming. I'm worried about my mom.* She considered her last option and goosebumps ran the length of her arm. *I think I'm in love with you.*

But she said none of these things and settled on something she knew he'd understand.

"Reggie is back."

He stubbed out his cigarette and motioned her to follow. She climbed through his bedroom window after him, as she'd done a thousand times. She donned one of his t-shirts to sleep in, as she'd done so many times before. Only this time she noticed him avert his eyes, though her body hadn't changed much since the last time he'd seen her naked. And she tried to pinpoint the exact moment when this behavior became the norm.

She sunk into his bed with its Batman sheets, settling into the groove that her own body had created. He rested his hand on her waist. It was no different from the million times they'd touched before. Except this time the air grew stifling hot, and it burned her throat to inhale. Her skin tingled from the pressure of his hand. She squeezed her eyes closed while she willed that hand to travel deeper beneath the sheets, to touch her where it never had before. And she suffered this way until she finally fell asleep, to the sound of his even, undisturbed breathing.

CHAPTER FIVE

Each time an offender walked into the courthouse, Richard looked for gray eyes and big hair. It'd been more than a month since he'd seen the girl rifling through his trash, and he checked off each day in his mind like a countdown calendar to what he feared was inevitable; he would never see her again. And if he never saw her again, then her fate would be feasted on by the mouths of wolves.

The Juvenile Court was located on East Alder Street near the Central District, inside the Youth Services Center. The white cement and slatted windows gave the building the look and feel of a prison. It was the middle of August, which could be the hottest time of year in Seattle. The air conditioning was broken, and the courtroom sweltered. There were circular desks where everyone faced each other, so no one could conceal their misery.

Richard wiped the sweat from his brow as he presented a case before Judge Tomlinson, a stocky man in his sixties who blinked like a broken Kewpie doll, his right eyelid heavier than his left. Most prosecutors served only a short time in the Superior Court's Juvenile Division. But he'd wanted to make a difference in the lives of disadvantaged youth, had hoped to break the cycle that turned troubled teenagers into hard criminals. However, the idealism soon wore off. His was an uphill battle, for the system that caged these animals was also the system that created them.

A fifteen-year-old boy sat across from him on the defense side of the roundtable. His black skin glistened in the hot court room, but otherwise there was no sign of duress. He wore a red hoodie and sat low in his chair, one hand covering his mouth. The defense attorney sat beside him.

"Your honor, the defendant would like to testify on his behalf."

Tomlinson nodded, popping his knuckles.

Richard clicked his pen as the defense attorney asked his questions, listening though not fully engaged. His opponent was heavily overweight, and there were sweat rings beneath his armpits. He spoke too fast, so even the defendant had trouble interpreting his words.

"Was your little brother difficult to handle?"

"Huh?"

"Was your brother difficult?"

"Um, yeah."

"Was he also prone to accidents? Accidents? Your brother, did he often have injuries?"

"Oh right. Yeah. Yes, hmm mmm."

"And you attest it was an accident, his falling down the stairs?"

"What you mean? Oh yeah, definitely. It was an accident, definitely."

But Richard knew better. He smiled at Tomlinson and tossed his head, moving a sweaty tendril off his face. The goal was to get a confession. Otherwise, the most the boy could be charged with was aggravated assault, which would land him in a rehabilitative institution or group home rather than detention. And the Judge had a firm stance on saving those spots for the "good kids."

Richard addressed the defendant.

"Mr. Allen, when did your brother get the cigarette burns on his arms?"

"I'm not sure," the boy said.

"Okay. Who was home when your brother fell down the stairs?"

"Just me and him."

"And what were you doing?"

"I was working my bag."

"Boxing, huh? You any good?"

"Yeah, I'm real good." He leaned forward in the chair. "I almost won the regional tournament last spring."

Richard looked up from his table. The defendant was sitting back in the chair again, his hands clasped together in front of him, his head cocked to one side. He wore his swagger in a sneer that wetted the corners of his mouth, which curled up towards his ears and left impish dimples in his dark cheeks. Richard had met many kids like Mr. Allen while he was in foster care, and could identify the sound of cocksure hyperbole better than a farmer could a rooster's crow. His next question was intended to break the defendant, but it was delivered half-heartedly, as Richard no longer believed the fissures in their community could be repaired with court-delivered justice.

"Almost, huh? Almost doesn't count."

"Well, I would've won if Jacob wasn't always interrupting my workouts!"

"Your little brother do that a lot, interrupt you?"

"Yeah."

"Does that make you angry sometimes?"

"Yeah.

"Did your brother get the burns before or after he fell down the stairs?"

"Before."

Richard paused, letting the boy's answer resonate with Judge Tomlinson, who cracked his knuckles even louder, each pop like a gavel thrum towards deciding the boy's fate. It was almost too easy, picking apart these kids. Their bravado always proved to be their weakness, their naivety their downfall, and once you got them talking it was like stealing a prescription from an elderly patient with Alzheimer's. They wanted to confess, wanted the world to know how and where and why they stood, the injustices that had befallen them and the measures they took to right every wrong they had experienced. The case was won the moment Mr. Allen decided to testify.

Richard looked back to the defendant. The boy's demeanor had changed. Instead of nonchalance, he now sat with his brutality coiled in his shoulders. Richard continued.

"Those burns were on his inner thigh. How did you know they were there?"

The boy stared back with defiance.

"Mr. Allen, why did you push your brother down the stairs?"

The boy leaned forward, menace dripping from his wide mouth.

"The little asshole wouldn't eat his cereal. Kept bugging me to make scrambled eggs."

The boy was sentenced to Juvenile Detention. He'd be released by the time he turned eighteen. Three years for shoving his kid brother down a flight of stairs in anger, which resulted in a fractured neck and brain trauma. The child was placed into a medically induced coma, but the damage to his developing anatomy was too great. At four years old, little Jacob Allen had reached the extent of his short life, one ended at the hands of his big brother.

It was hard to feel good at the end of a day like this, even after "winning." It didn't matter if the fifteen-year-old Allen boy was angry at the father who walked out when he was three. It didn't matter if the second child his mother had out of wedlock eight years later stole the love and attention which once belonged to him. It didn't matter if Ms. Allen was never home, had to work two minimum wage jobs to support her children, leaving the brunt of responsibility on an adolescent who was too immature to handle his own emotions, let alone those of a four-year-old. And it didn't matter that the Allen boy would go to juvie where he was unlikely to get the attention and guidance he sorely needed. Nothing would bring his little brother back, nothing could change the course his life took, and now Ms. Allen was bereft of two sons instead of one. Because when Allen left juvie, there was a more-than-likely chance he'd end up incarcerated again.

Richard left the courtroom heavy and spent, unsure of where his sympathies lay. He couldn't go home to his house in Magnolia, couldn't look at the unlined face of his beautiful wife or hear the pubescent whine of his handsome son. Why had this become his lot? Why had he been saved, and the Allen boy had not?

Richard drove along First Avenue in the downtown core of Seattle, the top of his maroon Mustang turned down so he felt the breeze. He liked to survey the area, watch the hustlers scrape and scramble for the day's fix, whether it be cocaine or sex or a bottle of orange pop. He felt more at home between the dilapidated brick buildings and the salty sea, cruising amongst the vice. Life was more exhilarating when you appreciated every meal, when you fought for a spot on the corner and earned your rights not by birth, but through bruised and broken knuckles.

He stopped at the light on First and Pike. A young woman wearing shiny, gold leggings and hoop earrings approached.

"You dating baby?"

He motioned for her to jump in. They drove around the block and parked at the Ethelton Hotel, a place Richard knew about from one of his cases. A Market Kid named Ronny Seid had been stabbed to death by his best friend over a stolen watch, his blood staining the red carpet so it had become ruddy and black. Outside the brick was riddled with moss, and an electric street sign with red letters read "200 Rooms. Transients Welcome." It was a place where one could rent by the hour or day or week, could shoot their last gram before slipping into a feverish dream that would never end, or in Richard's case, escort a young prostitute who smacked on bubble gum and looked more adult than any person should.

Once inside she began to lay out the services offered and their respective prices, but Richard interrupted her.

"What's your name?"

"Well, you can call me anything you like, Daddy. But it will cost ya."

He pulled out his wallet, fat with six, five-hundred-dollar bills that he took from Cassandra's daily allowance. She preferred cash instead of checks when she made one of her frequent trips to Nordstrom's department store on Fifth Avenue downtown, and Richard was certain she wouldn't miss it. The prostitute's eyes, thick and hooded with fake eyelashes, glanced hungrily at the bulging leather. She leaned against the dresser.

"Ok. What's your game then? You wanna play house?"

"I'll start with your name, please."

"It's Ebonique."

"I want your real name, not your street name."

"Forget you, whitey, that is my real name!"

Richard put his hands in the air.

"Okay. My mistake. You hooked on anything, Ebonique?"

"Why, you looking for something? I don't get high with my dates. It's a rule of mine."

"That's good. Rules are good. They help you protect yourself."

"That's right," she said, smacking her gum and pulling her chartreuse halter top down to cover her midriff.

"But do you have any rules that will protect you from the Headbanger Hunter? You're his type, you know."

She paused, stood straighter and uncrossed her arms. She glanced at the door, then back at Richard, as if deciding whether she could beat him to it from where he sat on the bed.

"Relax, Ebonique. I'm not here to hurt you. I'm not even here to fuck you."

"Then what you want?"

Richard sighed. "I want to know if you'd be willing to change your life." He motioned to the tiny fortune he'd laid in his lap. "You can have it all. But you have to stop prostituting."

Ebonique sucked air between her teeth and smacked her gum louder.

"Man, you think a few hundred dollars is gonna change my life? I got three kids at home. They're the reason I do this, not for drugs, not for no pimp. I can make $200 cash while they in school. I get to be there to pick them up, help them with their homework."

"And what if you're dead? What good would you be to them then?"

She leaned back against the dresser.

"Do you want to keep doing this?" he asked.

Her voice softened. "Hell no. I'm turning twenty-nine this month. But what else am I gonna do?"

Richard took the money from his wallet, glad to be rid of its weight.

"One thing I've learned, Ebonique. There's always a better choice."

CHAPTER SIX

IT WAS one of those Seattle summer days, when the wind was cold and made the tip of his nose itch. The heavy rain made his lungs feel soggy, made the red brick of The Bridgewater look moldy, and kept its residents locked indoors. The morning had passed so slowly that Sasha thought he might die of boredom. He'd seen the same music video for the third time before he finally turned off his television.

He was going to tell Monti. Later that night at band practice. He'd lay bare his secrets and she wouldn't hate him for keeping them. Because he had no choice. He felt it. They were running out of time.

He smelled pork chops and looked at his watch. It was three o'clock, on the dot. Daan always made supper at three, and expected his son to eat regardless of whether he was hungry or not. Once Sasha had gone to a birthday party at Chuck E. Cheese, one of those kid parties where the entire class was invited. By that afternoon he was nearly comatose from a pizza overdose, but when they arrived home, Daan practically force-fed him a meal of fried tomatoes and Vienna sausage.

"A disciplined mind is a holy mind," Daan always said.

Sasha stubbed out his cigarette and went to see about his supper.

He smiled at the portrait of his mother hanging over the fireplace. Their entire house was a shrine to her memory. Daan had refused to change anything after she died. The carpets were still a plush rose, thick shag that tickled the bottoms of Sasha's feet. There were Precious Moments figurines on every flat surface. They still had the antique dining room furniture with floral upholstered seating. They still had the bright yellow couch patterned with green ivy. The living room walls were paneled with russet, wood slabs. The kitchen and dining room were decked with golden light-fixtures. Blush-colored roses floated in a sepia background, papering the walls all the way to the second floor.

Daphne was gone. But the reflection of her tastes, her warmth, and her love remained. Sasha was spared by locking himself in his bedroom, tucked away behind the stairs at the back of the house. He was spared by the voices of Iggy Pop and Johnny Rotten and David Bowie, voices that were loud enough and ugly enough to drown out his own, the one in his head that told him the pain would never subside.

Daan walked out from the kitchen with two plates and laid them on the polished table in the dining room, still set the way Daphne would've liked.

"Have a seat, son."

Sasha sat and bowed his head, like a prisoner who clasps his hands behind his back without being asked.

Daan cleared his throat to pray.

"Dear Lord,

We thank you for these bountiful gifts we have received. We ask that you steer us away from evil temptation. Please show my son the path to righteousness and save his soul from eternal damnation.

Amen."

Sasha shoveled the food into his mouth, anxious to meet Tommy and Monti. Damn his damnation.

"There's a service at church tonight. I want you to come with me," Daan said.

"I can't." Sasha shoved bites of pork chop into his mouth.

"You can't, sir."

"Yessir. I can't, sir."

"And why is that?" Daan looked at him quizzically. Accusingly.

"Um, I don't believe in group worship?"

Daan cleared his throat, his eyes darting down the hall. Locking on Sasha's room. Sasha knew there was a limit to how much he would tolerate. And learning that his son was skipping church to get high and play in a rock band would be the tipping point. So Sasha added,

"And I don't believe in God, sir."

Daan choked on his meat, spitting it back onto the china plates, which had been his mother's favorite because they had elephants on them.

"You don't mean that," Daan said after catching his breath.

Sasha took his last bite of food and chewed it slowly.

"But I do," he said. "Hypocrites hide behind religion to justify their hypocrisies. They steal money from 'God's People' for their own sake. And control their flock by threatening eternal hellfire. Sir."

Daan waved a finger in his face.

"This is not my son's talk. This is not my son. I don't know who you are anymore. Look at how you dress. Like you're homeless."

Sasha shrugged. He preferred to shop at the Salvation Army. He liked to hunt for clothes once worn by hippies. He liked promotional t-shirts for bands that'd lost their radio-play years ago.

"I like clothes with a story."

"You keep your door locked. What are you hiding, son?"

What was he hiding? The poster of Sid Vicious licking Nancy Spungen's nipple, or the stacks of punk records and cassette tapes he kept in red, plastic crates were enough to give Daan an aneurism. He didn't want his collection of fanzines to be confiscated, and certainly couldn't risk his father discovering Monti in his bed. But admitting all this would put him at a disadvantage, so instead he said,

"It's for your own good. I didn't think it would benefit our father-son relationship if you walked in while I was choking my chicken."

Daan's face turned beet red.

"What did you say?"

"Well, don't you think it would be awkward if you caught me masturbating?"

Daan didn't respond, and Sasha thought he'd won the exchange. He didn't expect his father's next move to be so calculated.

"The tenants next door are late on the rent again. I need you to go see if they have it."

Sasha sunk lower in his chair.

"Why can't you do it?"

"Because. It's time you start becoming a man. Learning how to be responsible. You're sixteen, and soon you'll be the one managing the rental properties. And there's no time for learning like the present."

SASHA STOOD outside of Monti's apartment, allowing his new leather boots to get soaked in the rain. His fingers grew numb as he peeled chipped paint from the front door, stalling the axe he'd be forced to render. He'd thought of so many ways to save her from this indignity. When her electricity was shut off because Birdie didn't pay the bill, he'd rerouted the meter so that her unit received power from the main house. And every time Daan yelled at him about the increase in their electricity bill, Sasha would just apologize for leaving the lights on. When Monti asked why her apartment couldn't be repainted, he'd said it was because his mother had picked the colors and Daan was still too heartbroken to see them go. How could he tell his best friend that Daan wanted her family gone, and didn't intend to renovate their apartment until they had moved on?

Sasha knocked on the door, and to his dismay, Monti answered.

"What's up? I thought practice wasn't for another few hours?"

She was wearing an old, Seahawks t-shirt with scuffed galoshes and carpenter pants that hovered above her ankles, and this made him happy.

"My dad sent me."

"Let me guess. He wants you to dump me as a friend."

"No, I—"

"Wait, wait. He asked you to shove a crucifix up my ass to expel the black demon from me."

"Geez, no I—"

"I got it, I got it." She pointed at her teeth. "He wants you to tie me up in the courtyard so he can use the gaps for target practice."

"Monti!"

Her smile faded, and the only thing propelling him forward was the knowledge that Daan would be hateful, would relish the opportunity to cut her down.

"I'm just here for the rent."

She crossed her arms.

"What do you mean? It's the middle of the month. I'm sure my mom already paid."

"She hasn't. My dad said she's late."

"Your dad's an asshole!"

"That's true. But he wouldn't lie about this."

She chewed on her bottom lip and looked down at his shoes.

"You're ruining those, standing in the rain like that."

"I don't care."

She scoffed.

"Look, I'm sure it's all a mistake. But I'll let my mom know."

"If you need to borrow some money, I've been saving for a new Atari. I could lend you a hundred or two."

"We don't need your money."

"Okay, sorry I just—"

"You know what? We don't need your 'sorries' either."

She shut the door before he could say more.

Later that night, Sasha lay in his bed listening to the wind lift his blinds from the window, and winced each time it let them fall with a tangy rattle. Monti hadn't shown at band practice. And he hadn't been surprised. He knew what the flush in her cheeks had meant, and why she couldn't maintain eye contact. Though built with his grandfather's love and sweat, the walls of The Bridgewater were thin, and both he and Monti knew there were no real secrets between them. When Monti would come to school with haunted under-eyes and gaunt cheekbones, she'd say she had nightmares. And he would smile and accept, and pretend he hadn't been up all night, listening as she cried and begged Birdie to take her to McDonalds. It was a game they played, maintaining a child's perspective on all the conundrum they'd witnessed. They recorded their travesties in the storybooks of their imagination, preferring to remember events as they should've been, instead of how they were. The problem he faced now was that he was no longer a child, and didn't know if he could play the game much longer.

He pressed his ear to the wall, where her bed sat parallel on the other side. He knocked, two raps with his knuckles.

Are you still there?

The expanse of his solitude lay in the balance of that moment. The hush stretched before him so far he could see where his life took a detour into darkness. And in that darkness he was falling, with no control over the whorl in his stomach from having lost his best friend. Until she knocked back.

I'm still here.

SASHA RANG MONTI'S DOORBELL, and adjusted the guitar case he'd slung over his shoulder. He hadn't seen her in a few days. And he was afraid she'd never forgive him.

Reggie opened the door.

"What you want?"

His hair was disheveled and his eyes were red, as if he'd been rubbing them.

"Is Monti home?" Sasha asked.

Reggie stared at him, working his jaw back and forth.

"You her boyfriend or something?"

"No. I'm her best friend. We've met a few times, actually. Back when you guys first moved in. And a few times after that. I live right next door."

"I know where you live. And I know who you is," Reggie said, swatting the air. "What you need her for?"

"We've got band practice."

A look crossed Reggie's face. Almost pained. Almost proud. He pointed at Sasha's guitar.

"Let's see what you got."

"My amp's in the truck."

Reggie motioned Sasha inside and left him in the living room. The wood-paneled walls were splitting. There was a red couch mended with duct tape, a chipped coffee table covered in beer cans and an old record player. And not much else. Sasha couldn't imagine Monti, who was big and loud and colorful and striking, caught in such a lifeless place.

He knew she wasn't home. Because she'd never let him inside.

Reggie came back with an acoustic guitar and shoved it into Sasha's hands. He sat on the couch and stared. Sasha stared back.

"Go head and play, white boy."

Sasha played his favorite Sex Pistols song, "Anarchy in the UK."

Reggie stopped him after two bars.

"Man, that shit is garbage."

"That's kinda the point of punk rock."

"There's no point in that. And it ain't rock," Reggie said.

"It's a revolution. A political statement. An artist's rebellion. It's new and exciting and you wouldn't know anything because you're like, too old. Anyways..."

Reggie pointed at Sasha's Black Sabbath t-shirt.

"You think that shit was new when it came out? Just a bunch of doped-up white boys singing the blues. And that upbeat, happy, no rhythm shit music you call punk rock is missing the whole point."

"And what point is that?"

"Rage, son. And the point of rage isn't in the scream or the speed. It's in the howl. It's in them holes *between* the notes. That music y'all play ain't got no space. So it ain't got no soul."

Reggie took the guitar and played a few riffs. Sasha watched, slack-jawed.

"See how that made you want to dance, hit something, and cry all at the same time? That's rage, man. It's a combination of sorrow and the need to live. Because if you didn't need that life, then there'd be no point in raging."

"That was incredible. Who was that?" Sasha asked.

"Boy, that was me."

Reggie plucked lovingly through a stack of records that lay by his feet. He handed two of them to Sasha.

"Leadbelly for the howl. Chuck Berry for the basics. You need to know the story behind what you playing if you gonna play it right."

"Thanks," Sasha mumbled. He handed Reggie the guitar. Reggie looked at it, and his forehead creased together. And then he handed the guitar back.

"Keep it. I ain't using it anytime soon." Reggie stood. "You got something kid. So don't blow it like I did."

He walked Sasha to the door.

"Don't you make her play that garbage, now," Reggie said.

"I can't make Monti do anything," Sasha said. But it was as though Reggie didn't hear.

"She's too good to play that trash."

Sasha looked Reggie in the eye.

"She's too good for a lot of things."

CHAPTER SEVEN

MONTI STARED OUT THE WINDOW, watching the football team practice on a freshly cut field, their bleached jerseys glowing neon in the sun. Mrs. Henry wrote an algebra problem on the board, its dark, mossy surface smeared with pastel-colored chalk.

Solve for x: 4x + 62 = 347

There were six students in the class, juniors who'd failed the year before, and she was by far the smartest. She wasn't there because she struggled with math. Her guidance counselor felt it would be good to start her first semester with an extra study period. Just so she could transition successfully into a tougher curriculum. Monti was smart, but she struggled with her homework sometimes. It was hard to concentrate when she was hungry. And though, like the seasons, it came and went in varied force, she was always hungry.

She solved the problem quickly - *347-62= 285. 285/4 = 71.25 = x* - and showed Mrs. Henry her answer.

"Very good, Monti!" Mrs. Henry said. "I'm so proud of you!"

"Yeah. Cool. Whatever."

Monti was smart. She didn't need Mrs. Henry's praise.

The bell rang and she packed her school books into her backpack for the last time that summer. She chugged her milk, courtesy of the donation boxes from Mt. Calvary that appeared on her doorstep every few weeks, and tossed the carton into the garbage on her way out. Her steps echoed in the empty hallway, the white linoleum freshly mopped and smelling like lemon, glistening so she could see her reflection. She thought of where that girl on the floor was headed.

Bare cupboards, except for a package of old grits, until the next donation box came along. Filmy carpets with a decade's worth of grunge. Second-hand smoke. Empty liquor bottles. Reggie's mood swings. And Birdie. Crying or laughing or singing or sleeping. Or hurting. Lately, it was hurting more than the others.

She left the midcentury-styled high school, all red brick and geometric panes framed with white paneling, and headed for the football field. A group of players horsed around and practiced a play. From Monti's vantage, they were running the play entirely wrong, but it was nice to be on the grass and feel the wind in her hair, to feel the camaraderie of fellow athletes.

She watched Clarke Adamson, how his green eyes almost glowed against the gray, city backdrop and how he flicked the red hair off his forehead. The wind lifted his cut-off shirt, his abs wrenching as he twisted to throw a perfect spiral. But it landed on the ground because his friend Jared had terrible hands. She didn't like Clarke. He was stupid and popular and lived on the hill. But he was sexy, and lately she'd been wanting the feel of a hard body against hers. Lately she'd been noticing the dimpled chins and Adam's apples of her male peers, and had felt the way her body reacted when she stood near a boy who was taller and stronger than she. It was as if her body had its own mind, was wrought and ready to jump the first willing casualty.

Jared looked up as she walked by along the track. She hated Jared, too, hated how he breathed through his mouth and grabbed girls' butts as they walked to their seats on the bus. Most of all, she hated his nickname for her.

"No girls allowed, Oreo!"

It had been weeks since she'd been cut from the team for losing her temper, even though her temper had been no more intense than anything the boys displayed. But Jared wasn't clever and Monti figured this was the only insult he had in his pocket.

"I don't know why you're laughing, Jared. You guys are the worst team in the league. You won't win a single game this season with your butter fingers."

"Like you could do better," he said, rolling his eyes.

"Actually, I can."

Monti grabbed the football and shoved it into Clarke's gut.

"Call it out," she said, lining up in the slot back position.

The boys lined up, five on each side.

"Red 22, Blue 43, hut hut."

The ball was in Clarke's hands and Monti ran forward. She stutter-stepped her defender and cut across the middle. Clarke fired the ball and it landed expertly in her hands. Another defenseman flanked her on the right, and she spun the opposite direction, taking off down the field, her wild hair bouncing behind her as she gained more speed. She looked back. All the boys were watching and she could hear their incredulous clamoring from down the field.

"We were practicing that play all morning." A kid with terrible acne gave her a high five as she returned to the huddle. "You should totally have made the team."

Jared scoffed.

"Who cares? So she can run. Doesn't mean she can play with us. She might get her period and start crying on the field."

The words hurt more than she would've liked to admit. She had been playing football with these boys since grade school. She'd even gone so far as to have called them friends.

"I'll play defense this time," she said.

They lined up in the same formation, this time Jared in the slot back position. Monti took a position behind the defensive line as linebacker.

Jared made the same run, cutting across the middle. Monti

slipped past a block attempt, and just as he began to fumble the ball in his hands, she laid him down on his back with a hard hit to his chest. His teammates helped him stand.

"That was a fluke! No way a girl can play. Let's run it again."

"Don't be so upset, man. Oreo is not a girl, she's built like Sasquatch." Clarke patted Jared's shoulder.

She felt her nostrils flare. Of course she was a girl. She was strong with big thighs and ripped arms. She could hit hard and run fast and learn a play by simply watching from a window. She could hit her drums as fast and as hard as the guy who played on "Wipeout." She was a full-blown, red-blooded female. And now she was pissed.

Jared scowled and trudged back to the slot receiver position.

"Let's run it again," he shouted.

Monti took her position at linebacker and shoved her fingers into the damp earth. Clarke called the play, the veins in his neck straining as his deep voice rumbled. The ball snapped and she rushed forward, propelling straight from her haunches and through the offensive line. Jared happened across her path, and she exploited the opportunity by throwing an elbow and crushing his nose. Clarke looked down the field for a second option and didn't see her coming. Her shoulders hit him square in the stomach and she relished the sound he made as he gasped for air. She exerted the cache of strength from her legs, and just for good measure, lifted him off his feet. She threw in some extra elbows and a fist in his solar plexus before throwing both of their bodies to the grass. The boys crowded around them and Jared pushed his way to the front.

"What the hell, Monti! He can't get hurt, our first game is in a couple weeks!" He wiped the blood from his nose on his sleeve.

She looked down at Clarke, his beautiful face red and grimacing with pain. It was almost as red as hers on the day she earned her nickname, Oreo.

Her fifth grade class had gone to the Nordic Heritage Museum, a new community center which opened that year to showcase the neighborhood's Scandinavian history. After the field trip, Monti and her classmates walked back to the school, weaving through Ballard's Historic District of merchant shops, warehouses, blue-collar pubs and diners. Back to the intersection of Fifteenth and Market Street.

It was there, in front of the Denny's and smokeshop, that a familiar voice cut through her classmates' prattle.

"Hey sugar, why don't you come lick mine off me!"

Birdie stumbled towards a man who looked to be taking his smoke break away from the docks, a battered Mariner's cap hiding his face and his t-shirt covered in grease stains. They carried on in front of the store entrance. Birdie's alligator miniskirt hiked up, as if it was summiting the knolls of her jiggling thighs. One of her earrings dropped to the ground, and she shouted in mock frustration when the man picked it up, holding it away from her so she pawed for it like a kitten. Monti willed the crosswalk to change. Her classmates pointed and laughed at the loud woman making a spectacle of herself. She pretended not to hear the nasty things her mother said to a complete stranger, but then Birdie looked up and shouted,

"Monti, baby! Hey man, that there is my little girl. My sweet baby girl!"

Birdie bent over in front of the man, grinding her goods against the coarse crotch of his jeans. Clarke looked at her and said,

"Is *THAT* your mom?"

But what he'd meant was, *I thought you were like us. I thought you were normal.*

His teammates gathered around their quarterback, muttering under their breath, things like, *What the hell is Oreo's problem?* and, *That crazy bitch.* Monti didn't defend herself. Because it felt too good, putting Clarke in his place.

Clarke leaped to his feet. He grabbed her around the neck, almost hard enough so she couldn't breathe. He lifted her until only her toes grazed the turf. She saw it in his eyes - he was capable of hurting her. And instead of repelling her, this fact seemed to draw her in. His cologne smelled expensive. She looked down and watched his abdominals go taut as he shouted,

"You dumb Spook!"

She wanted the whole of him, if only to prove her own worth. She wanted to make him shudder until he realized she'd always been his equal. It was embarrassing to want the approval of her abuser, but she couldn't help herself. In that moment she wanted to win Clarke's heart so she could drop him the way Jared dropped his passes.

The boys murmured things like, *hey man, calm down,* and just as quickly Clarke's demeanor changed. He pushed her easily, playfully to the ground.

"You should be careful, Oreo," he said. "You can't hurt people and expect them not to hit back."

RICHARD WATCHED through the windshield of his Mustang while he waited in the parking lot. He'd planned to give Clarke a ride home after practice. Though sometimes allowed to drive out of convenience, Clarke still hadn't passed his driver's test. He was just getting ready to call Clarke over when he saw the girl with gray eyes walking along the track. She was unmistakable, and he sat back against his seat, watching as she gestured confidently at the group of young men.

He had enjoyed her brash physicality, and nearly doubled over when she took his son down to the ground. Watching her make a fool of those boys in her bare feet and cutoff shorts reminded him of his childhood in the Valley, back when he was Ricky Adamoli. He had spent his summers kissing black girls beneath the park's bleachers, so their brothers wouldn't kill him for it. Or playing basketball and skinning his knees on the hard cement. Or making sure that when his mother nodded off she didn't burn their house down with her lit cigarette.

He spent his winters in the classroom, always closest to the radiator to warm his legs, always exposed by his old basketball shorts. His was one of the only white faces, and he endured smack talk from his friends.

Man, ain't no girl gonna suck your dick. That fire crotch might burn her face off.

To which he'd reply:

Must be why your daddy's so mad, now that your momma's face look like the bald spot at the back of your head.

After school, he'd hit the corner store and pocket miniature pies and pepperoni sticks for dinner, then come home and make sure his mom was facedown and still breathing. This had been his life until he was put into the foster care system shortly after his thirteenth birthday. And sometimes he missed it.

Richard wiped his palms against his corduroy slacks, readying himself for when she entered the parking lot. He didn't know what he would say, but wanted to introduce himself somehow.

Hi. I'm the man whose trash you were eating. I was wondering if I could help you change your life?

But then Richard watched his son's reaction. He leapt from the car, ready to save this street angel who'd suckled from his scraps like a sweet, stray dog. He heard the words his son used, and felt his stomach coil and split open as if it would swallow Richard whole for the shame of it all. Where had Clarke learned such hate?

Richard watched as the girl left the field. He would apologize, profusely, for the ignorance of his ill-gotten offspring. But he saw in her eyes a look of wonderment and froze. He followed her gaze to a slender boy with long, blonde hair. The boy leaned against a Chevy Suburban, and wore black jeans cut short and frayed at the cuff. He pushed away from the car, revealing a t-shirt with a skull on the back. He blew smoke from his cigarette in her direction. She coughed and sputtered and feigned disgust, but still maintained her gap-toothed smile. He sauntered until he reached her feet, then bowed like she were royalty. Richard gripped his steering wheel as the boy brushed grass off her collar bone. He felt like an intruder. A voyeur, watching something he'd never experience for himself. Never again, anyway.

He started the car, deciding that Clarke could walk home. And on his drive back up the hill, he convinced himself that his disappointment stemmed only from a missed opportunity to help a child in need.

CHAPTER EIGHT

BIRDIE HADN'T COME HOME the night before, so there was no cake, no pastel-colored balloons and no wrapped packages when Monti woke on the morning of her sixteenth birthday. Instead she found a muggy day, partly sunny or partly cloudy depending on where you stood, and likely to change. She found an open box of condoms and empty beer cans on the living room floor. The coffee table, which was propped on a broken leg and a stack of old newspapers, was covered in dirty spoons, yet lacked the one thing she'd hoped to find: food.

She opened the front door to let in the fresh air and found a donation box on the stoop. This one was filled with the same as the last, cans of ravioli, packaged ramen, creamed corn, green beans, and tuna. But after stocking the shelves she found something else at the bottom of the box. A package of Twinkies, and nestled comfortably between the two cakes was a silver ring with an emerald stone. It was so big the stone nearly touched her knuckle, and she'd never owned anything so beautiful before. It must have been a mistake. Whoever packed the box had probably lost it. She slipped it on her middle finger for safekeeping, and made a plan to call Mt. Calvary to find its rightful owner.

The muggy morning was replaced by a heavy heat. Cruise ships barked their departure with a loud horn. And trains rattled against the tracks as they rolled through the yard.

Monti tore her room apart, rifling through her closet for something to wear. Sasha was taking her out for her birthday, and she wanted to look pretty.

Lately, all the time they'd spent together had been focused on the band. Everyday at five o'clock they would drive past the canneries, breweries and warehouses of Ballard to Tommy's house. She'd take her seat with her sticks in hand and count down a Black Sabbath song, even though she wanted to play funk covers. The one good thing about Reggie's return was that he would bring his albums along with him, and she'd grown to love artists like Parliament, Funkadelic, and Brass Construction. Sasha had the voice to sing black music, and she had the power and rhythm, but Tommy Pearson was hopeless. He was gangly and didn't know what to do with his body, could play only one tempo on the bass and somehow managed to play its deep, ruddy tones off-key. But after being cut from the football team, it was nice to participate in something. Monti learned early on that she had a natural affinity for activities that allowed her to hit hard and play dirty. And, though Tommy never left them alone, there was the added benefit of spending time with Sasha, doing the thing he loved most. Even if it meant playing tone-deaf, rhythmless, anti-melodic thrash rock the boys called "hardcore punk."

Monti settled on the only feminine thing she had in her closet. An old, pink baby doll dress with a thick, white collar, covered in blue and yellow flowers. She hadn't worn it in years, and it fit only because she still hadn't grown her breasts. After she ripped the stitching to make room in the waist the dress fit like a shift, and barely reached past her upper thighs. She found a pair of men's boxer briefs from Birdie's room, and donned her favorite tube socks with yellow ribbing to better hide her big legs. She combed her hair to one side and fastened it with a handful of colorful, plastic barrettes, shaped like rabbits and teddy bears and poodles. She painted her lips in deep plum lipstick, and to finish the look, put on the only functional pair of shoes she had besides her rain boots; faded, maroon Converse sneakers.

The doorbell rang. It was Sasha. He looked perfect in a salmon Hawaiian shirt, buttoned halfway, green army pants and black combat boots. His hair was loose so he had to flick it from his face, and each time the bright blueness of his eyes shocked her like a dirty game of peek-a-boo. She felt uncomfortable as his eyes casually tracked her head to toe. He chuckled.

"Quit laughing at me. I wanted to look nice."

"You look great," he said. "You have no idea how much. Like a punk goddess."

"I don't want to look punk. I want to look pretty."

He took her hand and led her to the Chevy. "Nah. This is way better than pretty."

They went to the Locks and had a picnic beneath the magnolia trees. They made up stories about the people in their yachts, waving like celebrities at the crowd who'd come to watch the lock chambers fill with fresh water, lifting the boats from the Sound into the city's canals. They ate fried chicken from Albertsons and drank grape pop. When Seattle's fickle summer unleashed a misty rain, they huddled together beneath the dampened blossoms. And when the rain subsided, they lay supine in the wavering sun, watching the clouds change the weather.

Sasha unbuttoned his shirt. His pale chest lit up like a road reflector. Monti noticed how his pecs had begun to square off, and before she realized her intention, had rested her hand in the grove of fresh hair, feeling his hot skin in the nape of her palm. It was as if she held his heart in her hands, as if it should be there always. He turned his face to the sun and peered at her with one eye through a blanket of lashes, his icy iris glistening beneath a raised eyebrow. Her cheeks burned as she pulled her hand away, but he caught her wrist in his fist like a heron would a fish from the canal.

"What's this?" he asked, turning her hand over to look at the ring. "Some dude stake his territory?"

Monti smiled. "Jealous?"

"Not in the least." He said it so casually, then let her hand drop like an afterthought.

She tried not to sound disappointed. "I found it," she said hesitantly. "In one of those deliveries."

He nodded and licked his lips in a non-committal way, as if they were merely dry instead of a delicious treat he was using to taunt her.

"What deliveries?"

She sucked on the inside of her cheek. She hadn't meant to tell him about the donations. She couldn't stand him knowing how pathetic she was. How poor. How hungry. How unworthy.

"I mean, I found it in the courtyard when I was checking for the mail."

He ran his fingers through the grass, his delicate, deft fingers, playing the harmony to the birdsong in the trees. His fingers, the pointer and middle, the ones she had wished would scrape her, probe her, and break her skin.

"But I'm not going to keep it," she added, taking it off.

"Why not?" he asked.

"It's not mine to keep." She turned it in her hand, and read the inscription. *My heart belongs to D.C.* She thought of two lovers meeting in the Capital, falling head over heels in love. She hoped their luck might rub off on her.

"Might as well keep it. It looks good on you, and you won't be able to find the owner now."

"I'll put it back where I found it. So at least whoever lost it has the chance to find it again."

He sat up and, to her dismay, buttoned his shirt.

"I think you should keep it. You deserve something nice. And you never break the rules." He grabbed her chin and lifted her face to meet his gaze. "Live a little with me, Monti. Finders keepers. Life is good on the dark side."

Sasha had one more surprise, though she'd insisted the picnic was more than enough.

"Don't worry. I know you would never let me buy you anything," he said.

He returned from the Chevy carrying an acoustic guitar in a black case.

She recognized it instantly.

"Where did you get that guitar?" she asked. He'd been inside her apartment. She could tell by the way his jaw clenched.

Sasha straightened his back and stared at her.

"Does it matter?"

A moment passed where neither said a word. Finally Sasha spoke.

"I wrote a song. My first one. No one has heard it before."

"Not even Tommy?" she asked.

"No. Not even Tommy. Can I play it for you?"

Monti leaned back on her elbows, afraid to watch as his fingers began to play. He was delicate as a sparrow's neck and deft as a writer's quill. His voice was soft and pretty, much unlike the way he sang in Tommy's basement, and it chimed in a tone pitched so it was heard by her ears only.

Nothing to lose, but no ending in sight
Flying too high but we're dying inside
Living on truth, but we're banking on lies
And no one says anything
No one says anything

He paused. His fingers stilled. And he cried through the silence.

Run from Mr. Brightside, run from Mr. Brightside
Or walk alone

He shifted his voice into a higher register, making the hairs on the back of her neck singe.

When no one's safe from grace, they're saved by the city
When no one's safe from grace, they're saved by the city
No place like the city
We're saved by the city

He stopped. She opened her eyes. The guitar rested against his

73

leg, the way Monti had seen Birdie do with Reggie. Like an old, tired lover.

"Have you ever kissed a girl?" she asked.

He smiled. "Was I that good?"

She felt her face get hot, the sun breaking through the clouds and landing her in a spotlight beneath the trees.

"Whatever. Never mind."

"Don't do that. I hate when you close off."

"I mean, the song was great. But it's not why I asked. I was just curious."

"Well, if it's, like, no big deal," he said, pulling his hair into a ponytail, "then yeah. I've kissed a girl."

"Who?"

He bit his bottom lip, as though he wasn't sure if he should say. He picked at the grass and sighed,

"Treesha."

She threw her hands in the air, knocking the pop over the checkered picnic blanket.

"Treesha Richards! What the hell! I hate Treesha," Monti said, crossing her arms.

"She's not that bad." Sasha righted the pop can and dabbed at the mess with a napkin.

Monti scoffed. "My asshole is cuter than Treesha. She looks like Gary Coleman with braids. Why did you kiss *her*?"

Sasha shrugged. "Why not? I'll try anything once."

Monti gathered the trash, muttering under her breath. Sasha put his guitar in its case.

"Why does it bother you? Jealous?"

Her head snapped up. His guitar was slung over his shoulder and little wisps of hair spun gold around his face. He grinned and winked.

"You're such a bastard," she said.

Monti stormed to the nearest trash can, knowing he'd follow, and as the fallen blossoms crunched beneath her feet, she said casually over one shoulder,

"And not in the least."

She heard him walking a pace behind, heard the jingle of his guitar case as it bumped against his lanky, bowlegged knees, a scene she could see though her back was turned. She'd had nine years to learn his movements, to become the expert of his antics. He would be looking at the sky no doubt, his nose like a perch for the singing birds he envied, though he could sing clearer and louder than all the fowl of the world combined. He'd say something like, *my mother's face is in that cloud,* then squint his eyes at the sun, a rule breaker at the expense of his own sight. He'd hum, and laugh at his untold jokes.

This is what she expected to see when she snuck a look over her shoulder, wanting to watch his Adam's apple move and pop as he awed over the sky above him, though it was the sky that should've been struck. Instead, he glared back at her, his eyes roving from the broken shoes on her feet to the frizzy hair the wind had blown out of place. It scared her, this look she'd never seen, this stark appraisal of her form and function. When they were kids and the boys at school teased him for being her friend, he would always say,

"She's not a *girl.* She's Monti."

She wondered if he still felt that way, if there was still a place for her left in the wake of his trajectory. She turned around quickly, somehow believing he hadn't seen her, that the heatwaves at their feet had grown high enough to blur her face. She held herself, closed her shoulders in, though it wasn't cold. And she pretended it was just another thing he said, so softly she convinced herself it was never said at all.

You wear your lies in your elbows.

The drive back to The Bridgewater was short, but Monti sweated the entire way. She'd come close to blurting it out,

I want to be with you! or

It should've been me, your first kiss.

But she chickened out each time. And by the time they reached her front doorstep, it was too late.

Taped to the door was a neon-orange notice. She didn't need to read it to know what it meant. She looked at Sasha, but he wouldn't meet her eye. Not at first. He crossed his arms, looked down at the ground so his hair curtained his face.

Eventually he did look at her, and his bottom lip quivered. A single tear eked down the bridge of his vulpine nose. Sasha lifted his arms and showed her his hands.

"What can I do? Ask me for anything and I'll do it. Whatever you want."

It would've been beautiful, looking down on his face from her perch on the stoop, had it not been for the unmistakable pity she felt in his deference. What did she want? It was simple, really. She wanted to be his equal. Her sense of stability and self-worth depended on it.

Her hand shook as she forced her key into the locked door.

"Nothing," she said. "There's nothing you can do."

TWO DAYS later Monti returned from band practice to the sound of funk music blasting from the record player. She walked inside and smelled hotdog mac n' cheese simmering on the stove. Birdie's voice belted from the kitchen, singing along to the music.

"What's up?" Monti said.

Birdie grabbed her hand and spun her around.

"We celebrating your birthday, girl!"

Birdie opened the refrigerator and pointed to a cake with white frosting and sprinkles.

"My birthday was days ago."

Birdie's smile wavered, then rebounded just as fast.

"I know, baby. I'm sorry I wasn't here."

"I was worried about you. You could've called."

"I know I know I know," Birdie said. She stirred the pot on the stove. "I got to working late at the bar. And then Reggie needed some help with something or other at his place. Cleaning, stuff like that you know. A woman's touch. And then I had to go back to work again...."

Birdie dished the macaroni into two bowls, pulling at the baggy sleeves of her sweatshirt to keep them away from the cheese sauce. When had her mother gotten so thin? Had it happened overnight, or slowly while Monti wasn't looking? She'd need to remember to save some of the food from the donation boxes. Birdie obviously wasn't eating enough.

"Well, it's almost seven now. Don't you have to be at the bar soon?"

Birdie kissed her forehead. She carried the food into the living room and motioned for Monti to follow.

"It's girls' night tonight. Ain't nobody in the world but me and you."

Monti filled her stomach with cheesy carbs and cake. They watched cartoon reruns while Birdie braided her hair. Birdie dug her fingers deep into Monti's kinks, pulling and braiding with such force that her eyes welled.

"Ouch!"

Birdie pushed her head back into position.

"Hush now and quit moving. Tender heads don't get fed."

"What does that mean?"

"It means if you want that white boy to think you look fresh you best let me get these braids straight."

Monti's mouth went dry at the mention of Sasha. The eviction notice had made band practice awkward, and she wondered why Birdie hadn't mentioned it.

Birdie finished Monti's hair and placed a package on her lap. It had been wrapped with the comic section of the newspaper.

"Where did this come from?"

"Go on and open it," Birdie said.

Monti tore at the paper, leaving it in shreds at her side. Birdie clapped and laughed when she pulled out her present. It was a Ballard letterman's jacket. Class of '75 and the color of burnt mustard.

"I know how disappointed you were when you didn't make the football team," Birdie said.

Monti brought the jacket to her face. It smelled like books and moths and dust.

"The world ain't kind to brown girls. But that don't make you unworthy. You are talented. You were better than a lot of them boys. And you not making the team don't mean you should give up."

Monti rubbed the leather sleeves. They were cream and polished with the wear of its previous owner.

Birdie touched her face.

"When it's something that really matters to you. When it matters more than anything else...."

Monti looked into her mother's honeyed eyes and felt the only type of love that mattered.

"Never. Give. Up."

Birdie let go of her face. Monti nodded and choked down a sob.

"Did you see what was on the front door?" she asked, wrapping herself in her new jacket.

Birdie sucked air through her teeth.

"There you go. Minding everything but your own damn business."

"But what are we gonna do? The notice said we have until the end of October. It says we owe three months worth of rent, plus late fees. It's like, almost $1,500."

Birdie kicked her slippers to the floor and stretched out on the pleather couch like a cat.

"You so worried about it, get a job."

"Minimum wage is $2.30 an hour." Monti did the math in her head. "Even if I worked sixty hours a week, it would take me three months to make enough."

Birdie rested her feet on the coffee table, the wood creaking unreliably beneath the weight.

"Well there you go."

Monti sighed. "Momma. We don't have three months. And I've got school."

"You know what I was doing at sixteen? Wasn't going to no

fancy school with a bunch of immigrant, crab-eating white kids. I was riding in the back of a segregated train, no toilets, no food, no water. And I was six months pregnant with you."

Birdie made the face that Monti hated. It was one where she was smiling, though it was obvious she just laughed away the pain. It was one that made Monti feel that if not for her love, there would be no one in the world who truly cared for her mother. It was the face of one who'd been beaten down for having turned the other cheek, and who truly believed their adversary was still an ally.

"You think you too good to drop out, that it? Already got more schooling than me. So you must think you're better than me."

"No, Momma. I don't think that."

Birdie smiled. "You should've seen the way they cheered for me in those nightclubs. Said I was better than Aretha. Thousands of people, screaming my name. 'Birdie James! Encore! Sing it Birdie!' So don't you worry, I'll be back on top like that. Soon. Real soon."

Monti nodded, a small movement of her head. She'd read the article about the performance Birdie recounted. She'd heard the story at least thirty times, and the number in the crowd grew with each iteration. Birdie had reached *thousands of people,* when the article said the audience had been no more than sixty.

Birdie walked to her bedroom, and Monti heard the sounds of drawers opening. She returned and handed Monti a faded shoe box.

"All my people's in the Central District, yet I sacrificed to move you here, just like I did when I left Alabama. You worried about losing a roof." Birdie chuckled. "When I was your age I was worried about getting lynched for not letting a white woman have the sidewalk."

Birdie pointed at the box, and Monti opened it. Inside was a stack of bills, multiples of ones, fives and twenties thrown in haphazardly like green confetti. Its metallic smell was as comforting as fresh baked cookies.

"Where did this come from?" Monti asked.

"Life is easier when you fine looking. The more men want your kitty, the more you can control them. That's how I get all them tips at the bar."

Birdie flipped her braids over a shoulder. "So don't you be questioning me again, hear? I love you. I'll take care of you. It's all gravy, baby."

Monti nodded. She felt like crying. A lump formed in her throat, like a cancer caused by exposure to despair. She couldn't bear another story of Birdie's former greatness. So she swallowed that cancer to let it nourish her belly.

Birdie sank back into the pleather couch and grabbed the remote control from the coffee table. "Hand me that *TV Guide*," she said. "I want to see if my soaps are on."

Monti sat on the floor in front of her mother. They didn't speak for hours. As midnight rolled in from the coast and Monti dozed in and out of sleep, she heard Birdie say,

"I'd give you the world, baby girl. I'd give you the world if I could."

CHAPTER NINE

IT WAS the end of August, drawing with it the dank smell of burnt and fallen leaves into Seattle proper. The long, summer days darkened, intensifying the anxiety and anticipation for the coming winter. The people of the streets were more desperate in winter, as were the single mothers struggling to keep the heat turned on. Drugs and crime were exacerbated by the weather, drawing everyone of means indoors and left alone to their own devices. The homeless were left to fend in the biting cold, the wet kind that seeped into the bones and froze from the inside out. No more long walks or barbecues, no more music festivals, no more jogging. And no more warm nights where sleep could be found on a nearby park bench. Just an endless expanse of gray and rain, and the stifling boredom that came with it.

There was a knock on the door. Richard put his newspaper down.

"Hello, Your Honor," he said as Tomlinson let himself into the office.

"Fancy meeting you here," Tomlinson said, a jovial smirk on his face.

Richard tapped the paper.

"Just thought I'd get caught up before heading home. I should actually get going." He reached for his suit jacket.

"Some pretty little number was wandering the halls looking for you today. I said I'd pass the message along since you were in court at the time." Tomlinson handed Richard a folded piece of legal paper. It read,

Mr. Adamson,

I'm writing to say thank you. With the money you gave me, I was able to take an intense, two-week GED course while my kids were in school. I stayed up every night to study. And guess what? I passed, and got a filing job at the King County Records Office. I spect that was because of you also. I don't make as much money as I did when I was dating, but I've got health insurance now, and the county building has a daycare service. We should be all right, for now I think. I never thought there were people like you in this world. I can only think it was God that brought you to me. If I can ever return the favor, you know where to find me.
555-2121
xoxo
Ebonique

Richard tucked the note into the pocket of his slacks, letting it mingle with his keys and spare change. Tomlinson regarded him the way Richard imagined a father might, with mild concern expressed in the warm crease of his pressed mouth. Richard concluded that he had also read the letter.

"Nothing wrong with being a sucker for a sob story," Tomlinson said, winking his Kewpie-doll eye.

The hairs stood on the back of Richard's neck.

"Not sure what you mean," he said.

Tomlinson stroked the stubble on his chin.

"Don't you though, Ricky?"

Richard had worked with Tomlinson in the Juvenile Division for a long time. And it'd started when Richard was still a juvenile, sitting on the wrong side of the conference table.

"I told you not to call me that," Richard said. "And I don't appreciate what you're implying. My family means everything to me, and there's not a woman in the world who could tempt me to stray."

Tomlinson sat in the plaid, upholstered chair in front of Richard's desk. The desk was made of glass, and half was covered with manila folders. And at the edge rested a Newton's cradle, which Richard had won at the office Christmas party. Tomlinson lifted one of the silver balls and let it drop, setting the apparatus into swing so it tap-tap-tapped the seconds down.

"Relax. No one here but old friends. It would do you well to be nice to me. Otherwise I won't tell you my news." Tomlinson winked. Or it might've been a blink. Richard could never tell.

He clenched his fist. He thought he'd made a clean break after he changed his name. After the details of his juvenile record had been purged. Why the defense attorney from his case remembered him twenty-years later was just a stroke of dumb-fucking luck. No one else from that life survived - either they were gone or were not credible enough to do any damage.

"What is it?" Richard asked.

"A private investigator contacted me. He wanted to know if I'd ever met a woman named Martha Adamoli. Said he was trying to solve a cold case."

Richard cleared his throat. Why would anyone investigate the death of his mother?

"Anyways. Just wanted to give you a heads up." Tomlinson rose from his seat. From the door he added,

"I always liked you. I could tell you were one of the good ones. Had *chutzpah* coming out of your ears. I just want you to know - I believe in second chances."

THE SKY WAS the golden color of a seagull's beak as the sun set behind cobalt clouds. Two ferries crossed paths in the bay, two shifts ending and beginning the day's work as the residents of Bainbridge returned and left the island. Richard drove up Third

Avenue and stopped at the light on Pike Street. Shadows and sweatshirts huddled together in front of the McDonald's, hands buried deep into pockets, white smiles against dark backdrops, mischievous like the Cheshire cat. It was where most of the city's drug deals happened, as it was easy to hop off a bus, shake a hand, and catch the next one as it peeled away from the curb, dime-bag in tow. He left downtown by way of Fifteenth Avenue, past the warehouses, building suppliers and the Seattle Grain Terminal, a concrete, prison-like structure with a plank that reached out into the bay.

Richard had called the school and reported the incident with his son and the girl with gray eyes. He wanted to teach Clarke a valuable life lesson. He'd convinced the receptionist to help, and gave her the name the boys used - "Sasquatch." The receptionist recognized the nickname instantly. And she trusted him enough to share the name and address of the guardian on file, Birdie James. After all, he was the Deputy Juvenile Prosecutor for King County.

He drove over the Ballard Bridge. Fishing fleets nestled together in the star-shimmered water and dockside pubs beckoned with neon bar signs. He stopped the Mustang on Leary Avenue, across the street from a place called The Bridgewater. He let the engine idle and ran a hand through his hair. He looked into the courtyard of the apartment complex. It was quiet, almost peaceful. The walkway was made of cobblestone and the grass kept neat. Lining the stone were cherry blossom trees, whose leaves had begun to turn fire engine red. The scene looked like an idyllic, Bavarian village.

"It's not my fault," he said to himself after a time, seeing the faces of dead black girls in his mind's eye. "It's not my fault if I save her."

❦

MONTI WOKE TO SHOUTING. Drowsy, she felt around for a pair of sweats, her hand feeling along the floor from the single, twin mattress on which she lay. Once dressed, she rushed from her bedroom to find Reggie standing over her mother.

"Fuck you!" he screamed. "You stealing from me now? You just a goddam ho!"

He raised a fist and struck Birdie in the temple, who lay cowering and whimpering on the floor.

"Please, baby, no!" she cried.

Monti charged him, as she'd done so many times on the football field, and shoved him into the old television set. He fell backwards, grabbing the yellowed curtains and ripped them as he crashed to the floor. He stood quickly, the whites of his eyes like syrup as the blood vessels pushed to the surface.

"I'll kill you if you touch her again," she said.

Birdie stood and tried to usher Monti back to her room.

"This is none of your concern. Git out of here."

"Hell no, Momma! You can't let him walk all over us like this." She turned to Reggie. "Hit me instead. See what happens."

He scoffed. "You need to learn some respect for your momma, little girl."

Monti chortled. "You first. Leave now, before I call the police."

Birdie grabbed her arm. "Don't you call nobody. Now git! This is grown folk talk."

"But he ain't talking!"

Monti watched helplessly as Birdie went to soothe Reggie. He stood still while she whispered in his ear, shushed him like a spooked horse. And then he pushed her again, knocking her into a table lamp. Reggie raised his fist and hit Birdie in the face. Her mother curled into herself and moaned.

Monti ran into the kitchen and dialed 911. A few minutes passed between giving the operator her address and the loud knock at the door. Monti assumed a neighbor must've called, and she wished the walls of the The Bridgewater weren't so thin. Before anyone could react, two police officers burst into the apartment, shattering the doorframe. They grabbed Reggie and dragged him into the courtyard.

"What the hell is going on?" he demanded, but they offered no explanation. His eyes wide terror.

Monti stood in the middle of the courtyard, watching the cops perp-walk Reggie towards the squad car. The neighbors, a young couple in their thirties with twin toddlers, stood in their window with the curtains drawn open. Their necks strained with morbid curiosity.

Monti felt vindicated, even as the younger officer slammed Reggie's head into the door of the parked vehicle. He fell to the ground, and the older officer kicked him in the stomach. He was getting what he deserved after what he'd done to her mother. Until the younger officer punched his face in rapid succession, making these sick, cracking sounds as Reggie choked on his own blood. His eyebrow burst open and his head snapped back against the concrete. Birdie shrieked in agony. She barreled past, and Monti grabbed for her.

The older officer locked Reggie in the backseat of the squad car, and Monti tasted bile as the young officer squared his body to the thundering, lovesick woman stampeding towards him. She reached for the door handle, but he wrapped his arms around her neck and tackled her to the ground. Birdie made gasping noises, her mouth opening and closing like a displaced goldfish. The older officer removed his baton and struck Birdie, who was now defenseless and held down by the young officer's knee. Her mother yipped and squealed like a beaten dog, and Monti's heart almost broke. She felt her mouth open, her throat grating as her voice carried across the courtyard, a name she hadn't uttered in years.

"Mommy!"

§

THE GIRL with gray eyes screamed and Richard's heart swelled against his ribcage. He saw the chords in her throat pull taught as she took off running, her rage conveyed in the speed at which she moved. He stepped out of the car, unsure of what to do.

The long-haired boy he'd seen in the school parking lot ran out of the house, wearing nothing but a pair of boxer shorts. He tackled her in the grass before she reached the sidewalk, before the officers could react to her pending assault. It seemed it took all the boy's strength to hold her back from harm, and they wrestled in the yard like angry siblings. Finally she gave in, and sobbed in his arms while he stroked her wild hair.

Richard envied the boy's youth and his ability to comfort the girl. Richard wanted to offer her comfort, wanted to take her from the life for which she'd had no choice in the making. Because she reminded him of himself, and that feeling of impotence he'd run from as a boy. She reminded him of someone he didn't save.

Richard started his Mustang and seeped his way back into the night. He drove past the Kingdome, the golfball-shaped stadium where the SuperSonics had won the Western Conference Championship during the 1978-79 season. He drove through the industrial swathe south of downtown, home to the Port and its orange and white gantry cranes, steel mills, business parks and bread factories. He took a deep breath and smelled the fresh and rising yeast in the air - a small comfort after what he'd witnessed.

Soon he was in Georgetown, a blue-collar community that, like Ballard, had been annexed into the city in the early 1900s. It had been known for its saloon-lined streets and twenty-four-hour vice. Now it was a small enclave of houses and bars, a community of families and artists and renters. Factories spewed pollution along the murky, toxic Duwamish River, where the first two Headbanger victims were found.

He parked his Mustang at the curb of a little craftsman. It was bright yellow and seemed to glow beneath the street lamps. He'd known he would come here, even before he found the address in the phone book he kept in his car.

Ebonique answered the door in a pink robe and black head scarf.

"Mr. Adamson? What you doing here?"

She wore earrings, gold and shaped like hearts. Her skin was scrubbed clean and oiled. She looked pretty without all the makeup, her natural caramel color offsetting her thick, pink lips. Her brown eyes were big and clear and doe-like.

"Just wanted to stop by," he said.

"Well, I appreciate everything you done for us. But we're good. I don't want to take nothing more from you."

"That's okay. The only thing I'm offering is my company."

He was homesick. It came and went with the waves of stress. Sometimes he could go for months without feeling it, other times just days. But lately, ever since the murders began, his taste for nostalgia was nearly an addiction.

"And what makes you think I want your company?" Ebonique asked.

"I'll be honest," he said, tugging lightly at his chin. "I'm not really concerned with what *you* want." He rubbed a smear from the corner of her mouth with his thumb. "You'll still get it, though."

Ebonique sucked air through her teeth and pursed her lips. She seemed at a loss for words.

He brushed his red hair off his forehead, the way he'd done so many times to win affection. He let his hand rest against the door-frame and leaned close so his designer cologne surrounded them in aphrodisia. Ebonique broke eye contact. She took in his suit and tie and polished shoes. She let out a breath. And he knew he'd won.

"By the way," he said as she let him inside, "this time, I *am* here to fuck you."

Monti woke in Sasha's bed the next morning, wondering how he could breathe and sleep so soundly after what happened the previous night. She couldn't sleep on her lumpy mattress, where merely inches separated her from civility and dozing like a dog on the floor. She couldn't listen to her mother's sobs as she cried out for Reggie, or for the bruised ribs and broken lip the police had left to tend.

She fingered the ends of Sasha's golden locks as they frayed against his pillow. She pulled the flannel he'd lent her closed around her face, and breathed in his smells; sweat, Irish Spring, and tobacco. She slipped quietly from the bed, and even quieter out the window into the soft mound of beauty bark behind The Bridgewater. She didn't want to wake him. Because he'd only try to make her feel better, or would give her that look of concern she'd grown to hate. She couldn't stand his feeling sorry for her, not when she so desperately wished he might feel something else.

She walked behind the apartments out to the sidewalk on Seventeenth Avenue. It was so early the moon set in the west while the sun rose in the east. The first risers in Magnolia had turned on their house lights, making little window stars carved into the ridge like gemstones. Up the street on Ballard Avenue, a line of sleepy storefronts with names like *Ballard Hardware, Metal Welding, Olson's Upholstery,* and *Marine Supply,* waited to be opened. A flock of seagulls danced and dove overhead, cawing in celebration of the morning's catch.

Once in the courtyard, Monti took comfort in the coming fall, and the leaves that brightened as a final, rebellious act before they shed and fell from grace. She was glad that school would start soon, and she'd be free from the drama and uncertainty. At least she hoped that was true - she could still hear her mother's screams and the crack of Reggie's skull against the pavement.

A trash can stood in front of her stoop. It had been set on fire. The remains looked and smelled like charred popcorn. Someone spelled a message in ketchup, probably meant to look like blood, on the walkway in front of her apartment. It was framed nicely with red and yellow leaves cut fresh by the wind, and read,

Nigger trash burns.

She walked inside and found Birdie pacing, muttering to herself and holding the shoebox.

"They think they can mess with us! Think they can scare us! They don't even know, don't even know what I'm 'bout to do."

"Momma?"

89

Birdie turned a wild eye, pointed and said,

"They ain't gon' get me girl. Ya hear? They think they can get away with this, but no sir, ain't gonna happen. Think I'll just bend over and take it. They couldn't pay me enough to take that shit."

She was raving, and the dark circles beneath her eyes made her skin look pale yellow instead of the bright toffee she'd always been.

"Momma, I think you should sit down." Monti moved to help her mother, but Birdie shrugged her off.

"Cain't. I gotta get down to the jail before they hurt him worse."

Monti noticed the pink shoebox in Birdie's hand. "Payless" it said, in gold, block letters. But she'd been paying her whole life. Each time she went to bed without dinner. Each time the rain soaked through the holes in her shoes. Each time her classmates snickered when she walked in wearing the same clothes as the day before. Each time she went without, Birdie insisted it was because her money went into that box.

"Momma? What are you doing with that? We need that money for rent." Monti grabbed for the shoebox, but Birdie pushed her so hard she fell over the broken coffee table. Monti watched helplessly as Birdie opened the door. She looked back, over a shoulder.

"Sometimes you make so much history with someone, the present just don't make sense. But that's my man, and I'm bailing him out. You'll understand. One day."

And then she was gone.

MONTI SAT on her stoop with only the moonlight to illuminate her thoughts. They needed to conserve. Electricity. Water. Food.

A soppy bucket sat beside her. She pulled out a sponge, stepped down from the top stair and knelt on the pavement. She smelled roasted marshmallows on the air, coming from a neighbor's fire pit though yards away, a smell carried on the wind to contradict her situation. Down on her knees, ashy and rough against the hard ground, she scrubbed out the words made of tomato and corn syrup,

Nigger Trash Burns.

She worked in the dark so no one could see the tear roll down her cheek.

A cruise ship horn sounded. A train bellowed as it rattled through Interbay, and Monti pictured it chugging away over a rail bridge past the Locks until it disappeared into the stark, blue form of the Western Mountain Ridge. Like the trains and ships that rolled through Ballard, she would roll too, away, away, away until no one called her "Spook" or "Oreo" or "Nigger."

Her stubborn pride could no longer soothe her, so she whispered, over and over as the city blared in the distance and the lapping bay beat against the shore,

It's all gravy. It's all gravy. It's all gravy...

CHAPTER TEN

Montgomery, Alabama
1949-1954

BIRDIE EULA JAMES was born in Montgomery, Alabama, and to the granddaughter of a former slave. If she had also been a slave, her mother Fannie once said, she'd have worked in the house, as her skin was the color of golden wheat in autumn, and her hair coiled loosely into springy, black curls. Her mother said this kind of beauty was evil, and would draw devils to her door like horse shit would a fly.

But Birdie thought this beauty was sacred. That it defined her. That it would set her free from the evils of Jim Crow, some strange little man who kept people like her separate from those with pinker, paler skin.

But if this beauty was indeed as her mother said, then the key to her shackles would be her voice, which could only have been a calling from God as bold as it was. From the time of her first words, Birdie sang gospel hymns each Sunday morning at the church in King Hill. She'd hear the word of God, sermons about staying humble and thankful, and how to turn the other cheek in the face of oppression. She didn't fully understand what those sermons meant, though suspected they touched on why she and her mother were forced to stand on the bus so a white person could have their seat.

Birdie didn't see much of her father, who found work in Detroit and only came home every other weekend. And her older brothers had trickled out of the house before she could name them without her baby lisp.

"It's just as well," Fannie said. "Better far from here than in the plot next door."

And for as long as Birdie could remember, her mother Fannie kept house for Mr. Jeffries, cooking, cleaning and laundering in a beautiful neighborhood called Capitol Heights. Sometimes Birdie wondered why Mr. Jeffries and his family lived in a big house made with clean paint, on streets that sparkled in the hot sunlight, with a wraparound porch on which to drink lemonade, while she and her mother lived on dirt, gravel roads in a gray shed and had to do their "unmentionings" outside in a backyard privy. But Mr. Jeffries was a pleasant man, and the only white person with whom Birdie was allowed to speak without being addressed first.

"Why?" Birdie asked Fannie. For so many things.

Why couldn't she walk through the front door of Mr. Jeffries' house when she came to help her mother with work after school?

Why was it that when she played with the white children while Fannie finished her work, she was made to wait outside like a stray when the rest were called in for cake?

Why did she have to stand on the bus when the front half was empty?

Why did she have to drink from "Colored" fountains and eat from "Colored" restaurants and go to "Colored" movie theaters?

Why did she get called names like "Coon," and "Spook" and "Nigger" when she crossed the invisible line that separated the shanties and juke joints in King Hill from the glimmering lawns of Capitol Heights, but when cars filled with white men came rolling through their part of town they locked their doors like hidden treasures lay just inside? And when Birdie was old enough, Fannie told her a story.

On a muggy, Spring day in Union Springs, Alabama, when Birdie's mother was a girl, she'd seen a black man hanging from a tree on her way to school. She'd seen the flies as they ate away the flesh between his eye sockets, the deep, black emptiness of the Devil at his work. She'd heard the grownups whisper about Wilbur Tomkins, how he got there in that tree. How he'd argued for a fair wage instead of the sharecropper's debt, which only made his people slaves once again. Because how could a man be free when he must pay for the seed by promising the crop? How could a man be free when he was tied to the land he toiled?

Wilbur's grandfather had worked the same land, only with a hard whip at his back. And that whip had been passed down to the current landowner, whose wife had insisted that not only did Wilbur forget his place like a good Negro, but had made his lascivious intent known by licking his lips the entire time he broached her on the subject of better pay.

The mob that took him had cut off his ears and let his organs spill free. They gave his toes to their children to keep as souvenir, and removed his manhood to hang from his neck, the neck they had tied a rope around, the neck they had taken his life from as he twitched and choked and begged his God for deliverance.

This scene had stuck with Birdie's mother, had given her nightmares for weeks. She decided then, somewhere in the middle of her girlhood, to avoid white people as much as possible, to cross the street when one approached, to nod and say nothing more than "Yessuh" or "No ma'am" or "I'll pick twice as much tomorrow."

Birdie shook with anger after hearing this story.

"But Mr. Jeffries is good, ain't he, Mama? Surely he can't think that way about us?"

"Thing is," Fannie said, "men like Mr. Jeffries will never have a problem eating bread made by black hands. But they will never,

ever see fit to break that same bread with those same hands as equals."

"I won't follow these rules, Mama. Jim Crow never even met me."

Birdie didn't know it at the time, but it wasn't anger in her mother's eyes when she scolded her only daughter. Fannie snatched her up, and shook her shoulders the way a desperate mother might of a girl she'd die to protect.

"You hush that mouth, child! You will do as I say! You keep your head down. And don't talk to no white persons other than the Jeffries'. They may still be white, but at least they's got some sense."

"Why?" Birdie asked, making an underbite with her petulant jaw.

"Because," Fannie said, "even when you shrink yourself up and do what they say, ghosts cloaked in white still come for black queens in the night."

❧

THE SUITS and skirts moved past her without acknowledgment and no change to spare. Monti smelled her desperation as it pilled and rolled down her neck. She rattled a beat on a kit of plastic buckets which varied in size and color, orange, white, blue and red. She'd collected them from the industrial junkyards of Ballard, wandering between the weeded alleys and salt-warped docks. She gripped her sticks as if she could milk money from them, convinced if she played harder and faster someone would pay her rent with a pocket of quarters.

A girl with yellow, feathered hair and a pink bomber jacket walked by.

"That ain't the way to make money. If you want, I can show you how."

"No thanks," Monti mumbled. She had an idea of what this girl did to make her money.

Monti watched the Market in Pike Place as she packed her

things. A group of kids huddled together on the corner, stomping their feet and shouting veiled insults at each other. They lit each other's cigarettes and danced to keep warm even though they wore puffy, color-blocked ski jackets with thick, wool collars. The girls flirted casually with the boys, twirling to music playing from a boom box. They drank from straws that stuck out of brown paper bags, special juice boxes for latchkey kids. There were white kids, black kids, and yellow kids, various shades crowding together like crayons in a Crayola box. Color didn't seem to matter, yet there was a palpable tension and camaraderie in the way they interacted. A fight broke out between two men with mullets and mustaches, and the kids cheered them on, dancing around the melee as if they had a stake in the outcome.

The girl with feathered hair meandered back, and she had a friend with her. The friend was petite, just a hair over five-feet tall. She seemed to be hiding inside a sweatsuit that hung off her frame, and her skin looked like dark chocolate. The two girls leaned against the wall of the doughnut shop where all the Market Kids hung out, and Monti paused what she'd been doing to listen.

"That killer got Evie," the feathered one said.

"For real? Dang…"

"You didn't notice she ain't been in the market lately?"

"Nah, I've been working The Strip last few weeks. Haven't had much luck around here. How'd you find out?"

"Scuzzo would stay at her mom's house sometimes. He went to crash and I guess she went crazy on him - blamed him for getting Evie into trouble."

"That's sad."

"I know. All he ever did was look out for Evie. Like he does for us."

"Do they know who killed her?"

"I went to the library to see what the papers had to say. They don't know anything. Just that he likes black girls."

"See, that's why I only date guys I know."

"And that's why you ain't having luck, though. Everyone's a

stranger at first. Can't make money unless you welcome new business, Coral. I've told you that before."

"But I don't want that killer to get me."

"That's why you gotta develop a sixth sense. Like me. I can spot a psycho the second I lay eyes on 'em. And I always get my money."

"But I'm not like you, Charlene…"

Charlene glanced at Monti, who'd been unabashedly watching the two girls.

"Hey pretty eyes, I told you I'd show you how to make money. No need to eavesdrop."

Monti ducked her head, finished packing her things and caught the next bus home.

She heard Birdie's wail before she entered the apartment.

"He's gone for good," Birdie said with tear-filled eyes. She collapsed onto the couch and it groaned against her weight. "After I bailed him out and everything. He says he's through with me."

Monti placed her mother's head in her lap, let Birdie's thick braids slide between her fingers. She focused on the course weaving of her mother's hair, instead of the hard, ripped pleather that scratched against her thighs.

"It's for the best, Momma."

Birdie wiped her eyes. She sat up and looked Monti in the face.

"Don't you dare say that."

Monti recoiled from her mother. Birdie's tears dried up in the intensity of her glare.

"He's helped put food in your mouth. And he's kept roof over us. And now we ain't got shit."

§.

RICHARD THANKED the housekeeper as she placed a platter of french toast and eggs on the dining room table. He sipped his fresh-squeezed grapefruit juice and peered at Cassandra as she read *People Magazine.* Clarke sat beside him, scrambling to finish his Algebra homework. There was no use in talking. He couldn't think about anything but the girl with gray eyes. She needed help. She needed him. And he couldn't abandon her again. If he opened his mouth, he would scream her name, though he didn't know it - he'd call her *Destiny!*, because it was the closest to the truth.

Finally, Clarke broke the silence.

"You coming to my game tonight?" he asked between mouthfuls.

Richard set his paper down. "You have a game tonight?"

"Yeah. It's a big one. We're playing Rainier Valley. It's an early game, starts at five o'clock."

Richard tugged on his earlobe. He really wanted to go, to see his old neighborhood.

"I can't. I have to work tonight."

Clarke spoke through one side of his mouth. "Whatever, what's new?"

Cassandra put her magazine down. "Can't you make an exception this time, sweetie?" She said it ironically, like a petulant girl trying to regain the power she'd lost in the backseat of his Mustang. Their marriage would be over once she stopped trying to win his affection.

"I'd really love to, but I've got a mountain of paperwork to get through, and I need to follow up with a probationary case at Everwood."

He also needed to decide whether to charge a 16-year-old boy who'd shot his abusive stepfather as an adult or a juvenile, the former resulting in at least twenty-five years of his young life spent in prison.

Both his wife and son rolled their eyes.

"Honestly, I don't know why you insist on staying with this job. It's not like we need the money," Cassandra said.

"It's not about the money, *dear.*"

"Well, I don't see why you can't skip work just this once and watch your son play."

Of course she didn't see. They never saw. They couldn't understand that some people weren't born with the world as a rattle they could shake and suck on and toss between their hands. Neither knew what is was like to have few or little choices. Or even worse, to choose between eating or keeping a roof overhead. To choose between dying or killing.

"Please, Dad? This is a big game!"

Richard picked up his paper, using it as a shield. "I'll catch the next one."

A hushed moment passed. Richard set down his paper.

"I've been meaning to ask, who is that girl you were playing football with? It was about a month or so ago."

"You mean Oreo?" Clarke said, his head bent over his homework.

"You call her Oreo?"

Clarke shrugged. "Yeah. Everybody does."

Richard shook his head. "Well. Who is she?"

"Her name is Montgomery Jackson."

Montgomery Jackson. Montgomery Jackson. Montgomery Jackson.

"What do you know about her?"

"I don't know," Clarke said, crunching his face into a smug expression. "She's a freak. She smells weird. She's always hanging out with some fag. She's a loser."

Richard folded his hands in front of his face, silently regarding his child, wondering how someone so callous could share his genes.

"Honey, don't say fag. It's an ugly word. It's best not to mention people like that at all," Cassandra said. "I'm getting a migraine. Have a good day at work. *Sweetie.*" And without a kiss for her husband, his wife left the table.

Richard snapped his fingers to regain his son's attention.

"I want you to stop calling her Oreo. And make sure she knows there's an open invitation for dinner. Anytime." He paused. His palms were sweaty. "In fact, you should invite her tonight."

Clarke's mouth hung open. "Whyyyah! I invited my friends over after the game. And she's a total reject. Besides, you said you have to work tonight."

Richard tried to put his reasoning into words Clarke would understand.

"Be like Nike, son. Just do it."

Clarke stared at him, fury turning his face vermillion. He wore a calculated expression, as if he resented being placed in a contemplative position.

"Why are you so interested in her, anyways?"

The lie slipped so easily from Richard's tongue.

"I'm afraid I can't discuss that. It's related to a case I'm working on."

Clark slammed his hands on the table, rattling the dishes and spilling grapefruit juice on the designer tablecloth.

"This is bullshit! You care more about those stupid niggers in juvie than you do about me!"

Richard slapped him with an open palm, leaving behind a rosy handprint, one that was redder than the ginger hair they shared. He left the table without acknowledging what he'd done, what he'd wanted to do, his breakfast unfinished, and begrudgingly went to work.

BENEATH THE THRUSH along the highway, the moss grew thick from the trunks of fir and alder wood. It hung from the naked deciduous trees like minty tinsel. It grew in thick patches from the deep, damp earth, and it provided the soft bed for the remains of LaRhonda Williams. The mythical beauty of the Pacific Northwest, the chattering finches and the emerald ferns with their rusted beads of pollen almost created a feeling of serenity. But LaRhonda had been in the brush for at least a month, unnoticed despite the heavy traffic of Aurora that whisked by merely yards away. The smell of her liquified decomposition overpowered the sweetness of the dank and must.

"How did you know the victim had a Black Mamba tattoo on her forearm?" the Detective asked.

"I guess I just have a good memory," Richard said. "Probably read it in her criminal file at some point."

Detective Colby Rawlings eyed him suspiciously. During an

investigation, people who unduly involved themselves could often be considered suspects. But when he'd heard the call come over his police radio on his way to work, he knew another Headbanger victim had been found. And he needed to help, if only for his own sanity.

Rawlings lifted his face to the sky. He clenched his fists. Finally he looked back at Richard with a smile and asked,

"Would you be open to coming downtown with me and taking a lie detector test?"

Rawlings confirmed Richard was a suspect. Because they'd found his business card in the pocket of LaRhonda's worn jeans. Of course there was a reasonable explanation for it. LaRhonda had circulated through the juvenile courts at least a dozen times, all for prostitution. Each time she was remanded to the Youth Center in the YMCA building south of downtown. And each time she'd found a way to sneak out. She was on the corner of First and Pike by the next afternoon, selling her hands and mouth to any bidder. There was no way to keep a child like LaRhonda off the streets. Runaways were not criminals, and could not be forced home by the law. The receiving homes they were sent to had no power to hold them. And the parents, the ones that cared enough to stay involved, had no legal option to keep their child from harm's way. So Richard gave his card to the multiple offenders, hoping that if they decided they wanted to get out of the life, they'd have someone to call. Unfortunately for LaRhonda, she'd never be able to reach that decision.

Richard watched the needle move on the machine, afraid to look Rawlings in the eye.

"Have you had any contact with the victim outside of court?"

"Of course not!" Richard exclaimed.

"How did the victim come to have your card in her pocket?"

"I gave it to her? I don't know."

"You don't think that's strange?"

Richard felt cornered, flustered, and didn't know how to explain himself to the young and strained detective.

"No, I don't. Kids like LaRhonda need help. She began prostituting because her boyfriend wanted new cross-trainers. I probably gave her my card because I felt sorry for her."

Richard felt the sweat percolate between his eyebrows and in the groove of his spine. Did Rawlings' suspicion have something to do with the investigator Tomlinson mentioned? Was someone trying to tie him to his mother's death to prove he was capable of violence?

After finishing the test, Richard parked his Mustang on the shoulder of Aurora Avenue. He'd failed the lie detector and was too stressed to go back to the office. So he returned to the scene and sat, looking into the trees, struggling to understand why some children ended up in places like the one where LaRhonda had been. He wondered what sort of man could hurt a teenage girl? What sort of man could leave her for the flies and maggots? He wondered what sort of man he was, and why he could no longer recognize himself.

Richard merged with traffic and drove a block north to the parking lot of the Georgian Motel. He let the engine idle as he peered out the window at a group of women pacing up and down the sidewalk. The youngest walked towards him. She had snags in her pantyhose and a hoop ring in her belly button that glinted in the light of a streetlamp.

He rolled down the window.

"I like men with black cars," she said.

"It's maroon, actually."

"Need a place to stay tonight?"

He turned off the engine and followed her beneath a covered, concrete walkway to room 207. In the light he saw she was pretty, in an offhand kind of way. Her front teeth jutted forward, her skin was smooth like milk chocolate, and her hazel eyes pushed out from their sockets with enthusiasm.

"It's twenty to blow, forty to fuck, and baby for two-hundred I can rock your world all night."

"Okay," he said, leaning back against the headrest of the creaky bed, removing his tie. "How much to bind your hands with this?"

The woman sized him up, and he could almost see her deciding whether or not he was just some kinky, repressed jerk-off or an actual threat. He hoped she had good judgment, because he wasn't sure himself.

"That's another twenty," she said.

"Okay. And what should I call you?"

She unzipped her bomber jacket and took off her stripper heels.

"Whatever you want."

She wiped her nose, a nervous tick. And then Richard recognized her, though he couldn't remember her name. Like LaRhonda, this young woman had been on the carousel ride of the juvenile court system until she'd aged out. He guessed she was in her early twenties now. His conscience told him to leave. But a greater pull held him fast to the bed.

"Okay," he said, removing his dress shoes.

Whatever you want, she'd said. And so he thought about this as if he hadn't known the answer, as if he hadn't wished for this young woman to be someone else. He pointed to the floor between his feet and called her by another girl's name. A girl for whom he was homesick.

"Kneel here, Eugenia."

CHAPTER ELEVEN

THE END of September was colder than usual. Salmon Bay was no longer cerulean, but a rolling and expansive, cast iron gray. Its surface danced as a dose of rain drummed into the Sound. The Cascade Mountains, which seemed to rise out of the bay like an iceberg, had already begun to whiten with snow.

The window was fogged, and it's sill had grown droplets. Their body heat sweltered the room as Sasha and Monti slept. The moisture seeped into Sasha's dreams, traveled through his veins until it reached a pinnacle beneath the sheets. He awoke with a start, suddenly aware of his body, what it was telling him, and how its message was pressed against his best friend's backside. He didn't want to move, but couldn't bear the embarrassment of her reaction.

The doorknob rattled, but it was Saturday morning, and he was too drowsy to consider that he'd forgotten to lock the door.

Daan walked in holding a plate of eggs.

"Mikael, it's getting late and I thought you might be hungry. I need you to help me fix a water faucet at your grandparents'…"

Sasha sat up just as Daan saw Monti asleep beside him. He watched as his father examined the room, watched the emotions ripple through his face. Fascination. Despair. Disgust. He rubbed the back of his neck as Daan stared at the picture of Sid Vicious, his tongue snaking from his mouth, his girlfriend pulling down her shirt to expose her breast. Monti stirred and opened her eyes. She smiled at Sasha, and he smiled back.

"What is this!" Daan cried, his face turning purple. Monti's eyes went wide with fear. Sasha watched as she scrambled out of his window, noting calmly how she left her shoes and clothes behind. He laughed at the thought of her running through the courtyard wearing only his flannel.

"And what did I tell you? A girl like that is more trouble than she's worth." Daan set the eggs on the dresser. "She on the pill?"

"You don't need to freak." Sasha yawned. "We were up late watching movies and fell asleep."

Daan pulled one of his records out of a crate. It was a Parliament record, covered with colorful drawings of busty, naked women. Monti let him borrow it.

"This is sinful."

"It's just music."

"I don't know what to say. What would your mother think?"

Sasha clenched his jaw.

"Don't pretend you know what she'd think," he said, but not loud enough to be heard.

Daan grabbed another record. It was David Bowie's *Diamond Dogs*. On the cover his face looked made-up and he wore no shirt.

Daan looked at Sasha, his eyes brimming. "This man is a faggot," he said calmly, as if one could be so easily identified. He began to pace, muttering, screaming, threatening to ship Sasha away to military school. Or a rectory. He fretted over mulatto babies and gay diseases until finally Sasha cut him off.

"You have to pick one vice and stick to it, Daan. I can either be a homosexual or sleeping with Monti, but I don't think it's fair to accuse me of both."

Daan shook his head. "You've left me no choice, Mikael. You know what's next."

Sasha sighed and threw back the covers. He followed Daan up the stairs and into the third bedroom. Sasha could almost feel his mother's presence on the second floor of the house. The shag carpet was pale yellow, and each room had either paisley print or sunflowers, like if Woodstock threw itself up all over the walls. Sasha knelt by the twin bed. He looked at the rocking chair in the corner, where his mother would sit and knit, or stare out the window for hours. He heard Daan washing his hands down the hall in the bathroom. The clink of his belt buckle. The cracking of knuckles.

He braced himself for what came next.

SASHA WAS six years old the first time his mother tried to run away. She packed his backpack with underwear and socks. A canvas bag filled with food, Mary Kay cosmetics, and Parliament cigarettes. Even at that age, Sasha knew they were missing key items. But he went along, her breezy constitution assuring him that everything would be fine. She looked beautiful that day, in a light, jean sundress that hung off her shoulders and navy saltwater sandals. She put big curls in her blonde hair, and colored her lips with a dash of pink lipstick.

"Sasha, we're going to see my sister in California," she'd said. "We'll put our toes in the sand and drink Icee's in the sun!"

He remembered her pearly teeth when she smiled, looking down at him from the driver's seat of their new Volvo. He remembered feeling excited to meet his other family, the Californian hippies that Daan referred to as "sinners."

They made it as far as Oregon before they were caught. Even at that age, Sasha knew it was probably for the best.

As Daphne pumped gas at a Texaco station in Eugene, she heard a sound. Sasha heard it too, and watched as her ears perked up like a fox. He followed her gaze to a semi-truck across the street, parked outside a Pacific Pride gas station. The trailer looked like the inside of a pillow, filled with chickens cooing and packed together tighter than an egg carton.

Though he was young, Sasha knew the inevitable would happen, and that no one would understand why.

Daphne walked across the street, leaving the nozzle hanging from the pump. Sasha jumped to the backseat so he could have a better view of his mother as she meddled with the trailer door. He couldn't see how she got it open, but she'd always been good with her hands, at knitting and crochet and the like. She grabbed furiously, cage by cage. She opened them, grinning in the tail feathers of each escaped chicken, and then smashed the cages to the ground. She made it through half the truck before the driver came running from the diner next door, his flannel flailing behind him in the sun and his meager hands grasping for his liberated fowl.

Sasha remembered sitting in the police station, and asking her why she did it.

"Because my love," she said, rubbing her warm hand against his cheek, "no living creature should be locked away like that."

Daan took a Greyhound and met them at the police station. He convinced the truck driver not to press charges. When he got in the driver's seat and saw the bags, Sasha saw a look come over his face that terrified him. His father looked angry. Violent. Broken. But Daphne remained stoic in the car, despite the hot, leather seats and Daan's heavy breathing.

Daan took her upstairs the moment they got home. Sasha remembered his father said, "You need to repent." But even at that age, he knew it wasn't a sin for an unhappy woman to leave her husband.

Sasha crept up the stairs and pushed the door to the third bedroom ajar. It was a simple room, with a single dresser and a twin bed for the occasional guest. Sometimes at night, when his nightmares were really bad, Daan would kneel by the bed and pray for his deliverance. And sometimes, he'd make his wife kneel too.

Sasha watched helplessly as Daan removed his belt. Daphne recited the Lord's Prayer, at her husband's insistence.

The Lord is my Shepherd, I shall not want...

Daan brought his belt down, hard against her shoulders. Sasha winced at the door, pushing it so it creaked loudly, but Daan was too busy to hear. Daphne looked at him, right in the midst of the stinging belt welting her bare shoulders, and lifted a finger to her lips.

Sssssh. And then she smiled.

SASHA GRIPPED the comforter on the bed as Daan's belt snapped against his skin. He felt the marks redden on his back. Whatever had blossomed for Monti that morning was wilted now, and he felt an anger for his mother surge like a hoard of wasps. Angry that she'd chosen the freedom of a truckload of chickens over their own.

Daan laid his belt on the bed. Sasha turned to face him, to receive the mark of Christ and His forgiveness. But that look on Daan's face was still there, the look he had when he discovered his wife was leaving him, or when a nightmare pulled him from sleep.

"Could you feel the wrath of God, son?"

Sasha shrugged. "If by wrath you mean a crappy, pleather belt, then yeah."

"Don't get smart with me. Your mother didn't take it seriously either, and look what happened to her."

Sasha turned his gaze on his father. His blood was hot, and he felt it rush to his cheeks.

"It's your fault she's dead."

Daan winced. He put a hand on Sasha's shoulder and pulled him close. Sasha saw the wrinkles etched into his weathered forehead, thick, dark and caked with the stains of war. He looked into his father's eyes, their color bleached to sterling. There was no love. But there was something else Sasha hadn't noticed before. His father's eyes were cloudy with fear.

Daan balled his fist and drove it into Sasha's stomach. He keeled over and coughed on the bed, bereft of air and lungs choked with terror. Tears stung his eyes.

"You clean that trash out of your room. And stop wasting your time with that girl." Daan's voice was shaking. He paused at the doorframe, the wrinkles around his eyes coming together in what posed as concern. "She'll be gone soon enough."

The door shut behind him, and Sasha closed his eyes. He breathed deep, and felt the ache in his stomach. He prayed, but not for forgiveness, and not for deliverance. And not of belief, but of desperation. Maybe to his mother, or some other guiding, universal force. He asked for answers, so that his anger might have something else to latch onto and infect.

Because, as it stood, his rage consumed him. He was so very angry, that it turned his knobby knuckles white as he pounded his fists into the bed.

He was so angry that his heart wrenched and snuffed out all feeling, disabling his body's mechanisms and clouding his vision. He was angry at his laughing, smiling, and accepting mother, at her warm hands and gentle kisses.

He was so angry, because she didn't take him with her.

DAAN SHUT HIS BEDROOM DOOR, and sank onto his bed. He sobbed quietly into his hands. Evil had infected him in Vietnam, and it was slow at first. But as he watched his newfound brothers die in an inferno of fire and bullets, it grew like a disease and tumored his lungs, his bones, his blood with hatred for anyone from the "other side." Daphne caught it too. From her time spent on the streets, ministering to the homeless. That evil tricked her into believing the people it infected could be cured. It was why she did things like carve her arms with the lids from tin cans, or walk to the grocery store wearing only her underwear. Or spend an entire week, lolling in bed. It's what made her take his family from him that day with the chickens.

And that girl next door? She'd been touched by evil too. And he knew it was only a matter of time before it took hold.

❧

THE DOORBELL RANG. Though her body ached all over, Birdie willed herself to move from the couch. One foot in front of the other. Head down and tits sweating like on those sweltering days in Alabama. She'd hoped the grayness of Seattle would be safer than the black and white world she'd run from. And in its own way, it was, though the quiet drum of rain and the passive disregard tore into her darkened flesh in a completely different way. At least in the South, her abusers were aware of whom they were abusing.

"Hello," she said, scratching her dried up scalp. A tall man with red hair and green eyes stood on her stoop, his hand holding firmly to a younger boy with the same hair and eyes. The man's white shirt looked professionally pressed, and his tan slacks had such a crease it looked as if a stick was running down the length of his legs. The boy wore a pair of jeans with designer bleach stains and a red letterman's jacket.

"Hello," the man said. "My name is Richard Adamson. This is my son, Clarke. He goes to school with your daughter. Is she home by chance?"

Birdie felt queasy. She knew this man. This Richard Adamson. And he knew her, in ways that should require he remember and feel sick to his stomach too. But he didn't. And that was some bullshit.

He'd stopped paying for her time, her body, her intimacy, years ago. But she knew he still trolled the streets of downtown. And she knew the reason he'd stopped patronizing her talents was because he preferred younger girls.

"What you want with my kid?" she said.

"My son and your daughter had an incident a few weeks ago. On the football field. And, well…"

Richard glared at the boy.

"I'm here to apologize to Monti," the boy said, barely moving his lips.

"Apologize for what?" Birdie crossed her arms.

The boy looked at his father, who creased his forehead and nodded.

"I came to apologize for calling Monti a 'Spook.'"

Birdie almost laughed. She hadn't heard that slur since she'd left Alabama.

"You got some nerve," Birdie said. "Whiter than rice boy, look more like a 'Spook' than my *beautiful* daughter. What she do, make you look like the fool you are?"

"Now hang on..." Richard said, but Birdie cut him off.

"Nah, you listen. Y'all must think you somebody coming up on my porch with some honky, fake ass apology."

"I'm trying to teach my son that behavior is unacceptable. That's why we're here."

Richard smiled. He was just as handsome as the first night he'd picked her up - downtown Seattle, 1972. She remembered the year. Because she was twenty-three and excited to have a clean, fine trick for once. And here he was, unable to recognize the tired woman she'd become. Bet he never had to spend a night in jail and lie to his kid about where he'd been. Bet he never got beat up or ate up or ran through just to make a dime.

Birdie pressed into Richard's face.

"Hear me now. You stay the hell away from my daughter, you alleybat mother-fu—"

"MOMMA!"

Monti emerged from the hallway, shame splashed all over her face. Birdie slammed the door shut.

"What was that about?" she asked. "Why were you so rude?"

"Because, baby girl," Birdie sighed and sank back onto the couch, "men cloaked in white be coming for black queens in the night."

"There's no KKK here. Not every white person you meet is racist."

"I ain't talking about no racists!" Birdie said. "I'm talking about evil. So you beware, hear me? The most evil of 'em out there know how to dress up pretty, come off the right way. Those are the ones to watch out for."

CHAPTER TWELVE

IT WAS the beginning of October, and Seattle's ridges from east to west, Capitol Hill, Phinney, Queen Anne, and Magnolia, all boasted the bright plumage of autumn leaves and evergreens. Orange, red, jade, yellow, and peach. Colors in exchange for the blue sky the fog, cloud, and rain had stolen for the next seven months.

Monti played her plastic drums on the corner of Pike and First. She played every song she knew, until the sticks left calluses in her palms and her shoulders popped and burned.

The plastic cup she'd set on the rum-splattered sidewalk held only a few coins for her efforts. She couldn't compete with the tavern across the street, or the adult movie arcade, strip club, payday loan, and liquor store that beckoned and glared around the block. There were better places to spend money for those who hung around downtown.

Monti watched as Charlene stepped out of a beige '63 Chevrolet across the street. She pulled on a pink sweatshirt and dusted off her white Keds, as if she'd just been hard at work, and smiled at a boy with dark skin as she leapt onto the sidewalk. Charlene pulled a wad of bills from her back pocket, her fingers curled over as though she were hiding a note to pass behind the teacher's back. The dark boy, wearing a Raiders jacket that looked expensive, kissed her cheek and accepted the money. Monti's mouth watered at the sight of cash.

She stacked her buckets inside one another and emptied her cup into shallow pockets. She thought back to a time when she and Birdie had been kicked out of their apartment. Birdie had taken her downtown with a cardboard sign and a practiced frown, begging for spare change. The cold cut through the cloth and Monti felt the shivers rattle her spine as they waited in line for an elusive bed in one of Seattle's shelters. She couldn't bear that shame again - to be a burden to the world.

"I can't stand to watch you like this. Do you want me to show you how to make some real money?" Charlene asked one day, relieving Monti from working up the nerve to approach her first.

Monti shrugged.

Charlene stuck out her hand.

"I'm Charlene," she said with a smile. Her face was cherubic, with rounded, high cheekbones, full, red lips and pale blue eyes. But the leather jacket she wore added a hardness to her appearance.

"I know who you are. I'm Monti."

"So what brings you to the Market, Monti?"

"What do you mean?"

Charlene lit a cigarette, then blew the smoke out in a pretty plume into Monti's face. She laughed in a way that made Monti feel seen.

"My step-daddy preferred me to my mom. That's why I'm down here." She pointed down the block to a girl wearing a black sweater patterned with white rabbits. Her hair was shorn and a thin braid hung down her neck. "Ratgirl ran away from her crazy foster family." The dark boy in the Raiders jacket stood a short distance from Ratgirl, talking earnestly with Coral, who now had a bulging belly though she looked no more than twelve. "Scuzzo is a dealer and a pimp, and doesn't talk about himself much. And the little one is Coral - she got thrown out of her house for getting pregnant. So what's your story?"

The roof of Monti's mouth shriveled and parched. She'd interacted with each kid Charlene mentioned at one point or another. They'd given her a hard time, and called her a fool for trying to make money on the streets honestly.

"There's no story. I'm just trying to help my mom pay rent," she said.

"What, she on drugs or something?"

"No," Monti said. "No way. She's just bad with money." She told Charlene the story about Reggie, and his needing bail. Charlene regarded her for a moment, and then shrugged.

"Whatever. Wanna smoke?"

"No thanks."

"Wanna drink?"

Monti shook head.

"Geez, they really got you with that 'Just Say No' campaign, huh?"

"You said you were gonna show me how to make money," Monti said.

Charlene stubbed out her cigarette with the toe of her sneaker.

"Right to the point. I like that. But I need to get to know you better before I tell you all my secrets."

Monti spent the rest of the afternoon with Charlene, and listened to her rundown on who to avoid downtown, who had the best weed, and which cops could be bribed. They gossiped with some of the girls in the Market, sitting on a grassy knoll overlooking Elliot Bay, and Monti listened intently as they exchanged stories about boyfriends and pimps and partying. Until someone mentioned one of the murdered girls. Then they slowly drifted away, back to their corners, one by one until only Monti and Charlene remained in the park.

Monti learned Charlene was no different than other sixteen-year-olds, but there was a sadness that eked around the bones of her eye sockets, a menacing way in which she carried herself. Monti was both intrigued by her and repelled, feeling that nothing Charlene said was wholly true, that there were pockets in her stories where she hid their real meaning.

A sinking, red sun hovered over the Cascade mountains, and its rays reached across the bay like burned and bleeding fingers.

"I said I'd show you how to make money," Charlene said.

She laid out the options on her hand, as if she were outlining a list of chores.

"You can either sell drugs, stolen merchandise, or your kitty. In my experience, the last one is the easiest, because you have sole proprietorship over the merchandise. Anyways, that's what Scuzzo says."

"I'm not going to do any of those things," Monti said. "So thanks for wasting my time."

"Oh I see what's going on. You think you too good to date."

Monti paused.

"No. I just want to be a good person is all. What you're talking about. Well, it's just wrong."

Charlene plucked grass from the knoll and gazed across the bay.

"My step-daddy is a good man. He has a good job working for Boeing's. Takes my mom out to dinner and disco every weekend. Always walks the dog." Charlene's shoulders sank as she ripped a large clump from the grass.

"None of that stopped him from sneaking into my room at night." She sighed, and a wad of cash appeared in her hand as if she'd just done a magic trick.

"So here I am. A high school dropout. Letting guys do things to me for money. Because they'd do them anyway and I might as well get paid for it." She looked at Monti. "Easiest money I ever made."

Monti stared at the wad of cash.

"Aren't you scared of getting hurt? What about the Headbanger Hunter?"

Charlene smiled. "Scuzzo keeps me safe." Her eyes roved over Monti, then dropped to the ground as she chewed on her lip.

"You've got a nice body, you know?" she said.

Monti pulled her letterman's jacket tighter around herself, covering the thin, sleeveless shirt she wore underneath. They came in a four-pack from the JC Penny in downtown Ballard, were white, and only cost $1.99. Monti looked at Charlene's mature curves while she lay in the grass with one hand behind her head.

"My legs are too big and I'm flat-chested," she finally said.

Charlene laughed. "Trust me. Some men are into that. You're a virgin, huh?"

Monti nodded.

"Men are into that too. In fact, I bet I could get you twenty-five just for that. You wouldn't even have to touch anybody."

"No," Monti said, though she didn't feel sure of her answer.

Birdie rounded the corner onto Western Avenue, and Monti gasped. She wore a baggy, houndstooth sweater and loose-fitting jeans. Her eyes were drawn, her cheeks hollow, and she stumbled over the cobbled road where merchants packed their crafts for the day. Monti's heart beat faster as she turned her back to the Market. She snuck a glance over her shoulder in time to see Birdie get into someone's car and disappear down the street.

"Is that your mom?" Charlene asked. Her tone was not judging the way Clarke's had been. Instead it seemed to wrap Monti inside a warm blanket, inside safety and understanding.

"Yes," Monti said.

Was that what her mother had to do now that Reggie was gone? She had looked so frail, so incapable of protecting herself from danger. Birdie wasn't strong the same way Monti was - she couldn't hit hard enough to make boys cry.

"Do you see her a lot?" Monti asked.

Charlene shrugged and looked down at the grass.

"Nah, don't think so." She patted Monti's shoulder. "You worried about her?"

Monti nodded.

"We might get kicked out of our apartment. I want to stay in school and part-time jobs don't pay enough. I don't know what I was thinking, coming down here."

"You seem real smart," Charlene said. "Maybe you knew exactly what you were doing coming down here."

Monti worked her jaw in circles. Twenty-five dollars could buy her a week's worth of groceries. Maybe more. She could make enough money to keep Birdie at the bar. She could make enough to protect her mother.

"I don't want to…date guys for money," she said.

Charlene rubbed her shoulder, and asked the question Monti had been dreading.

"What other choice do you have?"

A few days later Monti met Charlene at a hostel above the doughnut shop. Charlene's room was plain, with one window that opened over the cobbled square of First and Pike. There were clothes thrown atop an upholstered chair, along the hard carpet, and over a lampshade.

"Do you live here?" Monti asked, hovering near the door.

Charlene nodded, doffing her leather jacket and tossing it on the bed. "Yeah, most of the time. Whenever I got money." She lay back onto the bed, flipped her pretty hair and appraised her new apprentice.

Charlene smiled and patted the bed. Monti sunk into the spot beside her like it was quicksand. Charlene handed her a joint and Monti balanced the rolled grass between two fingers. She'd never smoked pot before, had only smelled it a handful of times on Sasha's body. And then she thought more of Sasha's body, and how marijuana had been inside it, how it'd felt the inside of his mouth, and how he'd shared that experience with Tommy so often. Often enough to make her palms sweat from the violence of her jealousy. She knew it was stupid, but somehow she thought by smoking that joint with Charlene, she could get closer to understanding this new boy. This new boy who'd taken her desires captive, who held them between his deft fingers as casually as a game of cats cradle. Winding and unwinding them until all formations had been exhausted, and then shoving that tired string into the pocket of his worn jeans, his to play with at will. She suspected he knew. Had begun to after the picnic at the Locks, after his eyes glistened and he smirked from the side of his mouth, after he'd said,

Jealous?

Yes. She was jealous.

But suddenly the image of Birdie entered her mind, and fear overtook her.

"I don't smoke," she said.

"Okay, as soon as you're ready, my friend is going to come in," Charlene said. "He isn't going to touch you and he won't say a word."

"Okay," Monti said. Her eyes darted to the window.

Charlene touched her face. "If you close your eyes now, you won't even see him. Just think of someone you want."

Monti closed her eyes. She heard the click of the light-switch and sensed the darkness. She heard the door to the room open and shut. A pair of feet scraped against the carpet. The sound of creaking wood and the sigh of a heavy body as it sank into the chair. And then silence.

She thought of blue eyes. She saw his cleft chin. She felt the tip of his nose that hovered over a pink, top lip. She savored his mouth that smiled, a grand, white smile, each time she walked in the room. She felt his ropy hands that danced and created, that pinched in playfulness and held fast for solace. Heard his voice so beautiful it opened the hearts of the most judgmental, the most unaccepting. She heard the flutter of wings, distant yet close. She could almost make out the soft sounds she imagined he'd make, the ones she'd heard as he slept beside her. The beating grew louder, as did hers in response, and her fingers moved with the deftness of his, and though he wasn't there she believed he could feel it, and this crescendoed her unto another plain, one filled with little beads of pleasure that popped in her mouth like ripe olives.

She stopped and heard someone flapping, the sound of a bird whose wings had been broken. She opened her eyes. The room was dark, only the moonlight shone the way to the door. She saw the glowing ember of Charlene's cigarette. And still, that flapping. She looked to the chair by the window and saw a man. A flaccid looking man with heavy eyes and swaying jowls, flaccid everywhere except for the flapping, made by the hurried movement of his fist.

He finished, his flapping fist stilled, and the wind behind his panting breath wheezed so loud. Loud enough to muzzle her song. Loud enough to tarry the spirit, the voice, the courage she had just begun to rouse.

She ran from the hotel, into the damp, mewling streets. Charlene followed, grabbed her hand, and placed something in her palm. But she couldn't focus on the object in her hand, only on the contents of her stomach, the sickness and shame that chewed away the lining.

"It's no big deal," Charlene said. "You didn't touch him. He didn't touch you. And you actually enjoyed yourself." She hailed a cab with a confident wave.

But I've got no money, Monti thought, until she looked in her hand. In it she saw what seven minutes could fetch. In her hand were two bills, which amounted to more money than she'd seen or touched in her lifetime.

"Remember. You had the power in that room. And that's nothing to be ashamed of." Charlene wrapped her pinkie around Monti's and kissed her fist, sealing the secret amongst friends.

Seven minutes. Nothing to be ashamed of.

Monti collapsed into the cab, told the driver her address, and wondered how long it would take to forget the flaccid man's face. How long would it take before the pull of easy cash made her do it again?

THE BASEMENT WAS EMPTY. Silent, except for the electric whir of the lamps in the back closet, feeding Tommy's pot. It was eight thirty, a school night, and she still hadn't finished her homework. But an essay about the American Civil War seemed trivial now. She had her own battle to wage.

Tommy had pushed his couch to the side of the room, opening the space in front of the television for their instruments. She sat behind her kit and picked up her sticks. She hit the kick drum once and let the thrum reverberate through her body. The thoughts softened to a harsh whisper. She played "Wipeout," her go-to song when she felt overwhelmed. It was a song that could take on different meaning, depending on how hard she hit or how fast she played. Tonight was somber, her kick drum precise and loud, stilted like the reaper's call. Sweat flattened the dark hairs on her arm. As she hit the symbols with her right hand, she let the stick spin in her left a half-second before striking the tom, just for fun. Her movements were fluid, her sound deafening, and soon her flurried thoughts dissipated.

She finished. Someone clapped, startling her. She turned and saw Tommy and Sasha standing in the doorway.

"That was pretty good, Oreo," Tommy said. "I'm going to take a leak. Anybody need a drink?"

Sasha shook his head no, but kept his eyes on Monti. His gaze didn't waver, not even when Tommy tripped and crashed on his way up the stairs. His blue eyes were like the laser shows played at the Seattle Center. Bright. Arresting. She couldn't look away, even though she wanted to.

He could see what she'd done. He could see she was tainted. His furrowed brow said everything. That she was dirty. That she was bad. That his father had been right.

Finally he let her go, dropping his gaze to the floor. He teased her by running his hands through his hair before reaching for his guitar.

"We should probably practice," he said quietly. She almost winced when he added,

"Since you're here."

CHAPTER THIRTEEN

D AYS LATER, Sasha had woken Monti from a dream with a loud *tat tat tat tat tat!*

She'd been running. Running on the football field at the high school. Running from the flaccid man, from Reggie, running so hard her ankles burned where her lungs should've been. When she hit the goal post she turned around, only to discover it had been Birdie chasing her the entire time. She heard clapping.

You're my hero, Sasha said. He opened his arms. Smiling. No. Smirking, a cigarette dangling from his mouth, the ash burning holes into the rubber toe of his sneakers.

My baby, he crooned, as if she were a crying child. But then she realized she *was* crying, that the salt in her tears was stinging her eyes. Badly. She had to close them. And when she opened them he was still there, digging a hole into the ground.

What are you doing?

Digging.

Digging what?

He smirked at her again.

Your grave stupid. Just go back to sleep.

Why are you doing this?

He threw the cigarette into the hole, a hole that was too small to fit even one of her big thighs.

I'm just trying to help you, he'd said.

And then he dug faster.

Sasha never knocked like that. Sometimes a *rap rap* just to announce his presence. Sometimes a *dink dink dink,* like a neighbor calling for company. But never the *tat tat tat tat tat tat tat tat!* It was as though he lived in her head. He could see the things she couldn't. Could see the things she'd hidden from even herself.

They drove north on Highway 99 in his Chevy. Monti kept her eyes on the window, watching the bowling alleys and bus stops, adult movie stores, and seedy motels. She gawked at the terrain as they crossed the highway divide into a coastal village even more idyllic than the one they'd left. They parked in the driveway of a large Tudor house that had a view of Puget Sound. Sasha fished a key out of a flower pot and let himself in. Monti wandered its two stories, examined the family photos, taking particular care with the one where his father held him as a baby.

"Where are we?" she asked.

"Edmonds. This is my grandparents' house. Let's go swimming."

Sasha led her to an indoor pool inside a cavernous room.

"Wow!" she said. Her voice echoed off the jagged, stone walls.

"Whatever," Sasha answered.

He undressed slowly, flinging his blue and brown flannel on the rocky, cement floor. He eyed her until she followed suit, and then cannon-balled into the water. Monti caught a glimpse of his back. His alabaster skin was marred by a network of bruises and welts, snake-skinning their way across his shoulder blades, hugging his sides. She jumped into the pool in her underwear and tank top, and watched him as he floated on his back, his yellow hair blanketing the blue space around him.

"Why did we come here?" she asked.

"Why not?" he said.

He swam in circles around her.

"This house is incredible. Your grandparents must be rich."

He made a noncommittal sound, and then changed the subject.

"Let's play Marco Polo. You're it."

She closed her eyes, sensing he was in one of his quiet moods. One of those moods where she could see the neurons fire off, each of his worries a slow-release capsule in his brain.

Marco.

Polo.

And then he didn't make a sound.

Marco.

Polo.

And then a splash from his feet. A brush from his graceful hands.

Marco.

His chin had come to rest on her shoulder.

Polo, he whispered.

It wasn't monumental, this position they were in. She could almost see the small cleft through the back of her skull, so familiar she was with his face. She remembered a time when they'd gone to Baskin Robbins. As they walked home, ice-cream dripped and pooled in that cleft. Without thinking, she licked it off his face and laughed at his horrified reaction.

So this was normal, what he was doing. But the way it made her feel wasn't. She held very still, until her thighs burned from treading, not wanting to scare him away. But then she couldn't help herself, for the burn in her thighs or the one in her groin. She smelled him. And felt his smell womanize the hidden folds of her body. She turned her head so slightly. Only to see if this was just another act of friendship, a casual intimacy that started when they were young.

But, like a mermaid he flitted away before she could see what he'd been up to, blinding her with a shot of water spit from his pink and pursed lips. She licked her face, hoping to taste more than just chlorine.

"I'm bored with this," he said. As he climbed out of the pool, Monti watched the hairs on his legs, how the water turned them into dark, tiny rivers transversing a milky, white plateau.

When had he grown so much hair?

Sasha pulled her into the sauna, a beautiful, sage tiled room with a view of the yard. A sign of high living. Of Sasha's living.

"It's the Scandinavian way," he explained, turning up the steam.

They sat and breathed together. In. Out. In. Ahh. In.

His steely gaze pierced through the steam. She looked where his eyes had focused, and saw her tank top was now translucent, exposing the brown silver dollars on her counter-like chest. He showed no modesty this time. And why should he? There was nothing for her to offer.

"Where did all the bruises come from?" she asked, pointing to his side.

"Went to a show the other night with Tommy. Got carried away in the mosh pit."

Monti clenched her teeth. "Oh. Okay."

"It's almost Halloween," he said.

"There's still time."

"But what if there isn't?"

Monti shrugged, unwilling to gather the elements of her predicament, to form a solid picture.

As long as the future remained unclear, she didn't have to worry. Or admit she didn't know what to do. Or that she was terribly frightened. She wouldn't have to acknowledge Birdie hadn't been working. Or that she'd grown so thin Monti thought she might blow away. That Birdie mistook the gawks when they went into town as compliments. That she could no longer blame their missing food stamps on Reggie, or the lack of food on her mother's forgetfulness. Birdie rarely left the house, and when she did, it was always after Monti had gone to bed, long after all the markets had closed for the night. As long as the future remained hazy, she wouldn't have to admit the only money they had amounted to ten dollars left over from the incident with Charlene. Because Birdie had taken it.

"Stop ruining this day," she said finally. "I'm having fun."

Sasha appraised her, sitting so still he looked like porcelain, and she could tell he was listening to her thoughts. Not literally. But in the way of friends, when one knows the other so well they can see the lies in the minutia of a facial expression. She feared if he looked hard enough, he would see the flaccid man from Charlene's room.

He would see that his father was right about her.

She was unsavory. She was trash. And she was beginning to suspect that people like her weren't given a choice to be otherwise.

Sasha shook his head.

"You're my hero," he said softly, so she almost couldn't hear.

"What?" Her heart pounded.

Was he transcendent? Surely. Because he'd bewitched her.

Did he know? Of course he did. Like the lines on her palms, he could read her.

"Nothing," he said, looking at her as if she'd accomplished something just by existing. His hero? Why, because she'd had yet to become a statistic? Because being a poor, black kid made ordinary effort some remarkable feat?

For a moment, there was no sound but for the drip of steam on tile.

"I don't understand why you won't tell someone," he said. But what she heard was, *tell me everything*. He scowled.

"Of course you don't understand," she muttered. Her breathing came out in rattling, panting huffs.

He crossed his right foot over his left knee. She looked at his pink, bulbous heel. She didn't recognize it anymore. It was much bigger, the skin older than the last time she'd seen the bottom of his foot. It was a man's foot.

He sighed hard enough to create a void in the steam. His nose was turned towards the ceiling.

"I'm not in the mood, Monti. Just say what you mean to say."

She bit her lip, but still, the words poured out.

"How could you understand? You've changed. I barely recognize who you are anymore, now that you spend all your time with a criminal."

"All of my time? Jesus Monti, I'm allowed to have other friends."

125

She shook her head. "No duh. That's not what I meant. It just seems like you're headed down the wrong path. Skipping school. Doing drugs. It's not you."

"You say wrong path, he says God's wrath..." the steam blurred his face, a sudden whir so she couldn't hear his mumbling. When it cleared, Sasha's face looked troubled.

"This *is* me, Monti. I love punk rock. I love pot. And Tommy's a good guy. I don't see the problem."

She closed her eyes, woozy from the heat. It was easier to be honest when she couldn't see his face.

"You have everything. Nice things. A nice house. You're good-looking. You could be the most popular kid in school. It's like you want to throw it all away. Did you know that everyone has been calling you a fag?"

Sasha's face turned pale and his jaw clenched. He'd never looked so angry, so Monti stared at her feet. But she peeked at him through the steam, his silence worse than his glare. He pointed a finger at her.

"See that? That's how *you've* changed. None of that bullshit ever mattered before."

Later that night, as he rummaged in the cupboards for dinner, Monti took the last of her money and thrust it into Sasha's face.

"It's not even close to what I owe you, but I figured you should have it," she said. "You know, for all the burgers and candy and movies you've spotted me over the years."

He looked at the money in her hand.

"Where'd you get that?"

"I, uh..."

"Because I know you didn't get a job." He crossed his arms and raised an eyebrow.

"What, you think I'm not capable of getting a job?"

"Don't be dumb," he said.

Her bare toes clutched the pearly grout in the tiled floors.

"Don't call me stupid!"

"Then don't act stupid!"

The open cabinets seemed to smile in agreement with their Betty-Crocker-box teeth.

"Just take the money, will ya!"

"No! Put it away."

The whir of the new refrigerator, which had meat in the meat box and red apples in the crisper, seemed to egg him on.

She took a step closer. Her voice broke.

"Please? Just take it."

"Why?" he whispered.

She threw it at his feet.

"Because I'm not your damn charity case, that's why."

He insisted they spend the night, though he wouldn't give a reason. He showed her to a guest bedroom, gave her one of his flannels to wear, and then padded down the hall in his bare feet and boxers. She had hoped they would sleep together, but he'd said there was no reason when they had their own beds.

Monti tossed and turned. She should've been thinking about her mother and their situation, but couldn't get his face, and how it had looked through the heat and fog, out of her mind.

She had assumed the rumors at school weren't true. But he'd hissed at her like never before - *that's how* you've *changed!* - and now she was afraid those rumors had weight. When they left the sauna and doffed their wet clothes, exposing their post-evolution bodies - pubic hairs, birthmarks, stretched skin, and freckles - it felt as if they'd reached an agreement. The first to look away would be the first to admit everything had changed. That nothing was the same.

She heard a door open down the hall, heard his feet padding along the plush carpet. The doorframe was lit from the hallway, a yellow line of light in the darkness. And then his feet broke that line as he hovered outside her door. She wanted to call to him, to invite him to her bed. But he walked away. She heard a door open and shut, then the click of a lock. As if he was keeping her out. Away from his secrets. And shielding himself from her lies.

CHAPTER FOURTEEN

Rainier Valley, Seattle
1960

IN THE WINTER OF 1960, Ricky Adamoli was fifteen years old. He'd made the basketball team, was in fact the only caucasian kid wearing green and white as the Franklin Quakers practiced on a hollow, hardwood floor. He'd made three shots against the team's best defender, and was told he might start the next game against Garfield.

He returned home with a new motivation for his school work, for success. A new motivation for life. That's where he found his mother on the couch, a bottle of whiskey between her feet. She would've had a thousand yard stare, if not for her drooping eyelids. And there had been dried vomit caught in the corners of her mouth.

"Where the hell have you been?" she asked.

"I told you I had practice."

She didn't hear. She never heard.

"Getting ready to leave, just like your father did. That it?"

There was no reason for these rages. No reason beyond the alcohol.

He held her off as best he could, absorbed as many of the blows and scratches as he could, and then put her to bed.

"It's not my fault," she'd always say the next morning. "I can't help myself. I need you Ricky."

The sirens came later that night. The investigator suspected the fire was caused by a cigarette, left to idle atop a stack of ads and newspapers. He'd found that once caught, the fire followed a trail of spilt liquor until it consumed the house. Richard's mother died, engulfed by the flames as the alcohol kept her mind numbed to all sensation. Ricky had been lucky to escape with only a few minor burns. Their house, a leaning shack which sat at the bottom of the valley with a view of Lake Washington, was completely destroyed.

No one came to the hospital to claim him, and Ricky became a ward of the State. He'd lived in two group homes in less than six months, and then landed in a foster home in the Central District. And that's where he met Eugenia Tucker.

She was tall, and her skin was like burnt marshmallow, toasted a rich amaretto and so very sweet. She wore her hair short and pressed, and liked to catch the twenty-five-cent matinee on Sundays. She made her own dresses out of discarded fabric, and spoke with authority though she never knew her parents or where she came from. His new home was a white craftsman with blue trim, owned by an older couple named Paula and Robert Tillman. And it was Eugenia who showed him the ropes.

"The Tillman's don't like mess," Eugenia had said as they sat on the floor of the girls' bedroom. "So always keep your stuff where it belongs."

Ricky thought it impossible for a house with five foster children to remain spotless, but all he did was nod. Even then, he could not bring himself to challenge Eugenia. She owned him at first sight.

The house rules were to be followed exactly and always. There was no eating allowed anywhere but the dining room. Only thirty minutes of television was allotted per day. Chores were to be completed before school, and all homework finished by dinner. After dinner, each child was required to work, sanding wood and building tables in the basement workshop for the Tillman's furniture store, and to go to bed at nine o'clock.

It wasn't long before Ricky learned what happened when the rules were broken.

One day he decided he didn't want to spend the night building birdhouses or rocking chairs. He didn't want to eat broiled beef tongue and lima beans for dinner. He didn't want to finish his homework, only to be banished to bed without praise, without comfort, without a single ounce of enjoyment. So he stayed away from that white house with blue trim for an entire, unfettered night. He went to see a movie on Broadway. Ate greasy burgers from Dick's drive-in. Sat outside a jazz club and listened to a smooth saxophone as the cold pavement numbed his backside. He wasn't doing anything bad, wasn't doing anything of meaning. He was merely existing, enjoying the peace and tranquility of unbridled solitude.

But the Tillmans didn't like the rules to be broken. And so Mr. Tillman attempted to break a two-by-four across Ricky's back. But the two-by-four remained unscathed.

It was Eugenia who nursed him that week he stayed home. Mrs. Tillman had called the high school and reported him sick, and so he suffered in bed, waiting for the time between classes and chores when Eugenia would visit. He should've reported his injury to his caseworker, had he been able to get in touch with her. Or he should've run away, as soon as his body mended. But he couldn't leave Eugenia, not when her fingers worked the tension from his sore muscles, and her honey, almond-shaped eyes twinkled as she teased and toyed with him.

"You look like a leprechaun, with that red hair. Are you good luck?"

To which he replied,

"No Eugenia. I've got the worst luck there is."

It wasn't long before he finally seduced her.

It was during the fall of 1961, the beginning of his junior year. It turned out that Mr. Tillman was a football fan, and allowed Ricky the length of the season to break away from the wood shop. The football field was one of the few places he found solace during his years as Ricky Adamoli. It was in the crack of skulls against helmets, in the power harnessed in his young, virulent body. And his only other place of solace? It had been the well inside Eugenia.

The night was dark and dewey. The team had just played the boys from the predominately white high school at the top of Queen Anne Hill. Ricky and his teammates shuffled out of the stadium, their heads hanging with shame. A mostly-black team had just lost to an all-white team, a team that grimaced and shouted from the line, phrases like "let's put these niggers in the ground!" They'd lost to a team whose crowd jingled their keys to add more injury to defeat, an action that meant "We have nice cars. You do not." Which to Ricky and his teammates also meant, "We have futures, and you do not."

For Ricky, it was just a game that ended badly. But for his team-mates, to win would've been an act of defiance. A statement of their worth.

Ricky was troubled by the pain and abuse his teammates suffered, pain that went beyond the yard-long sprints and hard hits to the body, pain that would not abate with a hot soak or massage. He'd been exposed to this pain, thrown to the ground by his face mask and called, by a young man who looked no different than Ricky, with the utmost vitriol, a "nigger lover." The action had quelled the protest mounting in Ricky's own performance, and he felt guilty for his passive play on the field. For not standing up with his teammates.

But he was able to put the unpalatable events behind him once he saw Eugenia standing near the bleachers. Her smile was soft and light, and her laugh rang out like a bell. It started to rain, and Eugenia shrieked and tried to cover her hair with her hands. It was the perfect opportunity, because the stadium was now empty, life-less, except for the remnants of sweat and turf and blood. Ricky pulled her under the bleachers and kissed up and down her neck. She resisted at first.

"I've got to get out of this rain! It's ruining my press!"

But he loved to watch the natural texture return, held his breath as the black locks coiled and danced into a soft, downy afro.

"You look beautiful," he said. "I love everything about you, Eugenia." And at the time, he meant it.

It wasn't his first time, but it was his most meaningful. Even while it happened, he knew he'd never forget the soft whimpers she made against his throat, or the gasp they shared as he punctured his way in. The rain tinged as it pattered against the bleachers, a song made to both enhance and hide the sounds of their lovemaking. Her dress became soiled as it rubbed against the earth. Brown staining white. He finished on her stomach, relishing the sight of his whiteness and how stark it looked against the rich ebony of her skin.

At the time, he was sure it was love. He believed they would be together forever. But what he didn't know, what he had failed to realize, was that his love would never be enough. Not when he'd been born with so little. Not when he had to survive. Survival always beat love. Always.

CHAPTER FIFTEEN

THE BRICK-LINED streets that weaved through Ballard's core were dusted with cobwebs and tree fodder. Halloween was a week away. A day when restless spirits could come home. And a day when Monti could lose hers.

The eviction notice remained taped to the door, but Birdie was unbothered. Every day, she perched on the couch in her black, silk robe, her braids tied up in a multi-colored scarf. She smoked cigarettes from embered end to end, yet kept a full pack stocked in case Reggie came back. She drank malt liquor and laughed at the television with a heavy nod between jokes. And she always, always, always insisted,

Everything's fine baby. It's all gravy. I'm working night shifts, see. Pouring drinks for tired, old fishermens. We ain't goin' nowhere. Been living here going on ten years, see if they can kick me out my own damn house.

When Monti asked for groceries, Birdie would chuckle and say,

When I was your age, shopping meant snapping a chicken's neck or picking collards from the garden. You'll see. Sure 'nough. You'll see you got things easy.

And then Birdie would leave all night, leaving Monti awake for hours as she tearfully prayed her mother would evade the Head-banger Hunter.

THE SIGN of the Crossroads Skate Center glowed against a deep, taupe sky, with the coming week's musical acts and hotdog specials spelled in block letters. It was the only noteworthy aspect of an otherwise modest, single story building that looked as lively as the Department of Motor Vehicles. But Sasha couldn't shut up about the place. He'd given Monti a brief history on the drive over to Bellevue, a suburb just east of Lake Washington. The Crossroads had been formerly known as the Lake Hills Roller Rink, and had served the outcasts of the Pacific Northwest for years, hosting teen dances and musical acts in an attempt to battle the seasonality of the skating business. It was also the landmark location where the band members of Heart first met.

Monti kicked at the rocks of the gravel parking lot and looked at her bandmates. One her best friend - the other her competition. They sat in the Chevy with their legs hanging out the back door, laughing and sharing a bottle of whiskey as their feet bumped together.

"You guys are assholes for drinking," she said.

"All the best bands play drunk!" Tommy insisted.

She looked to Sasha to back her up, but he only shrugged.

"He's not wrong," Sasha said.

"Whatever," Monti said. "I'm getting cold. Hurry up and finish."

Sasha snorted something from the inside of a bottle cap. His eyes turned from tranquil turquoise to neon indigo. In a matter of seconds, a fight passed between them, caught inside a passive staring contest. He motioned her forward with his strum hand. She hesitated.

Don't you offer me that crap!

He tilted his head and scoffed.

Seriously? Come here!

She moved until she was close enough to smell the booze on his breath. He reached for her. She startled. He shook his head and sighed, then pulled a small twig from her hair.

"You wanna mellow a bit?"

He chucked her on the chin and brushed past her as if it were any normal night, playing punk rock and huffing coke in a parking lot. He wore a ripped jean vest, faded black jeans, and an army beanie that plastered his hair down so it clutched at his back like an adoring fan. He opened both doors to the entrance of The Crossroads, arms outstretched as if he would embrace the whole world. Monti thought to herself,

Someday people will lick the pavement he walks on.

There were two stages on opposite sides of the auditorium. Near the main entrance was a concession stand that smelled of fresh popcorn and stale ketchup. Hundreds of kids milled about, some dressed like "squares," as Sasha called them, and others in chains and rags and all things black, playing video games and drinking pop. Metal-heads from across the region waited for the Battle of the Bands to begin.

Monti waited near the stage beside Tommy and Sasha. It was obvious they'd been there before, and were chatting casually with acquaintances. But she was too nervous, and barely registered the performances of the two bands that played before them.

The shakes kicked in after they set up their gear. Monti looked into the crowd from behind her drums. Hundreds of faces waiting to hear. Waiting to judge her. And she froze. These weren't her people. This wasn't her music. She didn't belong here.

Sasha came close and whispered in her ear. The tips of his hair brushed against the side of her face as he said,

"It's alright. I'll start us off. There's actually a song I've been wanting to play with you."

His cream and orange electric guitar wailed a somber melody. He swayed, slow and lean, as if his heart fueled only half his body's efforts. And yet everyone in the crowd looked possessed. The song sounded familiar, like something she'd heard at Mt. Calvary, slow and bluesy. Tommy jumped in after the first bar, and played a simple, walking bass line. Sasha stepped to his mic. He kept his head turned so she saw his profile, and his lips as they hovered over the mouthpiece. He sang and her breath caught in her stomach.

Black girl, Black girl please don't lie to me
Tell me why do you weep at night?
In the pines, in the pines where the sun will never shine
I will shiver and cry out for you

She was still afraid, yet no longer knew why. She couldn't look at him anymore. She didn't want to hear his voice, or watch as love and admiration replaced all doubt or uncertainty on the faces of the band's newest fans. So she began to play. Soft at first, just the tilting whisper of her sticks against the cymbals, on the one, two, three and four. By the second verse, she'd added her heavy kick on the one, and the tat tat of her snare, sporadic and full, like a military drum-march. The harder she hit the toms, the more the crowd danced, and the more she let go. Soon her armpits wetted with sweat, and her hair bounced around her face. She hit heavy. She hit sharp. She pulverized her drums.

As if to bait her, Sasha matched her fury with a roar.

You forced me to creep
You forced me to moan
And you forced me to leave my home!

And then he turned to face her, rested his foot against her riser and leaned in while he soloed. She softened her playing, mostly in awe, as his fingers ran the length of the guitar neck, an improvised series of mournful arpeggio's, soulful like the scats and slides her mother once sang. And he played so fast the crowd slammed their bodies into one another. All at once, she felt guilty. Instead of playing to the crowd, a sea of adoration and warmth, he played so only she could see the workings of the muscles in his face.

She put more force behind her hands, and played so loud she hoped to drive him away. And for a moment, she did, until he screamed his last words into the mic. They weren't the normal words of the song made famous by Lead Belly. They were his own, magical lines. Lines laid down by a strange boy who knew too much. They were prophesy, and she chose to believe they were not about her.

I'm in the pines, I'm in the pines
And the sun will never shine
I will shiver...
But I won't
Forsake you...

Silence, except for the screaming crowd. His indigo eyes looked sweetly into hers. They'd made something marvelous together. Even with Tommy's shitty playing.

Come to me now, she pleaded. *If you come to me now, I can forget that you're reckless.*

He smiled, and stretched out his arms as if he might hold her forever. But then he gave himself to gravity, and fell into the crowd. He put his faith in a hoard of strangers, screaming, angry punks who carried him away on their black-painted hands. And though Monti couldn't say why, this simple act terrified her.

Tommy decided to stay behind after their performance. He wanted to see who won. Sasha had become sulky once they'd finished, seemingly turned off by the loud whoops of praise.

"That was awesome, man!" a pale, acne-spotted kid said to Sasha as they waited by the entrance. "You'll be famous one day!"

"I sure fucking hope not," Sasha said.

"Why not? You'd be rich and get all the chicks you want!"

Sasha looked at the kid and scowled.

"I've already got money. And no use for baby chickens."

"Huh?" the kid said, and before Sasha could expound further, Tommy interrupted.

"Lighten up man, we won the battle!"

"So what?" Sasha said. Tommy looked wounded. Sasha grabbed Monti's hand so hard it hurt. He skulked out the door, dragging her with him.

They didn't drive straight home, and instead stopped near the Fisherman's Terminal, a swath of industry and commercial moorage that came right up against the bay. They found an empty bank of grass on the Magnolia side of Interbay, and watched as the full moon drew silver fish in an inky canvas of salt and water. The lit windows of the houses on Queen Anne Hill shone like stars and for once, Monti felt like one.

"What's up your butt?" she asked. "We sounded awesome!"

"I know," he said.

"So why the sad face?"

He pulled his hair into a ponytail and leaned back against his hands. His Adam's Apple dropped as he swallowed, and she imagined what it might be like to bite into his neck.

"Tonight was perfect. I'm finally a real musician, in a real band. I'm playing with the most talented drummer in the city, who also happens to be my best friend."

Monti felt a blush ripen her cheeks. She looked at her hands.

He continued, "And after we played, the first thing I wanted to do was tell my mom. But I couldn't. Because she's dead."

He grabbed her hand and looked out over the water, and the frank intimacy of that action made her want to jump into the bay.

"She killed herself, you know."

"What? I was there. You said it was an accident."

"When it happened, it didn't occur to me to ask why there'd been no water damage to her car. I was too young. But I'm not too young anymore."

"I don't understand."

"I realized the cop who came that night lied. He had more sympathy for me than my own father did."

"If the cop said it was an accident, then I'm sure that's what happened."

He kissed the back of her hand.

"I wish I could be more like you," he said.

They remained that way, sharing body heat on a cold autumn night, searching in the darkness for answers they'd never find. Finally Sasha pointed at the Ballard Bridge.

"She jumped off because she couldn't stand being with my father anymore. The war messed him up. And he refused to believe she was sick, something wrong with her mentally. No decent person would tell a kid their mom killed herself on Christmas Eve. And that's how I know the cop lied."

"But, he probably wasn't lying, you probably just—"

"Montgomery Laine..." Sasha clenched his jaw and pinched the space between his eyebrows. "I found an article about it at the library, okay?"

"Okay, sorry."

The bay lapped at her broken shoes.

"You remember the night we met?" he asked.

"Not really," she said, wiping her sweaty palms in the grass.

"Really? You don't remember anything?"

"I remember meeting you. Playing with your toys. Nothing significant."

"Wow. I always thought meeting you was one of the most significant things to happen to me."

He paused. He wanted her to agree - she could tell by the way he stared into the water. Blank space for her to fill. He cleared his throat.

"You were locked out. Caught in the rain. You were wearing a green dress. For Christmas. And you were the only person who was there for me after my mom killed herself."

"Why are we talking about this? Tonight was a good night. A great night. You're bringing it down, man."

She chucked him on the shoulder, then walked to the water's edge to skip rocks. She heard him over the rolling tide.

"Who else can I talk to about this, if not you?"

Monti skipped a rock so hard it hissed along the water.

"Do you remember that game we used to play as kids?" she asked. "We called it 'Man overboard!'"

"Yeah."

"We should play. Forget about all this sad stuff."

She walked back and straddled his lap, but he continued to sulk. She shook his shoulders until a smile broke across his face. As kids they used to play the game to decide who got the biggest slice of pizza or the last Mr. Pibb. Rock, Paper, Scissors seemed a stupid way to settle things. Monti preferred a contest which could be measured by more than just chance. One would sit on the lap of the other, and they would clasp hands. Using nothing but upper body strength, they would each try to push the other to the ground, and the victor would shout, 'Man overboard!' as loud as they could.

Monti took Sasha's hands in hers, surprised at how well they fit when once they'd been so small. They began to push each other, arms coiling and unraveling until she felt his resolve slacken. Soon she'd pinned him to the grass.

"You're not even fighting back," she said.

He crossed both hands behind his head, and his chest broadened beneath her. He looked at her pointedly, and in a voice that could barely be heard above the wind and the dry leaves that rustled, he said,

"What's there to gain from fighting back?"

She froze, suddenly aware of the position they were in. She jumped off his body and hugged herself in the grass.

"See that?" he said, sitting up. "You've been doing that a lot lately. Treating me like a leper."

"What are you talking about?"

"You don't touch me anymore. High fives, hugs. Not even a tap on the shoulder."

"That's not true."

"Okay. Then touch me, Monti."

She looked at him, at how the wind picked up his hair and blew it across his face. At how his upper lip stuck out just slightly more than the bottom. At how his nose was a little too big for his face, and yet still added to his beauty, as if in pointed protest. At how his eyes always looked sleepy and sad, the irises glowing turquoise in contrast to the sky so it looked almost navy in comparison.

"What do you mean?" she asked, laughing nervously. "Where?"

He looked down, pulled at her grimy shoelaces with lithe fingers.

"Anywhere you want."

She didn't move or meet his stare, and soon he took it away and gave it to the black-lit bay. She knew almost everything about him. *Almost.*

"Are you a virgin?" she asked finally.

He waited to answer, let her pant in heat like a forgotten dog in summer.

"Yes," he said.

She tried not to slump in relief. "Me too," she said. "I'm a virgin too."

He smirked. "No shit, Monti."

When they were kids, she had the potty mouth. But like two ferries passing in the bay, one heading east and the other heading west, he'd come to use profanity more often than she. Her elementary years saw many visits to the principal, initiated by complaints made by the parents of her classmates. Monti soon learned little girls weren't supposed to speak that way. She supposed Sasha had a similar experience, though in the opposite direction.

By the time they were nine she'd say things like, *I hate lima beans,* and he'd say, *No shit, Monti.*

By the time they were twelve she'd say things like, *I got this scar from tackling Johnny Ducco last year,* and he'd say, *No shit, Monti.*

By the time they were fifteen she'd say, *Sometimes I feel guilty for wanting to run away,* and he'd say *No shit, Monti.*

Each time had different meaning.

I know this. Because I know you so well.

I know this. Because I was there when it happened.

I know this. Because I've also had this feeling.

But when he said it this time, she detected something new.

I'm a virgin too.

No shit, Monti.

His smirk.

Because I'll be the one to take it.

She jumped to her feet. Her legs were running before she'd given them permission.

"I gotta get home. See ya," she called over her shoulder, unsure if he'd heard, and uncaring about the dangers of the night. Dangers like the Headbanger Hunter. At least she'd know what he'd want. And that she'd be justified in fighting him off.

꒰ ꒱

RICHARD RETURNED from court to find Detective Rawlings waiting in his office.

"Christ," Richard said. "What now?"

Rawlings waited for Richard to sit.

"We've found a connection between you and a Headbanger victim."

Richard rolled his eyes, loosening his silk tie.

"We've been over this. I prosecute crimes committed by juveniles. It's no surprise I've met the victims at one point or another."

Rawlings leaned forward in his chair. His eyes were puffy and weathered, making him look much older than his thirty-something years.

"This victim is different. Her name was Evie Tucker. I think you knew her mother." He played at looking indifferent, as if he pulled the name from his pocket-sized notebook. But Richard knew better. "Eugenia Tucker? You guys were in foster care together?"

"Yeah. So?"

"According to court records, Evie had been busted for prostitution multiple times. And most recently, armed robbery."

Richard made a motion with his hand. *Get on with it.*

"Normally Judge Tomlinson would've sent a kid like that to an institution. Normally, you would've presented an air-tight case. But you failed to inform the witness of the trial date. And so the case was dismissed."

"So far, all you've shown is that you know how to read a court file."

Rawlings gripped the handles of his chair, and his knuckles burned white-hot.

"Screw you, Adamson. Think you can't be touched just because you have money. But I'll dig up your whole life. I'll prove that you let Evie off just so you could exude your own form of justice. I'll prove just how sick you really are."

Richard looked at his hands. They were clean. Manicured. The hands of the well-to-do.

It was true. When he first saw Evie three years ago, he nearly fainted. She brought back all his memories of Eugenia, and the crossroads that had parted their ways. Was this the result of the paths they took? Was this child the product of the hardness Eugenia had experienced? He'd felt guilty, in his new suit, purchased by his beautiful, rich wife for his birthday. Even more so when he read the file compiled by DSHS.

Mother is an extensive user of heroin, alcohol and various hallucinogens, and is not presently active in the care of the minor.

That had been the incitement, when he began to question everything. Each choice he made, from the moment he left the Central District on a football scholarship, to the moment he changed his name to "Richard." Had it been worth it? He felt he owed Evie, for so many reasons he wasn't ready to face.

"So prove it," he said. Rawlings' face turned crimson. Richard continued. "In fact, I sincerely hope you do."

Rawlings chuckled. "Me too, buddy. Because there's no statute-of-limitations on murder." He stood and leaned so close Richard could smell his aftershave. "I'm going to burn you, Adamoli."

Richard choked on his own spit.

"What did you call me?"

"It's better to come clean now," Rawlings said from the door. "The longer you deny the truth, the harder your life will be when the time comes to face it."

CHAPTER SIXTEEN

IT WAS HALLOWEEN. The Ballard neighborhood was covered in gossamer webbing, and strung with orange and purple lights. Children dressed as goblins, ghouls and little Chewbacca's walked the leaf-stained sidewalks, scrambling for a last piece of candy before the sun set, before the tricks and antics of the older youth who waited for dark unleashed their depravity and toilet-paper-themed pranks.

Sasha sat at the coffee table with Tommy, breathing in the hot-boxed air of the basement.

"Tell me again why we can't buy this stuff from the store?" Tommy asked, packing a box he'd marked with the stamp Sasha had stolen from Mt. Calvary. "I'm getting tired of the food banks. And even though stealing is great for my street cred, I'd rather not go down for 'grand theft groceries.'"

"Because, it's like Robin Hood this way. You know, 'steal from the rich to feed the poor,'" Sasha said. "It's the only way I could think to help without offending her."

Sasha remembered how she looked when he'd offered to loan her money. How her beautiful face set into one of proud determination, and a storm of anger drove out the warmth from her eyes. Each time he drew attention to her situation, he betrayed the idea of their equality, and felt the fissure between them deepen. But each time he heard the sobs, which only came at night and through the wall they shared, he felt ever more powerless.

"Why would she be offended?"

"She's proud. I've known her for ten years, and I don't think I've ever heard her admit she needed help."

"So she won't get angry if she finds out we've been leaving these on her doorstep?" Tommy asked.

Sasha smirked. "Oh, she'll be angry. She'll be pissed. But at least this way, she won't feel indebted."

Tommy taped the box closed and sat back against the couch, his shoulder brushing Sasha's. Sasha leaned in. It felt nice to be touched and to not feel recoil. It was his mother who would touch him with love, and for years after her death, Monti had given him a form of that affection. But now she ran when he tried to get close. She was going to leave him, just as his mother had.

He didn't understand why everyone gave "the Pearson boy" such a wide berth. In the six months they'd been friends, Tommy had proven to be both loyal and kind. After Daan discovered the "sin" in his room, Tommy offered to keep Sasha's records and posters in the basement. And when Sasha expressed his concern for Monti's welfare, it was Tommy who suggested they take the food thrown out by grocery stores at closing each day.

"It's what all the Market Kids do," he'd said.

Tommy was only guilty of the same crime Sasha had been accused of, and most hurtfully by Monti. The crime of being different.

"So, is that story about the janitor true?"

Tommy stared at Sasha, his jaw clenching.

"Parts of it," he said finally.

"What does that mean?"

"Like, the gist of the rumors are true. But people completely missed the point, you know? Like, everyone thought I was a psycho when I stabbed that frog in the head."

Sasha nodded, noticing for the first time how Tommy's freckles made him look younger than seventeen, and how he chewed the inside of his cheek when he was nervous. He made Tommy nervous, and it was a good feeling.

"But, what people didn't understand was that I was saving that frog. I mean, what's more messed up? Stabbing something so it doesn't suffer, or prolonging its life for your own personal gain? What was I supposed to learn by cutting it apart? What would I get by watching its heart stop? That biology assignment was more depraved than I'll ever be."

"So, you and the janitor?"

"Yeah. It's true. But he was my friend. He cared about me. And then, things happened."

"Things happened," Sasha repeated.

"Yeah." Tommy leaned in closer.

They sat for a moment, no sounds but their breathing. Tommy let his knee fall against Sasha's thigh.

"Which do you prefer? Boy or girl?" Tommy asked.

"Boy I think. Just to spite Daan."

"What? Why?"

Sasha shrugged. "Why not?" He was posturing. He'd never tried "boy" before.

"I'm not sure you know what I mean," Tommy said.

"I always know what you mean."

Tommy gave Sasha a confused look, as if he couldn't believe what might be happening.

"Okay. But just so you know, 'girl' is slang for cocaine, and 'boy' means heroin."

"I know."

Tommy laid both options on the coffee table. Two small plastic bags, dusty and full of white powder.

"Pick your poison," Tommy said, going for the heroin. But Sasha didn't need a downer. He wanted to feel rapture and ecstasy, all the things that were harder to come by between Daan's fists and Monti's avoidance. And sometimes, the few times he partied hard enough, he swore he could hear his mother's laugh.

"Not that one," Sasha said, touching Tommy's hand. "I'd rather we stay up all night."

Cocaine was the drug used in all the fancy clubs of New York and Los Angeles. It was the drug for the rich and beautiful. It wasn't looked down upon like heroin or marijuana, because it wasn't addictive.

Tommy pulled his hair, which had grown long enough to graze his chin, away from his face. He pushed in closer, putting the weight of his body into Sasha's side. Sasha winced and pulled back.

"Jesus. I'm sorry, man." Tommy moved further down the couch. "I'm such an idiot," he muttered.

"It's okay," Sasha said, lifting his shirt and exposing the bruised and welted skin. "Daan just doesn't like sinners."

Tommy ran his fingers along Sasha's wounds, leaving behind a swath of goosebumps.

"You need to take care of that." Tommy returned from the laundry room carrying a first aid kid. Sasha watched quietly as he rubbed tiger's balm into the cracked skin. He lit a cigarette, and smiled at the clumsy hands that not only struggled with the bass, but also applying bandages.

"I want one," Tommy said, taking the carton from Sasha's pocket. But there were no more matches.

"Use mine," Sasha said.

And Tommy leaned forward, resting his hand on the back of Sasha's neck. The tips of their cigarettes touched. The fire caught Tommy's end ablaze. An erection strained against Sasha's jeans. He didn't question it. It happened all the time now, anytime someone he cared about came close enough to touch.

Monti. Tommy. They'd become his world. They'd become like ferries on the bay, fixtures of the sea. And as one of them slipped away into a dense, urban fog, the other emerged from the gloom with an open helm.

Nothing will go according to plan.

Sasha saw his mother's face. How she had grinned in spite of Daan's abuse.

I'm just the captive of a noble madman.

He feared he might die if he waited much longer. Like with nicotine, his craving for intimacy would compel him to chase one buzz after another, sucking the end of a butt while sicking his lighter to the next.

At least Tommy was a friend.

At least Tommy cared.

BANG BANG BANG!

Someone pounded on the door. Sasha nudged Tommy in the side, who rose drowsily from his chest. He looked at his watch. It was three o'clock in the morning.

"Go see who it is," Sasha said.

Tommy left the couch, wearing only his boxers, and opened the basement door. Sasha hid beneath a blanket. He heard a pleading voice. Begging. Needing. He heard Tommy say,

"I don't carry that stuff. I've told you that."

The heavy door slammed closed, followed by the sound of Tommy's feet padding back. He lay down and put his head in the crevice of Sasha's armpit.

"Who was it?" Sasha asked.

Tommy yawned.

"You know who it was."

Sasha moved Tommy aside and got up from the couch, relieved for the excuse to leave. He rummaged through his jeans until he found what he was looking for, and then dressed with his back to the couch.

"You don't have to go," Tommy said. "You could stay here, and you wouldn't have to feel guilty about it."

Sasha rested his hand in Tommy's hair, but didn't meet his eye. A last gift, one more touch to justify what he'd done.

"I'd never forgive myself," Sasha said. And then he chased down the night.

❧

IT WAS the beginning of November. Birdie felt the cold in her bones and her teeth rattled like snake-tail. She'd disturbed her nest, and now winter closed in like a swarm of hornets. It was her job to keep a steady home and food in her baby's belly. What kind of mother disturbed her own nest? The no damn good kind. But she still had some good left, right?

Catcalls sang in her ear, banshee music the city made which promised to make her happier than her own baby could.

"What you want today, girl?" asked a man in a devil's mask.

The yellow angel screamed from her elbow. He clutched it so tight she almost cried out.

"Your baby will die," the angel said. "I love her. I've made the world for her and you have no right to steal her away from me."

Birdie looked into the angel's face. She knew it, but couldn't recognize it.

"But I'm so tired. I just want a little bit."

"Losing her will be the end of us both."

And Lord, that angel was right.

"I got something for you," the devil man said.

The angel pushed her forward.

"I'll take nothing from you today, nasty fool." Birdie spat at the devil's feet.

"Alright then, I'll see you tomorrow, Birdie-girl."

The devil's chuckle followed her down the street.

The cold ground wetted through her worn sneakers, and her heels were sore and soggy but she made it to the bank nonetheless.

Inside the bank was warm - it smelled like hot carbon and burned coffee. Ten-keys rolled through paper reels, money coming in, money going out. Plastic, potted plants made the bank feel green. And Birdie belonged there, had money for once. The angel had shown it to her.

Birdie sat in a chair by the entrance and doffed her muggy sneakers. She rubbed the aches from her feet and stole three cookies from the nearby refreshments table. The tellers and customers gawked and the craving spread like wildfire. She felt hunger from the callused tips of her toes to the frayed ends of her braids. The dog of her addiction barked at her heels and the stares made her shrivel inside. She decided to leave the bank. The streets were calling with their sweet, banshee music. The angel would have to live without his baby, just as she would.

But one of the tellers spoke.

"Ma'am, may I help you?"

When was the last time someone called her *Ma'am*?

Birdie stood, took two steps and faltered. The teller smiled and waved her forward. Birdie reached the glass and leaned against the counter.

She spit cookie crumbs as she spoke.

"I'm here to pay my rent."

❧

"WE SHOULDN'T BE HERE!" Monti hissed. "We weren't invited."

Sasha and Tommy had dragged her along to crash the party celebrating Ballard's near-win in the football game earlier that evening.

Tommy rolled his eyes. "I'm a drug dealer who can do the routine to 'The Hustle.' When there's a party, I'm always invited."

The house looked like it'd been washed in cream. The shag carpet was so soft Monti's feet left imprints as she walked. Crystal chandeliers hung from the ceiling, and pink, floral curtains dressed the windows. The living room and kitchen were divided by a wall of clear glass cubes, frosted with shimmering paint. Monti felt as though she'd just stepped into a scene from *People Magazine*.

A group of girls from the high school stood by a portrait hung on the wall. They wore flared pants, turtle necks and tan leather jackets, or earth-toned sweaters, peasant blouses and Levis. Their hair was shorn or feathered or teased, and looked nothing like Monti's kinks. Someone pointed at her and laughed, making her regret she'd worn one of Birdie's dresses. It had a low cut halter top, sequins and a slit up the thigh. It was Birdie's favorite disco dress for when she went out, and Monti thought it would be good for her first party. She paired it with her only pair of formal shoes, scuffed, patent leather Mary Janes, and knee high stockings. The girls looked away and she slipped back into her letterman's jacket.

And then she noticed the portrait of a beautiful, perfect family. Two parents. One child. All stunning, all with perfect teeth. Clarke Adamson stood in front of his father, the spitting image of the man who'd caught her in the trash. Her cheeks burned and her heart pounded. She needed to leave.

"What's up with you?" Sasha asked, elbowing her in the side.

"What do you mean?"

"You seem tense."

Though the eviction notice had been removed from their door, Monti still didn't know how much time she had. And sitting in the living room of the people whose trash she'd tried to eat brought the calamity of her situation to the surface. She was drowning in her own sea of sorrow.

"Who invited the faggots?"

Jared bristled in front of them. "Nobody wants to catch your gay disease. Get out of here," he said.

Sasha, who was drunk, stood and poked Jared's chest.

"Aren't you the captain of the wrestling team?"

Jared squinted, his mouth hanging open.

"Yeah. So?"

Sasha smirked. "Well, that's more risky than me standing here. Don't you think? All that dry-humping on the mat…"

Jared stepped closer, menace raking his face. Monti prepared herself, ready to fight for her friend. Just like she'd always done. It didn't matter if she lost. She knew how to bear the brunt of pain, to let it whisk off her shoulders into a place she needn't think about. She was the strong defending the weak. The friend who would always be there, would always come through. Loyal to the end.

But it was Tommy who came to his defense. A wiry boy

drowning in an oversized jean jacket with a faux-wool collar placed himself between the stocky linebacker and Sasha.

"Just calm down, man. Let me give you some of this reefer, mellow you out?"

"How about you back off? Before I kill you, too."

Tommy cocked his head to one side.

"Screw you. You ain't tough. You ain't shit. You're just some rich boy with Farrah Fawcett hair."

Clarke had been summoned from another room, and came to Jared's side. Monti thought he might join in, but instead his bloodshot eyes focused on her, on the dress. She saw that same look the flaccid man had, as if he wanted her but wasn't sure why.

Jared lunged forward. Tommy dodged him and shoved him backwards in one swift movement. And then he pulled a knife.

But it wasn't the knife that shocked Monti. As Jared mumbled and backed down, and the altercation died, she focused on Tommy's hand. On the hand that held Sasha back, and brushed his stomach to make sure he was there. To make sure he was safe. It was a hand that would keep him from harm, that would enclose his being into its palm for eternity. A hand that would knead his naked skin into the soft dough of yearning. It was so obvious, but only because her hand would've done the same. As the party watched the knife in Tommy's fist, Monti willed Sasha to push his hand away. And when Sasha didn't, she willed her love to look more like hate.

Later, after the drama died down, Clarke approached the circle of chairs where she sat with Sasha and Tommy. In his red letterman's jacket and ass-tight jeans, he was almost too beautiful to loathe.

"Can we talk?" he asked.

Sasha perked up in her periphery.

"Go ahead," she said.

Clarke raised his eyebrows. "Alone?"

"Don't go with him, Monti." Sasha pouted. His t-shirt was stained and had a decal of Mickey Mouse taking a beer bong. "Stay," he insisted. He looked incredible. So incredible, all she wanted to do was hurt him. Because he had chewed through her heart and spit it back in her face for being just out-of-reach.

"What do you care?" she asked.

It wasn't fair. Not by a long shot. But she was angry.

Jealous.

Clarke's room was dark except for a small, green desk lamp. He grabbed her hand and pulled her to his bed. He sat down and motioned for her to follow.

"I shouldn't have said what I said, that day on the field."

"Okay." She crossed her arms.

"I was pissed about other stuff. My dad mostly. Anyway, I took it out on you."

"That's no excuse."

"I know it isn't. I was just really embarrassed. You made a fool of me in front of all my friends."

"It's not my fault they can't block."

"Yeah. It sucks there's no girls' team." He paused for a moment. "I just want you to know. That I don't think of you *that* way."

"What way?"

"You know. I'm not like, a racist or anything. And um, I wouldn't normally call you something like that. Because you're different."

"I don't know what you mean by that." She was lying. But she wanted to hear him say it.

"You're basically a white girl. And super cool." He sighed. "Beautiful, maybe."

He traced the pattern on his bedspread. White and blue checkers. He hung his head, and the weight of his vulnerability was evident in the tensing of his neck muscles. He was trying to be nice. It was supposed to be a compliment. She should've corrected him, but her tongue stuck to the roof of her mouth. Who could call a spade by its name when it dressed like the Queen of Hearts? Who could fight a wolf that believed it was a lamb?

Maybe this was the best she could hope for.

Monti lifted Clarke's chin and kissed him. Some of the hunger for Sasha faded, so she kissed Clarke harder. She kissed him so well she was certain he'd forget the stupid names he called her, and realize her blood ran hot and red beneath her brown skin, that she was pink inside like he was. That she was human, like he was.

"Wow," he said when she was done. He looked sheepish and unsure of himself. He pointed to her yellow letterman's jacket.

"This is cool," he said. "Vintage. But why do you want to wear someone else's jacket when you could get your own? You could play volleyball or soccer or something."

"I don't want to play those sports. I like football."

"But still, you could—"

"I couldn't," she said flatly. "Even if I joined another team, I couldn't afford to buy a new jacket." She wiped her nose. "My mom gave me this jacket."

"Oh," he said. "Sorry."

"I don't need you to be sorry. And I don't feel like talking anymore. So take your shirt off and shut up, or I'm leaving."

His green eyes flashed and his mouth dropped open. He raked a hand through his auburn hair that was still stained by leftover sun-streaks. He truly was beautiful. Not in the way Sasha was - not nearly like Sasha. Clarke had chiseled, athletic features and the misfortune of an abominable personality.

He pulled his shirt over his head, and every muscle twitched from the effort.

He flung her letterman's jacket to the floor and pushed her on her back so she bounced off the mattress, until he pinned her down with his hard body. He smelled like cake and cologne, and she surprised herself by pulling him against her, ignoring the textbook that jabbed into her shoulder.

"Do you know how lucky you are? I've done this with so many girls. What do you think of my bod?" he asked.

"It's nice, I guess."

"You're lucky," he said again. "Most girls would kill for a chance with the starting quarterback."

She smiled and nodded. She'd been to the last game with Sasha, and Clarke had been sidelined the whole night.

He slipped a finger inside her, but she was already turned off. He ripped at her mother's dress, the one she'd so carefully chosen. The kisses he left on her neck began to feel like bruises, and he'd shoved another finger in so deep she grimaced with pain.

"Stop," she said, but his shoulder muffled her mouth. She began to panic, and felt the fear choking her airways.

"STOP!" she cried louder, wishing she had stayed with Sasha.

His arm was against her throat and he rubbed her pubic bone so hard she thought it might bleed. She heard the clinking of his belt. She lifted her knee and drove it into his side. He reeled back, and she threw her elbow into the soft space between his eyes.

"What the hell is your problem!" he shouted, hunching into a ball.

She leapt from the bed.

"I told you to stop," she said, trying her best to rearrange her dress.

She couldn't see his face, but his words were like liquid nitrogen, giving her chills and scalding her self-esteem.

"I thought girls like you wanted it rough."

The textbook had fallen to the floor. Monti picked it up, felt the weight of it in her hand. And then she threw it at his head.

He muttered and cursed, and as she left the room she said,

"Guess you were right."

CHAPTER SEVENTEEN

THE GIRL'S hair was pulled on top of her head and fastened with a hot pink, doughnut-looking thing he'd heard called a *scrunchie*. Her jean jacket was bleached and her blue stirrup pants fluttered as the wind picked up. It was dark, so her features were hardly visible. But he'd watched her for a week, and could recognize her movements.

The Headbanger knew from her file that she was seventeen years old and her name was Naomi. Watching her walk up Aurora from where he'd parked excited him. And no matter how hard he tried to forgive himself, this excitement disgusted him.

He walked to the parking lot of a Baskin Robbins. Naomi was inside, peering into the ice cream buckets with her hands pressed against the glass. She made her selection and accepted her cone of some bright flavor, pink with balls of color throughout. Naomi left the store, licking her ice cream and humming "I'm Coming Out" by Diana Ross.

The Headbanger leaned against the wall of the store.

"Hey," he said.

Naomi turned around. "Oh, hey."

"You've got a pretty voice." He flicked the hair from his face and pressed his chest forward.

Naomi grinned, showing her sweet teeth.

"You think so?"

"No. I know so. A beautiful girl like you could be famous, with a voice like that."

"Oh yeah? What you know about beautiful girls?"

She was too easy.

"Enough to surprise you. You busy? We could grab a coffee or something."

She glanced at the highway.

"I can't. I'm supposed to hit the drugstore for my brother's asthma medicine."

"You shouldn't walk. It's dangerous out there. Let me give you a ride."

"Is that your car?" she asked, pointing to where he'd parked up the street.

"Yeah. That's my car."

She studied him, then smiled. It was a calculated smile, as if she had plans to take more than just a ride.

"It's really nice," she said. "I guess I got time for one coffee."

From her file he knew there were two possible outcomes for where the night would lead. He would ask her - *how much to fuck you?* If she told him to scram, she'd live. But if she set a price, she'd end up with a face her brother wouldn't recognize, in a muddy puddle at a nearby junkyard. It was her choice.

❧

RAIN PUMMELED against the window so Monti couldn't see out. The heater kicked on, rattled itself awake with the loud patter of a half-broken appliance. Her heart beat fast and she was anxious to break free of her desk, which was too small and felt more like a cage.

"But, I don't see why kids from the Valley go here if they don't live in Ballard?" asked someone in her Sociology class. Monti sunk low in her chair, still facing the window so she wouldn't see who spoke.

"There was never slavery or Jim Crow here. It doesn't seem fair that my neighbor has to catch a bus to the Central District and go to a worse school."

"Well," began Mrs. Brandon. She was a flittering, passive woman who'd look more like a student if it weren't for her sweaters and pearls. "The School District started the busing program a few years ago in order to desegregate the schools."

"But that's what I'm saying. There was never segregation here."

Monti felt the eyes of her classmates on her. She chewed her fingernails and pretended not to notice. She hated the sideways glances and curious stares that came with discussions of race. Some looked sorry. But others looked indignant, as if to say, *So what? It's in the past. You should be fine like the rest of us.*

"You're right," Mrs. Brandon said. "We didn't have segregation laws here. But promoting diversity is still important."

"Black people live in the Central District because that's where they want to be."

Mrs. Brandon sighed. "Monti, why don't you give us your perspective?"

The whir from the heater stopped. Sweat beaded her forehead. She didn't know what to say. This educator, who had her plaques and degrees on the wall behind her desk, had assumed her only black student was bused in from the "ghetto."

Monti's blood felt hot, as if it boiled over and seeped through her pores. She stared at Mrs. Brandon, then turned and looked behind her. Clarke sat forward in his seat. He smiled and smacked his gum, and was wearing her letterman's jacket. He'd refused to return it after that night. He brushed off the sleeve, popped the collar and winked. She looked away, and found Jared staring at her, open mouthed. In fact, the entire class waited for her response.

"No," she said finally.

"Excuse me?" Mrs. Brandon looked shocked. Affronted.

"I said 'no.' I don't have anything to say."

"That can't be true," Mrs. Brandon said. And she smiled.

That was all it took.

Monti leaned forward and hissed,

"What the fuck do you know?"

The principal sent her home for the rest of the day, and she was assigned a week's worth of detention. He threatened she'd be transferred to special ed classes, which were earmarked for the problematic kids. It didn't matter that she earned A's and B's, because she was *troubled*.

Monti stopped at the payphone in the school's foyer. She was so angry, there was no other option but to hit something or cry. She sobbed until she heard someone enter the hallway. She shoved her fist into her mouth and waited for the footsteps to retreat.

She dialed a number.

"You looking for a date?" someone answered.

"Who is this?"

The person on the other end hesitated. "You called me, so who the hell this is?"

"My name is Monti. My mom had this number, and..."

People murmured in the background.

"Well who you looking for Monti?"

"Do you know Birdie?"

More murmuring.

"This is a community phone."

The voice changed.

"Monti? This is Charlene. What's wrong honey?"

What could she say? She'd just been kicked out of school. She didn't know where her mother was. She felt alone. She felt afraid.

"Sounds like you need to talk," Charlene said. "Why don't you come down here? We're at the Market."

MONTI WENT to Pike Place after school everyday. She'd been surprised by the openness of the Market Kids, how quickly they accepted her into their world.

There was Diane, a fourteen-year-old Chinese girl who left home after her mother threw her out for getting arrested with alcohol. But all the Market Kids called her Yoko because she liked to pit a boy against another, and she spent her days hooking and her nights partying. Coral had given up a baby for adoption some weeks before, unable to care for a child because she was still one herself. And sometimes Tommy came around, carrying his little baggies of weed. They made eye contact once or twice, but both pretended not to see the other.

Kids panhandled for money, begging for the pockets of the suits and skirts as they walked to work. They snuck into the dirty movie arcades and peep shows. They jumped in and out of Lincolns as they rolled through Pike Place, the slam of car doors a rhythm to their worldly game of musical chairs. Some lived in abandoned hotel buildings, or used their street earnings to rent a room by the day in a nearby hostel. They spoke of horrors, of being raped at knife point, sometimes by fellow Market Kids, or getting robbed of the money they had just earned on their knees. They told stories of drugs, their only medicine for the long, cold days. They exuded the bonds they created, leaving behind the sludge of their affection like sidewalk slugs, street lovers who scored and injected into each other's veins. No one seemed surprised by, or even feared death. That is what happened when you lived in the gutters of downtown. And the Headbanger Hunter was just another danger on a long list of potential deadly outcomes.

But the campfire stories of street teens weren't enough to send Monti home. Instead, each day after school, she canvassed the tract that ran from Pine Street to University and between First and Third Avenue. She'd watch her mother take tricks to the Ethelton Hotel and waited until Birdie emerged again. She memorized the features of every man her mother talked to, the corners her mother worked, and the license plates of every car that took Birdie for a ride. And when it became too cold to walk the streets, Monti sat by the window of her apartment. She watched the courtyard with hawk-eyes until she heard her mother's tired steps ascend their stoop.

The leaves had turned brown, and the air smelled like the earth. Like death. The Headbanger Hunter had struck again, and the bodies left in his wake, the spirits of the five black girls, lingered like a desperate leaf in autumn. One day, a little more than a week before Thanksgiving, Monti found Coral sitting against a brick wall in Post Alley. Her face was bruised and welted. Her cheeks were lumpy and lopsided, and there was a gouged wound in one of them. The bridge of her nose was lacerated. Her neck had long, black marks running across it like tire tracks. Both her eyes were black and puffy, and one was swollen shut. She wore a pair of baggy sweats, and Monti wondered if her wounds extended beyond her face and hands. Coral shook, like her little, black body could no longer contain her spirit, like her soul needed to escape the confines of the world.

"You alright?" Monti asked.

Coral's lip trembled.

"What happened?"

Suddenly Scuzzo and Charlene appeared.

"She good," Scuzzo said.

Monti moved closer to Coral. "Don't look so good to me. She should see a doctor."

Scuzzo grinned and rolled his head, as if they'd just shared a joke. Monti scowled.

"Come on, girl. Why you gotta act all light-skinned?" He pouted with the big bottom lip he used to seduce the girls to work for him.

"She's just freaked out about that girl they just found," Charlene said. "But I done already told her, I would never let her go with a trick if I thought he was the Headbanger."

"Yeah," Scuzzo added. "Everyone knows some of these tricks be sick. But I got my eye out for her."

Coral stared into the ground. The smell of piss and beer made Monti sick to her stomach.

"Coral, come here."

Monti sank down next to the tiny girl, putting an arm around her shoulders. She slipped her last candy bar into Coral's pocket, and then glared at Charlene.

"Look," Charlene said. "There's no recess for kids like us. We do the best we can." She looked at Coral. "Family is just the people who experience the same things you do. We are your family, because we got that same pain."

Coral wiped her nose and nodded. A homeless man played a happy tune on his banjo where the Market met the alley, and Monti could almost hear the creak in his hobbled knees as he danced achingly to his own music.

Charlene continued. "I asked about that girl, Naomi. Because us ladies got to look out for one another, learn from each other. And you know what I found out? Naomi was out here on her own. She wasn't in the life like us, just every now and then for some extra cash. She didn't have people looking out for her like you do. You're going to be alright, Coral."

Scuzzo and Charlene walked back into the Market, and Monti held Coral tight in her arms until she stopped shaking.

CHAPTER EIGHTEEN

THE FLAME of the candelabra flickered under the breath of his wife's sigh. Richard chewed his filet and watched as the fire at the center of the table came close to extinction, then danced backed to life like scalding ballerinas.

"What's wrong, Mom?" Clarke asked, seemingly dutiful as he pushed his green beans around his plate with a fork.

Richard looked across the table, mildly curious about the answer to his son's question. The grandfather clock chimed the hour, eight gongs filled the low-lit room and then just the clink of Clarke's fork.

"Things have to change," Cassandra said. She took a sip of wine. "I'm not sure when everything got so messed up, but it's time for us to be a family again."

"Were we ever?" Clarke asked, flicking pieces of bean into the candlelight.

"I don't know," Cassandra said. "Probably not. But it's never too late."

"So, what does this mean? Are you going to stop drinking all day? Is your driver going to pick me up from school and take me to Nordstrom's with you? You going to start dragging me to all your society events and dinners and parties?"

Cassandra glared at Clarke, and then pinched the bridge of her nose.

"He makes a good point," Richard said.

Clarke straightened his shoulders and stopped playing with his dinner.

"My father wants to cut me out of my inheritance," Cassandra said.

"He can't do that," Richard said. "It's part of a trust. It's a legal contract."

"Unless I'm proven to be unfit. Then I don't get anything."

"But what about my trust? I need that for college," Clarke said.

Cassandra pursed her lips and shook her head.

"But that's so unfair!" Clarke slammed the table.

"Honey, why don't you go to your room and let me finish this with your father."

"But—"

"Go to your room," Richard said.

He waited until the slam of Clarke's bedroom door reverberated throughout the house.

"What's going on?"

"The school called the other day. Some girl accused Clarke of raping her."

"What? That's impossible."

Cassandra cocked her head to the side. "Is it?"

Richard scoffed. "We never should've been parents. We were just two, sorry kids looking to fill a void."

"Maybe so. But still. I loved you, though."

"Perhaps. But you didn't know me."

Richard stared into his wife's eyes until his own started to burn.

"Are the police involved?" he asked.

"No, I took care of it."

"How?"

Cassandra gulped her wine. "How do you think? I offered to pay them for five years as long as they kept it quiet."

"So then why is your father threatening to disinherit you?"

Cassandra tapped her wine glass with a crimson fingernail.

"He wants me to divorce you. He thinks you're a bad influence on Clarke. He thinks you're the scandal that will tarnish the family name. He went to a party last week and met Mick Jagger - his social status means everything to him."

Richard understood the sentiment.

"But I don't share your family's name."

"Well, there's more..." She finished her wine and fingered her diamond necklace.

Richard moved to the chair beside her and took the hand from her throat. "I already know about you and Lance," he said.

"You do? Why didn't you say anything?"

"I don't own you, Cassandra."

A reel of emotion flashed across her face - he was meant to be jealous of her affair. And then her expression settled on a combination of admiration and desire. She'd always believed he wasn't interested in her money or status. He was the only man at that frat party who hadn't tripped over himself to win her heart. But he'd only been playing the game he learned on the street, the one where you never revealed your true desires. Street kids learned the hard facts of life - no one would give them what they wanted.

"My father hired a private investigator. They're going to meet soon."

If it weren't for holding her hand, Richard's own would've trembled.

"He said if I divorce you, he'll stop digging. But if not, he'll use what he finds to disinherit our family." She looked down at the table. "He never wanted me to marry you. I guess he figured we'd be broken up by now. But he's getting older and... he doesn't want you getting 'one red cent.' That's how he put it."

"It's a lot of money. Why don't you just give him what he wants?"

Cassandra placed a hand on his chest. She rubbed it over the muscle, and her breathing became raspy.

She didn't know all of his secrets. But at the beginning, when he'd been infatuated with her beauty, body and brain, he'd showed her some of his scars.

"I still want you. I still love you, Ricky."

Perhaps it was time to put his guilt to rest. He'd made his choice years ago. There was no sense in destroying the life he'd made now.

"Don't worry," he told his wife, who'd buried her face into his neck. "I'll take care of it."

Later that night, as he whispered lovings into his wife's ear, Richard coaxed an address from her lips with each measured thrust. And when she slept soundly beside him, he slipped from their bed and dressed only in black.

THE LIGHTS FLICKED on inside an apartment in Belltown.

"My wife really loves me."

The private investigator jumped, dropping his keys by the door. His jowls flapped as he spoke.

"How did you get in here?"

"Don't ask stupid questions. I take it you've been following me. You should know by now who you're dealing with."

A fat, gray cat slunk by the man's feet, rubbing its body against his shins. It purred, and Richard had an urge to fling it from the window. He wondered if a cat would land on its feet from five stories high.

"What do you want?" the man asked.

"Again with the stupid questions. I. Want. Everything. You. Have. On. Me."

Richard had taken his time going through the apartment. It was basic, a single bedroom, single bath with a single couch and phone and answering machine. The wood floors creaked and smelled as old as centuries, and the baseboard heating wouldn't turn on. But the safe was sturdy.

The man glanced at the telephone. Then at the drawer of the table that stood against the wall near the kitchen.

Richard raised the object in his hand.

"You didn't even have the safety on. One shouldn't own a gun if they don't know how to use it properly."

The man's face blanched.

"Please…" he said.

"I get it," Richard said. "Some rich guy hires you for a job. Seems basic, cheating husband with a sordid past. But my father-in-law doesn't know me. You don't know me. You don't know what I had to overcome."

"I have an idea."

"You think so? So you know what it's like to get beat by your own mother? You know how awful it feels, once you're old enough to defend yourself, to still be defenseless because hitting a woman is wrong? You know what poverty feels like? It's like prison, except you don't always get to eat."

The man lunged for the phone. Richard sprang from the couch. He grabbed the man by the nape of his neck and slammed his face into the table. He cocked the gun and held it against the man's temple.

"Whatever Cummings is paying you, it can't be worth more than your life. Open the safe."

The man did as he was told. He turned over a stack of photographs, reports and notes. The photos were of Richard and the black girls he'd paid for, getting into and out of his car. The notes were of interviews with former neighbors and schoolmates, people who'd once known Ricky and Martha Adamoli. And the fire investigator's report, with a note written in the margins - *witness claimed Ricky left house before they saw flames.*

Richard paused by the door.

"Do you think people can change?"

The man stared back, blood oozing from a gash above his eye.

"Right, I don't think so either. Which means I'll be able to count on your discretion." Richard smiled. "Have a happy Thanksgiving."

AT THE INTERSECTION of Post Alley and Union, just south of the Market, Charlene prepared Monti for what was to come.

"You're lucky," she said. "For being beautiful and exotic. You could work as an escort and get paid for the girlfriend experience in fancy hotels. All you have to do is be who they want. Just do what he asks, and you'll be fine."

"You make it sound so easy," Monti said. She looked at Coral, to see if she'd agree. But Coral just stared off into a cloudless sky.

"It is easy," Charlene said. She brushed Monti's hair away from her face. "But you're sure you want to?"

Monti nodded. "I don't want my mom out here anymore." She glanced at Coral. "The little ones can't defend themselves."

Charlene reached into her jeans pocket and pulled out a tube of flavored lip balm. She removed the cap and held it out to Monti. There was white powder inside.

"It'll help," Charlene said.

"No." Monti pushed her hand away. "I don't do drugs and I never will."

Charlene stared at her for a minute, then closed her mouth and shrugged.

"Whatever you say."

A dark sports car pulled up to the curb. The window rolled down, slow for the anticipation like the beginning credits of a movie.

"You old enough?" a man asked. Monti peered through the passenger-side window. He wore a hoodie so it masked his face.

"Yes," she said.

"Get in," the man said.

Monti hesitated.

"You don't have to do it!" Coral seemed to spit the words out in shock. Her eyes were wide and she looked to be caught in some sort of trance, as if she'd just seen a ghost. "Don't get in that car if you don't want to."

But Monti's life was not about what she wanted. It was about survival, and two things were required to accomplish that feat. Money and education. And this was the only way to have both.

She hopped into the car and ducked her head the way she'd seen Charlene do. Once they'd left the Market, she sat up to look at her john. It was Clarke's dad.

"What do you think you're doing?" he asked, a shocked expression on his face.

"Same to you," she said.

They drove three blocks and the silence became unbearable.

"So what do you want?" Monti asked.

"Not what you think," Mr. Adamson said.

"So then what am I doing here?"

He stared straight ahead, looking very much like Clarke, only more handsome. He was dressed in a black sweat suit and wore a matching beanie. He wouldn't have been a bad first trick.

They reached the edge of downtown and turned onto Elliot Avenue.

"Where are we going?" she asked.

"I'm taking you home."

Monti sank into her seat. She hadn't known until that moment, but she would've done anything he wanted for the money. Birdie wouldn't make it on the street. And leaving The Bridgewater, where she and Sasha had intertwined their lives, was unfathomable.

Something caught the orange light of a street lamp near her feet. Once in her hand, Monti saw that it was a mood ring. The band was silver and etched with howling wolves, and the stone morphed between sage and rose as it warmed in her palm.

"Can I keep it?" She held her hand so Mr. Adamson could see.

"Um...no," he said. He snatched the ring from her palm. "Clarke borrows the car sometimes. It must belong to one of his friends."

Tension walled between them, like the see-through glass between the cabbie and the passenger. Richard sniffed loudly and wiped his eyes.

"I'll just go back tomorrow," she said.

"You shouldn't go through with it. You'll regret it if you do."

"Let me guess, you speak from experience?"

He glanced at her, then nodded.

"It's my body, and I can do what I want with it. I don't have to be ashamed if I don't want to be."

"But you can't always be in control. Look at what the Head-banger Hunter has done."

"You think I don't know that? I can't control anything."

"There's another way, trust me. If you need money, I—"

"I don't take handouts. And if you want me to trust you, then you have to be honest."

She took his silence to mean he agreed.

"What do you like about it? Picking up girls like me."

"What makes you think I do that?"

"So, you like, just happened to drive by and noticed me standing there? Yeah right. Besides, my friend recognized your car."

"I don't pick up girls," he said. "Just women."

"Fine. What do you like about it?"

He kept his eyes on the road. "The control over an outcome."

The car pulled to the curb in front of The Bridgewater. Mr. Adamson let the engine idle. "So what's your plan then?"

"Finish high school, go to college, get a job. Have a nice life."

"I had to leave home to make those things happen for me," he said.

He pulled a card from his wallet, wrote something on the back and handed it to her.

"I can't leave my mom," she said.

"Why not?"

She looked at the back of the card. He'd written a phone number. Monti thought for a moment. But the answer fell from her mouth as though it had always been there.

"She'd have nothing if I left. And I'm not cruel like that."

BIRDIE CRAWLED out of the fog long enough to notice Monti was gone. She'd been waiting by the window when a maroon Mustang stopped on the street in front of The Bridgewater. Two people exited the car. Richard waited by the driver's side, and Monti walked towards the apartment.

"That alleybat motha-…" she muttered to herself, watching her baby walk with her shoulders slumped. Her legs out, her face done up, a display for men to enjoy and pummel with their imaginings. Most mothers could be proud when they saw themselves emulated in their daughters. And that she wasn't like most mothers broke Birdie's heart.

"Where you been?" she asked as Monti walked into the apartment.

"Nowhere, Momma," Monti said.

"That man touch you?"

"No, Momma. Everything's alright. Go back to sleep."

"Girl, who do you think you are worrying me like this! What business you got staying out all night? I oughta come right upside that head, done lost your mind!"

Monti rolled her eyes and muttered, "Whatever."

Birdie reeled back on her heels. "I'm just as old as when you was first born. I'm still your momma!"

Monti's eyes flashed and they turned on Birdie in a way she'd never seen before. Her little girl was an ignited bomb of shame and fury, both swirling in her redbone eyes like a tornado.

"You are such a hypocrite. You're never here and we have no money. Yesterday I had to tape my shoes shut so my socks didn't get soggy. Tomorrow is Thanksgiving. Are you going to spend it with me?"

"I got to work, otherwise you know I'd be here."

Monti crossed her arms. "You can't work anymore. It's too dangerous."

Her baby was right. It was too dangerous to work. But that hunger reeled its angry head, and she had to feed both her baby and the devil. It was too dangerous not to.

171

"Hear me now," Birdie said. "Whatever it was you thought you were doing tonight. Put it out your head. Your job is to go to school. You want to work at McDonald's or something, I won't stop you."

"Whatever."

Monti stormed down the hallway, leaving Birdie alone and encased by darkness. She heard the bedroom door slam shut.

Everything wasn't alright. But it would all be gravy. Because right there, alone in the gloom she said to herself,

"That polka-dotted, ginger-headed poor excuse for a man will both remember and regret the day he messed with Birdie James."

CHAPTER NINETEEN

No more secrets.

When he passed her in the halls and she wouldn't meet his eye.

Don't do it.

When he saw her loitering downtown on his way to the shows his ilk held every weekend, in rundown warehouses and garages they rented on Capitol Hill.

Come to my bed.

When he heard her crying at night, praying for her mother to emerge from whatever forest she'd been lost to.

These were the things Sasha wished he could say, if he weren't such a coward.

THE YEAR WAS 1972. It was the week before Christmas. And his mother had taken him shopping. They were to buy evergreen wreaths, cranberries to string, and toys to donate to the local shelters.

"Don't spend more than what I gave you," Daan said. He looked younger then, the bags beneath his eyes still taut, his hair more blonde than gray. But still that foul mood, upset with his wife for renting the open unit next door to "those kind of people." He'd assured her they wouldn't pay the rent, as people on welfare couldn't be trusted.

But Daphne had a charitable heart.

"You should see the girl next door," she'd said, brushing Mikael's hair for the family's holiday photo. "She's the most remarkable creature. And her mother is a singer!"

Mikael had watched as his mother attempted to smooth Daan's edges.

"Look with a Christian set of eyes. The family is on hard times. That poor, sweet mother can't find work, and she has a daughter to support. We can afford to discount one apartment," she'd said as they argued over dinner.

They went to the shopping district downtown. They wandered the streets between First and Third Avenue, the sidewalks between Pike and Pine, and marveled at the Christmas lights and snow flurries, and the large Christmas tree that stood in front of the Bon Marche.

Mikael said his nose felt frostbitten, and they went to Woolworth's for meatloaf and hot chocolate. Mikael always loved going to Woolworth's, loved the cafeteria with it's orange, puffy stools. He would sit and spin for hours while his mother shopped, counting his Starlight hard candies against the counter. This is what he'd been doing when a commotion broke out in the cafeteria. He heard a woman's scream, a sound so blood-curdling that he jumped from his stool, leaving his candies behind. A feeling of burden overtook him, and suddenly he knew why he ran towards the screams, instead of away from them.

His mother lay in a heap on the floor, a jelly fish in white cashmere, surrounded by a sea of sage linoleum. She cried and flailed her arms, ripped at the skin of her wrists with her fingernails until there were red skid marks in the milky flesh. A crowd looked on, hushed and stunned by the frantic woman.

She was silent on the drive home, but he thought he knew what happened. Swept away with the Christmas spirit, Daphne had greeted each person who came her way, and had given most of their money to the homeless, or to the bellringers from the Salvation Army. There would be no wreaths, no cranberries, and no gifts for the shelters. And worse, there would be Daan to deal with. And so it was the fear of reprisal that overtook her. That, and as Sasha learned in later years, something called manic depression.

Christmas Eve of 1972. The best and worst night of Sasha's life. The morning before he'd walked in on his mother in the bathroom. The water spilled over the tub, cold to the touch of his shaking fingers. He could see the goosebumps on her neck and face, though she acted as if the water didn't bother her.

"Mommy?"

She looked at him but didn't see.

"Nothing goes according to plan," she said. "I'm the captive of a noble madman."

She muttered the phrase over and over. He moved to leave, to get his father, but then she turned her head towards him as if she could hear his thoughts. He held the doorknob as though it were a buoy and he'd drown alongside her if he let go.

She held a finger to her lips.

"Sssshhhh," she said.

He nodded.

"Promise me you'll always be true to yourself."

"I promise."

He didn't tell Daan about what he'd seen. And the next evening, Daphne Coen threw herself into the bay.

SASHA AND MONTI watched television in his bed. He hadn't seen much of her since the party, and she'd lost interest in the band. They were two ferries, one heading west into an emerald green jungle, the other going east toward the kiwi sky and cobalt ridge. Both would be lost.

They ate greasy pizza from Little Caesar's, taking advantage of a two for one deal. Monti devoured an entire pizza to herself, and he wondered if she'd been eating regularly, how she'd been eating, who was caring for her now that her mother wasn't stable, if her mother had been caring for her to begin with. He'd stopped leaving the boxes on her doorstep - she was rarely home to claim them.

"Monti," he said. "We need to talk."

The doorbell rang. Deep, hushed voices echoed down the hall. Someone jimmied the lock. The door opened and Daan stood with his arms crossed.

"What did I tell you, Mikael?"

Sasha blanched. "We're just watching tv. Nothing happened."

Daan stepped away from the door. "She's in here officers. And she's wearing the ring."

Two policemen entered the room. Sasha looked at Monti, at the fear welling in her eyes.

"Hi Montgomery," one of the officers said. "We'd like to ask you some questions. Is your mother or legal guardian available to bring you to the station?"

"What do you want to talk about?" she asked.

"Money was stolen from the home of William and Edna Coen, and a neighbor saw you loitering around the property. Will you please get your mom and come with us?"

Monti began to stammer, "I... I didn't steal anything!"

"Check the ring, officers. I saw it on her a month or so ago, when I caught these kids sleeping together. It belonged to my wife. It's engraved, and I still have the insurance policy on it." He pointed his finger at Monti, like it was a pistol, "And she stole it."

Sasha tried to shield her with his body.

"I found this ring. I've never stolen anything in my life," Monti said.

The officer motioned for the ring, and Monti handed it over. Sasha's palms were sweating. The officer frowned and said,

"'My heart belongs to D.C.'" He looked at Daan.

"D.C. for Daphne Coen."

The officer sighed. "Sweetheart, please get your mom. You'll need to come with us and answer some questions."

Sasha cleared his throat. If they saw the state Birdie was in, they would take Monti away.

"She didn't take the ring," he said. "I gave it to her. And she didn't break into Grandpa's house. I was there and I let her in." He stared straight into Daan's eyes, the veins popping red with anger.

"I stole the money."

❧

DAAN WASN'T A BAD MAN. Just one who'd been drafted to do bad things. But always out of love. The first one had been falling for Daphne. Because if he'd known what it would be like to love a "mentally ill" woman, he might've chosen differently. It seemed she broke and mended his heart every other day. Like when he returned home from war, a war he'd had no choice in entering, for any man who loved his country would surely have done the same, and she'd called him a baby killer and took to bed for weeks. And then, once she'd finished mourning, dragged him by the hand to the Ballard Bridge and tore at his body while cars rattled against the grates overhead.

He loved her through it all, through the outbursts and random acts of lust. He loved her though she always invited the undesirable to their doorstep. He loved her through his prayer when she refused to take her meds, hating the limbo they trapped her in. He loved her as he looked to the most extreme forms of penance, hoping to bring out the grace from the God he had to believe in, because what choice did he have if he hoped to go on? And then she had the audacity to leave him, despite his efforts, his patience, his attempts to quell her demons.

It was a father's job to make sure his children had better. And Daan hoped Mikael would see, one day, when he became the man he was meant to be.

❧

A WEEK INTO DECEMBER, Sasha waited in the Juvenile Court Room for sentencing. The process had been quick because he'd agreed to plead guilty to keep Monti from being dragged into the drama.

"I'd like to say something."

Daan stood, though the court room was set up like a roundtable conference rather than the formal, criminal proceedings he watched on television.

Judge Tomlinson nodded his approval, cracking his knuckles and blinking with only his right eye.

Daan cleared his throat.

"My son is headed down the wrong path. It's one of skulls and bones and that punk metal crap. I smell the drugs on him. Everyday. Our family believes that's why he stole the money. To pay for his habit. He's cutting school, and doesn't listen anymore. He needs to be taught a lesson. He needs to learn how to be a man."

The Judge looked Sasha over. His eyes had the brown staleness of dead tree bark. He smiled.

"Would you be willing to express your regrets to the court?" Tomlinson asked.

"No," Sasha said. "I have no regrets. I'd do it again."

Daan looked at Sasha as if he'd just been stabbed in the back. Sasha shrugged.

"I'm just being honest."

The Judge sighed. "Alright. The minor shows no remorse and the legal guardian has expressed he's no longer welcome in the home. Given his propensity for narcotics use, I am recommending the minor complete the three month counseling program at the Everwood Youth Center, as well has 200 hours community service. Next case."

MONTI WAITED on a bench in the hall. She'd expected him to be cuffed, or wearing a jumpsuit. But he looked like himself, his hair frayed around the edges and brushing his collar bones, wearing an

"I'm not a killer, just Vicious" t-shirt he'd made to commemorate his favorite rockstar. He looked like the Sasha she'd known. But he was flanked by two security guards, and this image solidified his transformation into something so beautifully dangerous and novel, like a lethal, unnamed species that left teeth marks in her skin.

"Why'd you do it?" she asked as he was led away.

He looked over his shoulder. His smile both scared and delighted her.

"Why not?"

⁂

"Don't go out," Monti said. "Please. I did what you asked and I stayed off the street. There are other ways to make money. You could work at the bar again."

Birdie looked over her shoulder at her baby in the doorway. The trees in the courtyard were bare and a murder of crows huddled together in the branches, judging.

"That's exactly where I'm going," Birdie said. "To the bar."

"Come on, Momma..."

"Don't you 'come on Momma' me. Girl, what you think you know?"

"I know things need to change. I know we can't go on like this."

"We? You don't know the sacrifices I've made for you. I was just a child when I got pregnant. I could've ended it all, ended your life before you had a chance. Then maybe I would've had one."

Birdie's voiced trembled. "I lost my man because of you, know that right? Couldn't have no more babies after you came. And Reggie won't come back long as you're here, making all them threats."

She pointed a finger at Monti. "So you don't like how things are? Well get on then. Let me handle mine."

Damn, if her baby weren't so strong and stubborn. Birdie felt proud when Monti squared her shoulders and looked down her nose.

179

"If you leave now, you might as well leave me for good."

It wasn't the mother who spoke next, but the disease secreting its poison. Poison that blackened Birdie's heart until its needs surpassed her own.

"I might just do that. Serve you right."

"I hate you," Monti said. "I wish I wasn't yours."

"Me, too," Birdie said.

She heard Monti crying and nearly turned back. Because she didn't mean nothing by what she'd said. It was the ache in her bones that made her want to hurt. But she kept moving forward, fearing that if she stopped she'd give in to the drug and never follow through on her plan.

It was late afternoon and almost dark when Birdie rang the doorbell.

"Can I help you?" Richard said, opening the door with a confused look on his face.

"You can stay the hell away from my daughter," she said calmly.

"I beg your pardon?"

"I saw you the other night. Dropping her off." She ran her hands down the front of her favorite dress. A peach, peasant frock that hung off her shoulders and had a tan, leather cinch. She'd tied her braids up in her red and white checkered scarf, and chose a pair of large hoop earrings.

Richard looked behind him, then stepped onto the deck. He closed his front door and said quietly,

"It's not what you think."

"Don't you tell me what I think. All I know is, you used to pay me to do stuff you can't do with your wife, and now you're sniffing around my daughter like some happy critter."

His face paled. "A what?" he asked.

"A happy critter. Running around, your face looking all nice and sweet when really you just a street rat in disguise. I know all about you. Girls share secrets on all the tricks. I know you're a lawyer. And yet you break the law, just like anybody else. A happy critter."

"Do you mean 'hypocrite?'"

"Don't you tell me what I mean."

He put his hand up and pinched his thumb and forefinger together, "You're daughter is this close to throwing her life away, but you're too far gone to see it. I don't think you should be lecturing me about anything until you get yourself to rehab."

Birdie felt her mouth drop open. Richard smiled.

"Yeah, I looked up your rap sheet. Prostitution. Possession of a controlled substance. Assault. Won't be long before you get your ninety days in jail. What will happen to Monti then?"

Birdie cleared her throat and regained her composure.

"I don't think you should be acting all mighty with what I know about you. You think your wife will be happy to find out what you really into when you 'workin' late?' You think you could still work if I tell the newspaper that one of the county's lawyers likes prostitutes with his morning bagel?"

His face darkened and he crossed his arms.

"How did you know where I live?"

"Pretended to be your wife and called the school. Wanted to make sure they had the right address on file because I never received Clarke's report card in the mail."

He regarded her for a moment. Then he chuckled.

"You don't have any proof."

It was Birdie's turn to smile as though she had all the power.

"You picked me up in June, right after those black girls were found in the river. I took you to the Ethelton. Cause I ain't getting in no man's car unless I have to. And after I heard what happened to them girls, I said to myself, 'man, fuck these tricks. They think they can treat us any which way they want to, like we're the nasty ones?' Half the shit I done, I never would've thought up on my own. So I decided I needed protection. And if any motherfucker went ahead and murdered me, I'd make sure he got caught."

His face was whiter than Mt. Rainier in February.

"So you know the security guard at the Ethelton is kind of a freak, right? And you know, since it's in a rough part of town, the hotel got security cameras. So I get all cute and I tell this security guard that if he sets up a camera in my room, he can watch what I do."

"What do you want?" he asked. His voice sounded like sandpaper.

"Pay me enough to get my daughter a better life, enough so we can start over. And then I'll be gone."

He glared at her. Birdie was afraid he'd call her bluff. It had been years since their last transaction, and she hoped his habit was bad enough to blur the faces of the women he used.

"Where's the tape now?" he asked.

"Nope. Money first."

He sighed out the tension in his body and pointed to the Mustang in his driveway.

"Go wait by the car, I need a minute to grab a few things. I'll buy you a drink." He smiled. "Maybe we can reach an understanding that will benefit the both of us."

CHAPTER TWENTY

AFTER THEIR FIGHT, Birdie never came home. Monti had returned to First Avenue, hoping to find her and fearing the worst. That her mother had actually left for good.

Standing next to a street clock, its beige face marked with Roman numerals and its hands frozen with neglect, Monti shivered, wrapping her new, black leather jacket around her body. Scuzzo had given it to her, and she'd agreed to work. Underneath she wore a tight pantsuit with a halter top from Birdie's closet, canary yellow with the pants rolled high to capris because they'd been too short.

The Market sign's red light made the street, which was slick with melted snow, glow orange. Every girl looking to date stood at her favorite corner, hovering over a square of pavement while her eyes bored into the windows of each car passing by.

A silver Lincoln pulled to the curb.

Monti jumped in and put her head down near the driver's lap. They drove away from the Market, up Third and stopped outside of the Ethelton Hotel. Monti thought of the girl Evie who'd been taken from her room, and found later with her face so pulverized it looked like carcass meat. For all she knew, this middle-aged, clean-cut guy with black hair and a mustache could be the Headbanger

Hunter. But she was out of choices. What hope did a sixteen-year-old girl without a high school diploma have of making any real money, enough to keep a roof?

"I need half," she said to the man. He handed her a wad of bills.

"I want everything," he said. "A good blow and a better lay."

Monti swallowed over the lump in her throat.

"Okay," she said.

The man reached behind his back. Her heart pounded, and her instincts signaled danger. She looked around the car for some type of weapon, a screwdriver or jumper cables or an empty pop can. She pictured her quickest escape and found the door handle. But he'd already locked it with the automatic feature. He reached for her, with something silver in his hand. A knife? She lifted a foot, ready to smash his nose into his mustache and scrap with her last ounce of strength when he said,

"Police! Show me your hands!"

MONTI WOULD'VE SPENT the night at the Youth Center had it not been for Mr. Adamson. He was the only person she thought would answer her call.

"I can't believe they let me go," she said on the drive back to The Bridgewater.

"It's your first offense, a misdemeanor at that. And you're a minor."

He smelled fancy and sweet, and sang along to songs on the college radio station. He was beginning to feel like a friend.

"So what I do doesn't matter," she said.

"It matters. The choices you make now could impact the rest of your life. But the system isn't built to help you."

"I don't know what to do."

"Here's what will happen. You keep doing what you're doing. You get busted and released. Busted and released. If you do end up going to a foster home or youth center, you'll most likely run away because there are both kids and adults there who might hurt you.

No one will be able to find you after you run, because no one is keeping track. Even if they did, they couldn't arrest you or make you stay somewhere safe, because the law protects your right to be a runaway. You'd most likely end up using drugs, because belonging nowhere is the loneliest way to live. And the way to make money on the street, you'll have to numb your mind to survive. You'll either commit a crime so bad you get locked up once you come of age, or a crime will get committed against you that you'll never come back from."

He had a distant look on his face. "Or, there's another option."

"What's that?" she asked.

"You stay off the street, finish high school and go to college."

"What if it's not up to me, whether or not I live on the street?"

He glanced at her and furrowed his brow. His thumbs tapped the steering wheel. He turned the music up and sang until they reached The Bridgewater.

He walked her to the front door. She didn't want it to open, fearing it would be just as cold inside as it was in the courtyard.

"Do you remember where I live?" he asked.

"Yeah."

"You're welcome to come stay with us. For as long as you need to secure the life you deserve."

"No offense, but your son is an asshole. He'd make my life miserable."

Mr. Adamson laughed. "True. But we're sending him to a private school for boys on the East Coast. His grandfather is going to whip some sense into him. He's leaving after the holidays."

"But I don't want to leave my mom."

He touched her shoulder, and the weight of his hand made her feel safe.

"You may not have a choice."

It was Christmas Eve. Birdie wasn't home, and for this Monti would never forgive her. What mother left her daughter to celebrate Christmas alone?

Monti lay on her mattress and listened to the rain. She stared at the eggshell walls and the popcorn ceiling. Her room had no posters from *Teen Beat*, no mirrors to do her makeup in, no bookshelves. It was empty of life, devoid of her person. Belonging nowhere really was a lonely way to live.

She looked out the window. The clouds were dense as charcoal, breaking over the streets and releasing their downpour in torrid sheets. She thought of the Market Kids, and the dregs of the city as they scuttled back into the sidewalk cracks, hid beneath the Viaduct or creviced between the skyscrapers, clearing the way for a fresh, new morning.

There was a flash by her window.

She opened it and found Sasha standing in the rain, his teeth chattering with cold, his golden hair plastered against his face, his leather jacket glistening wet. Once, her knees would've buckled to see him like this. Once, when they could laugh and play together, but not now.

"Are you going to let me in?"

She looked at her empty room, at the grungy carpet and battered doors. Once, she would've been embarrassed, but what did it matter now?

"I thought you were supposed to be in Juvie?" she asked.

He shook his head. "It was just a rehab facility. For troubled youth. And I jumped the fence."

They stared awkwardly at their feet.

"So, don't I like, get a hug or something. I haven't seen you in like, almost a month."

She reached out one arm and wrapped it around his neck. He squeezed her waist and sunk in until she supported his whole body weight.

He wiped the water from his eyes, then paced back and forth.

"We've been best friends since we were seven. And this is the first time I've seen your room."

"Yeah, so?"

"These walls are so thin," he said, tapping the one behind her bed. "I can hear everything. But I can't see it. And I can't touch it."

She felt it again, that sickness which formed in the pit of her stomach and doubled her over. It was there anytime Reggie came around, or when kids ranked on her for being grimy. It was the overwhelming shame that made her want to peel off her skin so she could beg for a new one, a new face, a new life.

"What do you want?" she asked.

"Come with me."

"What?"

Sasha grabbed her hand and pulled her down on the mattress.

"We'll die if we stay here, Monti. There's these punk houses in L.A. and New York. Musicians living and creating together, putting on their own shows. Rent is cheap when it's split six ways. We could make a life."

Her heart thudded against her chest.

"Why are you asking me?" she asked. Hopeful.

"Why not?" he answered.

It was the same answer he gave for the broken arm he got after skateboarding down Queen Anne Avenue, which was so long and steep the top couldn't be seen from the middle of the hill. He gave the same answer for the black eye he got during a punk show after he picked a fight with a guy three times his size. He was too reckless, too open to go unnoticed. He would never belong to her, and she knew what reckless men did to the hearts that loved them.

"I can't. I have to be here for my mom."

He clenched his jaw. "Jesus, Monti. You can't be that naive."

She jumped from the bed. "What's that supposed to mean?"

"Your mom's a junkie."

Monti froze.

"She has been since we were kids." Sasha's voice cracked, a pubescent slip that would've made her laugh under different circumstances.

"You don't know," she whispered.

He reached for her hand, but she yanked it back and covered her mouth.

"She came to Tommy's basement all the time, begging for drugs. She's probably getting high in some flop house right now."

"You don't know."

"Tommy has seen her buying from dealers downtown. It's why you never have money for rent."

Monti shook her head, making her hair bounce around her face.

"My mom gave you guys a deal on your lease. Not sure why Daan kept the rent so low, but that's what happened."

Her chin trembled and her sinuses congested.

"That day, coming home from church and finding her on your stoop like that? I thought for sure that would wake you up. But you were in such denial you lied right to my face."

"No way. That's not true. I have to be here for her."

He traced her cheekbone with a finger, "I know what you're planning to do."

She started, and pushed his hand away.

"Tommy told me. Don't do it. Not for her."

"If all this is true, then why haven't we been evicted yet? Because she took care of it, and she's out there making money for us now. She'll be back."

"Birdie doesn't look good. Didn't you notice how skinny she'd gotten?"

Monti paced and chewed her thumb.

"Please," he whispered. "Don't do it, Monti. Don't go down that road." He hesitated, looked down at his shoes so his wet hair slid over one eye.

"It should be with someone special."

It felt like a punch to the gut. She *had* wanted someone special. She had wanted *him*. But if what he said was true, then he'd been lying for months. He'd been pitying her for months.

"Come with me," he said. "I promise I'll take care of you."

She lifted her chin. "I don't need you to save me."

His eyes flashed teal, like lightening in a thunderstorm.

"Right. Because welfare's like, what? A job description for people like you."

Monti clenched her fists.

"Fuck you."

"No, it's cool. Because if that doesn't work, you can always make money on your back, right? Like Birdie did? Because it's so much better to be a prostitute than to accept help. Even from me, right?"

"Get out."

"And when you get hungry, you can just scrape through people's trash, or pretend the food-bank only brings you the leftovers so they don't go to waste!"

She slapped him across the face, so hard her palm burned as if his skin had been on fire.

He walked to the window, then stopped. *One last look*, his eyes seemed to say. They were wet. The pleading was palpable. But she realized what she'd been so afraid of, what she'd been unwilling to acknowledge. That he would hurt her the same way Birdie had. Whatever dreams they conjured, side-by-side on fragrant pillowcases, died with the last rays of summer. Just like those mahogany girls, the ones not so unlike herself.

She felt the void of his departure. He was a star, shooting high across the city, and would land wherever he wanted. He would burn long and bright and crash against the sky, and she would have to claw her way from darkness.

She packed her belongings in trash bags and headed towards Magnolia. Birdie made her choice. And Sasha made his. Neither picked her, and so she made her peace with the permanence of goodbye.

֍

It was a few days after Christmas. Detective Rawlings stood over the newest Headbanger victim, knowing deep in his gut this one would not be identified. She'd been tossed over the Aurora Bridge, had drifted with the current of the Fremont Canal until she caught beneath a grove of lily pads near Gasworks Park. It was a week before anyone noticed the smell, and a few more before it was reported. Most thought the stench came from the industrial archaeology that remained in the park, an intricate interweaving of rusted pipes and cylinders, once used by the Seattle Gas Company to light the city.

The body was too decomposed for identification. Most of her teeth were missing except for one gold tooth, from both the Headbanger's blows and, judging from the remaining nubs, what could've been extensive drug use. But the most alarming aspect was the fact the Headbanger had cut off the fingertips of his victim. Was the killer getting smarter? Would there be more and more bodies of young, black women to find?

Rawlings would take the body to the coroner, an autopsy would be done, but he knew the outcome.

Manner of death: Murder.

Cause of death: Blunt Force Trauma.

Name: Jane "Goldie" Doe.

But there was one item the detective made sure the forensic team took extra care to bag. A white and red checkered scarf. The water undoubtedly had washed it clean, but still. It could serve a purpose, could wind up being a pivotal clue. After all, it had been clinging to the ends of the victim's braids, had been the alert for the samaritan who'd finally seen her. It'd held fast, like a last effort to keep claim on her life.

PART II

1989

CHAPTER TWENTY-ONE

Los Angeles, California
1982-1987

AFTER HE'D HITCHED his way to the sunny banks of Los Angeles, Sasha changed his last name to Kent. He wanted a fresh start, taking a stage name, simple and transformative like the music he loved to make.

But he marked his past into his skin with ink. Dark, organic colors of blue and green and black. Skulls and crossbones of the punk sigil. A pill bottle with his mother's name on it, still full because, in the house he grew up in, mental illness didn't exist. Evergreens and roots for the cold forests that sprouted him from their bark. And a gap-toothed mouth on his pec above his heart. Most of his new friends, all part of the hardcore punk scene, thought it was just some rock symbol, inspired by The Rolling Stones or KISS, made imperfect to spit on the corporate ideals of the music industry. And he didn't correct them. Because he couldn't say he'd been in love once. It didn't feel right to share that secret when Monti didn't know.

He'd been happy in Los Angeles those first years, playing his creamsicle-colored guitar at small, rundown venues and junkyard buildings that smelled of piss and vodka. He snorted cocaine and took speed, and drank so much beer he blacked out on stage. He shared an apartment with his bandmates and threw parties to meet girls. He went on short tours with his band along the Pacific Coast, enjoying anonymous sex with pretty fans. He'd shaved his hair into a mohawk, wore blue lipstick and sang so loud he developed a permanent, husky tone. He punched the suburban fans who came for the fighting instead of the music, happy to give them the violence they craved. The violence he'd fled. And for a while, he'd forgotten the slick streets of Seattle, the mossy brick of Ballard, and the best friend he missed.

But on the nights he stayed home to rest his throat and liver, alone at the small apartment in Echo Park, playing his acoustic guitar on the deck and singing softly to silence his subconscious, he felt like an old woman who'd realized her real life, the one she truly wanted, had been wasted by someone else.

Eventually he grew tired of the L.A. scene. What started as a love for the underdog became an excuse for privileged white kids to fight and rebel, to exert hatred against those who were feeble and "other." A new scene was burgeoning, a pretty boy rock, all bandanas and eyeliner and sexy hip slinging. Everything he hated. It was all showmanship. He had no more fight left, and nothing to show.

The call came from his grandfather. Daan had a stroke and, after a trip to the doctor, was diagnosed with emphysema. And as quickly as he'd emerged from the forests of the Northwest to break the hearts of surfer girls and punk chicks, Sasha left the beach for home.

In a way, Sasha became the man his father had wanted. He took over the management of the family's rental properties, which had been sold down to two buildings and made just enough money for Daan's in-home nurse. He stopped wearing chains and black, stopped lining his eyes with sludge. He even became that defender of God's people Daan had named him for. At least, in the way it materialized in his mind. He formed a new band called Fungus Reign, and coined a phrase that would define the music they made, something that combined everything he loved. The heavy sound of Metal, the driving angst of Punk, and the veritable agony of Soul. And he called it *Gospel for the Faithless*.

ॐ

"Do it or I'll know you're a cop."

It was a soggy afternoon at the end of October. A line of cocaine stretched across the glass coffee table of a low-income apartment in the Central District. It was the good kind, purer and whiter than the Jordan sneakers Detective Jackson wore. Montgomery turned up her street voice.

"I ain't doing that shit."

The whites of the man's eyes looked yellow against his sweaty, dark skin. He slowly placed his .38 caliber pistol on the table, the mouth of the gun facing towards her. Montgomery didn't flinch. Instead, she leaned forward.

"When I was sixteen, my moms and I were about to get evicted. There was never no food in the house. I went to school hungry every day. I came home and my moms was either gone doing God knows what, getting beat up by her boyfriend, or passed out on the couch. At the time, I loved her so much I refused to see what was going on."

She leaned back in the chair and rested a hand on her right knee. The dealer had relaxed some, and seemed taken by both her story and "homegirl" appeal. It was either that, or the ass-tight blue leggings and mustard, low-cut crop top she wore beneath a baggy, broad-shouldered blazer. Montgomery continued.

"That year I got busted for solicitation. I wasn't using or anything like that, just trying to take care of the family. I come home and my moms is nowhere to be found. Just gone. Didn't even take none of her shit. And I knew right then I had to get real about why our lives were fading into nothing. Because she wasn't there for the scariest thing that ever happened to me. All them nights, she wasn't just sleeping. All them cats she let wandering in and out of our apartment, they weren't no 'special friends.' The shaking sweats, the 'I need to get well' whining and going on. Deep down I knew. That moms weren't supposed to leave their kids alone all night. That the only way I could not despise her was to lie to myself. Sacrifice all sense of my own deserving."

She lit a cigarette and sucked a waft of smoke into her mouth. But she didn't inhale before blowing it out into the dealer's face. She continued.

"So no matter what happens to me, one thing I know for sure. I ain't never going down as no junkie." She tilted her head and stubbed the cigarette out on the coffee table. "You gonna shoot me or nah?"

He didn't shoot. Instead he slid a package across the coffee table and Montgomery gave him the cash. She left the apartment and went to her car. She noted the decay of the neighborhood. Drug dealers had claimed the high traffic corners, and crack cocaine had bound the community in despair. Window shutters hung by rusted nails. The paint peeled away from barred-up corner stores. There was no laughter. Children played indoors, and if not then their voices were too soft, too innocent to be heard over the screaming sirens and *POP! POP! POP!* of gunshots.

She radioed her partner and drove away in an unmarked beater car. She had a report to write. Because a homicide detective was hoping to press this dealer, one Day-Tawn Marshall, for information on a drug-related shooting. And he'd asked Seattle's newest and only female narcotics detective for help.

TOMMY HAD SO MUCH MONEY, he'd begun to stash it around his apartment. Twenty grams of heroin returned $6,000 in cash. He just couldn't spend it all, and he didn't trust banks. Besides, no one would believe a rangy, black haired man with blue circles beneath his eyes worked in Finance, and bartenders didn't make that much in tips. So, in his little apartment on Capitol Hill, the rundown neighborhood east of downtown where all the gays, junkies, and poor artists lived in cheap, settlement-era apartments, he'd begun stuffing his money into obscene places. Inside a sock he'd continually used to masturbate. Beneath the creaky floorboards where the rats defecated. Between the stacks of dirty dishes piled high in the sink. Inside the pillow case where he lay his head at night, wondering if the man giving him head could tell he was surrounded by a fortune. Tommy preferred to take baths, but one day, while in a hurry, he discovered the reason his shower head was blocked was because he'd stuffed a wad of bills inside. Sometimes he forgot how much money he had, and where he'd stashed it.

Tommy had graduated from the skunky marijuana he'd grown in his mother's basement. Now he sold heroin, buying it wholesale from a man who lived in Georgetown.

He looked at the syringe on the coffee table, half-listening to the Sonics game. Shawn Kemp dunked the ball on a fast break. He was a rookie, but Tommy could tell he would be a star. Because he'd begun to recognize what stars looked like. His beeper went off, and his heart raced when he read the number.

An hour later, as twilight dawned and the Space Needle shone through the drapes, Sasha sat with him. They fumbled over pleasantries, but Tommy knew why he'd come. So he was surprised when Sasha said,

"You got any weed?"

Tommy laughed at his old friend.

"Nah man, that's kid's stuff."

Tommy watched Sasha more than he watched the game. Sweat beaded along his forehead. He was getting sick, but he'd wait it out, just to enjoy this fleeting moment. Though they'd kept in touch those years Sasha had been in Los Angeles, the dynamic between them was different. Ever since that night in the basement. Simultaneously, Tommy realized that he loved Sasha, and had essentially been used by him. But he wasn't angry. If Sasha wanted, he'd take him with open arms. No question. That using was just who Sasha was. He was destined to unwittingly exploit people, because he was so easily loved, so easily desired, and so easily generous in returning those feelings. So generous, though he could never sustain it. Except with Monti. God, how Tommy hated Monti for being too stupid to see it, blind to what had belonged to her all along. She was so fucking stupid, all those dirty looks she gave him, like he'd ever stood a chance. Making him believe he might've stood a chance.

Sasha pointed to the syringe on the table.

"You should put that up, man. Be done with it."

"Yeah," Tommy said. "I should." But they both knew he wouldn't.

Because he couldn't.

Tommy wanted to kiss him as they made their goodbyes, clasping hands and slapping backs as men did to show their love.

"Happy Halloween," he said, remembering a night when two boys could be who they wanted. One of them for keeps, the other just for fun. Touching and kissing and holding with care, the most innocent and dangerous act Tommy had ever experienced. But did Sasha still remember?

"Happy Halloween," Sasha said, a smile on his lips and sadness in his eyes. He put his hand on the back of Tommy's neck, and Tommy felt his fingerprints against his skin. "I'll see you around."

But Tommy knew this would be the last time they met.

After Sasha left, he plunged the syringe into his last remaining vein. Some people chased the dragon. What he chased was a lion, a golden lion with blue eyes, a lion who was part sad, strange boy, whose cynicism, disdain, and perverted sense of things only brightened the light that'd been bestowed on him by gods.

He nodded in and out, and felt his heart palpitate.

Damn, he thought. *I didn't mean to take that much.*

But even that was a lie, a dope-sick lie that fiends used to convince themselves they didn't want to die. Because of course they did. The only thing that kept them going was the dragon, or in his case, the hungry, golden lion.

Darkness came swift, and though he knew he would die, he felt serene. His eyelids closed on the beautiful face, one that could take over the world with his pout and scowl, a face made of the ocean and sand mixed together like summer. And then he was gone.

&

LATER THAT EVENING, Montgomery walked into Police Headquarters at the Public Safety Building, downtown between Third and Fourth Avenue. The smell of hot fax paper and stale coffee permeated the regurgitated air, air that hadn't been rinsed by daylight for at least twelve hours. She made her way through a pen of cubicles before she found Detective Rawlings at his desk.

"What you got for me, Jackson?" he said.

"Good news. Made my first buy. Not enough to make Day-Tawn snitch, but I can work my way up to a kilo. A three-year prison sentence might be enough to scare him."

"You have trouble finding him?"

"Not at all. One of my informants made the introduction. I let my enviable charm do the rest."

"Right. Well only one more to go."

Montgomery scoffed. "And the thousand who'll replace him."

A door opened from somewhere behind her. Montgomery kept her cool, but her eyes darted around the room for anything on which she might catch a reflection. A window. The glass from a picture frame. A black coffee mug. Getting made by someone on the street could mean her life, and she needed to be ready to turn her street persona, which happened to be one *Scarlett Vermillion*, on a dime.

Rawlings had begun talking about a co-ed softball league he played in, how they were down a girl and needed a fill-in when Montgomery noticed a line of photos tacked to the cubicle wall. She recognized the Headbanger victims from the summer and fall of 1981, a time she only thought about when memories of Birdie and Sasha trespassed through her nightmares.

Rawlings' voice faded into her periphery as Montgomery's eyes settled on a photo of the last victim, or rather, the remains of the last victim. She was too decomposed to be recognizable. But the dress she wore, which was peach and peasant-style, and the white and red checkered scarf caught in her waist-length braids were distinctive enough. Montgomery bit her lip, but a sob erupted from her mouth. Her jaw tightened until her molars groaned from the pressure. She was devastated. But then, in an instant, all her sorrow morphed into rage.

Rawlings waved a hand in front of her face.

"Earth to Jackson?" His head tracked her gaze and settled on the photo.

"Not my only unsolved case, but it's the one I can't forget," he said. "I keep them up no matter what else I'm working on."

"Why?" she asked.

"Because they were so young. They made mistakes, but still had a chance to turn it all around. The Headbanger stole that opportunity from them."

"That last one wasn't so young."

Rawlings snapped his head around. "Do you know who that is?" he asked.

"Yeah," Montgomery said. "She's my mom."

COLD AIR BLASTED through the vents. Montgomery cowered over the photographs taken of her mother's beaten body under the florescent lights of a pewter-painted interview room.

Rawlings' tired eyes suggested he was used to the drama, numbed by the sudden influx of corpses that had littered the Pacific Northwest since the seventies. Ted Bundy, the Green River Killer, the I-5 Killer. And the Headbanger Hunter. All were named, and yet all were faceless by either their hidden identities or vacant stares. And then there were those silent killers, the ones who had many names. Heroin, boy, smack, girl, china white, dope, blow, snow, crank, and crack. The ones that would've taken Birdie eventually, had the Hunter not killed her first.

"You're certain this is your mother?" he asked.

"Yeah," she said. She pointed at the checkered scarf, its brightness dimmed by the industrial murk of Lake Union, the white of it caked with grime, the red of it blackened with blood.

"She tied her hair in that scarf every night before she went to bed. And that dress..." She pointed at the picture. "It was Birdie's favorite. She was strutting her stuff in front of everybody at Woolworth's. She was laughing so loud, everybody was watching her. I wanted to be just like her..."

She pointed to her mother's arm in the photo and, despite the decay, could almost envision the tattoo of a microphone and butterflies that looked like musical notes.

"I was nine when she came home with this tattoo. It was so ugly. She shoved me to the floor because I'd grabbed her arm, not knowing it was there. I remember telling her it looked stupid. Then she laughed. So did I."

Rawlings didn't respond. It was a tactic to keep her talking.

"I'm sorry," she said. "I don't know why I said that."

Rawlings pulled the pictures back.

"We'll need you to formally identify belongings found with the victim at the medical examiner's office. But I'd like to ask a few questions and get the ball rolling."

He leaned forward on the table. Montgomery recognized the signs. No doubt his heart was beating faster. His knee bouncing and his mind racing through all the evidence he'd memorized over the past eight years. The identification of Birdie James was a new lead to chase down, and Rawlings looked as though he strained against a leash. Detectives worked all-nighters, drank too much, and ostracized their loved ones for moments like these.

"Did your mom have any aliases?" Rawlings asked.

Montgomery thought for a moment. She could almost hear her mother's voice saying,

Baby girl, Kitty Blues needs another cocktail.
Kitty Blues can't find her T.V. Guide!!
Kitty has the blues, Kitty Kitty Blues...

"She called herself Kitty Blues sometimes."

Rawlings scribbled in his notepad.

"When was the last time you saw your mother alive?"

"I'm not sure of the exact date. But it was after Thanksgiving. Sometime in early December."

"Do you remember anything significant about the last time you saw her?"

Of course she remembered. She and Birdie fought. She begged her mother to stay, then basically shoved Birdie's nose in her own dirty laundry and told her not to come back.

Montgomery cleared her throat. "We had a fight."

"What about?"

She shrugged. "Just mother-daughter stuff."

"How long was it before you noticed Birdie hadn't returned? Were you concerned?"

"I'm not sure."

Rawlings scribbled. "Okay." He paused. "Why didn't you report her missing?"

Montgomery pressed her tongue against the inside of her cheek. His face was impassive, but she knew he was judging her.

"I did report it. After a few months went by, but she was a drug addict and a prostitute. The cop told me they couldn't investigate unless I had proof of foul play."

Rawlings rubbed the back of his neck, shaking his head.

"And you didn't pursue it?"

"No, I didn't. Did you pursue it?"

"There's no reason to get defensive. I'm not assigning blame. I'm just trying to figure out why it's taken eight years to identify her."

"Well," Montgomery said, crossing a leg over the opposite knee. "It wasn't unusual for her to take off and leave me for weeks."

He scribbled on his notepad, nodding silently.

"She was also hooked on heroin. I got that from looking up her record." More scribbling. She'd never been on this side of the table. Her voice rose and bounced off the empty walls.

"And eventually I just realized I needed to focus on myself and get my life together."

Her emotions simmered. Soon they'd spill over and she wouldn't be able to control herself. She squeezed her eyes shut and breathed in the smell of the room - ghetto tears and stale cigarettes. The HVAC clicked on and rattled before sending a stream of dry air overhead. She calmed after a moment and opened her eyes.

"Any other reason you thought eight years, with no word from your mother, wasn't something to investigate?"

At this she broke down crying. She covered her face with her hands and wailed into her palms. Detective Rawlings gave her the space to mourn.

"Will you bring me a photo of Birdie?" he asked once she'd settled. "I don't want to canvass with a mugshot."

"Yeah. Okay."

"Detective?"

"Yeah?"

"I'm sorry for your loss."

"Thanks."

Montgomery pulled out her wallet and removed an old photo strip. She was ten years old when Birdie had taken her to the Seattle Center. They'd gone into a photo booth and made funny faces, bunny ears, kissed each other's cheeks. And for the final frame, a glamour shot with their cheeks sucked in to heighten their bone structure. Birdie looked incredible. She looked happy.

Montgomery slid the photo across the table.

"Don't lose it. It's all I have left of her."

CHAPTER TWENTY-TWO

DUSK SETTLED on a November night in front of the Velvet Room Strip Club. The twilight-purple sky accentuated a pink, neon sign that read, *SHOWGIRLS*. Montgomery waited in a cafe on First and Pike, drinking an espresso. She was responding to a complaint from a woman who said her eighteen-year-old daughter was getting drugs from work. Her partner was across the street, having a conversation with the club's manager, a spindly, pockmarked man in his late thirties named Dennis. Victor would be explaining that his girlfriend Scarlett needed to be on the rotation. And though Montgomery thought her partner looked as friendly as a St. Bernard, she knew the manager would not question the authority Victor's tall frame could enforce.

"Alright girl, it's showtime!" Victor said after he'd hustled into the cafe. "Scarlett Vermillion is scheduled to dance in less than an hour. Better get over there and change!"

He rubbed his hands together and waggled his eyebrows.

"You're enjoying this too much," Montgomery said.

"Yeah right. It'll be like watching my sister up there. And then I get to explain to my wife why I had to see my partner get naked." He held the door open. "I'll be at a table. You see if you can get one of the girls talking, and I'll see if I recognize any dealers."

"Got it, Vic."

It's what narcotics detectives did. They went undercover. They looked for the vice. They seduced the johns who wanted to pay to beat and penetrate women. They enticed the girls who offered more than just a private dance. They looked to score, and worked their way up the chain until they knocked off one more supplier. All in a day's, week's or year's work.

Victor put a hand on her shoulder.

"You sure about this?" he said.

"Sure about what?" Montgomery asked.

"You know." Victor cleared his throat.

"No, partner. What?"

Victor rolled his yes. "You don't have to go all the way, you know... Naked."

"I know I don't."

"In fact, this might be a bad idea. This might put the Sergeant on your ass again. And I feel like kind of a jerk right now, to be honest."

Montgomery crossed her arms.

"You bought three lap dances when you inspected the Sands club last week. Just to see if one of the dancers offered you sex. How is this any different?"

"Okay. Okay, girl," Victor said, nodding his head. "When you right, you right."

INSIDE THE STRIP CLUB, the air was thick with cigarette smoke. The floor ripped at the bottoms of her shoes, sticky with spilled pop. A thick bouncer asked for their ID's.

As Victor dealt with the bouncer, Montgomery caught the blue eyes of a stranger. He leaned against the wall just inside of the main showroom, gesturing wildly and laughing with Dennis the manager. His hair was long and sandy blonde, nearly half-way down his back. His jeans were loose fitting and had holes in the knees, and he wore a green and brown flannel over an NWA t-shirt.

Their eyes locked. His mouth dropped open. Her heart pounded against her ribcage, and her tongue stuck to the roof of her mouth.

Sasha started to speak, so she closed the space between them in two strides and punched him hard in the face.

"What the hell!" he shouted.

Montgomery glanced back at Victor, his head tilted to one side and a confused expression on his face.

Dennis with the bad skin doubled over in laughter.

"Guess you won't be getting lucky with this one!" he said, patting Sasha on the back.

She rushed to the dressing room before they could say more, but still felt their bewildered stares on her back.

They were supposed to watch. Follow their instincts. Pick out the guy who kept whispering in a girl's ear. The guy who kept giving everybody dap. The dilated pupils, the skittish glances, the tweaking fingers. They asked the girls which customers would "pay extra," where the best dope was, swapped stories of near encounters and getting busted. And if that didn't, as Victor often put it, "shake loose some change," they went to another block or club or street corner and tried all over again.

Montgomery had just enough time to change and ask one of the girls where she might score. The girl blew her off, which wasn't a surprise. New faces drew suspicion. That's why she'd keep coming around like a bad cold sore. A good detective had to out-shit the bullshitters.

She walked on stage in a pair of clear stilettos and a red, satin robe over black lingerie. The song "Mistreated" by Deep Purple played over the speakers, and she swung her hips to the rolling rhythm and grinding guitar. She felt her pulse in her wrist as she grabbed the pole and looked over the room, praying Sasha wasn't watching.

He was.

She hadn't the time to practice a routine, and felt grateful to be in good shape. The beat of the song dropped. She let her robe fall to the stage and kicked it into the viewing area. Sasha grabbed it from the floor and held it like a trophy. She swung her leg around the pole and spun, and then used the strength in her arms to pull herself upside down, wrapping her legs as she slithered back to the floor. She did a succession of twirls and slunk around the pole, and then hoisted herself up again, letting her legs hang open from the side and using her core to lower and raise them, bicycling her muscled thighs mid-air. Men whistled. Money was thrown at the stage. She played at being sexy, but relied on her athleticism, and all the while she watched for anyone who looked suspicious.

Her routine was halfway finished. She had to do it, even though Sasha's ironlike gaze tracked her every move. Because it was well known; the more you took off, the more money you made. How could she play a desperate stripper with a habit if she didn't go full nude?

Montgomery pulled the straps of her bra down, ripped it from her chest and flung it at Victor. If she had to be uncomfortable, then so should her partner. He hollered and threw money at her, but wouldn't meet her eye.

Sasha moved his chair to the front of the stage. He pulled a bill out of his wallet. Folded it into a small rectangle. Put it between his teeth and leaned forward on his elbows. She hesitated for a moment, but knew that if she wanted to be believed, and therefore trusted by the other girls, she'd need to play along with the customers' desires.

Montgomery crawled towards Sasha on her hands and knees. His eyes looked purple in the red glow cast by strobe lights. He still smelled of Irish Spring and tobacco. She took the bill between her teeth and felt the heat of his breath on her lips. He winked, and then let the money go.

"It's throbbing."

That familiar drawl snuck in from behind her, and when Montgomery spun around, she half expected Sasha to be clutching his groin.

"My eye," he added, she assumed in reaction to her stammering. "It hurts. I'm going to bruise. Why'd you hit me?"

She looked around the dressing room. Girls fixed their hair and did their makeup in front of a mirrored wall, seemingly unbothered by Sasha's presence as they slipped into their nether-wear. A few even snuck glances at him, and the knowing look in their eye made Montgomery clench her fists.

She stepped closer to him. Once they'd been the same height, but now he looked down at her, taller by at least three inches.

"When I'm in here, my name is Scarlett," she whispered. "Nothing else. Got it? Scarlett Vermillion."

"Okay," he whispered back. "And I'm Count Chocula." He looked down the length of her body, and though she'd already changed back into her sweatshirt and jeans, she crossed her arms over her chest.

"What are you doing here?" he asked.

"I'm a stripper."

"Quit lying." His face was impassive, but his tone was hard.

"What makes you think I'm lying?"

He smirked. "You're a terrible dancer. It was like watching a bodybuilding competition."

"No one forced you to watch," she said.

"No one said I didn't like it."

She felt her cheeks ignite. Butterflies grew in her belly.

She had no response, until one of the girls tried to catch his eye during their standoff. He gave the girl a subtle nod, and suddenly Montgomery felt she had to follow her instincts. He was welcome in a room of half-naked women. Sure, he was still gorgeous, but she guessed there was more to his appeal than just his looks.

"You holding?" she asked.

A wave of emotion passed so quickly across his face, she couldn't interpret its nature.

He hesitated, squinted his eyes.

"Meet me in fifteen minutes," he said. "Under the Viaduct."

"So FIRST YOU sucker-punch the guy. And then you bust him for a half-gram?"

Rain drummed against the skyscrapers and minimarts, and left water streaks streaming down the windows of the downtown precinct. Victor sat at his desk, filling out a report. Sasha had been willing to sell her a half-gram of heroin down by the waterfront, and she'd radioed Victor to pick them up afterwards.

"I had no choice," Montgomery said.

"You didn't even give me a heads up. You just disappeared, went to meet a stranger under the Viaduct. Not cool."

The Viaduct was a raised portion of Highway 99 that separated the city's downtown from Elliot Bay. It created an area under cover of darkness, where it was easy for people to drive on the street below and catch whatever vice they wanted for the night. It was a place where dealers flourished, and a place where women disappeared. Women like the Headbanger Hunter victims. She never believed she'd see Sasha among the street types that skulked there.

Victor continued. "What if he attacked and you weren't able to defend yourself?"

"But I'm trained to kill."

If she had been a man, they wouldn't be having this conversation. She'd proven herself over and over again. She graduated from the Academy with the highest test scores of her class. She had one of the best arrest records in her unit. And no one could shoot better.

But her male colleagues would always have doubts. They laughed and called her "AA" because she could drink with the worst of them. And she went along and talked shit back, pretending she hadn't heard what they really meant when they thought she wasn't around. "AA" for *Affirmative Action*.

"He knows me," she said. "We used to be neighbors. And I had to do something or else he would've blown my cover."

Victor still frowned, so she tried to cheer him up.

"He sold me some black tar."

Victor raised his eyebrows. Black tar was a stronger form of heroin, and had been responsible for an influx of overdoses just four years prior. Busting whoever was trafficking it into the city would look great on their stat sheet.

"Let me do the talking," he said.

Inside the interrogation room, Sasha smoked a cigarette and sat with his feet resting on the table. The smell of burnt dandelions flooded Montgomery with memories, but she swallowed them down to the place where she kept Birdie, and all the other pain she knew.

Victor pushed a piece of paper across the table.

"We can get you on the possession and distribution of a controlled substance. Or you can sign here and agree to help us out. What we really want is your supplier."

"Sorry. He's dead. Just found out earlier today. Overdosed."

Sasha looked at Montgomery. She kept her face calm, unreadable. He sighed.

"You remember Tommy, don't you?"

Montgomery stammered, and tried to swallow over the lump in her throat. She did her best to conceal her emotions. Sasha let his ridge-colored eyes well, and his tears looked like melted ice.

"I'm sorry for your loss," she said finally.

Victor looked at Montgomery, the frown returning.

"Tommy who?" he asked.

"Pearson," Sasha said.

Victor tapped his thumb against the table.

"Any idea who Tommy's supplier was?"

"Nope," Sasha said.

"Well, shit. That doesn't help us, man. And I'll be honest with you. You're way too pretty to be going to jail."

Sasha shrugged. "Sorry. Can't help ya."

Victor gave Montgomery a look that seemed to say, *fix this.* He said he needed to use the restroom and left them alone together.

She leaned back in her chair.

"When did he die?"

"Few days ago."

"Wow. That's fresh. But you're not acting like someone who's just lost his best friend. And Tommy might've been more than that."

Sasha nodded. "Maybe he was."

She clenched her jaw. "Then I'd expect more tears. Maybe some sobbing."

He lifted his feet off the table and sat with one knee bent, bouncing it rapidly.

"It's not the first time I've had to say goodbye to a friend."

She took a deep breath and chose to ignore him.

"Help us," she said. "That stuff you sold me kills people. It probably killed Tommy. We need to find out who's bringing it into the city before more people die."

"You're wasting your time." He said it slow, his R's somewhere between a menace and a purr. "People are going to use regardless. Tommy wasn't a victim. He knew the risks. Everyone does. This crusade against drugs is misguided. Are you going to arrest the guy from Arco for selling me a forty ounce? You going to arrest me for drinking myself into an early grave?"

She pursed her mouth.

"No?" he continued, running a hand through his hair. "Pot, Cocaine, Heroin, Sex, Meth… They're all part of the human condition for self-destruction. No victim, no crime."

Montgomery felt the cords in her neck tighten. She bit down on her lip, until the tannic taste of blood smothered the rage enough to keep her composure. She cocked her head to one side and leaned across the table.

"No victim? My mother is dead! She had a $400-a-day habit. She had sex with men so she could pay for it. And then she got into bed with a murderer."

Tears spilled down her cheeks.

"I have no family because of that shit you sold me tonight. So *I* am a victim. And if I hear you say otherwise again I swear to God I will rip your throat out."

He opened his mouth to speak, but dropped his head instead.

Montgomery bristled. "Nothing to say? Figures. I guess you'd have to be heartless to be the type of person who'd steal from his own grandparents."

His eyes shot up, electric blue like dish soap. His knee bounced faster.

"Fuck you, Monti," he said.

Victor returned and sat down. The set line of his mouth indicated he'd been watching the video playback in another room. The silence became uncomfortable.

"What's the call?" Victor asked.

Sasha stared at the ceiling. "Tommy had the best stuff in town. His regulars will be freaked about losing access to it. I'll see what I can find out."

"Alright then!" Victor said. "You're free to go. But don't leave the State, and keep yourself available. And if you find out who Tommy's supplier is, come straight to us." Victor patted him on the shoulder. "Let us know if you need anything."

"Actually, there is something." He looked at Montgomery. "Next time you bring me in, have the balls to cuff me yourself."

Before they left the precinct for the night, Victor pulled Montgomery aside.

"Were you going to tell me about your mom?"

She shrugged. "Eventually."

He regarded her for a moment. "Neighbors, huh?"

She nodded and mumbled yes.

"Make sure it doesn't get personal. Sergeant Wilcox won't give you another chance."

"I swear," she said firmly. "It won't get personal."

CHAPTER TWENTY-THREE

A WEEK LATER, and Sasha thought of one thing only. Montgomery Laine Jackson half-naked on a stage, her back arched, her gray eyes stormy. Beautiful and deadly. Forever untouchable.

He'd wondered what might happen if they crossed paths in the city, if enough time had passed so they'd no longer recognize each other. But he'd been kidding himself; he would have recognized her if she'd been in clown make up, though the blue eyeshadow, pink lipstick, and teased, side swept bangs weren't much better.

He could still read how she moved, could see the detail in the minute ways she raised her eyebrows and creased her forehead. Maybe it was because he'd been high and drunk, but he could see the burden that had curled around her shoulders and clutched to her neck, a demonic sloth composed of black spirits made by dead girls, junkie mothers, imprisoned fathers and all things unjust. It would either eat her alive, or she'd tear it apart in her strong, deft hands.

Blood and water drown me out again
I'll sink beneath the docks
There is no Heaven
I sit beside myself, I have no friend
And when the evening comes

There's no redemption

The sound technician cut into the session. His name was Gary, and he wasn't Sasha's first choice.

"The timbre of your voice is off. You're breaking at the falsetto parts. Can you fill it out, make it sound more clear?"

Sasha rolled his eyes. His bandmate and bass player, Penn Christiansen, gave him a look through the window that said,

Dude. Suck it up.

The drummer, Jay Randall, was harder to read. But Sasha knew what he was probably thinking.

Don't fuck this up.

Jay was happy about the band's record deal, and couldn't wait to share their music with the mainstream. Penn saw it as an opportunity to become true artists. But Sasha had been offended by signing with a major record company. He liked the small, independent label that released the band's first singles, singles he'd had to finance with his side-job selling dope to musician friends in the scene. He liked the underground shows advertised on neon fliers and telephone poles, or in the obscure fanzines read only by their small community of rejects. He preferred to watch his friends play after their set and liked when he recognized most of the faces in the audience. This DIY band of misfits, these carpenters and waiters and line cooks and warehouse stockers, had stumbled upon some wicked kind of magic. Music that directly related to and emulated their perfect lifestyle of "otherness."

Fuck the man. Fuck you. Fuck me.

They were anything but mainstream.

But the tides had shifted. Someone started tossing around the word "Grunge." Seedy entrepreneurs began patronizing the local bands because they liked the music and party scene, and so offered to pay for demos or studio space to further insert themselves into the underground world. Mudhoney, Seattle's golden garage band, had broken into the European market, doing real tours and playing sold out shows. And music executives began looking for "the next big thing" by walking the halls of the Rain

City Lights building, a nondescript warehouse south of down-town, once owned by the City's public utilities company that now rented practice spaces to local bands. It was there, under those same circumstances, that Fungus Reign was discovered. The scene was changing, and Sasha didn't like it. He'd finally found where he belonged, and sensed it would soon be pulled out from under him.

It would be tainted. Polished. Commercialized.

Sasha looked at the technician.

"More clear, huh? Do you mean like, more Julie Andrews Sound of Music?"

Gary sighed.

"Just sing it again, okay?"

He sang it again, and received the same feedback.

"Tell you what," Sasha said. "If I wake up tomorrow with a Madonna-sized beauty mark, you can bug me about my timbre. Until then, let's approach this shit like it won't be the theme song for a tampon commercial."

"Look, I understand if you're worried about sounding like a pussy, but—"

Sasha interrupted him.

"Did I say that?"

Everyone stared at him from the recording booth. Penn dropped his head into his hands.

"Who here isn't ruled by pussy?" Sasha asked, picking at his cuticles.

Jay chuckled, flicked his long, black hair out of his face. But no one answered.

"Pussy is like, the most powerful thing in the world. I'd be honored to sound like a pussy," Sasha said.

Jay had brought two girls with him to the studio, and they giggled and bleated like sheep. The brunette one was attractive, with hair past her waist and Kelly-green eyes. She wore a black, lace dress and an oversized, gray blazer packed with shoulder pads. Sasha had barely noticed the other one, a cute blonde in a Fungus

Reign t-shirt and jeans. Women looked like starched, stock-board cutouts to him now that he'd seen Monti again.

Gary cleared his throat.

"Sorry, what I meant was—"

Sasha interrupted him. "What *I* meant was, whenever my best friend got her period, she wasn't dancing on the beach in a white dress listening to George Michael. Because she always felt like shit, and didn't pretend otherwise. *I* felt like shit when I wrote this, and that's how it should sound."

"Okay. Got it," the technician said.

The Kelly-eyed girl focused on Sasha now, in a way that made it clear it didn't matter she'd come for Jay. She undressed him with her gaze, so obvious it was almost boring.

Sasha pushed the microphone out of his face.

"Screw this. I can't sing in front of groupies."

He glared at the two women sitting on the couch as he walked into the control room.

"Dude. I don't think you can call them that to their face," Jay said under his breath. "It's un-feminist or something."

"It's un-feminist to pretend they're anything but what they are. They like your record deal better than they like you. We're not some cock rock band, and they shouldn't be here."

"You get more action than any of us," Jay protested.

"So what? I don't go looking for it. And I definitely don't bring it into the studio."

Jay stared at him, then cleared his throat.

"That was harsh, man. Maybe you should take five."

"I think I'm just gonna go. My timbre is kinda sore. And this all just feels so pointless." Sasha slipped his arms out of his sweatshirt sleeves and hugged himself where no one could see.

"I know you're upset about Tommy," Penn said, placing his hand on Sasha's shoulder. "We all are. But we've got to get this album recorded. We signed a contract."

Penn was the reasonable one in the group. The mature one, and he was getting married in the coming Spring. Sasha would be the best man.

He looked at his bandmates. They'd become his family, and this record deal meant the world to them. He didn't want to be responsible for obliterating their dreams. If they didn't meet their deadlines, the label could drop them for the next band. He didn't want to help the police, but if they found out about his dealing, or if charges were filed against him, it could put everything in jeopardy. The pressure was crushing him, and there was no way out except to scream his way through.

"Fair enough," he relented.

"Let's just get through this song, and we'll call it a day. Okay?"

Penn, with his kind eyes and bowl-cut, ever the peacemaker, was trying to be empathetic. But he'd never understand. Because he wasn't the last one to see Tommy alive. He wasn't there, sitting in that cold apartment, empty and lifeless except for a view of the Space Needle and the drone of a Sonics game, a revolving door for the most desperate and alone. Penn didn't see the look in Tommy's eyes when he said goodbye, as if it were for good. He didn't know what it was like to be too much of a coward to ask his friend to get clean. He didn't have that deep, gutted feeling as he shut the door on a friend who he knew was going to die.

"I've got to use the bathroom," Sasha said.

Penn sighed. He hesitated, then stepped out of Sasha's way.

"Make it quick man," Jay said.

After he locked the door, Sasha ran cold water over his face. He lifted the cuff of his jeans and removed a baggie from his tube sock.

Girl, Blow, Snow. Cocaine.

Whatever it took to get more "clear," as Gary had requested.

He took a thick line of coke off the sink's ledge. And then another. And then another. He cleaned white dust off white porcelain. He licked his forefinger to gather the remains from the cold, white ledge for one more taste. Quickly, he felt like he was up. Lively. As though he could take on the world, let alone some corporate, pop-song mongering Judas who wouldn't know creativity if it punched him in the face and called him a pussy. Jay might be bothered, and Penn wouldn't like it. But everyone took a hit of something every once in a while, his bandmates included. It was part of the lifestyle. Partying, fucking, drinking. Drugs and Rock n' Roll. It expanded the mind and tore down the pretense.

That's how it started anyway. A game he played as a teenager just for kicks. Now he used so much he needed to sell heroin to finance the habit. And it'd been an easy transition to make. He asked Tommy to recommend a supplier, gave his beeper number to a couple of friends in the scene, and boom. He had enough money for rent and cocaine and a practice space for the band. Sure, now his nose would bleed and run, and he avoided the doctor to stay ignorant of the damage he'd done to his body. Sure, now this thing he'd started just for kicks felt impossible to kick. But he was going to be a rock star, according to the band's A&R guy. There was nothing to write home about.

He splashed cold water in his face, tied his hair back into a ponytail, and walked into the sound booth with a smile. He put everything he'd been feeling into the next parts of the song.

I'm gonna fall
I'm gonna fall, not too long
Bone marrow seeps through the nose
Torn inside out so it shows
When you throw. Me. Away!

CHAPTER TWENTY-FOUR

THE HEADBANGER MURDERS happened between the summer and fall of 1981, and were soon forgotten. Because the next year, during the summer of 1982, a new killer staked his claim on "The Strip," a part of State Route 99 located in South King County and known for its prostituted women who worked by the hundreds. The remains of over forty teenage girls and young women had been found between 1982 and 1984, and the need to catch this new killer eclipsed the six victims taken by the Headbanger Hunter.

Evie Tucker had been the first, and was last seen working on the corner of First and Pike. The next five had been seen either on or around Aurora during the weeks before the discovery of their bodies. All had been prostitutes. All had been black. There hadn't been much evidence collected at the scenes, but there'd been some. Carpet fibers and semen were found on Naomi Watkins and LaRhonda Williams, the girls found in an abandoned junkyard and underbrush of an undeveloped lot. They'd all been raped. Testing of the semen revealed the assailant was blood type AB negative, which Rawlings believed to be a stroke of luck since it was the rarest of blood types. The victims had been killed in another location, as there was no blood at the scenes where they were found. Except for Evie Tucker. Her body lay beneath the Ballard Bridge in a pool of her own gore. Rawlings believed she was the instigator somehow, and something about her had set the killer off on his brief but horrific killing spree.

For eight years, Rawlings stirred the pot of evidence to keep it from hardening. Every quarter, he pulled the file and followed up on interviews, posing the same questions from different angles to squeeze out new information. There was no telling when or how a case would break open. Sometimes it happened with persistence, after pouring over the same information for years. Or sometimes it happened when a beautiful, hard-ass woman walked over to your desk and casually gave you leverage on your drug-related shooting while blowing your cold-case wide the fuck open.

Rawlings went to The Bridgewater and asked each neighbor if they could remember the day they'd last seen Birdie James. Most didn't know who she was. That was the problem with time - once enough of it passed the dead ceased to exist even in people's memories. But the owner of the building remembered Birdie and her daughter. He couldn't speak to the last day of her life, just to the evil that had taken hold of their household. The devils they brought to his doorstep.

"Certain things went on in that house," Daan said, tied to an oxygen tank and choking on his own words.

"What kinds of things?" Rawlings asked.

"It's no surprise she turned up dead. Demons always take what's freely offered. And Birdie had no trouble offering herself. I can't help you other than to say she had all kinds of men coming in and out of that apartment. And she was always keeping long, sinful hours. Gone for weeks at a time. Leaving me that little girl for an extra mouth to feed, who thanked me by infecting my son with her wickedness. Ask me, you're wasting your time. God will punish the wicked however He sees fit."

"What kinds of things?" Rawlings asked again, his voice louder.

Daan started coughing, a fit that took over his wretched body and left him just enough air to say,

"The kind you don't come back from."

Rawlings sighed and looked at the dying man in front of him.

"None of us will be coming back. But we all deserve to keep the time we get. We all deserve a peaceful end. My God believes in that."

Rawlings continued to canvass, knocking on every door in Ballard for information. Then he went downtown, to all the known corners "Kitty Blues" favorited. He worked with a reporter at the *Seattle Times*, hoping a tragic story would entice people forward with information. And by the end of the week, once he'd exhausted all his options, he drove by a large, white house and parked his car along the curb of Magnolia Boulevard. A house he'd been watching, a house his gut told him held all the answers. He'd chased down leads over the years, but always believed his true killer hid in plain sight. A tall, handsome man who would run in the next term for Seattle's City Attorney. Richard Adamson was responsible for the Headbanger murders. Rawlings just couldn't prove it.

A woman in paint-splattered jeans and a brown crochet sweater emerged from the house next door. She held a professional looking camera and began taking pictures. Rawlings' palms sweated against the steering wheel. He could almost taste the turning point of the case on his tongue, he was so hungry for it. He approached the woman on her porch.

"May I ask what you're doing?"

The woman flipped her long, gray braid over her shoulder. She had to be in her fifties, but had a child's whimsy in the soft wrinkles of her smile.

"I should ask you the same thing."

Rawlings showed her his badge. She laughed and pointed at his car.

"You see the way it's parked? Somewhat diagonal from the curb, like whoever drove had too much on their mind to straighten out. And the streetlight pouring over the black car like it's trying to shed some light on someone who's lost. And the full moon over the dark, blue bay. It's like Seattle noir coming right to my doorstep. I'm a photographer, and it's my job to notice moments like these."

"Do you always take pictures from your house?"

The woman smiled. "My name is Margaret. Why don't you come inside for some tea?"

Moments later, Rawlings had a mug of green tea in front of him on a bamboo coffee table. He sat in a living room with walls coated in still portraits and candid photographs.

"Taking pictures is my passion," Margaret said, her eyes working over Rawlings' face as though she were piecing a puzzle together. "I'm always focused on the details, on those mercurial moments when the true essence of a situation shines through. If I see something worth photographing, I don't hesitate."

He smiled, and he heard the click of the camera as she snapped a quick picture of him rifling through his case file.

Rawlings handed her the photo booth array of Birdie and Montgomery.

"Have you ever seen this woman?" he asked, pointing at the picture.

Margaret's face was unreadable, which told the Detective she knew something.

"Why are you asking?"

"Because she was murdered eight years ago, and just recently identified by her daughter. Her name was Birdie James. Does that ring a bell?"

Margaret nodded her head.

"I need all the help I can get. Even if it's small," Rawlings said.

"Just a minute." Margaret left the room. A door opened, and Rawlings heard the hollow sound of basement steps creaking beneath her weight. She returned holding a portfolio in her hands and handed him a picture.

"I'm really good with faces," she said. "Once I see one that means something to me, I never forget it. I was sitting on my porch with my camera watching the bay when she fluttered up to the house next door like an exotic bird. I was so upset, because I thought I'd missed my opportunity. But then she came back down to the driveway and just stood there, waiting. It was like she was asking me to capture her."

Rawlings studied the photograph. He felt the excitement ripple from his shoulders to his toes. In the photo, Birdie James stood next to Richard's maroon Mustang. She wore a peach dress and checkered head scarf, the same clothing found with her body in Lake Union.

"I saw her sing at a club in the Central District during my drinking days. She had the most beautiful voice I've ever heard. Incredibly talented. When she walked up to the Adamson's place, I was so excited. I remember thinking she was so gorgeous," Margaret said. "And yet, so broken too."

She moved to the couch next to Rawlings. "See those hollow eyes? And her frayed braids trapped in that scarf? She looked out of place up here. And I don't mean that in a snobby way. There's just not much color in Magnolia. I remember her leaning against the car, running her hand over the hood like she envied it or something. Like a fallen movie star taking one last glimpse at her former life, and seeing her true reflection for the first time. So I just started shooting."

"Did you take more?" Rawlings asked.

This was it. He could feel it. Putting cases down was all about dogged effort, community cooperation and pure, fucking luck.

"I did. I still have the negatives, but this is the only print I made."

"Why is that?"

"Because my neighbor came out and I could only get a few shots of the woman alone. He ended up in one of the frames and ruined the picture."

"What happened next?" Rawlings asked.

"Well, she and Richard - that's my neighbor - they got in the car and drove off."

"I know it's a long shot, but do you remember what day this photograph was taken?"

"I can't remember the specific day, but I know it was close to Thanksgiving, 1981." She pulled the negatives out of the portfolio.

"Right. If you look through these, you'll see photos from my niece's Thanksgiving play."

"Would you be willing to testify to this?" Rawlings asked.

"Of course I would. It's terrible she's gone."

Rawlings took notes for the report he'd write later, and they exchanged contact information.

As he was walking out the door, Margaret said, "It's ironic."

Rawlings stopped. "What is?"

Margaret sighed. "That photo has been my most successful one to date. It inspired me to take pictures of people downtown, and to look for the most tired and beautiful souls I could find. I had featured shows at galleries all over the country, and that one was the favorite by far. You know what I called it?"

"What?" he asked.

"Shattered Stars Shine the Brightest."

"Right."

"Is the girl okay?" Margaret asked.

"What girl?"

"The girl from the photo booth."

"You know her too?"

"I never spoke to her, but she lived with the Adamsons for a couple of years. Hey, maybe that's what Richard and that woman were talking about?"

Rawlings bit back a curse. A damning piece of evidence and a possible defense all at once.

"Thank you, Margaret," he said. "Let's keep in touch."

JAB. JAB. CROSS PUNCH. HOOK. UPPERCUT.

Montgomery worked the punching bag she'd hung in the loft of her house. It was a two-bedroom craftsman, and the wind strained against the mint-green siding. The front door was painted coral so that each day or night, when Montgomery returned home from a shift, she was greeted by something bright and cheerful. The wallpaper was white with green pinstripes, and the hardwood floors shone with lemon-scented oil. During the warmer months, college students walked home from keg parties, and their laughter leaked through the panes of the push-out windows. In the summer the sun baked the house until it smelled like cookies the families who'd come before had made together. The little craftsman was Montgomery's most prized possession, a place of security she had saved for since entering the police force.

JAB. JAB. RIGHT KICK. SHOULDER THROW.

She panted and grunted a path through her anguish, but still, Rawlings' question regurgitated and contaminated her thoughts, unwanted like vermin.

Did you pursue it?

And the question he didn't ask, the one she could see as it scrolled across his brow.

Why not?

JAB. LEFT KNEE. UPPERCUT. JAB.

As the years wheeled her forward and out of her teens, Montgomery realized just how close she'd come to losing her childhood, that tender piece of the heart where whimsy trumped reason. She would've sold her body to save her mother's, and for what? So Birdie could put one more score on the board of her addiction, like it was just a game with broken pieces to pack away if she lost? Once she became a cop, Montgomery did pursue it - she pulled her mother's arrest records to find names or leads to follow. Instead she found a mother she'd never wanted to meet. And realized that on those long nights, when she stayed with Sasha out of fear or loneliness, her mother wasn't working to stock their bare cupboards.

JAB. JAB. SPIN, LEFT ELBOW. BACK KICK. CROSS PUNCH.

The chains holding the bag rattled, a tinny cry for mercy that she could not give. She hit with such force the bag seemed to jump. She dropped all form and let her body wail against it, fists and feet in a flurry to erase the image of her mother's body torn apart, caked in maggots and mud. The ceiling groaned from the weight of the beating, and with one final kick the bag fell to the ground.

Montgomery looked at the drum kit in the corner of the loft. It had been so long since she'd played, the cymbals gathered dust. Watching Sasha sway to her beat had been like something close to mastery, because in that moment he belonged to her tempo. Playing without him felt like playing one-handed.

But she needed to hit something. Montgomery picked up her sticks. She rolled them in her hands, poked the the tips into her callused palms. Sometimes she wondered what might have been had she run away with Sasha that night. Would he have become the drug dealer he was now? Would she have ended up like her mother? Or would they have lived happily ever after? She could never know the answer. But for every story she told over beers with her fellow officers, the happy stories adults shared of their childhoods to find common ground, Sasha was at the center. And that would never change.

She played slowly at first, the song they won the Battle with, the song to which he'd changed the lyrics.

Black girl, black girl, don't lie to me. Tell me why do you weep at night?

She played it over and over until her thighs burned and her shoulders ached. She couldn't remember the exact words they used that last night together, just that he'd left her for good. But playing the song brought his voice to her ear, and in the slow drawl that she could savor like honey she heard one word,

Denial.

There'd been two possible outcomes. Either Birdie was dead, or she'd deliberately stayed away. And denial had been the salve for that double-edged sword.

CHAPTER TWENTY-FIVE

MOUNT PLEASANT CEMETERY was at the top of Queen Anne Hill, surrounded by reaching, hunter pines and antique oak trees. The sky looked as though it would break and bleed heavy cobalt over the stone and gray tombstones. A herd of russet leaves danced around the plot where "Goldie Doe" had been buried. Reverend Pritchard stood next to Birdie's grave, his head bowed and his mouth proclaiming kind and hopeful words of Birdie's deliverance.

"We can thank the Lord she has been found! And we can trust she's found her place in Heaven."

The Reverend nodded at Montgomery, resting his hand on her shoulder, and then left her alone in the graveyard. The wind gnawed her ears and the trees whispered overhead.

She had printed an obituary in the *Seattle Times*, not believing many would come. To her surprise, a handful of former Seattle musicians and friends Montgomery never met had come to pay their respects. There'd been a tragic pall over the entire event, and Montgomery was frustrated at the lie of it all. She hoped Reggie might be hurting in whatever corner he cowered in, whispering love songs to the needles, grams, and spoons he called his friends and introduced to the only woman who truly cared for him.

Shortly after her interview with Rawlings, a story came out in the paper.

Eight years ago the last known Headbanger victim was found floating in a cluster of reeds in Lake Union near Gasworks Park. The victim could not be identified by police at the time, due to advanced decomposition and measures taken by the killer to keep the victim unknown. Fortunately for the lead detective on the case, that victim has finally been identified as Birdie Eula James.

Unfortunately for Seattle, one of its most talented artists has been lost to tragedy. Birdie James was a well-known Blues, Soul and Funk singer, and made her rounds through the clubs in Seattle during the late sixties and early seventies. She recorded her first album in 1969 with a small, local label in Seattle. One Seattle musician described the album when he said 'take Ella Fitzgerald, put her with Jimi Hendrix and then add the groove of Parliament. That's what listening to Birdie James is like.'

After the success of her first album, James and her band received a record contract with Eden Records, one of the top seven record companies in the country. But before the second album was finished and for undisclosed reasons, James was suddenly dropped from the label.

James, who was also a single mother, turned to prostitution in order to support herself and her young daughter. The lead detective on the case believes she'd been solicited by the Headbanger Hunter, as like with the first five victims, and is asking anyone with information about the case to contact Seattle Police Headquarters.

"I ever tell you how I joined the choir at Mt. Calvary?"

Sweet smoke coiled in from behind her, making shapes in the air before succumbing to the breeze. She didn't need to look to know it was Sasha. The smell of his tobacco took her back to the Ballard lots where they played "Ring around the Rosie," spinning until their arms felt like snapping and they fell into the dandelions, crying with laughter, or sometimes just crying, holding each other until they found peace and snoring into the weeds until the pines turned black against the thickening, violet dusk.

"I was in the courtyard one day. Daan and my mom were fighting. I was singing to myself when Birdie walked by with her groceries. 'Help me with these,' she said. I carried them to the door, but was too afraid to go inside because I wasn't allowed. When she came back out, I thought she would yell at me. 'Come on then,' she said, and we drove to the church. She walked straight in, shouting over the choir. They were in the middle of practice. 'Y'all need to let this white boy sing with you,' she said. They gave me a chance. I was terrible, because I was so nervous. They laughed and told us to leave. This was a serious choir, one that traveled around the country and won competitions. I started to cry. 'Quit that,' Birdie said. And then she told the choir, 'he's got more talent in his littlest finger than all of you combined. Quit rolling those eyes at me, DeMarcus! I'll come upside that head and fuck you up.' I couldn't believe she swore in church. I was so embarrassed, but also proud. She said, 'Either you let him in or I will come to every single practice, every single service, every competition and talk so much shit, no one will be able to hear you!'"

Montgomery heard the grass sizzle as Sasha threw down his cigarette. She couldn't turn around. Because she'd become the cop again, and he'd become her target. He slipped his arm around her chest and rested his chin on her shoulder. She put both hands on his arm, gripping like it was driftwood and she was caught in a maelstrom.

"You shouldn't be here," she said, staring down at her mother's grave. There were tears in her eyes, but she sniffed them back so they burned her sinuses.

"I know," he said, and kissed her hair. They stood that way for a moment, Montgomery marveling at how time had changed everything. How it had turned them into different people. How he'd literally grown while they were apart, so she couldn't help wondering if she'd been holding him back. And how he'd chosen to throw his opportunities away.

"Tomorrow, I'll want to kick your ass again," she said. "Tomorrow, the clock starts ticking."

He sighed. "Tomorrow, I'll be furious you put me in an impossible situation."

"Then quit the drugs."

"Too bad it's not that simple."

"Will it ever be?"

"Maybe. On another plain."

He squeezed her.

"I'm sorry your mom died," Sasha whispered. "When my mom died, I didn't cry either."

Her heart tripped over itself. She remembered a Christmas night when a quiet boy gave her cookies. How her mother had locked her outside and said, "Go on and play for minute." The memory felt incredulous now. It had been raining. It had been cold. A strange man had knocked on their door. And now, as an adult she knew her mother had been selling her body, getting high. Now she could name the culprit behind the seasonality of their struggles, and saw that throughout her childhood Birdie had slipped in and out of her addiction like a wavering tide.

"It's easier to make believe when you're young. But we should stop that now."

Sasha kissed the back of her head. She could hear him breathe in the smell of her hair, feel him press his nose into its coarse thickness, and was reminded of the joy before that summer. Playing dress up with Birdie. Riding bikes with Sasha. Roasting hot dogs on the beach at Golden Gardens on spring nights when Birdie wasn't "working." Allowing Sasha to butterfly kiss her cheeks as they lay out in sleeping bags while camping in the courtyard of The Bridgewater.

"We should cry, right now for our mothers," Sasha said, his chin resting on her shoulder.

She bent her head and nestled her face into the hairs on his arm. She sobbed three times, and then made herself stop. He was still too reckless. He could be the antidote, but also the disease.

She shrugged him off.

"You should go."

She listened to him retreat behind her in the soggy grass.

"At her worst, Birdie was absent and addicted," he said, his voice strained over the distance he gained. "But at her best, she fought. She fought hard for the people she loved."

Montgomery took the scenic route back to the main road, and stopped her Geo Tracker abruptly when she reached Kerry Park. On her right, the city loomed tall against the chalky sky, the building lights already twinkling in the subtle darkness though it was still afternoon. Mt. Rainier rose out of the fog as if it floated on the bay. The Space Needle had just begun to glow, as though it warmed itself up to shoot into the sky.

Her skin itched as she looked at Seattle's skyline - somewhere, in the urban sprawl, one man's desires could be the end of one woman's desperation. Somewhere, the secrets of her mother's death were buried beneath the rain-soaked pavement. In her nightmares, she'd seen her mother walking, her golden face turned towards the sky, the sun washing her smile, her hand trailing over the tall grass. Each time she turned and looked at Montgomery, her smile contorted itself into a skeletal grimace, and her skin peeled back away from the eye sockets in a bloody rosette. And her wailing voice cried, *Find me baby, girl! Find me!*

Montgomery cleared her throat and spoke towards the city that had chewed her mother up.

"I'm mad at you, Momma. I'm so fucking mad at you."

She slammed her fist against the steering wheel.

"He never should've found you. The Headbanger never would've got you if you'd just quit the drugs."

She was screaming at the top of her lungs, and ignored the older woman who startled as she walked by with her dog.

"I want to hate you! I want to blame you! But I can't because then I feel guilty. And then I hate you more, because this guilt isn't mine!"

She slammed her hand against the dashboard, over and over and over while saying,

"This guilt isn't mine! This guilt isn't mine! This guilt isn't mine!"

She keeled over the steering wheel and cried until mascara burned her eyes and blurred her vision. Once finished, she started the car. She took three deep breaths, and turned back to the skyline.

"But don't worry," she said, her voice congested. "I'll still kick his ass for you."

·❦·

"USE A COASTER," Richard said.

Clarke poured a large glass of Scotch. "Relax," he said. "I'm drinking it straight. No water marks."

They were seated at the dining room table. Cassandra smoked and ran a finger lazily back and forth over the lit candelabra. She looked bored, and Richard wondered if it was because she'd lost interest in the game of winning his affection. She no longer dangled her affairs in front of his face like catnip, and was free to sleep with whomever she chose. As long as she remained discreet. Voters were less likely to elect a man with a troubled marriage as Seattle's next City Attorney.

The housekeeper walked in and out of the kitchen, leaving dishes of potatoes, green beans, steamed eggplant and pot roast, all on trivets to avoid destroying the finish on the antique, wooden table.

"Ugh," Clarke said. "I hate eggplant. It tastes like butt."

Richard shook his head. Twenty-four years old and his son still lived at home. It was embarrassing. Especially after Clarke had been afforded one of the finest educations the Eastern Seaboard had to offer, and a job working for his late grandfather's real estate and development company.

"When have you ever tasted butt that wasn't your own?" Richard asked.

Clarke paused mid-drink. "I don't know what that means."

"It means you've spent your whole life kissing your own ass and haven't done a thing to deserve it."

"Mom! Did you hear what he just said to me?"

Cassandra sighed and poured a large glass of wine.

"I have a headache and I'm going to bed," she said. "You boys figure it out." And so exited the mother of the year.

"Have you given more thought to grad school?" Richard asked.

Clarke shrugged and swirled the Scotch in his glass. It spilled over the rim and splashed onto the table, but he seemed too inebriated to notice. Richard clenched his jaw and eyed the puddle of alcohol, which now scored the finish on a table that cost as much as a mortgage payment.

"I think I should travel first," Clarke said. "Maybe help the less fortunate. I could do that 'Houses for Humans' thing."

"You mean Habitat for Humanity?"

"Right. I could go to Mexico or wherever and build a house for a poor family. Sample the local tequila and señoritas. A win for me and a win for them."

Richard stared at his son. He couldn't believe how much he'd given up to be part of this family. Parents were supposed to love their children unconditionally. But he was never able to love his own.

"You can't even drink 150-year-old Scotch without spilling it all over yourself. You're a walking liability, how are you going to build a house? If you want to help, send them a check."

Clarke rolled his eyes. "Shows what you know. What good would a check do when they don't even have a bank account? They need me."

Richard leaned forward. He smelled the alcohol on his son's breath.

"Nobody needs you."

Clarke stared back. He picked up the bottle of Scotch and poured it over the candelabra. Flames shot out from the center of the table, and Richard fell back in his chair.

"Jesus!" he shouted.

Richard leapt to his feet. Clarke was still seated at the table, now engulfed in flames that nearly reached the ceiling. He was inanimate and expressionless, and his face glowed orange in the firelight.

"What did you do!" Richard shouted. He ran into the kitchen and grabbed a fire extinguisher, and nearly slipped on the floor as he rushed back into the dining room. He sprayed the flames until the room filled with smoke and dry chemicals.

A slow chuckle emerged through the smog. It was Clarke.

Richard couldn't take anymore. His hands shook as he reached for Clarke's neck, ready to end it all. He pulled so hard he thought Clarke's head might pop off, and dragged his son to the floor. He hit Clarke in the face, over and over, wanting to cave it in, wanting to end the beauty he never should've made. This young man wasn't his child - he was the devil, sent to punish Richard for his own selfish choices.

"Stop it!"

Richard heard the shrillness before he heard the words, but he didn't heed the cry. Suddenly he saw someone's manicured nails clawing into his hands. Someone weighed on his back.

"You'll kill him!" Cassandra cried.

Richard stood so quickly she flung off his back and hit the wall behind him. He towered over his wife and son, his breath coming in heaving, roaring gasps. Cassandra weeped and crawled her way to Clarke. She cradled his head in her lap and crooned while he whimpered. But she didn't see the look on Clarke's face when Richard reached for his keys, the leer as Richard closed the door on his family. She didn't see their son for the spoiled piece of shit they'd allowed him to become.

He opened the garage and removed the tarp from his Mustang. Cassandra had wanted him to sell it, but he couldn't put a price on the memories. He started the engine and ignited his sordid tastes all over again.

CHAPTER TWENTY-SIX

"Do you have something for me?"

The night was so foggy, Sasha couldn't see who stood on the opposite side of the metal fence of his house on Capitol Hill. But he recognized the voice.

"Depends on what you're looking for."

Monti joined him on the porch. She was dressed in a white crop top, a red Troop jacket and baggy jeans. Her hair was teased, and her red-rouged lips accentuated the gap in her teeth.

"It's loud in there," she said. She looked at the house. He could see an opinion form on her face as she took in the peeling paint and unkept yard - the grass had grown so long it almost reached his knee.

"The Hard Rock Buffet?" she asked, pointing to the words spray-painted on the front of the house in angry, black letters.

"It's what our friends started calling the place because of the all-nighters and rock bands we host here. So we decided to make it official."

She sat next to him on the bench swing Penn had found at Goodwill. His entire body buzzed with excitement, and it bothered him that he couldn't tell if it was because of her proximity or the drugs in his system.

Someone from inside the house screamed, and the music blared louder on fuzzy speakers.

"What's the occasion?" she asked.

"My band got a record deal and just finished recording an EP. We're going on tour in a few months." He paused, brushing the cigarette ash from his torn jeans and exposed kneecap.

"No shit?"

"No shit."

"So then why are you sitting out here by yourself? Shouldn't you be celebrating?"

"It feels too fake to celebrate right now. I feel like a poser." *Like I don't deserve to be here when Tommy can't be.*

She scoffed and stood up. "Leave it to you to turn something positive into a damn tragedy."

"I didn't expect you to understand," he said, wrapping his jean jacket tighter around himself.

"What's that supposed to mean?"

"I'd invite you inside, but I'm afraid you'd arrest my friends. That's what it means. You're a damn sellout."

"Excuse me for trying to make a difference. I guess it'd be better if I sat around getting high and smashing guitars, right?"

"Doesn't it make you feel bad, arresting people like Birdie? She was your family."

"I'd bust a parasitic, preppy little white boy as much as anyone. So give me something by next month or I'm going to arrest you."

"Did you just call me preppy?" Sasha said. "Because that's unforgivable."

"Whatever," she said, making her way through the yard.

He raised his voice over the music. "That last summer, all you cared about was being there for Birdie. You would've done anything to keep your family together. And now it's your job to do the exact opposite."

She spun around at the fence.

"Okay, you want to be real for a minute? You said I could trust you. You promised to take care of me. But you can't even take care of yourself. Your pupils are so dilated right now you look like a blue-eyed lemur. Yeah, I know a junkie when I see one."

"So do I," he said.

She squinted at him.

"What have you been doing all these years?" he asked.

She shrugged. "I finished high school, went to the Academy. Worked patrol for a few years, then I—"

"I'm sorry, let me clarify. When I said 'what have you been doing' I actually meant 'who.'"

"Excuse me?" She took a step towards him, her fists clenched.

"Do you have a boyfriend? Friends? Like, any kind of personal life besides work? Who are you fucking, Monti?" He relished her silence, drank it slow like a peaty Scotch that burned.

"You want to know what I think?" he continued. "I think you're torn up. I think deep down you know you can't change the world as a narc, but you work yourself to the bone anyway. I think you know the only difference between a crack user and a cocaine user is the color of their skin, and you know why one gets a harder deal than the other. You're just a thorn on the scourge, and we both know what will happen if you arrest me." He stood up and threw his cigarette into the grass.

"Nothing."

She stood by the fence, staring at him. He could tell she wanted to argue. Her mouth opened and closed, her bottom lip trembled and he nearly leapt across the yard to catch it with his teeth.

Someone changed the music inside the house, and Sasha squeezed his eyes shut. He couldn't have known this would happen. He would've prevented it otherwise.

A tortured voice bled into the night air.

"Cain't no more
My body's achin'
Cain't no more
These hands is shakin'
Cain't no more
This soul is a yearnin'

Cain't no more
Cuz you left me reelin'"

"What the hell is that?" Monti asked. She rushed inside before he could answer.

Sasha followed the trail she made, pushing through a crowd of functioning alcoholics that hovered around a keg in the living room. She stopped in front of the L-shaped couch, which was gray with holes where the cushion poured through. Penn sat with his eyes closed, nodding his head to the music. The record player was on a bookshelf behind him, and without looking he reached back to turn up the volume.

"Cain't no more
These lungs ain't breathin'
Cain't no more
This heart stopped beatin'
Cain't no more
This hell is a burnin'
Cain't no more
Cuz you left me reelin'"

"Turn this crap off!" Monti hollered, startling poor, sweet Penn.

Sasha put a hand on her shoulder, but she shrugged him away. He felt sorry for both of them. Monti had no way of knowing Penn's parents were professors and music fanatics, or that he'd grown up listening to Ella Fitzgerald, Billie Holiday, and Charles Mingus. She had no way of knowing he'd graduated from the Cornish College of the Arts with a degree in Jazz, or that Birdie James was one of his favorite singers.

And there was no way Penn could've known Birdie had broken Monti's heart at the age when hurts stopped healing.

Penn was drunk, and so more confrontational than he would've been otherwise.

"This crap?" he said. "This woman was a goddess!" He turned the music up louder. "She was a genius, and sang me to sleep every night when I was a kid. I love her! And I miss her!"

Penn threw his head back and started to sing along. Monti

walked around the couch to the bookshelf, grabbed the record from the player and snapped it in half, throwing it on the scuffed, wood floors. Everyone at the party stopped what they were doing and stared.

Penn stood up. "That was so mean!" he cried. He tilted his head and regarded her for a moment. "Who the hell are you, and why are you in my house?

Sasha interjected. "Penn, this is Monti Laine. We grew up together. She was the drummer in my first band."

Monti looked as if she might kill him with just her glare alone. He'd broken her cover. Sasha shrugged. "I'm not going to lie about who you are to me," he said quietly. He looked at Penn. "Birdie James was her mother."

Monti's eyes were red and she looked as though she might cry. Sasha moved to embrace her, but Penn beat him to it.

"I'm so sorry for your loss," Penn said, stroking Monti's hair. To Sasha's surprise, she didn't push him away. Instead she leaned in and whispered in his ear.

Monti wouldn't make eye contact as she brushed past Sasha and out the door. But he followed her anyway. He couldn't be afraid of honesty any longer. He'd lost too much for being silent.

"So that wasn't normal," he called out. "What happened back there?"

She turned those gray, feral eyes on him. "Enlighten me."

"I think you feel guilty. You blamed your mother for leaving you. You didn't look for her. And now that you know the truth, maybe you're thinking there's more to what happened."

"I know what happened," she said.

She held her elbows in opposite hands and ground her teeth into her bottom lip. He knew she wore her lies in her elbows - she was deflecting.

"Either way," he said, talking to her back as she walked towards the street. "You can't run around smashing people's records every time you hear her sing. And I can promise you, that won't be the last time."

"And how do you know that?" she asked with a shaky voice.

"Birdie's music is playing on local radio. Indie scene types are buying her record, and I heard the label is going to reissue." He shrugged. "It happens sometimes. Tragedy turns an artist into an icon."

Monti laughed. "Unbelievable." She uncrossed her arms, and her shoulders settled as she calmed. "That was the first time I'd heard her album," she said. "I always thought she was exaggerating when she talked about her performing days. Because she lied about the stuff that counted."

He would've jumped from the porch. He would've trampled the grass beneath his Converse sneakers. He would've pulled her into his arms and gone back to the days when they were kids and chose each other over everything else. But she shook off her vulnerability with a toss of her head and said,

"Next month. I mean it." And then she was gone.

Sasha went back inside. The party had resumed its clamor, and he knew how the rest of the night would go. He'd drink more beer. He'd do more cocaine. He'd stay up for hours, maybe fuck one of the girls that had been flirting with him, and he'd think about the look on Monti's face when she heard her mother sing until the sun came up.

Sasha sat next to Penn on the couch.

"What did she say to you?" he asked.

"That if I let anything happen to you, she'd kill me." Penn looked worried. "She's kind of intense. Do you think she meant it?"

Sasha smiled. "Hell yeah she meant it."

❧

CASSANDRA BRUSHED a stray curl from her face. She breathed into her hands, which were gloved in cashmere, then cursed herself for the lipstick stain she left behind. With a heavy sigh she exited the car and activated the alarm with the auto-lock feature. She wrinkled her nose and stared at the sidewalk, making sure to avoid the urine stains as she walked into the police station.

"Can I help you?" someone asked.

She couldn't see faces or make out the details of her surroundings. She couldn't remember how she'd got there, just knew in her bones she had to put one foot in front of the other in order to save her son and protect her family's name.

"I think my husband is the Headbanger Hunter, who can I speak to about this?"

A flurry came, of forms and faces and voices, and a pair of strong hands led her to a blank slate room.

"Mrs. Adamson? Can you hear me?"

She focused on the man in front of her. He was stocky and eager and had the look of someone who'd aged too quickly, supple skin with a deeply creased forehead and a frosted gray hairline.

"Yes," she said. "I'm sorry. Who are you?"

"Detective Colby Rawlings, ma'am. Can I get you some coffee or—"

"I can't believe I'm doing this."

"—water. We have some leftover Halloween cookies—"

"I should go. What am I doing here, this is madness."

A hand clamped over her trembling fingers.

"Why don't you tell me the reason you're here today?"

The detective's eyes were warm and friendly, the color of hot cider on a cold day.

"I remember you," she said. "You came by once, wanting to ask me questions. But my husband is a lawyer. He said you were fishing and that I didn't have to talk to you."

"Yes. I remember."

Cassandra noticed the coffee that had been placed on the table, just within her reach. She stared into the blank face of the cup, still and smelling burnt.

"We never should've been parents. We didn't come from good families. We never learned how to care about anyone but ourselves. I thought that meant we'd be good together. I thought that his aloofness about who I was and my family's money meant that he could truly love me."

"Nobody is perfect," the detective said.

Cassandra sipped the coffee and grimaced at the taste. It was bitter and stale and gritty like pumice. She took another drink.

"The last eight years or so... they've been wonderful. Richard and I were like lovers again. Our son was away at school. Richard's career was going well. He made a name for himself — do you remember that case a few years ago, when he prosecuted some cop for abusing street women?"

"Yes, I remember."

"He's using that notoriety as his platform for City Attorney. He's promised justice for all."

The detective leaned forward. "He seems like a good man. On the surface."

"Yes!" Cassandra cleared her throat. Her mouth tasted like gunmetal. "May I have some water please?"

The detective hesitated. "Of course you can." He left the room so quickly his chair clattered to the floor.

Cassandra unwound and rewrapped her scarf. What was she doing here? Of course Richard wasn't capable of the travesties done to those girls. Though she never thought him capable of many things, and had since learned otherwise. The walls closed in, the cement blocks came with jagged edges. She couldn't breathe, and stood to leave just as the detective hurried into the room, sloshing water from the cup he carried.

"Please," he said. "Take a seat, Mrs. Adamson."

She did as she was told and gulped the water until her stomach ached. The detective smiled with confidence, as though he could judge her but had chosen not to.

"I was just his beard," she said, lighting a cigarette. "All this time, I was just this pretty, rich beard he could use while he slummed it downtown. My husband has screwed a hoard of black whores, who knows what diseases he's given me over the years. I could have AIDS."

"How do you know this?"

She crossed a leg over the other and focused on the beige heel that bounced in the air.

"My son told me. The other night he and Richard got in a fight. My husband put his hands on our son, almost beat him half to death. Clarke, that's my son, he told me he's hated his father for years."

The detective nodded slowly, as if he already knew the story but was letting her tell it. Letting her narrate so she could confess too, share her weight of the guilt so it would no longer be hers to carry.

"Once, when he was little, Clarke decided to tag along on one of his father's late work trips. He snuck into the back of the Mustang and waited to surprise him. And that's when he…"

Tears welled in her eyes. The detective pushed a box of tissue across the table.

"I need proof," he said.

Cassandra sucked in a breath until her lungs were full. She let it out slow.

"That first girl, Envy or Ivy or—"

"Evie."

"I found a photo of her in my husband's things."

The detective's head cocked to one side and his neck veins thickened.

"It was in a box with this…" She spit a sob into her hand, wailed into the cashmere until it was destroyed. "It was like he…like this, they way it was arranged…"

The detective moved to her side of the table and slipped an arm around her shoulder. Cassandra crumbled against him.

"It was like he'd kept a trophy!"

CHAPTER TWENTY-SEVEN

THE WIFE HAD GIVEN him access to the house. She welcomed Rawlings' investigative team inside while the suspect was at work, and they tore through the mansion like hungry wolves. Tucked into the back of a bedside table was the smoking gun, the damning piece of evidence no jury could deny. Rawlings moved quickly, and bulldogged his way to an arrest warrant from a judge who'd been eating Thanksgiving dinner with his family.

Now it was so dark he could see the cold roll by in a wavering mist. Sleet assaulted the pavement outside his unmarked vehicle. Rawlings waited until the rumble of a Mustang pulled into the drive. He had backup nearby, but knew he wouldn't call. He'd been anticipating this moment for eight years, and wanted to savor it alone.

He stalked up the driveway, his eyes on the target, a beautiful man with his red head bent over a leather briefcase.

"Richard Adamson," he said. The suspect's head jerked up, a deer caught in the sight of a predator. Rawlings flashed his badge. "You're under arrest for the murders of Evie Tucker, Shandra Hornsby, Kameel Prince, Naomi Watkins, LaRhonda Williams..." He paused as he cinched the handcuffs around the suspect's wrists. "And Birdie James."

❧

A WEEK WENT by and Sasha didn't call. It wasn't abnormal. Informants took their time, and only came forward after they'd been squeezed or needed something in return. But there'd been another overdose, another drug-related death from the stuff Sasha sold. Another death that could've been avoided if Montgomery could just sweep narcotics from the streets as easily as fallen leaves.

The doorbell rang.

"I need your help."

Richard stood on the porch, with his hands clasped together in prayer and worry lines burrowed into his forehead. His reputation had been dragged through the headlines of all the local newspapers.

COLD CASE IGNITES: LOCAL ATTORNEY TRIED FOR HEADBANGER MURDERS

Richard stepped forward, like he'd planned to come inside. Montgomery braced herself. He looked at her with pleading eyes.

"Surely you know better than anyone that I only wanted to help those girls."

What she did know was that Richard had offered his pool house to her at the most desperate time in her life. From her experience with the Market Kids, she knew what happened to the juveniles who ran from abusive foster homes. And in her work as a narcotics detective, she saw who some of those kids grew up to be. The ones who couldn't find their way out ended up in handcuffs.

Richard had showed her a way out, and without making her feel helpless. He'd understood why she needed control over her own well-being, why she had to rely on herself so no one could ever disappoint her again. He gave her the pool house, and left her to figure out life on her own.

"Come inside," she said, opening her home as he had done for her. She owed him the benefit of the doubt. He wasn't perfect, but he'd had a reputation in the Market. She knew there were dozens of women he hadn't murdered.

"So you made bail, obviously," she said. Montgomery took her place on the couch, a mauve, floral sofa large enough to sit three people. She sipped the mug of tea that had been sitting on the coffee table, and offered Richard none. "That couldn't have been cheap." She spread her long arms across the back of the couch, claiming her territory. Richard took his cue and sat on a bean bag chair in the corner of the living room.

"I'm innocent," he said. "I didn't kill those girls." He glanced at the television, which played the evening news. But she didn't turn it off.

"Then why did they arrest you?" Montgomery asked.

"Everything they have against me is circumstantial. They are pressing me to confess in exchange for taking the death penalty off the table. But I'm not admitting to something I didn't do."

"How am I supposed to help you?" she asked. Though she was grateful, she hadn't forgotten the type of man Richard was. Maybe he wasn't a killer, but she never felt he was wholly trustworthy either. After she graduated high school, she went straight to the Police Academy, cutting all ties except for Christmas and birthday cards.

"I can't imagine how this must feel for you," he began. "Finding out your mother died, and then hearing I've been charged with her murder. I know it must seem crazy that I'd come to you in the first place."

"My mother has been dead to me for a long time," Montgomery said.

"Right. Well, I know how that goes." Richard paused for a moment. He stretched forward, grabbed her hand and placed it face-up in his. He slowly traced his thumb over the lines in her palm. It was soothing, a touch she hadn't realized she'd been craving.

"You remind me so much of myself when I was young. Stubborn. Tough. Self-made. I saw something in you that night, when I found you in my trash. And I wanted things to turn out differently for you."

"I appreciate what you did for me," Montgomery said, pulling her hand away. "But Detective Rawlings is good at his job. If he thinks you're guilty..."

Richard licked the corner of his mouth. "You don't think cops make mistakes? You're so young, you still see the world in black and white. I think it's interesting that even with your background, you became a cop."

She leaned forward. "The world is black and white. I'm black, and you're white. You have no idea what it was like for me. I was poor. I was hungry. I was hopeless. But I never did drugs."

"You don't know what would've happened to you."

"I know that drugs kill everything they touch."

"I am innocent," he said. "I didn't kill those girls. I'm not perfect. I know I'm a hypocrite, but it's only because I'm human. I pay for sex, but I don't get off on hurting people."

"I want to know the evidence they have against you," she said.

"Alright. I guess that's fair." He ran a hand through his hair. "All of the teenaged victims were cases I tried at one point or another. But that only proves I did my job and tried the cases I was assigned. They have witness descriptions of my car in connection to the victims or the areas they were last seen." He cleared his throat. "But we both know the explanation for that one."

"That doesn't seem like enough probable cause," Montgomery said. "What else?"

"They served a warrant on my wife. Searched my car and found carpet fibers that were 'microscopically similar' to ones found on two of the victims. They have the blood type of the perpetrator from semen found on two of the bodies, AB negative. It's the rarest of blood types, and I also happen to be AB negative."

"Well that doesn't help."

"I'll admit it doesn't look good. But none of the evidence alone can prove, beyond a reasonable doubt, that I committed these murders. I'm not the only man in the world who pays for sex and drives a Mustang. We both know witness accounts are fallible. The car they saw could've been red, could've been brown, hell it could've been green. And carpet fibers? Find another car with the same type of carpet and you've got nothing."

"So then why do you need me?"

He paused. "You'll be subpoenaed as a witness. And I was hoping you'd be willing to leave out certain information."

"I'm not going to lie."

"And I'm not asking you to lie. I'm just asking you not to say anything that will damage my reputation. I don't want to hurt my family. There are certain things about you and me that no one needs to know."

She leaned forward on her knees. "Be real with me, or else I won't even consider helping you."

"I know it will be hard for jurors to believe I killed your mother if you testified to my good character. And if they can't prove I killed your mother, they can't argue I killed the other victims either."

"Okay then," she said, standing and motioning him towards the door.

"Are you going to help me?" He didn't say it, but she heard it all the same. *Like I helped you?*

She hesitated. She was angry at Birdie for so many things. But Sasha had been right. Learning her mother had been murdered cast their past in a new shadow, and the tender memories rewound through her head like a VHS tape.

"I came here knowing you could easily kill me," Richard continued. His green eyes began to water. "I swear to you, I didn't kill those girls."

"I'd like to believe you."

"Eugenia Tucker," Richard spit out. "She can prove my innocence. Please, just talk to her before the trial starts."

"I'll think about it," she said, closing the door before he could respond. Because she owed him that much, at least. But Montgomery was owed something too, and the debt was so long overdue she would now take it for herself. It was time she knew the truth.

CHAPTER TWENTY-EIGHT

Montgomery, Alabama
1959

REGGIE JACKSON HAD BEEN fifteen years old when he first saw Birdie James.

He'd been playing in the band at Dexter Avenue Baptist. People sang and danced, speaking in evangelical tongues, and Reggie watched while waiting for his turn to play saxophone. He took it with him everywhere, like an overgrown boy might his baby blanket. He chewed the insides of his cheeks as he watched the sweat pool in the armpits of the prettiest girls, and thought of all the places where that sweat might percolate and gather. Between thick thighs, or sliding down those heavy, black breasts. He wasn't there to find God, but to dance with the prettiest of God's children. And as his eyes roamed and marked his targets, he heard the faintest voice coming from far and beyond. So quiet it was, he thought it might not be real, as no one else seemed to hear its chime. Like a dog following a hunter's whistle, Reggie left the church and walked across town.

A girl sang on a slab of sidewalk in front of a white-owned department store. And a crowd of white people had stopped to listen. No one shouted hateful epithets. No one told her to move along. Those faces Reggie had been raised to fear showed nothing but awe, a peace he'd never seen himself when looking into the pale eyes of his oppressors. Reggie almost fainted. It was four years after the Montgomery Bus Boycott, and the city had turned into a combustible fury of bigotry and violence and rebellion. Sit-ins and school integration brought on bombings, dogs, and hoses. Demands for equality were met with billy clubs and murder. Little black boys were beaten, jailed and threatened with lynching when little white girls kissed their brown cheeks. An innocent, black man named Willie Edwards, Jr. was marched to the Alabama River and forced to jump to his death, because a group of Klansman had heard, without specificity, that a black truck driver had been carnally engaged with a white woman. And Willie just happened to be a truck driver, black, and within their barbaric reach.

But now, on the pavement of a city embroiled, a high-yellow angel sang so pure that people seemed to forget their hatred.

He ducked into the alley beside the department store, and braced his shoulders against the brick. He played his saxophone, melding his brass voice with her crystal song. They finished on the highest note and the crowd reluctantly dispersed. She joined him in the alley.

"I'm Miss Birdie James," she said, extending her hand. "You almost as good as me."

And he said, "Well lucky for me then. Cuz' you might be pretty enough to make a man try harder."

It'd been a slow courtship. He'd walk Birdie to school on his way to work in the cotton fields in the rural counties outside Montgomery, listening to her prattle about her plans to become a famous singer. And he'd tell her about his plans to quit the fields as soon as he'd saved enough, to travel and become a world-class musician. Two poor kids with big, rich dreams. On Saturdays, he called on her to picnic with him by the river while her mother was at work. But as he was four years older, he'd had to be patient. So patient, that at times he forgot all about her, and wouldn't see her for months.

By the time he'd turned nineteen, Reggie began spending his weekends in the shanty juke joints, playing his saxophone for tips and then drinking them away. Until one night, Birdie walked in with her curls pinned back, wearing red lipstick and a teal dress that brought out the yellow in her skin, and an inch too high above the knee too. She'd walked straight to the table where he sat with his friends, pulled the woman who'd been sitting on his lap to the floor by her hair and said,

"Reggie Jackson, quit screwing around and marry me already."

She was pure and sweet, and just bad enough to tempt him into setting down roots. But he wanted to get out of the South. He wanted to walk on the sidewalk and look anyone in the eye. He wanted to vote without having to pass a literacy test, one that would be rigged for him to fail. He wanted to be called "sir," instead of "boy." He wanted to speak his mind to anyone he pleased, and he wanted the ache in his fingers to come from playing the saxophone raw, instead of stooping in the fields picking cotton for pennies by the hour.

"YOU HAVE A VISITOR," the guard said, rattling the bars of Reggie's cell at the King County Jail. He had nine years left on a fifteen-year sentence for his third offense for possession of crack.

He nearly pounded on the door to be dragged back to his cell when he saw who waited on the other side of the glass.

Montgomery picked up the receiver and spoke loud enough so he could hear, even though he hadn't yet picked up the other end.

"Sit," she said.

But it was something in her eyes that made him stay. For once, they held pity for him, instead of hatred. He sat down and picked up the receiver.

"Did you know she was dead?" Montgomery asked. Her eyes

were red-rimmed, as if she'd been crying. And they were hard, as though she was too stubborn to show she cared.

Reggie nodded, staring at the sleeves of his orange jumpsuit.

"They think she was murdered by the Headbanger Hunter," she said.

Reggie tried to control his face, and not betray his feelings.

"Yep. I heard that too. It's too bad."

"Too bad? That's all you have to say?"

She looked straight into his eyes. She'd never done that before, had always treaded lightly around him. As though she were afraid that if she got too close, he'd spook and run away. It made him feel guilty to see she loved her mother so much she'd do anything not to stand between them. He couldn't look at her any longer, so he leaned back and stared at his lap.

"I want to understand what happened to our..." she hesitated and looked at her hands. Had she wanted to say *family*? "I want to understand what happened to my mother."

There was a prolonged silence.

"I don't want to talk about it," Reggie said, harsher than he'd intended.

"Okay. Can you tell me about why her record deal got dropped?"

Suddenly, the heat went into Reggie's hands and his heart beat like a war drum. What business did she have, coming into his cage and rubbing his face in his own shit as if he were a damn dog?

"Why are you here?" he asked. "What business you got, coming up in here and dragging this shit out?"

"Because I lost everyone before I was old enough to understand why. And now my mother is dead and I might never know the truth. I want to know."

"Ain't shit to know, girl!" Reggie said, slamming his hand on the table.

"I want to know why you couldn't be a father to me. I want to know why my mother kept using until it put her on the streets so she could be abused, killed, and thrown away like trash."

"Let me ask you something. You think I deserve to be up in this prison cell for fifteen years?"

Reggie's defense attorney had tried to get him a shorter sentence. Yes, it was his third drug offense, but he wasn't a violent criminal. And there was no difference between crack and cocaine, except the former was cheaper, used by poor folk like himself, and so worthy of a steeper punishment. It would've worked, until Montgomery testified for the prosecution.

"It's not my fault you're in jail," she said quietly.

"Well it didn't help none, you coming to court and telling my business."

"I told the truth. You were a violent person."

"You know," he said, rubbing his cheek, "I been hearing about this new girl selling dope. A high yellow girl with gray eyes. Now how many of them you think live in Seattle?"

"I'm not sorry for what I said. You beat my mother." She leaned back and wrung her hands together. Reggie could tell she was nervous.

"And I'll be paying for it my whole life. I was paying for it before they put me here. And I'll be paying for it when I get out. You kids think you know about the world. Think you know about life. You don't know shit about the world your momma and I come from."

And then Reggie told her a story.

THE PLAN HAD BEEN to marry Birdie once he saved enough to take them both to Seattle. It was more expensive to travel that far, but he'd heard Washington was the most progressive and free state where black people could live. On a brisk day in the fall of 1964, he'd finally saved enough, and went calling at her mother's cabin.

"She's working at the Jeffries' house just now," her mother said. "I twisted my ankle, so she's covering me today."

He saw it all in his mind. He would finally become the man God had intended him to be. He'd finally make a life for himself, and the woman he loved. But when he reached the back door of the house, he heard the most ungodly sounds. He peered through the window, and into the dining room on the other side of the kitchen. The black legs of the piano were scraping against the floor, and the keys groaned and cried out in an awful, stilted pulse. A white man held Birdie by the throat, his suspenders hanging limply at his sides. His slacks were pulled down, and he held the entrails of her dress in his other hand. Her beautiful curls had become limp and frizzy, and she grimaced as he pushed himself into her against his polished, baby grand. He heard her saying, over and over,

"Please, Mr. Jeffries."

And then she saw him, standing helpless in the window. The look in her eyes still haunted him, each night as he slept on the cot in his cell. He could still see that look, the one that embittered him to her for the rest of their lives. The look that said, *Don't just stand there.* But that's exactly what he did. Because white men had been raping black women since the days of slavery. And white men would kill black men for standing up for their women, families and dignity. He could kill Mr. Jeffries. Or he could report the crime. But it would be up to a white jury to defend Birdie's dignity. It would be up to a white jury to defend his right to protect his self and woman. A white jury was always given the choice of whether to hold their assailants and murderers accountable. It didn't matter what the Civil Rights Act said. What good was law when those enforcing it didn't believe in it's merit? He'd either hang, or suffer yet another denial of his right to exist in peace.

Birdie had made him love her more than he loved himself, in a time when he was powerless as both a man and human being. He left without her, but Birdie followed him to Seattle. She'd made that white man Jeffries buy her a train ticket, holding a knife to his throat until he agreed. Reggie knew why she done it, but in his mind it hurt less to call her a whore.

She showed him a baby whose skin was as light as stained canvas. A baby as beautiful as her mother. A baby he would fail to protect, and forever wonder whether she was truly his own. And for this, he would never find forgiveness.

. . .

MONTGOMERY'S FACE BLANCHED. She held the receiver limply in her hand as Reggie told the guard to take him back.

A few days later, as his fellow inmates made phone calls home to their families and friends, Reggie thought about who he could call. There was no blood family left, and this made him angry. So he called the son of one of his old musician friends, a friend who remembered the clubs and shows and parties before drugs tore them apart.

"Hey Day-Tawn, what's good?"

"Wassup Uncle Reg?"

"I need you to do something for me."

"Anything, you name it."

"I need you to be on the lookout for somebody. Light-skinned. Gray eyes. Name is Montgomery Jackson."

CHAPTER TWENTY-NINE

IT WAS NOW MID-DECEMBER. The city was like a globe of sleet and pine and wool-shaped clouds. The earth was a deep brown, enriched by the decayed leaves of autumn. The bay's reflection had changed from cornflower blue to choppy slate, and a constant drizzle sprayed the city.

Sasha's truck smelled like stale beer and cheese puffs, and Montgomery had to focus on the fuzzy dice that hung from the rearview mirror to keep from getting nauseous. Candy wrappers and fast food containers covered the floor. The back seats had been removed, and there were amps stacked so high you couldn't see out the back window.

"Can't believe you still drive this thing," she muttered.

"There's too many good memories to give her up now," he said.

They'd met at his house in Capitol Hill, and were going to meet his supplier. Before she'd set up the buy, Victor had expressed his concerns. He wanted to take the meeting, but was called to court to testify for one of his cases.

"I picked up on some vibes during that interview," he'd said. "Whatever history you got, you can't let it cloud your judgement."

"I don't know what you're talking about," she'd said. "I'm a good cop. I know how to do my job."

"You're a great cop. The best partner I've worked with. Which is why I don't want to see you suspended. Or worse. So I'm just gonna say it. There can be absolutely no nakedness. Not while he's our informant."

Victor had every right to be worried. Their sergeant had given Montgomery one more chance to control her temper. That summer, she'd been working Aurora undercover as a prostitute. She didn't think it was fair that the girls got busted more than the men who paid them, and so focused her energy on getting the johns off the street. The girls trusted her while she pretended to be one of them, enough to tell her about their experiences, about men getting too handsy. About rape and degradation behind moldy dumpsters and rat-infested alleys. About beatings that took place in the backseat of cars. There was one john in particular who liked to leave the girls black eyes as souvenirs, so it'd be harder to get work from anybody but him. So they'd have to say 'yes' when he wanted to hire them again, submitting them to more abuse - fecal, probing, gory abuse. All so he could exert his power over them.

Montgomery made it a point to get picked up by this particular john. They went to the Marco Polo motel off Forty-Second Street and made the exchange for flesh. For a brief moment, she'd forgotten about the cameras they'd set up in the room, and had just enough time before Victor arrived to shove her gun into the man's mouth and threaten to paint a mural with his brains if he hurt another girl. Their sergeant had been so furious he nearly ripped the phonebook he kept on his desk in half. But he'd convinced the john to forget the incident by appealing to his base nature - a formal complaint would be admitting he'd lost his power to a woman.

They rode in silence. Montgomery kept stealing glances, unable to resist looking at her former best friend. He was a man now. His face had a five o'clock shadow, and his lips held a determined scowl instead of the playful smirk he wore when they were kids. His hands were larger, and thickly veined. She felt the calluses on his fingers when he'd tapped her arm to remind to wear her seatbelt. He was dressed simply in a yellow Sonics beanie, a long-sleeved thermal t-shirt and ripped, dirty jeans, and he tapped his silver thumb ring against the steering wheel to a song in his head.

"How's the record?" she asked.

"It's good. A little cleaner than I'd like, but whatever." He gave her a shy smile. "My bandmate Jay is a great drummer. But he's no Montgomery Laine. Do you still play?"

"Sometimes. Just for fun."

"Cool. Well, maybe you could come on tour with us. As back-up or something."

"I've never heard of a back-up drummer."

"No. Of course not. That's just a pretense. We'll be gone for a few months, and I want you to come with us so I can seduce you before I die."

She was speechless for a moment. Was he being serious? She stared at him until he broke his straight face into a smile. She rolled her eyes and changed the subject.

"I don't understand why you're selling drugs when you have a record deal."

"We're a new band. They paid us when we signed, but it isn't a fortune and tours are expensive. I need the money and I can't stand authority."

Montgomery sucked her teeth in disgust.

"Seriously," he said. "Why should I work at a minimum wage job I don't care about? I only sell enough to pay the bills and eat. I spend the rest of my time playing music. And as soon as we start selling records, I'll stop."

In her heart, she believed he sold for another reason. But it scared her too much to think about.

"Why'd you sell to me?" she asked.

He raised an eyebrow, glancing in her direction. She sensed he hadn't trusted her under the Viaduct, hadn't believed she used even though she made fake track marks on her arm with a sterile needle.

His answer cut to the bone.

"I figured it was the only way you'd tell me the truth."

"Where are we going?" Montgomery asked minutes later as Sasha pulled into the driveway of a small, gray house in George-town. Buys were typically set in the open, so the cop working undercover had means for escape if something went down. She'd said this specifically to Sasha, that the meeting with Tommy's supplier needed to be in a public space, like a park or shopping center.

He turned off the Chevy and looked at her. His blue eyes froze her mounting objection, turning her outrage into a breathy petulance.

"Don't you trust me?" he asked.

"Not really," she said. "You blew my cover with your friends."

"I didn't tell them you were a cop. As far as they know, your name is Monti Laine. You're a childhood friend and local musi-cian." He patted her hand with his fingertips. "You know I'd never do anything to hurt you."

A man with a kind smile and deep, brown skin answered the door. He wore a red tracksuit, and was in a wheelchair. He led them through the front hallway into the kitchen. Montgomery noted the pictures on the walls. A happy, biracial family smiling in front of the Woodland Park Zoo sign, three girls clamoring to sit on their father's broken lap, his fair wife wrapping her arms around his neck and kissing his cheek. The same family running along the ocean, their father's wheelchair sinking into the sand, and a bonfire smoking in the distance. Wedding photos, the man and his woman standing together beneath a vine-covered awning, kissing in the sun.

"Percy, this is Scarlett," Sasha said as he sat at a small card table. The kitchen looked like a soda shop, with black and white check-ered wall paper, and the sink held a stack of unwashed dishes, many of them made of colorful plastic and covered with Disney characters.

"How do you do, Scarlett? Can I get you something to drink?" Percy asked, grinning. He had perfect teeth.

"No, thank you," Montgomery said, sitting in the chair opposite Sasha.

He wheeled to the table to join them, handing Sasha a sports drink.

Montgomery tried to look bored, like a girlfriend who'd been dragged along against her will.

Percy looked between Montgomery and Sasha.

"So, how's Carmine? She know you here?"

"Carmine's good," Sasha answered, drawing out his words. "Still dancing at the Velvet Room."

Percy eyed Montgomery with what looked like fatherly concern. He cleared his throat.

"Excuse me for being so frank, but boy, let me give you some advice. Keep it simple with the ladies. One good woman is half the drama and worth ten times more than twenty girls you don't care for." Percy looked at Montgomery and nodded. "I'll put him on blast, not even worried about it."

Montgomery smiled politely. "I can take care of myself."

Percy chuckled. "I think you got your work cut out for you with this one."

Sasha shrugged. "I'm slowing down, I swear. Besides, I think Scarlett might be 'The One.'"

"Is that so?" Percy asked, looking to Montgomery for confirmation.

"Well, I'm not sure," Sasha continued, rubbing his chin. "How did you know Tina was right for you?"

"Easy," Percy said. "She told me so."

Sasha nodded and looked at Montgomery. He smiled with a corner of his mouth, and his eyes crinkled, as if they were all playing a game and only he knew the rules. But then there was a moment, when the dishes in the sink settled with a clang, drawing Percy's attention away. A brief moment when Sasha's eyes softened and his bottom lip trembled as if it took all his strength to ask,

"Are you 'The One' for me?"

Montgomery felt her face flush, and her hands shook beneath

the table. She pressed them into her lap, but didn't answer. The smirk returned.

"Scarlett don't know what she wants," Sasha said to Percy, laughing.

Percy patted Montgomery's shoulder in solidarity. "So, what brings you here? And I mean besides you needing advice about your commitment issues," he said to Sasha.

"Well, I'm assuming you heard about Tommy?"

"Nah, I ain't talked to Tommy for a month or so now." Percy glanced at Montgomery. "He usually calls me at the beginning of each month. He alright?"

Sasha leaned forward and rested his forehead against his hands.

"He OD'd on Halloween."

"Oh, what? Oh no. Aww, man..." Percy shook his head. His eyes watered, but he sniffed them dry.

Montgomery was taken aback. Percy was visibly distraught, something she hadn't expected. Most dealers she'd arrested up to that point had been cold-hearted. They pimped out their girl-friends. They beat and murdered people who didn't pay. They created gun wars over the right to stand on a slab of pavement.

"Anyway," Sasha said, eyeing her. "I just thought you should know. And I wanted to make sure you knew I was around. In case you needed anything."

Percy nodded his head, drumming his fingers against the table. He shrugged his shoulders and motioned sheepishly at Montgomery.

"She's cool man," Sasha said. "I trust her with my life."

Montgomery felt the hairs on her arms raise like quills. Once Sasha made a couple buys, she could arrest Percy and negotiate a deal - information about his supplier for a lighter charge. Like rungs on a ladder, she would climb over each person responsible for infecting the city with a drug so strong it could kill even the most hardcore of addicts. But then Sasha changed the subject.

"How are your girls?"

Percy's face lit up. He wiped his eyes. "They're good, man. Real good. My oldest is going to Harvard. Costing me a fortune, but hey, she's my princess. They're so smart, much more than me. Get it from their mom. My youngest was just accepted into a private school for the creatively gifted."

Percy's whole body radiated with pride, and Montgomery's high, the one she felt right before a break in a case, suddenly tasted like bile in the back of her throat.

"You were supposed to make the buy," Montgomery said later through clenched teeth. "You messed up."

They were driving back to Sasha's house when her beeper sounded. It was Victor, and he was waiting at the precinct to hear her report. But what could she tell him without validating his concerns about her relationship with their informant? That she'd been flustered by Sasha's flirting? Surprised by Percy's kindness and family-oriented lifestyle? That when the moment came for Sasha to make the deal, he looked to her for confirmation, confirmation she couldn't give because he'd manipulated her emotions?

She didn't feel right about busting Percy, and Sasha knew it.

"Bullshit," he said, pulling into his driveway. He turned in his seat to look at her.

"You want to know why Percy sells to people like me? He broke his back falling off a roof after Boeing laid him off during the recession, working for a shady contractor with shit equipment because there were no other options while his wife was in nursing school. He dotes on his girls. He's there for them everyday when they get home from school, so his wife can work crazy hours at the hospital. He wants them to have every opportunity in life and is willing to risk jail for it. He doesn't use and he doesn't drink. He's not violent, and if you stubbed a toe the man would give you his only wheelchair. We both know the world won't be saved by putting Percy in jail. Because someone else would just take his place."

She stared at his rundown house through the windshield. Match point. He'd slammed it down her throat and she had no rebuttal.

"So... Is Carmine your girlfriend?" she asked.

He grinned. "Jealous?"

"No. Just making conversation." A pause. "What's your band's name?"

"Fungus Reign. We're playing at the Central Tavern in a few weeks."

"Cool."

"Cool," he said.

"When do you think you'll stop using?"

He sighed. "I'm just doing what young guys in rock bands do. It's not a problem."

They watched the windshield wipers streak against the glass.

"So what do I do?" she asked finally.

He put his hand on her knee.

"Focus on those who do the most harm."

But Sasha's advice wasn't that simple. Because she wasn't sure who had done the most harm. And she wasn't sure she could forgive those who fed the monsters created by addiction.

That night she dreamt of a train in a tunnel. It was dark, she saw only headlights. They grew brighter, expanding like a ripple as the train barreled towards her. She couldn't breathe. She couldn't scream. It was coming, and the truth of its weight would grind her into the tracks.

❧

RING RING RING! Ring Ring Ring!

The car phone, a novelty that cost a fortune to install in his off-duty vehicle, rang so loud Detective Rawlings nearly hit his head against the roof.

"Hello, honey," he said into the receiver.

It was his wife, Jen. It was always his wife.

"I just wanted to know when I should expect you home," she said.

"Not until tomorrow morning. So try not to worry about me until then, okay?"

"Okay. I'll do my best, Colby."

"Okay. I love you."

"I love you, too."

Rawlings turned off the ignition. He was lucky. Some families weren't as understanding of the long hours and foul moods, the hushed conversations that ended whenever an innocent walked into the room.

He was parked outside the Marco Polo motel. The windshield fogged with each breath he took, but he could see his target with hawkish clarity. Richard Adamson had been staying in room 107 with his son. Sex workers walked up and down Aurora, but Rawlings wouldn't lose sight of his target. Deals exchanged hands in the middle of soggy side streets, and desperate feet climbed fire escapes towards their demise, but Rawlings couldn't lose sight of his target.

Another woman had gone missing. A woman whose street name was Coral.

❧

THE PILLOWS WERE COVERED in coarse hairs. The grout between the bathroom tiles was stained a rusty orange. The television screen was gritty and everything smelled as if it festered with mold, remnants from the subspecies of mankind. And for some reason, Clarke decided to go with Richard when Cassandra threw him out of the house.

"This tv sucks," Clarke said. He was sprawled out on one of the full-sized beds.

"Then go home and watch," Richard said.

"I can't leave you," Clarke said. He sat up and glared across the space of sticky carpet between the beds. "You need me. I'm all you have left."

Richard sighed. "I know that."

Clarke rolled onto his stomach and held his chin in his hands. He looked like a little boy again.

"Everything will be okay," Clarke said. "You're not guilty. Once the trial starts, everyone will know the truth."

Richard had shied away from the subject each time Clarke tried to discuss the trial. But something was different tonight. Maybe it was the new year, the new decade that was a few weeks away, or the fact that a crazed detective was parked outside waiting for him to slip. He saw no point in lying anymore.

"I don't think that's going to happen. There's a lot of evidence that makes me look guilty."

Clarke focused on the television, but Richard noticed a shift in his body, as if a weight had been dropped on his back.

"Really? Like what?"

"I'd met most of the victims through cases I prosecuted. One of the victims had my card in her pocket. And there's a photograph of myself with another of the victims, wearing the clothes she was later found murdered in. Stuff like that."

"None of that means you killed them."

"No. But all those things, combined with the smoking gun…"

Clarke looked at Richard. The glare from the television made his bruised eyes look as if they glowed, yellow like a cat's.

"What smoking gun?"

"They found a ring in my nightstand. It belonged to this girl named Evie. She was the first one killed."

"Why did you have the ring?"

"I don't know. I shouldn't have kept it. But I couldn't help myself. There's a lot of things I shouldn't have done."

They watched the television, ignoring the obvious.

Finally Clarke spoke.

"Did you ever love me?" he asked.

"No," Richard said.

"Why not?"

"I'm not exactly sure. When you were a baby, you cried at all hours, day and night. You cried whenever your mom left the room. As a toddler, you were so defiant. Your mom swore you didn't know what you were doing, but I could see it in your eyes. This one time, you threw your applesauce across the kitchen floor, explicitly after I asked you to finish your food. You didn't laugh. You didn't whine. Just stared at me with nothing, like you and I were nothing."

Richard popped open a lukewarm beer. He drank half in three, long gulps.

"You required attention at all times, and would throw a fit if you didn't get what you wanted. When you started school, we had to meet with the principal at least once a month. Because you would do these horrible things. Like stab a kid with a crayon so hard that you left behind dark, purple welts in his thigh."

Clarke chuckled. "Why would I do that?"

"Because you lost at Chutes & Ladders. I remember it like it was yesterday. It was so ridiculous to me."

"But none of that makes me unworthy of love." Clarke sniffed, as if he was trying not to cry.

"No. Of course it doesn't."

"You guys never cared about what was best for me."

"Yes we did. That's why I sent you to that private school, to your grandfather."

Clarke buried his face into the crook made by his arms. His body convulsed, and to Richard he looked grotesque.

"I know it's not your fault, son. It's mine. It always has been. But I've done my best. I've done what I can."

Richard finished the beer and crushed the can beneath his foot.

"And my feelings will never change."

CHAPTER THIRTY

MONTGOMERY ALWAYS HAD TROUBLE SLEEPING, but it'd become worse since she officially buried her mother. Playing her drums or punching the bag wasn't helping. So she resorted to organizing.

The month after she'd turned eighteen, after she'd officially begun her adult life by joining the police force and listing herself in the Yellow Pages, Montgomery received a phone call from Mr. Coen.

"I put your stuff in storage when you moved out," he'd said. "It's been almost two years. You need to take it or it's going to the dump."

"Thank you," she managed to say.

"You owe me for the cost of the storage unit." He then gave her the address and unit number.

"Mr. Coen, I hope you don't mind my asking. But you didn't like us very much. Why did you save our stuff?"

He answered her question with one of his own.

"Have you heard from Sasha?"

"No," she said. "Have you?"

"No." And then he hung up the phone.

. . .

MONTGOMERY SORTED through the storage unit, box by box until she found her mother's album. It was called *Southern Rain*. She listened to it over and over, on the old record player she left behind. She hadn't noticed when she was a child, but her mother's voice was saturated with sorrow, gravelly like the bottom of a lake. The story Reggie had told her haunted her thoughts as she remembered the last fight she'd had with Birdie. *I wish I wasn't yours.* She shuddered at the possibility that the man who had hurt her mother had also sired her existence. When Birdie was the age she was now, twenty-four years old, Montgomery was nine. Even as a young adult, Montgomery couldn't fathom the responsibility of another human life. Her mother had been a child rearing a child.

Maybe Sasha was right - there was more to Birdie's death. Perhaps she had been more than just a reckless woman who met a dangerous end. Perhaps parents only kept their pasts hidden to protect their offspring. Perhaps Birdie's lies had been told out of love.

Montgomery turned the record over and read the credits.

Birdie James, vocals

Reggie Jackson, saxophone

Lyles David, drums

Milton White, bass

Lyles David wasn't listed, but Milton White's phone number and address were in the Yellow Pages. Montgomery scribbled Milton's contact information onto a scrap of paper, and tucked it into her wallet with a photo of her mother.

The drone of traffic that sped by on Fifteenth Avenue echoed off the cement walls. Her former life, packed into boxes, was stacked snugly into a four-by-eight-foot room. Only a mile or two away from the last place she'd seen Birdie alive. Was her mother's ghost trapped at The Bridgewater? Or did she haunt the strips of sidewalk where she'd left pieces of her soul like lost pocket change? No - her mother's ghost haunted the people who allowed her to fade away, be forgotten and perish in the dark.

. . .

THE NEXT DAY, as the sun began to settle behind the mountains in a smeared, purple haze, Montgomery woke three hours earlier than usual. She'd been on the night schedule, sleeping during the day to play make-believe in the shadows. She was only two years into the job, and had been warned of the dangers. Not just the physical ones that ended in death, but the moral dangers that could turn a family man into a kingpin. To protect herself from the psychological onslaught her work entailed, she wore her anger like the badge she kept in her desk. Each time she busted an addict for possession, she pretended she was busting her mother. It was her resentment that kept her from sliding too close to the edge. As long as she hated Birdie, she would never become her.

Now Montgomery was groggy from lack of sleep, and stood at the door of a little red house. It was in the Madrona neighborhood, just east of the Central District. The lawn was gated and well-kept, the grass beginning to frost in the cold air. The wraparound porch had metal patio furniture and hanging baskets, turned dormant for the winter. There was a welcome mat that read "Season's Greetings."

The man who answered the door was tall and lanky. His hair was coarse and peppery like a scouring pad, and his dark eyes were ringed in blue. His skin had the quality of leather - deep and brown and smooth, with the aged look of experience.

"May I help you?" he asked in a gritty voice.

"Are you Milton White?"

He nodded.

"My name is Montgomery Jackson. I believe you knew my mother, Birdie."

He motioned her to sit on a couch wrapped in plastic, and brought her a cup of tea from the kitchen.

"Oh, Birdie, Birdie, Birdie," he said. "Now that's a damn shame. My condolences, sweetheart. The world's a lesser place without her, I know that."

"Right..." Montgomery looked around the room. There was a fireplace in front of her, and it smelled warm and ashy, as if it'd been used lovingly. Bass guitars hung on the walls, floating in the air like dragonflies. She pointed at one of the guitars, black with flecks of gold that bounced in the waning light shining through the window.

"Do you still play?"

"Sure sure, a lot of local stuff. The last ten years or so have been mostly session work, traveling around the country. I do alright, played on a few well-known albums."

"I got your name from *Southern Rain*. Never really heard it until recently."

"Really? Birdie never played it for you?"

Montgomery shook her head. Milton pursed his mouth and made a low rumble in the back of his throat.

"Yeah, well..." He breathed out the words as if he hoped they'd be the end of the conversation.

A clock ticked the seconds by, and Montgomery could only stare at her feet

"I ain't got nowhere to be, so you go on and take your time."

"What?"

"You know, for whatever it is you came to ask me."

She wasn't sure herself, but Milton's eyes were kind so she spoke without restraint.

"For the last eight years I assumed my mother abandoned me. When I was sixteen I found out the reason we were so poor, the reason she was never there for me was because she was a junkie."

Milton handed her a tissue. She hadn't realized she was crying.

"I figured she was either caught up in her drugs or dead from an overdose. Either way, I didn't want to know and I didn't want to care. But then I found out that all this time she'd been murdered...."

"Alright now," he said. His voice was like a melody, and he rolled his hand in the air as if he could pull her words forward.

"I want to blame her and forgive her and save her all at once, but I can't do any of those things because I don't understand what happened. If she was that talented, so much that now she's all over the radio, then where was everyone when we were starving? What the hell happened?"

Milton grabbed her hand, wrapped it in a blanket made by his large palms and held it until she stopped crying.

"I can't tell you what happened," he said. "But I will tell you everything I know."

He went back to the kitchen and returned with two glasses and a bottle of whiskey. He poured two drinks and handed one to Montgomery. He took a sip, made that breathy sound with the back of his throat as if he'd been quenched.

"You were still a baby when I met your mother. I was playing in a band at the Black and Tan club over on Jackson Street. She walked up to me with this crazy looking fellow and told me I needed to join her band. I was skeptical at first, but man, that first time I heard her and Reggie play together…"

He ducked his head, then looked back at her with a gleam in his eye.

"You ain't heard nothing until you've heard them two voices together - that's how good his sax sounded, like it was part of his throat. They made these harmonies that intersected, dissected, rolled and waved. Your ear would get lost in it."

"I don't remember any of this."

"Well, you were still so young. And kids weren't allowed in the types of places we played at."

"I read in the paper that your record deal got dropped."

The lightness in Milton's eyes faded, and his eyelids grew heavy.

"I wouldn't say dropped, necessarily."

"Then what would you say?"

"I was about ten years older than Birdie, so she was always like a sister to me. We'd play these shows and men would just lose themselves for her, she was that beautiful. And Reggie was always so jealous, sometimes there'd be fights. Now, when I was around he never got too out of hand because I don't get down like that. But sometimes Birdie would come to shows and you could see the black eyes beneath all that makeup. So there was already that tension with the band. It was toxic, and me and Lyles didn't want no part in it."

Milton finished the rest of his whiskey and poured another. He went to tap Montgomery's off, but stopped. She hadn't touched it, and her tea had grown cold.

"The band went to L.A. for this signing party, you know, industry stuff."

A vague memory dislodged itself. Montgomery in pajamas, staying at the neighbor's apartment watching movies and eating popcorn when they still lived in the Central District.

"Now, this next part is just what I heard. Me and Lyles left the party early. Neither one of us were into the hard drinking or drugs. I wanted Birdie and Reggie to come back to the hotel with us, but they wanted to keep partying."

Montgomery shifted in her seat. Had her mother been sober at any point in her childhood?

"I guess one of the executives told Birdie he wanted to sleep with her. And you know, these guys have this way of making you feel like they own you. Like if you want to make it, you have to do what they say. But your momma wasn't never going to do what she wasn't fitting to do, so she told him, and again, this is just what I heard, but your mom goes, 'I wouldn't fuck you even if your dick shoots diamonds.'"

"Yeah, that sounds about right."

"Of course, when Reggie found out what happened he went off on the guy. The band couldn't get momentum after that. Producers kept cancelling on us, they kept bumping us off tours and eventually Lyles and I had to move on. We played to eat, you know?"

"And then my mom had to turn to prostitution to support her drug habit."

Milton's face softened.

"Now I don't know about all that. For as long as I knew her, I didn't get any indication your mom did drugs. Maybe a drink here and there. Now Reggie, he used anything and everything, like a lot of musicians back then he thought the drugs elevated his playing. But your momma never touched the hard stuff."

"That doesn't make sense. Why wouldn't she just get a job then?"

Milton rubbed his chin and looked at the ceiling.

"I remember her telling me about this new apartment. She was so excited, because it was in a white neighborhood. She wanted you to have good schooling. You know back then, certain neighborhoods were hard to get into because landlords wouldn't rent to black folks. It was around the same time we were getting stonewalled by the record label. And like I said, we played to eat. Some folks just ain't made for clocking in and clocking out."

Montgomery thought of the day they moved to The Bridgewater. It was the summer before she started second grade. She sat in the courtyard in a grove of blooming rhododendrons while Birdie and Reggie moved boxes from a U-haul truck. Birdie kept wrapping her arms around his neck, her braids loose and fresh down her back, kissing his cheek while he tried not to smile and all the while saying,

"We'll see. We'll see how it goes."

LATER, in the cold morning hours valued only by night-stalkers, Montgomery and Victor worked a "john patrol" near a Denny's diner on Aurora. Montgomery dressed the part in tattered jeans, a low cut top and heavy bomber jacket, strutting up and down a section of walkway and peering into the cars. Johns kept stopping and she busted them one by one, padding her and Victor's arrest records. A maroon Mustang rolled up the highway, headlights in her eyes so she couldn't see through the windshield. The trial was coming up, and she still hadn't followed up on Richard's request. Was this him checking up on her? But he couldn't have known she'd be here, he didn't know she worked undercover vice. The car drew closer and sidled to the curb. Montgomery leaned down to look through the window. Suddenly, the engined revved and before she could see the driver, the car sped away.

CHAPTER THIRTY-ONE

EUGENIA LIVED in a purple-painted house in the Central District. She welcomed Montgomery into her living room with a smile and an offer of tea. Montgomery watched as the woman, who was in her forties but had lived life so hard she looked to be in her sixties, fluttered through her empty cupboards for something they both knew never existed.

"How 'bout some water instead?" Eugenia asked, handing Montgomery a cloudy glass filled to the brim.

"Thank you," Montgomery said. She took a sip and set it down on the coffee table. "Eugenia, I'm here to ask you about Evie."

Eugenia rocked in her chair.

"Evie was an angry child. Right from the beginning. Couldn't do nothing with her 'cause she wouldn't hear nothing you said." She chuckled. "She was my star, though. After I lost her, I cleaned up my act. Not soon enough, though."

"Can you tell me what was going on in her life at the time she was murdered?"

"Well, she was acting wild. Dating, smoking, drinking. Teenage stuff. I wasn't able to keep an eye on her because I had to work nights." Eugenia paused. "I mean, I had my own issues with drugs, but I got better. Anyway, Evie got caught shoplifting at the Bon

Marche downtown. The store pressed charges. Everything went downhill after that. She started prostituting, using harder drugs. Wasn't taking advantage of no opportunities offered to her."

"Why was Evie so angry?" Montgomery asked.

Eugenia stared out her window. A light snow dusted the street outside.

"Same reason I was. Her father abandoned us."

"I'm going to be honest with you, Eugenia. The man arrested for the murder of your daughter told me you could prove he was innocent."

Eugenia scoffed.

"He's exactly where he deserves to be!"

"Can you tell me why he'd send me here?"

Eugenia pressed her lips together and looked down her nose at Montgomery.

"This ain't your business."

"My mother was the last victim, Birdie James. She had a drug problem, and I often went hungry for it. I almost ended up on the streets like your Evie, but Richard gave me a place to live. I just want the truth."

Eugenia chewed her thumb. She sipped from the cloudy water glass, and her eyes rimmed red.

"Alright then," she said.

§

EVEN AFTER FOUR YEARS, Eugenia came to him. After he'd won a championship his senior year in college. After he'd stopped writing and said he couldn't afford the long-distance phone calls. Even after he'd changed his name to "Richard Adamson" and met the woman he was going to marry. Despite all this, Eugenia showed up on his doorstep on a warm summer's night in 1966. Because, as Richard remembered, she'd said there was no other choice.

Eugenia looked beautiful when she came. The sun was setting behind her, and made her ebony skin glow orange and red as though it burned from within. He wanted to touch her face, like he had each time he came home from college for the summer, unable to afford living on campus until his scholarship began the next year.

Cassandra never came with him. At first he thought it was because she was steadfast, dedicated to her tennis and academic clubs. But as they settled into their life together, he realized she never wanted to see where he came from, never wanted his past to be that real. She wanted him for his sex, and for what he represented. Open rebellion against a conservative father who didn't believe a woman should inherit his multi-million dollar enterprise. And so, during those summers in Seattle, Richard turned to Eugenia, to her arms and smile and warmth, to the musky place that made her cry out in pleasure. It felt like coming home, because she'd known him when he was simply Ricky Adamoli.

On that warm evening of 1966, Richard was engaged. He and Cassandra had used some of her trust money to buy a beautiful, white house on the bluffs of Magnolia. And he'd recently had the talk with her father.

"Success isn't just about who you know," Mr. Cummings had said. "It's also about who you portray."

"You don't even know me," Richard had said.

"I know you're not like us." Mr. Cummings took Richard's hand in his and squeezed until the knuckles popped. "I can't stop Cassandra from marrying you," he'd said. "But I can stop her from making a fool of me."

And Richard understood. A man who built homes for the East Coast elite, a man who dined with movie stars in New York's finest restaurants had an image to maintain. And Ricky, with his Motown twang and slow Northwestern drawl, didn't fit that image. It's why he'd changed his name after he turned eighteen. So people like Mr. Cummings wouldn't find out about his alcoholic mother and the abuse he suffered. Or about Richard's father, who had disappeared after getting arrested for driving a pool cue into the eye of the man who'd cheated him out of twenty dollars. Or about his run-ins with the Seattle Police, arrests for vandalism and robbery and cat mutilation.

Richard changed his name with everybody, except Eugenia. Until the summer of '66, when she knocked on his door holding a baby.

"This is Evie," she said, kissing the infant's forehead. "She's your daughter."

He hadn't seen her since the previous summer. After they made love, he told her about his plans to marry. She cried, but he steeled himself against her tears. He needed Cassandra. And he wanted her. For the house they were able to buy. So he could pay for law school, and focus solely on the demands of higher education. He needed Cassandra. Because his lust to be somebody would consume him otherwise.

"Ain't you gonna say something?" Eugenia asked.

Richard just stood there, staring at the mulatto baby he knew he'd made. But it was 1966. Racial tensions in the city were high. Blacks fought to desegregate their schools with organized boycotts, angry at the city for neglecting their youth, for perpetuating a structure of substandard, underfunded schools in their communities. A structure created by Seattle's laws and outright discrimination, which forbade blacks from living anywhere in the city besides the Central District and South Seattle. A few years before the citizens of Seattle had voted down an open housing ordinance by two to one, not wanting their neighborhoods overrun by those who sought equality.

"Everyone thinks it's so progressive here," Eugenia had said during one of those sweet summers, with her downy afro against his pillow and her long lashes petting her cheekbones. "Everyone thinks it's not racist like the South. But it's a lie. In the South, someone might spit at the ground and force you off the sidewalk, calling you a nigger to your face. Up here in the North, they may not spit and they may not call you names. But they'll smile and say a position's been filled after they've called you in for an interview. And that almost hurts worse. At least in the South you know where you stand. Here they allow you to hope while pulling the rug right out from under you."

It made him uncomfortable when Eugenia tried to talk to him about her experiences. In order to be with her, he'd have to take a stance. And he feared he'd find himself on the losing side of the fight.

"Well?" Eugenia asked, rocking the fussing baby in her arms.

Richard breathed deep until his chest caught. He expelled the air from his lungs.

"Everyone knows you get around, Eugenia."

But he knew she didn't.

"That baby could be anybody's."

But he knew she wasn't.

"Even if it is mine, I don't want it. This was fun, but it's better this way."

Once more, he steeled himself against her tears.

"That ain't true. I know you don't think that's true," she said, wiping her eyes.

Richard clenched his fists. He began closing the door, closing her out, and said the most honest thing he had in months.

"I don't want to raise a black baby, Eugenia."

"You can't let him go to jail, Eugenia."

Montgomery reached for the woman's shaking hand. A tear slipped from Eugenia's eye, guided down her face by the creases in her dark skin.

"He wasn't a perfect man. And I'm beginning to wonder if he was ever a good man. But I know him well enough to believe he'd never murder his own child."

"Oh, of course he didn't kill her!" Eugenia said. "She told me he was trying to give her money, trying to keep her out of trouble. But forget him, you know? He was too damn late to do anything for us!"

Montgomery pulled Eugenia into her arms and held her while she cried. The woman calmed, and Montgomery felt she was ready to hear the truth.

"If you don't tell Detective Rawlings the reason Richard took interest in Evie, you're no better a person than he was when he left you."

"What kind of man does that?" Eugenia wiped her face.

"Does what?"

"Just flips a switch, shuts off his feelings for the people he loves. How can someone do that?"

Montgomery struggled to speak through the dryness, as parched as the cotton of an abandoned field.

"I don't know."

&

IT WAS ALMOST CHRISTMAS. A cloud of smoke billowed from Sasha's pursed mouth as he stood alone in the alley behind the Central Tavern. It always happened before a show, no matter how many gigs they played. But tonight it was worse. His nerves were wrought, like acidic, brassy vines, so thick in his stomach they unfurled and burned his throat. These vines were pulling him down, depressing the muscles in his face, arms and heart. It was cold - his worn flannel did nothing to thwart the chill. But Sasha relished the city's icy embrace, and rubbed the goose bumps that prickled his forearms. He took the final drag of his self-roll, then ground it into the slick pavement beneath his boot. He wasn't looking forward to this show. It was the first time Fungus Reign would be headliners.

"To promote the band before the tour," their manager David had said.

But when Sasha looked at the deep, black sky, he saw a shooting star. And instantly he knew salvation was coming. It was either that, or his demise. Both were welcome, both were good, and he felt it in his toes. And this was as good a reason as any to take another bump. He pulled up the cuff of his paint-stained jeans, his favorite pair courtesy of The Salvation Army, removed a vial of his stash from inside his sock, held it up to his nose, pinched one nostril closed and inhaled until his lungs were full and his brain caught fire. And as quickly as that shooting star, now a dead rock lost to the universe, those metal vines loosened their hold.

The creak of the brass door cut into the silence.

"You ready man?"

It was Jay, holding the door open wide, his long, black hair tossing in the wind.

"Hell yeah," Sasha said.

The faces in the tavern were obscured by darkness from where he stood on the small stage. He was blinded by the contrast of black walls against neon beer signs, which hung behind the bar and in the windows facing the street. He knew Monti was out there. Because he felt her presence. Also, because he hadn't returned her flurry of pages.

"Hello," he said into the mic. "I'm Sasha Kent. This man here on drums is Jay Randall. And this is Penn Christiansen on bass. We are Fungus Reign."

He stepped away from the mic and played with his guitar strings. He usually gave the nod and Jay would count them down, but tonight he had doubts. He should be focused on their fans, on the friends who stayed after their sets and graciously delayed the hour-long drive back to Olympia to offer their support. He should play the songs he knew they loved. But instead he leaned towards his bandmates and said,

"I'm changing the opener."

Penn and Randall exchanged a look before nodding.

Sasha returned to the mic.

"This is a new song from our album, recently released, never played it live before. But it's playing on the radio now, so watch out I guess. And it's about, um…well its about this girl…the one who got away."

The crowd cheered loudly, but he drowned them out with a

hard riff. Jay picked up the beat, a heavy sound with open space, and Penn swayed and bobbed his head.

Sasha sang, quiet and low. He played his guitar so it wah wah'd, wailed and harmonized with his voice.

Blood and water drown me out again
I'll sink beneath the dock there is no heaven
I sit beside myself I have no friend
And when the evening comes there's no redemption

Jay smashed the cymbals and picked up the tempo. Sasha played a rhythmic phrase and Penn held the melody with his bass.

I'm gonna fall
I'm gonna fall, not too long
Won't be my dead mother's pride
And there'll be nowhere to hide
When you throw me away

He sang it loud, getting pulled into the song, stomping his foot the way he learned while playing gospel music in church. The venue was full, and the crowd pulsed and pushed against the stage's edge. Some people dove from the edge of the stage into a moshing sea of punks and rockers, carried on the slow, deep tide of Penn's bass.

I'm gonna fall, fall, fall
Bone marrow seeps through the nose
I'm torn inside out so it shows
When you throw me away!

He couldn't see her, but somehow he knew she was out there. His Salvation. Or his Demise. And the thrill of Monti Jackson was in the fact he didn't need to know which.

❦

MONTGOMERY STOOD in the back of the Central Tavern near the bar. It was as old as the saloon, which dated back to the 1890s according to the painted sign on the front window. She primped in the mirror behind the bartender, and it was so hazy it made her look antique. Liquor bottles lined the vintage wooden cabinet, blocking a portion of the cloudy glass. The walls were covered with photocopied posters in various shades of neon, advertising upcoming shows with local bands. Mixed between the posters hung pictures of artists who'd once come to play and who had since "made it." Artists like Jimi Hendrix. The air itself smelled haunted by the ghosts and stories of the past. Barstools sprouted from the cream and black tiled floor, and Montgomery took a seat at one of them.

She was two beers in before she heard that voice. God, that voice.

Blood and water drown me out again

Goosebumps raked down her neck. Her breathing became shallow and torpid. She felt as though she'd been given a sedative, and her mind went completely blank. The voice that sang those words grated against the steely sound of his guitar. She couldn't make out his face from where she sat, as he swung his long, blonde hair and thrashed around the stage. He possessed her, by the memories he'd dislodged with that tormented voice.

He stood so still in front of the microphone, and she was certain their eyes locked.

Drink the broth I made for you my friend
Or push the hand away that burns it's own skin
Keep the crutch you leveraged from my ribs
Just leave the broken glass you watched me cut with

She saw a flash of images. A boy in red pajamas. A Christmas tree. The rain. A door locked, her hand slipping on the knob as she tried to get back inside. A broken shard of Christmas cookie. Her tears. Sasha's sad eyes, darkened by circles beneath them. His pained, knowing smile. Sasha Coen. Always Sasha. The boy she'd met that Christmas Eve, a night shrouded by absent mothers, was now a ghost. And the man he became looked like one - pale, ethereal and with gaping holes where the eyes should've been. Acid rose in her throat, and she pushed it down by gulping her beer. She stared into her empty glass, but Sasha's voice forced her to see.

I'm gonna crawl, I'm gonna crawl, I'm gonna crawl
Sun rising over my grave
Forever I'll be your slave
When you show me the way!

After the show a girl jumped onstage and wrapped her arms around Sasha's neck. She was wearing a short black skirt, a frayed and cropped t-shirt, and a long, leopard-collared trench coat. Her hair was cut into a pixie and dyed hot pink. Sasha kissed the top of her head, and suddenly Montgomery felt very plain, very normal in her oversized yellow sweatshirt, jean jacket and plum leggings. She'd seen this same girl working at the Velvet Room, and had a feeling this was the "Carmine" Percy had asked about.

Montgomery pretended she wasn't disappointed to see Sasha with another woman. She pretended she hadn't come because of what he'd said about her lack of a personal life. And that he hadn't been the best performer she'd ever seen, and made her so immensely proud her eyes stung. She'd gotten so good at pretending.

Montgomery went home alone. She made a pot of coffee, and curled up beneath a blanket on her couch. Every time she closed her eyes, she saw faces. Faces she loved. Or faces she loathed. She could no longer tell the difference.

Sasha had opened Pandora's box with his music. Images from her childhood came flashing across the dark space between her eyelids like a silent reel of home videos. Flashes of Reggie and Birdie and Daan, adults who had failed her in one way or another. And Sasha, the only one who didn't yet the only one she feared.

CHAPTER THIRTY-TWO

IT WAS the beginning of happy hour on a Friday afternoon, capping the second week of January. The eighties were officially over, and Sasha was glad to see them go. He sat with the members of Fungus Reign at a wooden booth inside the Comet Tavern near the corner of Pike and Broadway. The electric, red sign that hung in the window like a trap for beer flies reflected off the sheen of Jay's black hair. Penn tapped a notepad with the eraser of his pencil.

Sasha drummed his thumb against the table, bouncing his knee in time with his pounding headache. He pulled his black hoodie tighter around himself, which he wore as an excuse for the chills. It had been an entire day since he used cocaine. Seeing Monti at the Central Tavern felt like striking a match. There was a glimmer of fire, a small flame that wouldn't last unless it found something to burn. And God, was he burning for her. He'd played cat and mouse with his baggies for weeks, until he reached a moment of clarity once he'd snorted through his stash. He had no hope of being with her while he continued to use. Not after everything she'd been through.

"Here's the tour schedule," Penn said, passing a copy to Sasha and Randall. "We leave next month, and I'm going to be honest guys... I don't feel like we're ready. We should be practicing everyday so we don't embarrass ourselves."

Jay read over the schedule. "I think we sound fine. We've got the songs down cold." Sasha could tell Jay was only half-listening, because his head turned away from the table and his eyes bored into the backside of a girl playing pinball across the bar.

"But practice has been sporadic the last few months," Penn said. "I don't feel like we're as in sync as we used to be."

There was a pause, a gap that Sasha knew he was meant to fill. But he was too busy spiraling, sinking into a cold, black sea. And there, in that black abyss he saw Tommy's face, grimacing with the pain of unrequited love. That last night before Tommy overdosed was the moment for Sasha to get real, and he'd been too chicken to take it. He'd been unable save his friend because he was no better himself. Jay and Penn were at that same crossroad, the one where Sasha had veered right and left Tommy for dead. But instead of speaking up, they left these little gaps like breadcrumbs, as if Sasha was lost in a forest and could follow the silence until he found his way home. If they had something to say, then they should scream it. He loved screaming. It had been the only thing, other than cocaine, that made him want to leave his bed in the morning. Until Monti walked into that strip club.

"I don't think I want to go on tour," Sasha said quietly. Jay jerked his head around, and Penn rubbed the point where his nose met the space between his eyes.

"But 'Blood and Water' is playing on all the top rock stations, and MTV just put the video into rotation." Jay tapped the table until Sasha looked up from his lap. "At this point, we can't afford not to go," he said.

Penn chewed the inside of his cheek and stared at his beer. There was a power dynamic, and everyone knew what it looked like. A tall, lanky singer with blue eyes and a bluesy voice who composed and wrote nearly all the band's music. The label had said, "Fungus Reign is our biggest priority." But what they really meant was *Sasha Kent is our next revenue stream.*

"It's too late to cancel now," Penn said, though his lips barely moved. "It's only for a few months, and I could really use the money for my wedding. Lisa is really stressed out."

"What if we just go back to the way things were?" Sasha asked. "I liked playing in the small clubs, for people who were my friends. These label guys, these so-called fans are nothing but leeches."

The waitress came by.

"Another round?"

"No thanks," Jay said. "We'll take the check."

Penn wouldn't meet his eye.

"This started as a democracy..."

Sasha sighed. "Whatever. Let's just go then."

"It will be good," Penn said. "For you to see there's more to life than this Seattle scene."

"I know there's more," Sasha said. But what he didn't tell his bandmates was that he'd already lost it.

The band's house reeked of nightfall and havoc when Sasha returned home. People slept over stale toilet bowls and dressed themselves in vomit, singing anthems and declarations for chaos. The cabinets may as well have been filled with bras and dope, because that's how easy it was to get the vice everyone thought he wanted. Someone slipped a baggie into his hand as he walked by. He didn't have to ask anymore.

"God you smell so good," a pretty, drunk girl said.

"It's the smell of success," Sasha said. He sunk onto the couch and the girl curled into his side.

"Really?" she asked.

"No, not really. What you smell is just my body odor."

"Well, I really like it," she said. But what she meant was, *I'll give you all my love for free.*

Lines of coke stretched on the coffee table in front of him, like rowed fields ready for planting. And from those lines he could cultivate euphoria. It wasn't long before he broke the promise he'd made, the one Monti never knew about. And when those dope lies started preaching their sermon, they convinced him she never cared in the first place. What good would he do her, spiraling down into the wet darkness where even the sea monsters drowned?

❦

THREE WEEKS after the show at Central Tavern, Montgomery met Sasha at a restaurant in Greenwood, a small neighborhood just north of Ballard and west of Aurora Avenue. It was quiet like the suburbs, the perfect place for young families with its cluster of coffee shops, restaurants, and storefronts.

The Rickshaw was a popular American/Chinese dive with a red, pagoda-shaped roof. It had a red neon sign and a message board showcasing the specials. To add more flair, the top of the sign glowed bright yellow and there were decals shaped like men in sunhats pulling small carts.

Montgomery and Sasha sat in a small booth near the bar, hidden in a fog of cigarette smoke, and leaning close to be heard over the karaoke singers. It was two o'clock in the morning and Montgomery had just finished her shift.

"This place has the best almond chicken," Sasha said, shoving a piece into his mouth. He chewed slowly. "I was surprised you called. You usually just page me."

"Yeah, well you don't answer your pages. And I needed to talk to you. I want your advice about something."

"Are you worried you're dressed inappropriately?"

He grinned, then eyed her fishnets and low-cut blouse. She hadn't bothered changing back into her normal clothes.

"No." She licked the froth from her beer.

"So you dressed like that for me, then." Sasha winked.

Montgomery stared into her hands while her stomach flip-flopped.

"So what did you want to talk about?" Sasha asked.

"You been following the news about the Headbanger?"

"Of course."

"So you know Clarke Adamson's dad is the one accused of killing those girls that summer? And my mom?"

"Montgomery Laine Jackson, what kind of friend would I be if I didn't know? Get to the point." His admonishment was soft, and he placed his hand over hers.

She pulled her hand away.

"After you left—"

"After you rejected me."

"Whatever. After you left, I got busted for solicitation. Birdie was...gone, and Clarke's dad bailed me out. I'd spent enough time with the Market Kids to know how my life could've turned out. But Richard helped me. And now he's asked me to help him."

She told Sasha about how Richard had let her live in his pool house and work as a file clerk at his law firm.

The waitress came by, and Montgomery ordered two beers.

Sasha moved his chicken around the plate. "I'm not sure what it is you're asking me."

"The reason why Richard was able to help me was because he was trolling for prostitutes. He picked me up one night. And's he's asked me not to mention this when I testify. The fact that he solicited prostitutes would make him look more guilty."

"Well, don't they have any of the women he's 'worked' with as witnesses?"

"I'm not sure, but I doubt it. There's no way for the prosecution to find out who he's been with, and women working on that side of the law rarely come forward with information. And even if they did, it would be hard to make them seem credible in front of a jury."

"Do you think he's innocent."

Montgomery didn't hesitate. "Yes. He had a reputation as one of the good tricks. He was never violent." Montgomery stared into the frothy face of her beer. "I loved my mother, but she wasn't there for me when I needed her. She chose her addiction over her own daughter. I want to get the guy who killed her, so bad, but... I know

Richard never hurt anyone. And my mother left me. She left me the second she started using."

Sasha pursed his lips together and grabbed her hand again.

"I think you should cut Birdie some slack, but I can't tell you what to do."

"I testify tomorrow morning."

He pinched the bridge of his nose, then took a long drink, getting froth on his upper lip. His tongue whisked it away.

"Focus on those who do the most harm," he said.

They drank in silence, and just as Montgomery readied herself to leave Sasha said,

"I want to play a game."

He explained the rules, and called it "Secrets or Shots." Montgomery suspected he'd made it up on the spot.

They'd each take turns sharing a secret. If the secret came as a surprise, the listener had to drink. If the secret was known, the teller had to drink. The first to share seven secrets successfully, or to get the other too drunk to continue, was the winner. And the loser had to sing "Bohemian Rhapsody" in front of the entire bar.

Sasha ordered two more beers and six shots of tequila.

"The shots are for the big secrets. If I think I've got a juicy one that I'm certain you don't know, I can bet you one of these."

Montgomery knew she shouldn't play. Sasha was still her criminal informant.

"I'll go first," he said. "Remember Julie Pataky from third grade? I'm the one who cut her ponytail off during 'Heads Up, 7 Up.'"

Montgomery struggled to drink her beer because she was laughing so hard. "My God, why did you do that? She wouldn't come back to school for a week!"

Sasha shrugged. "I heard her call you a jungle bunny at recess the day before and it pissed me off. Your turn."

Butterflies formed in Montgomery's stomach. He was making the game more personal than she was comfortable with.

"Clarke Adamson had a small penis," she said.

"Drink," Sasha said.

Montgomery raised an eyebrow at him, so he continued.

"We had gym together and I saw him in the locker room. He was trying to compare himself to Jared Abrams in the shower. Plus, it was so obvious he was overcompensating for something." He smirked at her while she sipped her beer, but didn't ask the obvious question, which was whether or not she'd slept with Clarke.

"My turn," he said. He pushed one of his shots towards her. "I hooked up with Tommy..."

"Drink!" Montgomery said.

"Let me finish. I hooked up with Tommy. Sometimes, I feel like I did it just to spite you. It pissed me off that you might judge me for being gay, or that your feelings for me held any sort of contingency. Other times, I feel like I did it so he'd always be tethered to me. So I'd never be without some form of adoration. And I've never felt worse about anything in my life."

"Why is that?"

He wouldn't look her in the eye as he spoke. "Our friendship was never the same. There was always this imbalance to it. I knew he was in love with me, and that what I'd done gave him false hope. We'd talk on the phone or he'd come visit, and he'd always say 'Find me once L.A. is out of your system.' I lied every time, 'You already know I will.' I couldn't tell him I wasn't in the closet, that I actually liked hooking up with all those girls on tour. I wouldn't tell him that I could never return his love, but still needed it for myself. That him being the only man I'd been intimate with didn't mean anything."

"When you say intimate, what do you mean exactly?"

"It was innocent. But I was being cruel."

"Why did you do it?"

He looked at her pointedly. "He was the only person I had in my life who loved me for me, and not for what I could do." Sasha stared into his beer again. "But getting used by someone who is supposed to care for you... It's almost impossible to reconcile. And then once you do, it shatters the globe you thought was your world. It's my fault Tommy's dead."

"Tommy overdosed. That's not on anybody but him."

"It's not that simple, Monti."

"How do you know?"

"Because nothing is."

Montgomery threw the tequila back.

"Did you think you might be gay back then?" she asked. Bar glasses clinked loudly over the karaoke, but her ears honed into the vacancy made by Sasha's pause.

"No," he said finally. "But I've never believed in labels either. Your turn."

She pushed one of her shots towards him.

"You remember that night when Reggie got arrested? Well, the next day I was cleaning up that burned mess someone left on our porch. Daan came over. He called me a nigger and said I'd only cause you trouble."

Sasha clenched his jaw. His hand rested on the table. She didn't realize she'd been holding her breath until he picked up the shot and drank.

"When I told you I kissed Treesha, I intentionally left out the part about hating it. Just to see if you'd be jealous."

Montgomery took a swig from her beer. Her head was spinning and her hands tingled. She watched Sasha drum his fingers against the table, a soothing rhythm tapped out by his thumb ring, and she felt her composure getting pulled into his hands.

"It broke my heart when you left," she said.

Sasha drank.

"I could hear everything through the walls. Every time you cried. I heard every lie you ever told me. You didn't trust me. And it broke my heart."

Montgomery drank.

"I don't want to play anymore," she said after a pause.

Sasha took one of his shots.

"I left because my family basically disowned me after I got arrested. Because they assumed the worst about me instead of asking what was wrong."

"No more," she said.

"I never cared if you were a prostitute, or if you screwed a thousand guys. I only cared that none would be me."

"You win!" she said, throwing up her hands.

"Last round." His mouth was red and his eyes sparkled. "Just one more each. You next."

There were three words she wanted to say. Because anything else seemed pointless. Three words she'd known nothing about until that summer. But once she said them, there'd be no going back. And because he was her criminal informant, acting on her desire would mean putting her career on the line, the stability she'd fought so hard for. So she pushed one of her shots towards him, and in a rush of words said,

"I treasured those nights when we were kids and I was so hungry I licked the crumbs from your face while watching you sleep in a bed that felt like my own."

Sasha smiled, and drank his last shot.

"Since the day we met, I've been a complete dumbass…"

"Nope, drink!" she said.

He held up a finger.

"Let me finish." He sipped his beer. "Since the day we met, I've been a complete dumbass, but also just… just dumbstruck in love with you."

She sighed, and clasped her hands in her lap. She couldn't look up from the table. And so Monti drank.

They left the restaurant together, and walked into a dark and misty night. Their cars were parked on the street behind the Rickshaw. As they rounded the front of the building, Montgomery thought of one more secret she needed to know. She grabbed Sasha's hand.

"Why did you steal that money from your grandparents?"

He chucked her on the chin.

"To pay your rent, stupid."

She grabbed him by the sheepskin collar of his jean jacket and kissed him. He pushed her into the back wall of the Rickshaw, and the brick pressed hard into her shoulder blades. She savored the tobacco on his breath as his tongue felt the roof of her mouth and flicked the space between her front teeth. Her fingers fumbled with his belt. He pressed his forehead against hers and groaned.

"Hell yeah. Take it off, Monti."

Her fingers were cold from the winter rain, and she struggled with the buckle.

"Take it off, Monti," he said with more urgency.

His hair smelled like the ocean and sand and sweet magnolia blossoms, and it brushed against her face and tickled her collarbone so she struggled with the buckle.

He grunted and grabbed both her hands, pinning them above her head and holding them there with one palm. He used the other to snake up her skirt and rip at her fishnets until he could rub his thumb over the sensitive flesh of her mound, making her gasp against his neck.

Suddenly, a loud crash startled them and they jumped apart. A raccoon emerged from the dumpster behind the building, chewing and holding its bounty between little, black fingers. Montgomery laughed, realizing how cold she was and wrapping her leather jacket tighter around her. But Sasha wasn't laughing. He seemed agitated and anxious, and his hands trembled.

"Jesus," he murmured, turning his sad eyes on her. "I'm so sorry, Monti. You deserve better."

He walked her to the main street, waved down a passing cab and, before she could protest, disappeared into the night.

CHAPTER THIRTY-THREE

IN THE SUMMER OF 1981, Montgomery had felt abandoned. She'd felt forgotten. Discarded. Unseen. Now she sat in a sterile courtroom downtown and had the attention of what felt like the entire city. It was a cold morning, and she was hung over, distracted by the memory of Sasha's kiss. The rows in the gallery were filled by the Headbanger victims' families, reporters and spectators, and she couldn't bring herself to look at a single one.

The prosecutor looked flustered, hair disheveled as though he'd been raking his hands through it. The defense attorney looked smug, as if he knew he'd found enough reasonable doubt to get his client acquitted. Montgomery wasn't allowed to hear testimony or follow the trial until after she testified, but it seemed the favor leaned towards Richard. And she was still unsure of where her loyalty should lie.

"How did you first come to meet the defendant?" the prosecutor asked.

Montgomery looked at Richard. He leaned forward in his seat, his brow furrowed and his eyes earnest. He'd abandoned a family that needed him for a wealthy one that didn't. He cheated on his wife by paying black women for sex. He was a weak man who couldn't choose between Ricky from the Streets or Richard from the Hill. And she knew exactly how he felt - torn between the life he once belonged to and the person he wanted to be. How could she blame him when he'd been the one to offer the stability she needed?

Montgomery cleared her throat.

"I went to school with his son. We played football at the park together, and I met Richard at some point."

"Did you have any other type of interaction with the defendant?"

"I got into some trouble when I was younger. Richard helped me."

"Do you remember when this occurred?"

"It was either December of '81 or January of '82."

"And do you remember the date when you last saw your mother?"

"Not the exact date. But it was a week or two before Christmas."

"How did Richard help you?"

"He let me live in his pool house."

A murmur erupted from the gallery.

"What kind of trouble were you in?"

The defense attorney stood.

"Objection, your honor. Juvenile records are expunged once the offender turns eighteen. The witness shouldn't be obligated to disclose this information when it's not relevant to the case."

The judge looked at Montgomery. "I'll let you decide. Do you want to answer the question?"

She shook her head.

The judge nodded. "Sustained."

The prosecutor continued.

"Did the defendant have any contact with you before he invited you to live in his pool house?"

"No... No he did not."

The prosecutor tapped his knuckles against the table. The smile he gave strained across his face. He walked towards the witness stand.

"Detective Jackson, can you tell me what you remember about the last day you saw your mother alive?"

Her eyes smarted as she recounted the details and the fight they had. The prosecutor went to his table and returned holding a photograph.

"Will you please identify the people in this picture?"

She looked at the photo. Birdie and Richard were in his driveway, his maroon sports car behind them. They looked as if they were in a deep discussion.

"My mother and Richard," she said.

"And this outfit she's wearing. Was this the outfit she wore the last day you saw her alive?"

"Yes."

"Thank you. No further questions."

The defense attorney stood and approached the stand.

"Detective Jackson, did the defendant ever harm you in any way?"

"No, he did not."

"Did you ever get the sense that he may have wanted to harm you?"

"No, not at all."

"Did you ever have any type of interaction that was inappropriate, or sexual in any way?"

Montgomery hesitated. "No," she said.

The defense attorney looked at his client. He looked into the gallery, and then at the jury.

"Just to reiterate, your mother was Birdie James, the last victim, correct?"

"That's correct."

"I'm sorry for your loss." He turned towards the jury and dropped his head, then looked back at the witness stand.

"How would you describe your life with your mother?"

Montgomery licked her lips. "There were good and bad things. My mother was a talented singer, so there was always music playing. We danced a lot. Watched cartoons. But we were very poor. I often didn't have enough to eat and was left to fend for myself."

"Were there any extenuating circumstances that led to your family's struggles?"

"I believe my mother had a significant drug problem throughout my childhood. She uh, she worked as a prostitute downtown."

"Did the defendant ever meet your mother?"

"I'm not sure…"

"During the summer of 1981, did you try out for the Ballard football team?"

"Yes I did."

"And how did you do?"

She shrugged. "I was the best on the field. Not the strongest or necessarily the fastest. But I knew the game better than anyone out there."

"And did you make the team?"

"No."

"Were you angry about that?"

"Yes, I was. It's a no cut sport, but the coach said I had a bad attitude."

Montgomery heard a familiar snicker, and noticed Clarke sitting in the row behind his father. She made eye contact, and he popped the collar of the mustard letterman's jacket he wore, the one he'd stolen from her that night at the party. The one Birdie had given her for her sixteenth birthday. It was as if he'd known she would testify, and had worn it specifically as some kind of trophy or way to taunt her. Judging by the discoloration of his face, Clarke had recently lost a fight, which soothed Montgomery enough to ignore him.

She remembered Sasha's advice. *Focus on those who do the most harm.* The person who had harmed her the most was Birdie. Because Birdie was the one who mattered.

The defense attorney continued his questioning.

"Now, can you tell me if you remember a time when the defendant and your mother may have met?"

Montgomery sighed. "Yeah. I got into a fight with Clarke. Um, Clarke Adamson, the defendant's son. Richard brought him to my house to apologize."

"So your mother and the defendant met before her murder. And how long was it from the last day you saw your mother to when the defendant invited you to stay at his pool house?"

Montgomery shrugged. "A few months maybe."

"So, it's possible that your mother had gone to Richard, a man who worked to get troubled juveniles the help and guidance they needed to become viable members of society, because she wanted help for the child she couldn't take care of."

Montgomery bristled beneath the collar of her blazer. The prosecutor spoke before she could answer.

"Objection, calls for speculation."

"Withdrawn your honor." The defense attorney looked at Montgomery and smiled. "Do you remember how your mother received the defendant?"

Richard leaned forward in his chair. She looked into his eyes, and knew what he wanted. But she'd paid her debt. And her gut was telling her that something was off. Why had her mother been in Richard's driveway that day, and why was he lying about it?

"Yes," she said. "My mother was angry and told them to leave."

The defense attorney turned and looked at Richard. "Are you sure she was angry?" he asked.

She remembered what her mother had called Richard that day. *Alleybat.* She didn't know what it meant. And she didn't like the way Richard's chin lifted with entitlement as she prepared to answer.

"Yes, I'm positive she was angry. The reason Clarke and I fought was because he called me a 'Spook.'" The color drained from the defense attorney's face. He started to speak, but Montgomery cut him off.

"It's a racial slur used against black people. It's highly offensive, and my mom was ready to beat some ass when she found out what Clarke had called me."

"Young lady, I don't condone swearing in my courtroom," the

judge said. Montgomery barely heard, she was too focused on staring Richard down - his face had turned redder than his hair and he clenched his jaw until a vein emerged, throbbing, from his forehead.

"No further questions," the defense attorney said.

"Redirect your honor?" the prosecutor asked.

"You may proceed."

"Detective Jackson, from your experience, where do you think people learn to be racist, or to use words like the defendant's son used to hurt you?"

She shifted in her chair, and thought of Daan Coen. She'd been so afraid that Sasha's kindness was merely pity, and wondered if that would've been the case if Daan hadn't been so brazenly bigoted.

"Society plays a large role, the history of this country and misinformation. But in my experience, when I was young and bullied and called 'nigger' by a classmate, I always assumed they'd learned that word at home."

An idea was beginning to form, though it was still shapeless. But good cops learned to follow this instinct. She looked at Richard. He held a pencil in his hand and squeezed until it snapped.

"I always assumed those little assholes learned that word from their parents."

"YOU EMBARRASSED ME IN THERE. My family too. After everything he did for you, I'd expect you to be grateful."

Clarke had followed Montgomery outside onto Third Avenue. Likely for the same reason she had felt Richard's green glare on her back as she left the courtroom. A sheet of drizzle hung down from the sky, and it sizzled as it touched her hot skin.

"I just told the truth."

"The truth? Your mom was a welfare queen who tried to scam my dad out of his money. Those girls were trash and wouldn't have died if they'd made better decisions. That's the truth."

Montgomery spun so quickly her sneakers screeched against the wet pavement. Clarke stood in front of her, with a beaten face in the process of healing, yet still so painfully handsome it didn't seem fair he'd also been born into privilege. And such a waste of space that he wore a second hand letterman's jacket he'd stolen from a sixteen-year-old girl who had nothing of value she could call her own, just to remind her she was powerless.

She lunged at him, grabbing the bottom of the jacket and pulling it over his head so he couldn't move his arms. She kicked out the back of his knees and pushed his face into the soggy cement. She tore the jacket from his body and held it triumphantly as he struggled to regain his composure.

"What the hell was that!" he said.

"This is mine."

"Give it back!" He whispered the command, though it sounded like a scream. Her blood curdled at the menace on his face. How dare he? This was the last gift her mother had given her, the last good memory. She squared her hips and took a deep breath.

"You want it? Come and get it."

Clarke spit on the ground and waved her off, slinking back into the courtroom.

AT THE WANDERLUST Saloon on Aurora Avenue, Montgomery nursed a beer at the bar. She and Victor had been working around the corner, this time at a place called The Georgian Motel, busting johns with her as bait. She was dressed simply, wearing jeans over a pink leotard and a black leather jacket, but had that look, the desperate attempt at making eye contact with any man who came into view.

A tired prostitute sat on the stool next to her. She wore a spandex dress with ruffled sleeves and exposed shoulders, and the folds in her shape caused the dress to bunch around the midriff. Her deep, red skin was flat, her black hair was thinning and her fuchsia lipstick marked a set of wine-stained teeth.

"It's slow tonight," the prostitute said. "You have any luck?"

"Yeah. You?"

"Got a couple earlier this afternoon. But nothing since then. I guess it's just one of those nights. The rain is keeping everyone at home. You'd think it'd drive more people out here, out of boredom and whatnot. Course, if I was still young and pretty like you I might've got more work. You like music?" the prostitute asked.

"Yeah, I like music."

The prostitute extended a hand. "My name's Esmerelda."

Montgomery introduced herself.

"I'm Scarlett."

"You got a quarter?" Esmerelda asked. She took the spare change Montgomery gave her and walked over to the jukebox. Montgomery listened as the pages turned, *whick, whick, whick*.

A voice came from behind her.

"Your name is Scarlett?"

Montgomery turned and saw a familiar face, one that had come from the direction of the bathroom. It was Charlene.

"Cain't No More" began to play.

"Kinda depressing, don't you think?" Montgomery said when Esmerelda returned. Her mother had become a "thing," a fad, a sad story with a beautiful soundtrack. But where were her fans when Birdie was strung out and penniless?

"Slow night, slow song," Esmeralda said. She took her seat at the bar again. Charlene sat on the other side of Montgomery.

"You're just riding the bandwagon, like everyone else," Montgomery said.

Esmeralda gave her a sideways look and pursed her mouth together as if she'd said, *the fuck you say?*

"I would've been playing Birdie James years ago. Not my fault they only just added her to the playlist. That was my girl."

Montgomery sipped her beer, real slow so she had time to think.

"You knew her?"

Esmeralda chuckled. "Hell yeah, I knew her. We were working this strip when you were still eating your Lip Smackers."

Esmerelda motioned at Charlene.

"We got a new one. This is Scarlett."

"I see that," Charlene said, giving Montgomery a knowing look.

"So how'd she go from singing to this?" Montgomery pointed to the space between herself and Esmeralda. She'd heard what Milton said, that Birdie hadn't used during the years he'd known her. But she had got the impression he may have been trying to protect her mother's memory.

Esmeralda shrugged. "You think I'd be here if I knew the answer?" She sighed, swirling her drink in a tumbler stained with soap. "I do know she took it real hard when she lost her record deal."

A man walked into the bar, and Esmerelda perked up. She sidled over to his table, leaned close to his ear. Her boisterous laugh filled the room, and she sat across from him, bobbing her leg and stiletto heel.

"Scarlett, huh?" Charlene stirred her drink with a straw.

"Yeah. What's your name?"

Charlene turned and looked at Montgomery as if the action itself exhausted her. It had only been eight years, but her appearance made it seem like twenty-five. There were lines around her eyes, and they didn't look to have been made by her smiles. Her voice was raspy and her cuticles were brown, as if stained by tobacco.

"You must be new to this line of work," Charlene said. "Because the girl I met would've been hard by now."

"I don't know you," Montgomery said. She threw some cash onto the bar and readied to leave.

"One of two things. You're either new because you quit before getting started back then, or you're a cop. Either one I could do damage with. So how about you stop playing games and stop acting like I ever did anything but try to look out for you."

Montgomery sat back down.

303

"I saw your mom on the news," Charlene said. "I'm sorry."

"Thanks."

"Did you testify?"

"Yeah."

Esmerelda sauntered back.

"Guy was a dud," she said. "This sucks."

"So quit," Montgomery said.

"Excuse me?"

Both Esmerelda and Charlene looked at Montgomery with the bitter rage of someone who'd just been slapped in the face.

"Quit dating. Neither of you seem to like it, or are better off for it."

"Oh, and you do?" Esmerelda asked.

Montgomery looked at Charlene, who merely shrugged in response.

Esmerelda eyed her. "You a cop or something?"

A breaking news headline scrolled across the screen of the television behind the bar. It was a segment about the coming verdict for the Headbanger Murders, and silenced the few barflies sprinkled around the dive, as well as Esmerelda. There was a clip of Richard testifying in court, looking both handsome and sympathetic. Eugenia followed, admitting he'd been trying to help the first victim, his daughter Evie Tucker.

And then the reporter spoke.

Another twist in the case happened when the daughter of the last victim, local singer Birdie James, testified that the defendant had helped her get off the streets. Now it will be up to the jury to decide whether the former candidate for City Attorney is a cold-blooded killer, or a misunderstood philanthropist.

Charlene gawked at Montgomery.

"You said that?"

"It was true."

"Yeah, but like, did you tell them the other stuff? Like how he picked up girls downtown all the time?"

Montgomery shook her head.

"What is wrong with you? Where's your respect for Birdie? When I met you all you wanted was to protect to her."

"Sending an innocent man to jail won't bring her back."

"I don't get it," Charlene said, shaking her head.

"You want to know what I don't get? Why beautiful women like you and Esmerelda and my mother put yourself in harm's way just so you can get high."

She stopped them before they could speak the addict's lie.

"Yeah, I can tell both of you are into something."

"Honey, you think that's why we do this?" Esmerelda put her hand over Montgomery's and stroked it the way Birdie would have done.

"It's true, some of the girls out here are working to support their habit. But just as many of them only start working for one reason," Esmerelda said.

"And what's that?"

Esmerelda slapped the bar. "Bitch, money!"

Charlene chuckled and flagged the bartender for another drink.

"My mom always told me she worked at this bar," Montgomery said, after a pause.

"The girls on Aurora come to this spot, before and after," Esmerelda said. "Commiserate and share knowledge. Honestly, I'd be disturbed if your mom hadn't lied to you about what she did for a living."

"I turned to the streets because for me, no home was safe," Charlene said. "I started dating because living outside made me feel less than human. Rifling through garbage to eat made me feel less than human. At least if I dated, I'd only be subjected to one thing that made me feel less than human. And then I started using, so I wouldn't have to feel at all."

Montgomery gulped her beer to stave off the creeping dryness in her mouth.

"Women like us get paid to let men abuse us. The habit takes the sting off our suffering." Esmerelda touched Montgomery's face. "It was no different for your mother."

The man from the table motioned for Esmerelda to leave with him. Montgomery had to control the urge to trail them and make sure she stayed safe.

"I still don't get it," Montgomery said.

The chime from the bell hanging on the door rang out for one more happy customer. She knew this meant Esmerelda was gone, her life in the hands of someone who'd make her an object.

"I was poor. I had no money. I was willing to do whatever was necessary. And I never did drugs."

Charlene rolled her eyes to the ceiling, then dropped her head so she peered into Montgomery's face.

"You always seemed to think you could have one without the other. That you could toe both lines, the straight world and the one I live in. And maybe you could've. Maybe you would've been strong enough to keep from getting hurt. But the fact is, you barely got a taste."

"But I—"

Charlene grabbed Montgomery's neck and pressed their foreheads together. She smelled like wet pavement and despair. "We're not all born with the same amount of fight."

Montgomery felt Charlene's tears against her face. She felt Birdie's tears. She felt her own. She thought of the day they moved to The Bridgewater. Reggie was skeptical, talking about corporate mongrels and spineless bandmates, words that were meaningless to Montgomery back then. But Birdie was dancing, and she'd pressed her forehead against Montgomery's and whispered, *This is our castle. And I'm going to make it work. It's all gravy, baby.*

Was it truly that simple? That Birdie's choice for a life on the street had been economical, a result of lost income and great expectations? Perhaps those afternoons when Montgomery came home to a locked door, or Birdie's hushed insistence that she *git!*

when someone rang their doorbell, were evidence of a love language Birdie couldn't translate.

"Okay," Montgomery whispered. "Okay. I get it."

Charlene pulled away and sipped her drink.

"So what's the gang up to now?" Montgomery asked. "How's Yoko and Scuzzo and Coral?"

"Scuzzo got shot a few years ago, robbed for his product. And the cops think the Green River Killer got Yoko."

"That's terrible."

"That's the life."

"And Coral?"

"Coral's been missing for a few months now."

"Did you tell the police?"

"Of course. Took long enough for someone to take me seriously, though. Some detective, Rollings or something, he's worried the Headbanger got to her before he got to him."

An image of the lanky black girl, her pretty face broken and beaten in an alley, dislodged from Montgomery's memory.

Richard's face came back onto the television for another news segment.

"Know what the word is?" Charlene asked.

"What?"

"Someone got away from the Hunter. Someone knows who killed your mother."

"You think he's guilty?" Montgomery asked, pointing at the television.

"I don't know," Charlene said. "He looks straight enough, but then again... Sometimes the straight ones are more messed up than we are."

CHAPTER THIRTY-FOUR

IT WAS FEBRUARY. Rawlings squeezed his stress ball tight in his fist, but it wasn't helping. He was furious. The Headbanger jury was hung and the judge declared a mistrial. Richard Adamson had skated past his fate, and now the County Prosecutor was hesitant to retry the case. His smoking gun, the mood ring found in Richard's possession that once belonged to Evie, had been explained away. Richard wasn't a killer, just a bad father who found his daughter's ring in his car and wanted to keep it to remember her.

All the victims had been dumped at the locations where they'd been found, all except for Evie, who had died in a pool of her own blood beneath the Ballard Bridge. The others had been killed in unknown, dark and lonely places. Then moved to another dumpsite, which made finding another smoking gun all the more impossible. Something needed to break the case open again, otherwise Richard Adamson would get away with murder.

Rawlings squeezed the stress ball tighter. After Margaret had given him the photo of Birdie and Richard in the driveway, he'd interviewed Detective Jackson and felt she was hiding something. It hadn't bothered him at the time. When he first began investigating the Headbanger Murders in the summer of '81, he made a point to interview as many Market Kids as were willing. And Detective Jackson had the kind of face that was impossible to forget - gray eyes against skin the color of a sun-bleached, brown paper bag, black, kinky hair down to her shoulders, and the handsome set of a stubborn jaw. He watched her face during her testimony, saw the subtle change in her expression as knowledge settled in. Her body seemed to buzz with adrenaline, like every good cop who's just found a missing piece to a secondhand puzzle. And now Rawlings wanted inside her brain so he could connect the dots she was hesitant to connect herself.

He picked up the phone and asked her to come to Headquarters.

An hour later, she breezed over to his cubicle with her eyebrows raised.

"What's going on with Day-Tawn?" he asked. "I'd like to put that shooting down."

Jackson sighed. "I think I've been made. He completely ghosted me. Won't respond to my calls or pages."

"I've got a fourteen-year-old kid with a bullet in his face because he sold a few grams while standing on the wrong slab of pavement. His first day on the job. Day-Tawn is my only eyewitness."

"I hear you."

"Do you? Because you can't be good at this job and play it safe. You can't play the middle Jackson, you pick one side or the other. Whose side are you on?"

"I said I hear you."

She turned to leave.

"Those Headbanger victims? They were your age when Richard let you live in his pool house. Imagine they weren't too different than you were, at that age. Imagine you and your mom had more in common than you thought."

She clenched her jaw. If she hadn't heard before, she was definitely listening now.

"You didn't prove your case."

"All the evidence points to him."

"But it's not enough. You must be missing something."

"I had a smoking gun." He thrust a school photo of Evie into Jackson's hands, and pointed at the mood ring she wore. "I found that ring in his bedside table. Her mother confirmed it was her ring."

"Like I said, you must be missing something."

Her voice had grown louder. He sensed her desperation. Sometimes, when interrogating guilty suspects, there was this moment where they began to believe there was still hope. Not all people who'd done bad things had done them because they wanted to, and when pushed just the right way they gave it up faster than a prom date on ecstasy. He'd give her a bite and sit back while she proceeded to gorge herself on the leftovers.

"Yellow fibers."

"Yellow fibers…"

"Right. We found them on Naomi Watkins, the girl left in the junkyard. The only piece of evidence I couldn't tie to Richard Adamson."

She nodded, biting her bottom lip as if she were trying to decide something.

"I heard someone got away."

"Doesn't surprise me. I've always believed someone out there knows who committed these murders. Problem is, working girls don't always report their assaults."

"Problem is, people call them 'working girls.'"

"Then what would you call them?"

He knew she'd taken his bait by her answer.

"Survivors."

"Ey, what you doing here?"

Day-Tawn had answered the door of that low-income apartment on Yesler in the Central District, with bloodshot eyes and malt liquor on his breath. Montgomery had shown up without calling first, without an invitation. This was her first mistake.

"I need to re-up," she said, matching his hostile tone with her own entitled one.

"Let her in," a voice called from somewhere inside the house.

Day-Tawn sucked his teeth and opened the door just wide enough for her to slip through. Montgomery followed him down a set of creaky, wooden steps into a den filled with smoke. The beams were exposed and insulation pushed its way between the bare wall studs. A young man wearing a Sonics sweatshirt and matching green Reeboks sat on a bean bag chair playing Nintendo. He was stocky and had racing stripes buzzed into his fade.

"This is Rico," Day-Tawn said, picking up the second controller and sitting on the open bean bag chair.

Both men proceeded to play Mario Bros, and seemingly forgot Montgomery was in the room.

"I gotta be somewhere, so..."

Rico threw the controller down after his Mario died.

"You messed me up!" He glared at Montgomery. Without looking at Day-Tawn he said, "Run to the store. I want some Jujyfruits and a strawberry pop. I'll take care of this one."

Day-Tawn muttered under his breath and trudged up the stairs. Montgomery listened as the front door opened and closed with a slam.

Rico pulled out a vial of cocaine, held it to his nose and snorted. He offered it to Montgomery.

"No, I don't do that shit. I'm all business." This was her second mistake.

Rico stared at her face, and not because he liked what he saw. Montgomery felt the hairs on the back of her neck raise and recalled what Reggie had told her.

I been hearing about this new girl selling dope. A high yellow girl with gray eyes. Now how many of them you think live in Seattle?

"Know what? I'm just gonna go. I'll call Day-Tawn later."

As she moved towards the stairs, Rico reached out and grabbed her left wrist. Her reaction was automatic. And it was also her third mistake. Montgomery rotated her arm and grabbed Rico's tricep for leverage as she spun around to strike him in the face with her opposite elbow. He grunted, but like the bait in a dog fight, he seemed to feel no pain, keeping his grip on her wrist. Blood oozed from his broken eyebrow and he grinned with menace as he pointed the gun he'd been holding at Montgomery's face.

"I knew you were a cop."

Montgomery put her hands up.

"My partner is around the corner."

Rico frisked her, running his hands along her waist and thighs, and crouching down to check her ankles.

"No radio. No badge. No gun. If you're telling the truth, it won't matter. I'll be long gone before anyone finds you," he said.

As he moved to stand Montgomery pushed the gun away and head-butted him in the space between his eyes.

"You bitch!" he screamed as she ran for the stairs.

She'd only made it a few steps before Rico grabbed her ankle and yanked her violently back onto the floor of the den. He held one of her arms behind her back and used his knees to hold her legs still. He ripped at her jeans, forcing them away from her waist.

"I'm going to split you in two and then I'll blow your fucking head off."

He pushed the gun hard against her temple. Montgomery tried to scream, but the weight of his body pushed all the air from her lungs. She squeezed her eyes shut and said a prayer for Sasha when a shot reverberated through the hollow den. Montgomery's ears rang, and it took her a moment to realize she was still alive.

She pushed Rico's dead body away. Day-Tawn stood at the bottom of the staircase, holding a gun.

"Dude is crazy," Day-Tawn said. "Out of his mind. Shot a four-teen-year-old kid a few months ago over some bullshit. Makes us all look bad." He helped Montgomery to her feet. She was too stunned to speak, could only stare questioningly at the young criminal who had saved her life. But as though he could read her mind, Day-Tawn answered her question with one of his own.

"Ain't you Reggie's girl?"

Montgomery gave Day-Tawn her blood-splattered clothes and accepted a pair of sweats. She'd decided she was okay with his street form of justice after he'd told her all the terrible things Rico was capable of, including the shooting Rawlings was trying to solve. She drove to Headquarters and told her sergeant she was taking personal leave, that her mother's death and trial had taken a toll on her mental well-being. And then she went home, curled up on her couch with a cup of chamomile tea, and made a phone call to the King County Jail.

"Thank you," she said.

"No need." Reggie's voice sounded congested.

"Is it okay if I call you every now and then?" she asked.

"I think I'd be alright with that."

They were silent for a moment, just listening to each other breathe in and out of the receiver. And then Montgomery asked a question.

"What's an alleybat?"

CHAPTER THIRTY-FIVE

IT WAS a cold morning at the end of February when Sasha got a page. He recognized the number of the band's manager David, the liaison between the artist and the death of creativity, otherwise known as the corporate label. Sasha went to the kitchen to call him back.

"The tour is cancelled," David said.

Sasha leaned against the counter. Peach tile, his mother's favorite color.

"Alright," he said slowly. He'd learned that if he didn't react, if he didn't let on that the success of the band may have mattered to him, the music executives would inevitably cave. It's what people did when they faced losing something valuable.

"Well, it's not cancelled. Just postponed. The label loves the tracks you guys finished so far. They love your voice, your whole package."

"My package...," Sasha trailed off, his voice cracking into the receiver.

"They want you guys to record six more songs and turn *Faithless Gospel* into a full length album. The "Blood and Water" video is getting heavy circulation on MTV, and it's important to capitalize on that momentum. The label wants the band to fill in as the opener for smaller tours. When big names come into the area, or bands have to drop out or can't perform, that sort of thing. They want to ease you into this."

"So thoughtful."

"Here's the thing, though. Randall quit. And Fungus Reign is supposed to open for Iggy Pop in Portland next week."

"He broke his arm at the end of our last show. He's only quitting because it doesn't make a difference right now. He'll be back."

"Okay..." David trailed off. "You know, you've cost the label a lot of money in missed studio time. And if you guys can't play this gig..."

"We'll play it."

"You know a drummer who can learn all your songs in a week?"

Sasha smiled and lit a cigarette.

"Just so happens, I know the best drummer in the city."

Sasha joined Daan in the living room, who was watching infomercials for fishing gear. He sighed, and hung his head in his hands. His bandmates had been looking forward to the tour. And playing his music live was the next best thing to getting high, the only good thing about being signed to a major label. The label expected the band to work, and wanted Fungus Reign to open for their more well-known artists. The band had been scheduled to tour with Black Sabbath because their dark sound was a good fit and the exposure would help sell records. It would've been an amazing opportunity. Now it was gone, and Sasha knew he was to blame. He was beginning to feel that a band of sellouts was better than no band at all.

For Sasha, the best part of playing live was the uncertainty on people's faces. He loved converting non-fans into idol worshippers. Loved how he was able to mold that look of reservation into something much like devotion. He would solo on his guitar, flinging his hair until his sweat rained over the crowd, until he could feel the pulse of his emotion reflected back to him. And when he sang, it felt as if the whole world could hear his cry.

He watched Daan watch television in the room where everything changed. Though they had new furniture, a tan, suede couch and matching recliner chair, and had removed the Precious Moments figurines, Daphne was still present. She was in every cobwebbed corner that nobody cleaned. In every tile crevice that had turned black with mold. In the smoke that hung in the air, because even so close to death, Daan refused to hand over his cigarettes. Suddenly, nothing mattered anymore.

"Do you know why I come every week?" Sasha asked.

Daan looked at him, his face heavy and weathered. His eyes had lost all color, and flashed bright against his pupils like silver lightning. He didn't respond, and looked back to the glare of the television.

"Of course you don't."

Sasha grabbed his backpack from beside the couch. From it he pulled out a syringe, a cotton ball, a bottle of water and a baggie of cocaine. He placed them on the coffee table, and prepared the syringe in front of Daan, who looked incredulous.

"It's because I forgive you."

He lifted the sleeve of his brown and blue flannel, showing Daan his track marks. They were somewhat hidden by his tattoos, but only if you didn't look hard enough.

"And I don't want to hide anymore."

Sasha let the syringe sit on the table. He stared at Daan.

Daan's face contorted into a grimace, like a man who might cry if he only knew how.

"Will you answer something honestly?"

Daan nodded.

"Why did you wait until that summer to evict Birdie? You let them rent from us for a long time. Did you do it for Mom?"

Daan tilted his head, furrowing his brow.

"I did it for you, son. What kind of father would take away his kid's only friend?"

"So then what changed?"

Daan coughed in a torrential fit, and between his hurls and stuttering he said,

"You can't save them, Sasha."

The sound of Daan's rattling phlegm.

"Some people can't be helped."

The sound of Daan's lungs erupting.

"I've only wanted what's best for you."

"What changed!" Sasha shouted.

Daan took a series of deep breaths. He looked at Sasha with tears in his eyes, shaking his head as though what he would say was so painfully obvious.

"You fell in love with that girl."

Sasha took the syringe from the table and hit in his arm.

"I never used that money for drugs. I didn't use anything harder than pot at the time. Sending me to Everwood was the worst thing you could've possibly done. I only stole that money because I wanted to help Monti."

Daan let out a sob.

"Please, son! It wouldn't have ended well. Look at what you were willing to do for her. Regardless of your intention, your grandparents were devastated. You were throwing your life away. And I couldn't let you experience what I went through with your mother."

Sasha dropped his head into his hands, rubbing his palms over his forehead. He looked at Daan.

"Mom never meant to break your heart. But you definitely meant to break her."

IT WAS ONLY NINE O'CLOCK, but the dampness made the night feel older, as if it were ready to die and give way to dawn, exposing his secrets. He saw the sign. *PUBLIC MARKET PLACE.* A beacon for the denizens of Seattle, the roaches and feeders of the underground. And he'd become an inbred of the cycle. He walked through the market, down a flight of metal stairs and onto Alaskan Way. He idled beneath the viaduct and felt a rush when the moon broke free of inky, black clouds. He watched the bay come alive with silver ripples, but the last of his resolve waned when a voice said, "Looks like snow tonight." He and the dealer shook hands. He wouldn't be able to stop now. Not if he was going to do what he planned to do. Because he needed to feel good about himself, if he was to see her again.

He found a payphone and dialed.

"Hey," he said. He felt relieved, more than he liked to admit, to hear Monti's voice again. He sighed into the receiver, resting his chin on the hard plastic. He said the most honest thing he had in months.

"I need you."

A WEEK later Montgomery found herself sitting at the back of a tour bus. It was black and sleek, with a back room where Sasha slept. Everyone else had bunk beds, stacked on top of each other with a curtain for privacy. Everything about the bus signified wealth, that Fungus Reign was heading towards superstardom. As trees and truck stops and coffee stands whirred by, Montgomery couldn't help but feel proud of her friend. She couldn't help but feel regret also, for the times she told him he was reckless to pursue such a lofty dream. Because here he was, living it. And here he was, true to his word, bringing her along for the ride.

Montgomery sat on the couch in the common area of the bus, where Penn and David were playing cards at a small table. Sam, a long-haired, hippy-looking kid in his late teens working as the band's roadie and technician, sat beside her and watched as if everything Penn did would reveal the secrets to becoming a rock star.

"This is a fancy ride for a three-hour drive," Montgomery said.

"Yeah, well… it's been paid for," David said.

Penn shot him a look.

"We'll be touring soon, so we thought we'd test it out. I think we'll call her Bertha."

"So when did you start playing?" David asked, looking at her over his cards.

"When I was young, about seven years old. My mother was a singer."

"But you don't sing though. Why the drums?"

Montgomery smiled.

"I like to hit things."

David nodded. "I think that's awesome." He looked at Penn. "And drums are a much safer choice than the bass. It's always the bass player getting the band into trouble."

Penn scoffed. "I wish..." He ducked his head and shrugged at Montgomery. She'd given him another copy of *Southern Rain*, and so he'd forgiven her for smashing his favorite record.

Eventually everyone dozed off. Montgomery looked at the back of the bus. Sasha had been in his room since they left. And the narrow hallway between them felt insurmountable and ominous. But she needed to speak with him.

She knocked on his door. He didn't answer. She opened it. He was sitting on the bed, and had just finished tying off his arm. He didn't try to hide what he was doing, and seemed to almost welcome the discovery. He looked at her with the sad eyes of a naughty boy.

"Are you going to arrest me?" he asked.

THE SHOW WAS at Starry Night, a night club in Portland's Chinatown neighborhood inside a brick building that had been converted from an old church. There was an eery pall over the music community and regulars, as one of the club's promoters had disappeared after someone leaked the club had been involved in a counterfeit ticket scam. But everyone's mood began to lift once they realized Montgomery was able to learn six songs in time for sound check, and that Fungus Reign was going to put on a great show. It helped that she already knew what Sasha meant when he said,

"There's too much space," or "Can you make it snap more?" Or his incessant, repetitive requests of, "Make it so loud my heart stops!"

Those years of listening to punk records, listening to his drawl as it deepened with puberty, as he talked slowly over the screaming on his favorite songs, had stuck with her more than she realized.

Fungus Reign had a short set, only thirty-five minutes. And though he looked as if he'd rolled out of bed, threw on the nearest pair of torn jeans and a mangy, dark green sweatshirt, though his hair was unwashed and the bags under his eyes said, 'I wish I was anywhere but here,' the crowd loved Sasha. It was as if he had two voices, one commanded by his hands, the other manipulated by some higher power. Sitting behind her kit, Montgomery was reminded of that day at Mt. Calvary. Of how, after a non-believer had evoked God's presence for the staunchest of worshippers, she believed she would lose him. She could feel it, that he was meant to belong to the world, and that she would only hold him back.

But just as he garnered the love of Iggy Pop's fans, he turned his back on them. It was time for the guitar solo of their last song. Sasha faced Montgomery, resting his foot on the riser where her drum kit sat. He was taller now, and rougher around the edges. But in this position, he floated below her, his hair hiding his eyes until he looked up with an icy scowl, rather than the softness she'd remembered when he was a boy. And this change was evident by his playing. His guitar sounded bigger, angrier, and his fingers moved faster. He banged his head in rhythm with her heavy beat, his body movements evoking her to react in the same, hitting her drums so hard she felt it in her lower back, in her ankles, and in the severe ache of her rotator cuffs.

He went back to the mic, but she could still feel him, as though he held her hands from behind her, moving her arms so their sound became one. She looked at Penn, and from the way he moved she could see Sasha was with him also.

Sasha sang.

Damn delights from the flock

Let the rain wash our names from the sidewalk
Don't pray for the crows who cry alone on the plain
The flame and and field, left to waste.

Suddenly, Montgomery felt angry. At what might've been, had they continued making music the way only they knew how.

She stomped her kick drum on the offbeats.

Boom Ba Boom-Boom Boom Ba Boom-Boom

What might've been, had she run away with him like he'd asked?

She slapped her high hat so it nearly whisper-screamed.

Tstss Tst Tst Tstss Tst Tst Tstss Tst Tst Tstss
Boom Ba Boom-Boom Boom Ba Boom-Boom

What might've been, had they seen the pit that stretched between them was only manmade, and so could be just as easily undone?

She was so angry, it made both Penn and Sasha stop playing. She thrummed out the beat over and over, faster and faster, until her sticks began to shred and sweat pooled down her back and she saw her mother's face and how hard she fought and fought and fought so she hit and fought until she could barely breathe.

She pounded her toms so they battle-cried.

Tstaaa! Tstaaa! Tstaaa! Tstaaa!

DAA da da da DAA da da da

BOOM BOOMBOOM BOOM

Tstaaa!Tstaaa! Tstaaa!Tstaaa! Tstaaa!Tstaaa! Tstaaa!Tstaaa!

DAA dadada DAA DAA dadada DAA DAA dadada DAA

BOOMBOOMBOOM BOOMBOOM BOOMBOOMBOOM

And once the rage was gone she ended with every ounce of sound she could possibly make with all the force in her legs and arms and heart and being as the lights dimmed and the crowd screamed and Sasha stared at her slack-jawed,

CRACK CRACK CRACK!

The crowd erupted. Sasha got down on his knees and bowed to her in worship, and soon the crowd's wave of arms followed suit. Penn clapped and cheered. But she wasn't finished.

She tore apart her kit. She threw the mic stand down. The

crowd thought it was for show. But she was for real. She kicked her toms. She wrestled Penn's bass from his hands and smashed it on the ground. She only stopped when Sasha wrapped her in a bear hug.

He stroked her hair and said,

Sssh Sssh Sssh.

The lights went down.

AFTER THE SHOW, Penn approached Montgomery backstage and gave her a hug. He smiled and mumbled, "thanks for playing with us." David couldn't believe she'd been able to fill Jay's shoes, couldn't believe a woman had been able to play loud enough and hard enough to balance Sasha's blaring, fuzzy guitar solos and his Rock n' Roll scream. Members from Iggy Pop's band gave her props and shook her hand, asking what her plans were. She was gracious and answered their questions. She was only a part-time musician and no longer had a plan. But her main concern was Sasha, who leaned against the wall by the dressing room. Three girls surrounded him, smacking on gum and flipping their teased bangs out of their face. He was laughing with them, flirting as she'd never seen him do before. He slung an arm around one of the girls, while signing another's bra as she lifted her Fungus Reign t-shirt with his free hand. He looked up, and caught her watching. Her face burned, but she didn't look away. He winked. As though life itself was just a game.

She walked to where Sasha stood, fraternizing openly with his fans, and shoved him as hard as she could.

"You're an asshole," she said.

Everyone stopped talking, some with raised eyebrows, others open-mouthed, waiting for the drama that would unfold. She must have looked like a scorned lover. And in a way, she was, only his betrayal meant the difference between life and death.

She rushed outside into the alley behind the venue. Sasha followed.

"We're not in grade school anymore. At some point you have to stop hitting me and tell me how you feel."

"I feel cheated. You were supposed to have better. I was the one headed for trouble and you were the one who had everything." She turned to face him. "How bad is it?"

Sasha tucked his hair behind an ear. "It's not bad. I promise you. I'm just having fun, you know. Living like a rock star." He smiled, but it didn't reach his eyes.

"Can you stop?"

"Of course I can."

"Are you going to?"

He touched her face. "Eventually."

"I don't believe you," she said. "But I want to."

"I know. I don't believe me either."

THE NIGHT WAS clear and stars littered the sky. The city was quiet, except for the tavern music that spilled onto the streets, and the prostitutes that worked them. They walked around downtown Portland, making small talk and filling in the gaps for the eight years they'd been apart. He told her about his punk days in L.A., the craziness of the shows and the parties and the women. She told him about high school, how she'd graduated at the top of her class and went straight to the Police Academy. And about Richard, how he'd given her a home and stability and guidance.

They stopped by the fountain in the Pioneer Courthouse Square, a city park in the center of downtown. At the east end stood the courthouse, the oldest Federal Building in the Pacific Northwest, built in the colonial style of the 1800's. There was an old dive bar in the distance, and its green, neon sign gave the park a Beetlejuice-type eeriness.

"You're missing your idol," she said, motioning back in the direction of Starry Night.

"I'd rather be with you."

They sat on a park bench.

"After you ran away and I moved into the Adamsons' pool house, your dad moved all of our stuff into a storage unit."

"No shit."

"Yeah. I think he was hoping I'd be able to tell him where you were."

"Wow. That's a trip."

"When did it start?"

"Gosh, I don't know. That summer it was just now and again, you know? Like, just for fun. But I don't know how it starts, only how it ends."

"But if you had to put a date on the day you started using drugs, what would it be?"

"I guess when my dad sent me to Everwood."

"God," she said. "I feel so responsible."

"Why?" he asked.

"Because if it weren't for me and my drama, you never would've gone there."

"Your drama? Monti, I love you. Even if I'd known what would happen, I wouldn't have done a single thing different."

MONTGOMERY LAY IN HER COT, listening to the snores around her. It was after two in the morning, a time when she'd usually be awake and working the streets. She couldn't stop thinking about Sasha. About what he'd told her. About how things might've been different.

When they'd returned to the bus, David and Penn were visibly upset. Sam wanted to stay, and was pouting because the band had been invited to an after-party at a local punk house that opened it's doors to traveling musicians.

"No party," David had said sternly, and Montgomery could sense something was wrong.

The bus started smoking about an hour outside of Portland, and they pulled into a truck stop off the freeway. The nearest town was Castle Rock, an old timber village whose 2,000 residents had turned in for the night. The only payphone at the truck stop had been vandalized, its cord cut so it was inoperable, and David's cell phone was unable to get a signal. Eager to please, Sam had offered to walk into town to get help, but they'd all decided it was best to wait until morning.

Montgomery thought about going to Sasha's door. Pulling the lever quietly, to see if it was locked. But Penn was asleep in the bunk beneath her. David and Sam were in the bunks on the opposite side. Someone would hear.

But then the curtain moved, and Sasha hopped stealthily onto her bed. He was shirtless, and his boxers creeped out from the waist of his jeans. In the shadows, his black, winding tattoos looked as if they alone kept him rooted to the earth.

"What are you doing?" she whispered.

He unbuckled his belt as quietly as he could. He pulled the covers away, exposing her bare legs. He rubbed her calf, then pulled on it until she lay supine.

"Wait," she said.

"No baby." He laid his weight on top of her and unbuttoned her nightshirt, the soft cotton leaving behind goosebumps as he pulled it across her skin.

"No more waiting," he said. "It's now or never. And I'd quit playing music before I'd let it be never."

He kissed her body everywhere, his hair trailing behind him as he made his way down her stomach. He stopped between her legs, and she bit her lip to keep from crying out.

He slid his way back to her face and kissed her so deep she could hardly breathe. He hooked her knee in the crook of his elbow and pushed it towards her face and kept a hand over her mouth as he slipped inside. He moved slowly, quietly, kneading against the grain until her eyes watered. Soon she moved with him, and they rocked in and out of each other like the bay and the shore.

They stayed together until sunrise. They whispered and held each other, and Montgomery traced the tattoos on his body. Trees and roots that wound down his forearms. A skull on his shoulder.

And a mouth over his heart. She looked closer, and realized what she thought was some sort of logo or Rock emblem had been something else entirely.

"Why did you get this?" she asked.

He grinned. "Why not?" After a moment, he kissed her forehead. "Because I love your smile."

"And these," she said, tracing the scars along the angular landscape of his abdomen. "I don't remember these. What are they from?"

"Daan thought he could beat the punk out of me."

"You never said anything."

"Didn't feel right, burdening you with my issues when you couldn't admit your own."

She kissed his neck. "I can't believe you went to juvie for me, that you were willing to sacrifice so much."

He kissed her nose.

"You should believe it. And I wasn't the only one willing to make sacrifices for you."

"What do you mean?"

"I stole the money for you. But I gave it to Birdie."

"Even though you knew how addicted she was? Why?"

"I had faith that she'd do the right thing, that she loved you more than anything. I knew what that felt like. Know what she said?"

"What?"

"If I could hide from it, I would."

And for the second time that night, the stars shed light and made a path through water. One she'd have to follow.

Someone stirred in one of the bunks. Montgomery clutched Sasha tighter, as if being discovered could mean she'd lose him.

"I'm sorry," she whispered. "About that summer."

"Montgomery Laine," he said, his breath steaming hard into her ear. "Stop being ridiculous."

He nestled her face into his neck. "We were just kids."

When the birds trilled in the trees and the sky brightened, when Montgomery hovered on the edge of sleep she heard Sasha say,

"You were supposed to be my first. And I hope you'll be my last."

A TRUCKER CALLED for help on his radio the next morning, and the bus was on its way. Sasha rode in the front seat with the driver, his sneakers resting on the dash, his arms moving as he pointed at things they passed and made up stories.

"That motel's where Jimi Hendrix had a three-way with conjoined twins."

He had snuck back into his room before anyone had woken, and Montgomery was yearning to be close to him again.

"That was really messed up last night, David. The label was supposed to send us a new bus," Sasha said over his shoulder.

David looked tired, and rested his head on a yellow throw pillow.

"Yeah, whatever man."

"I'm serious," Sasha said. "Making me sleep on a queen bed when a twin will do? With no air conditioning so that my feet don't get too warm? Feet are supposed to be cold in the winter, you know that, right David? Anything else is just posing. We're a punk rock band, for God's sake." He looked at the man driving the tour bus. "It's no way to treat a rock star."

David was smiling now, though from the strain around his face it seemed he was trying not to. Sam chuckled and shouted,

"Gin!"

and Penn threw his cards down, contorting his face in mock disgust.

"I need you guys to be quiet," Sasha said. "I got terrible sleep last night. Seriously. The worst. I'll be contacting my lawyer, David. This just can't stand."

Sasha turned around and winked at Montgomery, making her blush.

And just like that, whatever tension had been present amongst the band members the night before was gone.

Before the bus reached Seattle, Penn pulled Montgomery aside. They sat together at the table furthest from the front. He slipped a small envelope into her hand.

"I'd love for you to come to my wedding," he said. He looked nervous, and kept looking over his shoulder.

"Oh, I couldn't do that. I don't know you that well, and..." She glanced at Sasha, who was still cajoling with the driver. "I don't know if it's appropriate I be there."

"Hold on," he said. He returned from the front of the bus with a notebook in his hand.

"I've been organizing all the notes for the album's dedication. I think you should read this."

She looked at the notebook, at Sasha's scratchy penmanship.

This album wouldn't exist without my best friend, Montgomery Laine. Monti, wherever you are, I'm sorry for making the chicken-shit move. I guess it's easier to say it this way than to your face. You are my muse. Every song on this album is either about you or for you or from you in one way or another. You never understood my music, but you are punk all the way. You do it all yourself. You never sell out. And God help anyone who meets you in a mosh pit. If not here, then on another plain, I'll be seeing you.

"You see? You're a part of this band, whether you like it or not." Penn touched her knee. "And I have a feeling.... It's really important you be there."

CHAPTER THIRTY-SIX

CORAL ALWAYS FELT the Headbanger Hunter would try to find her. Because he'd told her so much, during the fall of 1981.

She'd been working overtime on all the thoroughfares: Rainier Avenue, Broadway Street, The Strip, First Avenue. She needed the money to pay for an abortion. The baby's father didn't want to be involved, and she wasn't sure she could give another child to the State.

The Hunter was tall. And handsome, with the prettiest red hair and green eyes she'd ever seen. He took her to dinner, and seemed to find any excuse to use her name.

"How's the shrimp, Coral?"

"Would you like more water, Coral?"

"Coral, you have the most beautiful skin I've ever seen."

She'd been flattered, that this handsome white man would find her attractive. That of all the girls working that day, he'd chosen her. Because he obviously wasn't like the others. In fact, he was so kind she considered not charging him. Whatever happened between them that night would be because she wanted it.

But after dinner, he didn't open the door to his maroon sports car as he'd done before. He'd grown silent. She pointed out the street to the downtown hotel they were supposed to drive to, and he hissed at her to "be quiet!" Instead, he drove her north on Highway 99 into Shoreline, a quiet, unincorporated area of King County. He parked in an abandoned lot off the main street. It was dark. No streetlights. No windows. Just groves of evergreens that grew into the sky. And no one close enough to hear her scream.

"How many bastards have you made?" he asked, shutting off the engine.

Her jaw dropped, and she instinctively put a hand to her stomach. He saw this, and his face broke into a cold sneer.

"I bet your gash is filthy. I bet you don't even wash it between johns."

He slapped her hard across the face. He walked around to the passenger door, dragged her from the front seat and made her lie on her stomach in the back of the car, the door left open so the wind chapped her skin. And he forced himself into any space he could, even the ones that made her cry out in pain. Afterwards, he hit her with a closed fist, over and over until she felt the dried pulp on her face. She couldn't move, because he held her down in the seat with a forearm across her throat. She'd heard johns could be rough. And so she endured him, because she needed the money. It wasn't until he stopped, walked to the back of the car, and pulled a baseball bat from the trunk, that she realized he meant to kill her.

"You know what they call me?" he'd shouted from behind the open trunk. "The Headbanger. Or the Hunter. Sometimes both. Which is stupid because I'm neither."

The trunk slammed shut.

"I'm just a good samaritan, cleaning up the trash. Trash like you has no place in this world, Coral. And it's time to take you out."

He'd underestimated her. She was all knees and elbows, but knew how to use them, and was the fastest girl on the Rainier Varsity Basketball team before she'd dropped out of school.

Coral scrambled out of the car. But he was quick too, and used the bat to trip her feet. She fell to the ground. He swung the bat, missing her head by just an inch as she rolled her body hard into his shins. He lost his balance, and she sprang forward, knocking him to the ground. He grabbed her ankle when she tried to run again, and when she fell her cheek snagged against a rock. He was on top of her, trying to position the bat against her throat. His hand brushed against her mouth. She opened wide and bit, grinding her teeth until she tasted blood. He screamed. As he raised his hand to hit her again, she grabbed a handful of dirt and threw it in his face. While he struggled, she elbowed her way free. She ran into the grove of trees, ignoring as he shouted,

"I know where to find you!"

Coral ran until she found a main street. She called Scuzzo from a payphone, and he picked her up. She spent the night alone, in the bathroom of the old apartment they shared in the Valley, bleeding into a towel, the abortion no longer necessary.

CORAL JUMPED when someone knocked on her door. She'd been staying with her boyfriend in Capitol Hill. They were squatting in an abandoned home. The roof leaked, there was no heat or running water, holes in the walls let in the weather and the tile floor was so worn it looked more like dirt. But Coral's boyfriend had a warrant out for his arrest, and no one knew they were there. It was as safe a place as any.

"Who is it?" she asked, trying to sound tougher than she was.

"You probably don't remember me," a woman's voice said. "But I've been walking around downtown, all day everyday for a whole week now, trying to find you."

Coral leaned against the door, bracing herself for any violence that awaited her.

"Me and you, we used to know each other. Not long enough for me to get a street name, though. LaFuschia Martin, my name is Montgomery Jackson. I knew you as 'Coral'. I gave you my last candy bar, and held you in Pike Place one time. Do you remember that?"

Coral moved away from the door. Her hand hovered above the knob.

"Oh and Charlene wanted me to tell you 'hey.'"

Coral opened the door to find a tall, light-skinned woman with kinky black hair that went past her shoulders. Her gray eyes were friendly, and she wore a baggy Seahawks sweatshirt and jeans.

"Do you remember me?" Monti asked.

"Maybe a little," Coral said. Years of drug use made it hard to remember things.

"You think we could talk for a minute? About the Headbanger?"

Coral nodded. She let the woman inside. And after an extended moment of silence, she told the woman her story.

"Why didn't you tell the police?" Monti asked.

"I was pretty strung out those days. Got busted for possession and solicitation. It just worked out that I was arrested before I had a chance to go in on my own, you know? I was planning to, but I still had to make that money. Anyways, I tried to tell the cops that arrested me, but they just thought I was lying to save my ass."

Monti rubbed her forehead and tapped her foot, as if she was trying to shake out a thought.

"That night, when I was getting ready to do my first turn. You told me I didn't have to if I didn't want to. You told me not to get in the car."

Coral had her own thoughts to shake out, but this memory was the kind she could never forget no matter how hard she tried.

"I wasn't certain, but it looked like the one I got into the night I was attacked."

Coral looked at Monti, really looked at her for the first time since she'd walked inside. She dressed as though she'd spent time on the streets, but her skin didn't hang on her cheekbones with dead weight, and her fingernails were too clean. She wasn't working anymore. And the warmth in her frost-colored eyes suggested she never truly did. Not in the way Coral had, in the way that made it impossible to reenter the real world. You couldn't get a mortgage when your money was illegal and you slept through the day. You couldn't get clean when the only way to get through your job was to numb yourself to the abuse.

"Did you know a man was tried for the murders? It ended in a mistrial. Some of the jurors felt there wasn't enough evidence to prove he did it," Monti said.

Coral sucked her teeth. "You see where I live? You think I watch the news or read the paper? I don't got time to be worried about nothing or nobody else but myself. Because if I don't, I'm dead. I'm not gonna let you make me feel guilty when I tried to do the right thing and no one believed me!"

Monti touched her hand. "I didn't spend enough time in the Market to experience what you've been through. And I'm not going to say anything about what you should or shouldn't have done. But I'm a cop now. And *I* believe you. So what are *you* going to do to put this piece of shit down?"

IT WAS POURING rain later that night when Montgomery knocked on the Adamsons' front door.

"What are you doing here?" Clarke asked.

Montgomery held out the letterman's jacket. "I wanted to make amends. I shouldn't have taken this off you the way I did."

"I don't want it," he said, thrusting out his chin.

Montgomery smiled. "That's a shame. It looked really good on you."

Clarke stood a little straighter. "Really?"

"Yeah. You look sexy wearing it."

He shrugged, and took the jacket from her hand.

"You want to come inside? Have a drink?" he asked.

"Sure."

Montgomery hadn't spent much time inside their mansion during those two years she lived in the pool house. They never offered, and she wouldn't have accepted if they had. She had been a tenant and they her landlords. So Clarke's comment about Birdie that day at court not only struck her as odd, but had shattered the impression that her personal life had been unknown to him.

"Is Richard here?" she asked, taking a seat on a barstool in the kitchen.

Clarke reached into the cabinets and brought down two tumblers, setting them on the white counter island. He took a bottle of whiskey from the pantry and poured them each two fingers' worth.

"No. He's working. Trying to save his career. Some people still think he's guilty even though he wasn't convicted."

"Do you think he's guilty?" Montgomery sipped her drink.

"Of course not!" Clarke took a large gulp from his glass.

"How is your mom handling everything?"

"She left, moved back home with my grandma. She's selling the house and I'm technically not supposed to be here, but I forgot something."

He swirled the whiskey in his glass. Montgomery knew if she didn't speak, he would soon fill the silence.

"She wasn't happy to hear about his daughter, Evie. I stayed because I know he needs me."

"That's very…understanding of you."

"Well, I really love my dad."

"How did you feel about having a sister? And that she'd been murdered?"

"I don't know. It's not like I knew her or anything."

"What makes you so sure your dad is innocent?"

"He wouldn't have looked so guilty if he hadn't tried so hard to help those girls. He was always working late, bringing case files home. He tried to get them off the streets, back into foster care. I think he would've fostered some of them, but my mom would never allow it."

"Was that hard for you? Him working so much?"

Clarke shrugged. He put on the letterman's jacket and grabbed the collar, standing as if he was being photographed.

"I don't want to talk about this anymore." He finished his drink and frowned as if he was working through something in his head.

"Would you like to go out with me sometime?" he asked.

Montgomery tried to keep her face neutral.

"I'd love to, but I can't."

"Why? You have a boyfriend?"

She thought hard about that question. It had been a week since she'd been in Portland with Sasha, seven long days since he'd held his hand over her mouth to keep her from moaning too loud on the tour bus. She could think of nothing else. And then she pictured him with that syringe, the look in his eyes, and she could think of nothing else. And these two images kept her paralyzed.

She looked at Clarke. "I don't have a boyfriend. But I do have strong feelings for someone, and going out with you just wouldn't seem fair."

Clarke stared into his empty glass. "I really appreciate you being honest with me."

At the door Montgomery spun around and looked into Clarke's eyes. She had one more question.

"What did you mean when you said my mother was a welfare queen?"

He ran his hand through his hair. "I really shouldn't have said that. I don't actually think like that."

"I know. But why did you say it?"

"I was angry when the prosecutor tried to act like that photograph of them together meant he was guilty. I remember that day she came over. I was eating a snack in the dining room and heard them talking."

"What happened?"

"Well, I think she was like, still angry about that 'Spook' thing. She told my dad to stay away again, which I thought was kinda stupid since I'd already apologized. I couldn't hear the whole conversation, but I remember my dad grabbing his checkbook." He pointed at the drawer in the console table behind him. "So I figured she'd asked him for money."

He paused. "Sometimes I felt like those girls were taking advantage of him. He wasn't perfect, but you know, nobody was like, forcing them to be out there prostituting themselves. It wasn't his duty to help them."

Montgomery clenched her jaw. "Okay. Well, thanks for telling me."

"You're welcome."

She turned to leave.

"If you ask me," Clarke said. "It was probably a pimp that killed your mom."

She squeezed her eyes shut and turned slowly on her heels.

"Hey Clarke?"

"Yeah?"

"That jacket really does look great on you."

RAWLINGS WANTED to make sweet love to Detective Jackson after she brought him his witness. And she looked as if she needed it too, as if she'd been dragged through the mud and wanted to be bathed by loving hands. He wouldn't have minded doing that for her, not after she'd helped him put down a murder case, eight years cold.

It was those yellow fibers. The lab had narrowed down the wool fibers by comparing them to known clothing types. Then they tracked the yellow dye used to color those fibers, which was a unique blend of red, yellow and brown used by a local jacket company in the seventies, and discontinued since. That, combined with the witness's ID of his suspect out of a photo lineup, was enough to make the arrest.

"What made you piece it together?" he'd asked her.

"It was a lot of little things. A lot of luck. I was in the right places at the right times."

"That's bull."

"You weren't wrong when you said all the evidence pointed to Richard. That mood ring, I was the one who'd found it. When you showed me that picture, something bothered me about it. The explanation for his keeping it made sense but..."

"What?"

"When I found it, his reaction was one of surprise and…well, he looked defeated. Ashamed. If it was meant to be a keepsake, he wouldn't have been ashamed of it."

Rawlings was also bothered by something. "Where were you when you found the ring?" he asked.

She'd smirked. "Don't worry, boss. I'm done playing both sides."

Jackson called him over the radio, and Rawlings rolled out with his team of investigators. He knocked on the door of that white mansion atop the ridge of Magnolia. And he smiled when his suspect answered the door in a mustard-yellow letterman's jacket.

CHAPTER THIRTY-SEVEN

THE FIRST MURDER was Evie Tucker.

She was five feet, five inches and red like desert sand. She'd started smoking and drinking by age eleven, and had made her way downtown while looking for her mother, Eugenia.

The money was too easy to make. The drugs were too fun to use. And nobody seemed to care about what she did to get them.

Until she got busted, agreed to undergo counseling in exchange for probation, and finally, after thirteen years of hard living, learned who her father was.

After her appearance at court, he followed her in his fancy, red car, right into the lobby of the Ethelton Hotel where she sometimes stayed. He begged her to change her life. But he was too damn late. She just didn't care anymore.

But she was also curious. One day, almost three years later, she went to his house at the address he'd given her. In case she ever needed anything. And boy did she need it. She'd been sick for two days. And if she didn't get well soon, she thought her insides might leak through her eye sockets, the pain was so bad. She thought she'd shake right out of her clothes.

Her last trick had almost strangled her to death, because that's what he liked. And she was still too scared to start working again.

She was caught someplace between needing the high more than she needed to breathe but not so hooked she was willing to die for one more hit.

She went to the house.

A boy answered the door.

"Is Richard here?"

"No. Who are you?"

She didn't want to say. She hated this boy already. Hated that he lived in this house. She knew who he was. But the shakes were so bad, she could barely see. Nearly deaf, she was. And all she could think about was that sweet escape, that heavy nod that shuttled her to something even sweeter than peace. Oblivion.

IT WAS STRAIGHT OUT of Penthouse. He was finally going to get some. He liked the tight, white shorts she wore. And the gray dust all over her knees, as if she didn't mind standing on them in the dirt. He liked how she seemed to shiver all over, and believed just being in his presence excited her. He liked the flowy, green shirt that hung off her shoulders and showed off her belly button, a small black hole from which he couldn't force his eyes.

Girls at his school were so stupid. They'd date him for a few months, let him get under their shirts, a hand down their pants, and then they hardened like some stuck-up, Barbie bitch. He'd been voted most likely to become a supermodel in his junior high yearbook, but somehow, he was still a virgin. But he wasn't willing to be like his dad. Not yet. And he wanted this girl to want him.

Just looking at her standing there was sending the blood to his crotch. It made him feel excited. And it made him feel dirty. Shameful. Like when he'd been caught in the back of the Mustang. He watched while his father cheated on his mom with some black whore he'd picked up downtown.

"Don't matter who I am," the girl said. "Your dad owes me some money, and I'm here to get it."

"What's your name?"

"Evie."

"My dad has never mentioned you."

Evie glared at him. She was pretty. In a trashy way, a way that he'd never admit to his friends.

"I need my fifty dollars," she said.

Clarke invited her inside. He wasn't sure how to go about it. But he didn't hide what he'd been thinking, and he could tell Evie had picked up on it.

She stepped closer to him, and he smelled the sweet butter that glistened in her straightened hair. She grabbed his hand and rested it against her warm thigh.

"If the money ain't here, you can bring it to me later. I'm staying in room 217 at the Ethelton."

೪

EVIE DIDN'T THINK the boy would come. In fact, she'd almost forgotten about him. Her body hurt too much to remember anything but what it felt like to not be hurting. She answered the door. He played with his hair and thrust flowers into her face. He wore a button-up, as if he was on some sort of date.

"You got the money?" she asked.

"Yeah. I got the money."

She grabbed his hand and led him into the room. She pushed him on the bed. She almost felt sorry for him, the way his green eyes widened with excitement. But she felt even sorrier for herself.

Afterwards, she tried to rush him out. Because she needed to score. But he wanted to babble on as if he was her boyfriend or something.

If she'd been more sound of mind, instead of so dope-sick she couldn't think straight, she would've put everything away before she let him in. If she'd been more sound of mind, she wouldn't have let him in at all. But her room was a hoarder's box of mess, covered in things to make it feel as though she had a home, even though she never would.

"Who is this?" he asked, grabbing the photo she kept on her dresser. She took it everywhere she went. Because it reminded her of that photo of two people kissing in a black and white world during world war times, with a man in the sailor hat dipping a girl so it looked as though her back might break in ecstasy.

"That's my mom," she said without thinking. Because this photo was from a different war, though the world was still black and white. And her mother was the girl whose back would break in ecstasy. But the man who kissed her wasn't no hero. The man in the photo who kissed her mother would never be a hero no matter how hard he tried.

"Who is this!" the boy with red hair cried again. He was staring at the photo, holding it close to the television because it was the only source of light. He kept looking at the photo, then looking at her, then looking at the photo, then looking in the mirror that hung beside the television.

"Who are you!" he yelled.

If Evie'd had more sense, she wouldn't have gotten angry. She would have seen this boy maybe hurt like she did, and maybe didn't deserve his lot in the same way she never deserved hers. She might have seen that no amount of money or jewelry or nice cars or nice houses could ever replace the trust the world sometimes took from a child without permission.

Evie looked at the boy whose name she should've shared and said,

"How about I tell you in thirteen years?"

The boy's eyes clouded black. But she kept going.

"Because that's how long it took for the man in the picture to let me know he was my dad."

CLARKE HAD BLACKED OUT. He was driving the Mustang home when

he came to. Someone was in the car with him. She moaned, grasping at the air as though she struggled to find her way out of a dense fog. He looked at his fists. They were sore and bloody. The girl scanned the car, her eyes darting as landmarks passed. She screamed. She hit him, and called him filthy names, as if somehow the situation was entirely his fault. He continued to drive up Fifteenth Avenue, heading towards the Ballard Bridge. But she grabbed the wheel and swerved him down onto the intersection of Leary Way. She was fighting and screaming, and he kept driving until they'd reached Shilshole Avenue, surrounded by the quiet and abandoned warehouses that serviced the Fisherman's Terminal.

He stopped the Mustang under the Ballard Bridge. He pulled the girl out, and dragged her into the gravel just beneath the grates. All he could think of were her hands as she pulled down his pants, and how it still excited and disgusted him to think about. How he still didn't know what it meant, his father kissing that woman in the photo. How maybe he actually knew exactly what it meant. And the only way to stop the feeling, the one of excitement and disgust, was to forget the girl's face ever existed. He found a rock beneath the bridge. And he lay into the girl's face, over and over and over, until it could no longer be seen.

CHAPTER THIRTY-EIGHT

PENN'S WEDDING was on a cool afternoon at the beginning of March, and Montgomery had missed the ceremony. She hadn't been able to decide whether or not to go. Sasha never called, and she hated how it made her feel, pacing the hardwood floors of her house, punching her bag or pounding her drums so hard her sticks and shins splintered. Finally she decided she had every right to attend a wedding she'd been invited to. And she had every right to rub Sasha's face in his own shit if that's what needed doing.

Montgomery walked into Discovery Park, Seattle's largest at 534 acres and converted from the former Fort Lawton. It had a network of forested trails, meadows and historic military buildings. On a western-facing plain one had a view of Elliot Bay from the top of Magnolia. The trees were just beginning to bud, and it looked like the miles-wide field, which was caught between two rows of canary yellow barracks, one decorated with wedding tulle and white twinkle lights, was framed by a wreath of green pussy willows.

Montgomery smoothed the lap of her maroon, velvet dress as she walked down the cement path towards the rental hall. Her dress had a turtle neck that opened over her chest into a keyhole, and hugged her body from the ends of her wrists down to the ground. She didn't have a jacket that matched, and so carried one on her arm and shivered in the dewey air, heavy with the scent of spring rain.

On her right, atop a small knoll was an old, white chapel, and a stone wall encased it within a small grove of oak trees. At far the end of the field was a WWII era bus stop and horse stables. Colonial-styled houses, painted meringue with white trim, made a stoic line on a distant hill, and Montgomery thought to herself, *what a beautiful place to get married.*

Just as she approached the reception hall, Sasha came ambling from between the brush and trees. His black tux was creased and dirtied, and his white button-up looked as if it'd been torn open. He stopped short when he saw her.

"What are you doing here?" he asked.

"I was invited."

He quickly reassembled his face into a smile.

"I like your Reeboks."

Montgomery held up the shoes she carried in her hand.

"I can't walk in heels. I was going to change them once I got inside."

"Don't. You look better this way." He pointed at the jacket slung over her arm. "Shouldn't you be wearing that?"

She rolled her eyes and donned the navy blue police jacket she received when she first joined the force.

Sasha's smile widened. "Put on a pair of aviators and you're my dream girl."

"I always have been."

"So true."

The door to the rental hall opened with a clang.

"Where the hell have you been!" Penn shouted, jumping down the stairs and storming over to where they stood. He looked handsome with his hair gelled down on the sides. He wore a baby blue suit and neon yellow suspenders.

"You missed the ceremony! You're the best man! We didn't even have the rings!"

Sasha seemed to shrink beneath the scolding.

"I got lost in the park."

"Cut the shit. After we finished taking pictures, Jay said he watched you walk off into the park with Carmine and some other chick. Someone complained to park security that they saw people from the wedding having sex by the lighthouse. They almost made us leave."

Montgomery felt the blood drain from her face.

Penn's voice softened. "Would you really rather get high and have a threesome with people you don't care about than show up to your best friend's wedding?"

"Of course not." Sasha stared at his shoes.

Penn gave Montgomery a sympathetic look and then turned back to Sasha. "You're ruining everything. Don't you care?"

Sasha sighed and tilted his head back. He spoke at the sky. "Not really."

Montgomery stifled a sob and ran into the grassy plain, towards the cliffs that stopped at the beaches, which stopped at the ocean, which flooded towards the mountains. She'd wanted to believe Sasha would never make her cry, would never fall ill like Birdie had. She heard him following her in the grass, and when he grabbed her arm she covered her wet face with her hands.

"I can't believe you," she said. "And I'll never forgive you for this." She tried to push him away, but his will was stronger than hers. He wrapped his arm around her waist and began a slow waltz to the wedding music that swam through the park, and she could feel the sun against the back of her neck as it broke through the clouds.

"I never expected your forgiveness," he said. "I knew it was hopeless when I saw you at the Velvet Room, but I couldn't help myself. I'm sorry for needing you, and that it could only happen once."

"It doesn't have to be that way," she said, resting her face against his collar bone. His shirt smelled like fresh linen, and his skin salty like the sea.

"It does."

"How do you know?"

"I played a show in New York once. I was young and pumped up by the city. Everything was so loud and diverse, and I loved that you could find anything or anyone you wanted, at anytime of day. I met this really cool bartender after the show, and I told him I was jealous he got to live in such an amazing city. And he said to me, 'Growing up here is great, except for one thing. It completely ruins you for anywhere else. Anywhere you go, you'll always be thinking, *But I have that in New York. And it's better where I'm from.*'"

He lifted her chin, and with his other hand pulled her closer by the waist.

"You are my New York, Monti. You are my cabin at Mt. Rainier. You are every wonderful place or thing or experience this world has to offer and I am ruined. What seven-year-old should have the burden of meeting his soulmate? What sixteen-year-old should suffer the pain of losing her? Over and over again, I told myself it was just partying and I'd stop once I had New York again. So holding you here in the sun while there's clouds in your eyes and holes in your smile should be the only thing I need. Except it's not. There's something I want more. And that's why I know."

She dropped her head.

"Look at my eyes, Monti."

She obeyed, and the blue was nearly eclipsed by the blackness of his dilated pupils.

"I'm not a good guy right now," he said. "And I won't stop."

She watched as the tail-whipped ends of his yellow hair flayed over the black of his tux, watched as he walked away on the dirt path and into the trees until he was gone.

Penn waited by her car in the parking lot.

"I honestly thought having you here would keep him in line," he said. "I don't know what to do."

"It's your wedding day. Go enjoy your wife. That's what you do."

"You said you'd kill me if I let anything happen to him."

Montgomery started the engine. Penn gripped the open door as if he might hold the car hostage.

"Just focus on your family," she said. "And I'll start handling mine."

§

"So, we've got a problem," Rawlings said as he ushered Montgomery into his office. He'd paged her to meet him, and was stunned by her running mascara and swollen eyes.

"Yeah, you said that on the voicemail you left. What's going on?"

He almost regretted calling her, because now he didn't want to pile more misery onto what she was obviously dealing with.

"Clarke confessed to stalking his victims. He used the information found in the case files Richard would bring home. He'd get their names and ask for them while cruising First Avenue."

Montgomery shook her head. "I can't believe he's been the killer this whole time. I thought I knew him. An entitled son of a bitch, sure, but a killer? Did he say why he stopped?"

Rawlings crossed his arms. "He claims he never did."

Montgomery shuddered.

"So what's the problem?" she asked.

"It's your mother. Clarke confessed to all the murders, except for hers."

§

In that big, white house in Magnolia, Richard drank at the dining room table alone. The cold air whipped at his neck from the open window he'd had to break to get inside. He had no money. His career had tanked after the trial. Cassandra moved back home to the East Coast, leaving divorce papers for him to sign. And he had no claim to his house since it'd been bought with his wife's trust fund before they were married.

All he'd wanted was to make something of his life.

He was fifteen when he'd smelled the smoke. He'd walked downstairs and found his mother passed out. Her head lay sideways on the kitchen table, and there was a puddle of drool beneath her cheek.

Smoke billowed in beckoning wisps from the corner of the living room. He went to investigate, and found a burning cigarette left on a pile of old newspapers. What if he hadn't been awake? He would've died alongside his mother, who started her second bottle of tequila before three o'clock that afternoon.

He grabbed the bottle from her hanging hand, heavy and lifeless like the death she welcomed, and spilled a trail from her feet to the burning cigarette. He'd opened the front door. Smelled the fresh air. And never turned back.

Richard walked to the window and pulled back the blinds. There was an unmarked car parked just up the street. Everything was falling apart.

His mother. His lover. His daughter. And now his son. And for what? Who the hell was he supposed to be now?

FOG CROWDED the *RAIN CITY LIGHTS* sign atop the building of Fungus Reign's practice space, and it was still cold enough to wear a winter jacket.

"What are we doing here?" Carmine asked. They'd already used up her stash, and were on their way to Pike Place to get more when Penn paged Sasha.

"Don't worry, we'll make a stop afterwards."

They walked into the the band's practice room. The music gear had been pushed aside, and in its place was a circle of chairs. Penn, Jay and David sat next to each other. A couple of the band's mutual friends were there, as well as two executives from the label. And then his grandparents, huddled together at the edge of the circle, eyeing the beer cans, pin-up girls and bongs that were scattered around the room.

"What's going on?" Sasha asked, still reeling from the drugs he'd used with Carmine.

Jay stood and cleared his throat.

"Carmine, you need to leave. This is about the band."

Carmine took Sasha's hand and gave Jay the finger.

"She's cool man. Whatever you guys need to say, she can hear it."

Jay shook his head. "No dude, she needs to go."

Carmine sulked. "I don't understand where all this animosity is coming from."

"Because you look like you jumped straight out of a funhouse, " Jay said. "And I hated those as a kid, they freaked me out."

Sasha looked at Carmine. Her hair looked brighter than usual, a neon fuchsia, and in her Periwinkle sleeveless dress, she actually did look like a funhouse character. He tried but failed to stifle his laughter.

Penn stood up from his chair.

"You see Carmine? You are literally a walking nightmare. And we need to talk to Sasha alone. You can come back once we're done."

Carmine crossed her arms.

"Well, why does *she* get to be here?"

Sasha followed Carmine's gaze, and his breath hitched in his throat. Monti stood in the corner of the room, leaning against the wall where the amps were stacked. She wore a black blazer and a pair of black jeans, and out of the light she practically blended in with the amps. Was that how messed up he was? Where once he felt as though he'd orbited her sun, now he walked into a room too high and drunk to notice his best friend. She wouldn't meet his eye, just stared at her boots. She looked as uncomfortable as he felt.

"I don't want her here," he said, his voice hoarse.

Jay cleared his throat, and began reading from the piece of paper he held in his hands.

"Sasha,

You are the most talented person I ever met. When I saw you perform at the Nosedive in L.A., your hair was blue and in a mohawk. You were covered in beer and you didn't even sing, just screamed into the mic. But the way you played the guitar was unlike anything I'd ever heard or seen. And I knew I had to be in a band with you. It felt like destiny when I saw you walking these halls four years later, looking for someone to jam with. I know you don't believe in destiny, but I do. It's probably because you're too close to see it, because you and destiny are one in the same. That's how I know Carmine is not your destiny. And neither are the drugs you two do together…."

Sasha looked to his side and found that Carmine was no longer there. He moved to the door, but Penn beat him to it.

"Just listen," he said.

Sasha turned back to the circle. Monti frowned at him now. Jay continued reading.

"I thought that if I quit the band, you might wake up and see everything you were going to lose. I thought that if I quit the band, the choices you make would no longer affect me. But I was wrong on both counts. I have three brothers, but none feel like blood the way you do. That's why I had to come today, because I can't sit back and watch you throw your life away. I'm afraid you won't show to the gig that will be the band's big break. I'm afraid you'll bail on the studio, or will disappoint our fans with a bad performance. I'm afraid you'll disappear for weeks and not tell anyone if you're okay. I'm afraid that if I walk into a bathroom after you, I'll find you passed out over the toilet, blue in the face, hanging on to life by only a breath. I'm afraid of these things, because they've all happened, time and again in the years we've been a band. And I'm afraid the next time you get high will be your last.

The End."

Jay folded the paper and sat down in his chair.

Sasha undid his ponytail and let his hair fall over his eyes. He couldn't stand Monti looking at him that way. As though he'd betrayed her.

David spoke next.

"The label has decided to put the album and tour on hold until you finish at least one month of treatment."

Sasha scoffed. "I'm not going." He looked at Monti, who stood motionless in the corner. "You shouldn't have invited her," he said.

"This was her idea," Penn snapped.

"Whatever," Sasha mumbled, pulling at the sleeves of his sweatshirt. He made eye contact with each person in the room, saving Monti for last.

"I'm not going to rehab."

Penn's face turned red.

"Fuck you Sasha!" he screamed. "I was supposed to get married with my best friend by my side. I needed you to be there, SOBER! You're my brother, man. But ever since you got together with Carmine, you haven't been yourself."

"Are you seriously blaming her? That's so cliche, man."

Jay stepped forward. "Dude, we're not blaming her. It's just, you two are toxic together. It's not a relationship. If you weren't so hooked, I guarantee you wouldn't even like each other."

Sasha thought about his next move. And then he thought about the comedown, the deep, suffocating depression that took his mother before he'd mastered cursive. What they were asking for was too much. He rushed outside, into the rain. He was halfway across the street, headed for his truck when Monti called out to him.

"So that's it? You're not even going to try?"

She stood on the sidewalk in front of the building. The sky grew dark, and the sign that read "Rain City Lights" glowed indigo against the clouds, dense and dark like chalkboard.

Monti's body was haloed in bluish-purple light. A body he'd studied his whole life, a body of which he was now an expert. Her long arms, the muscle of her triceps as they bulged in time to her kick drum. Her lips, doughy like the pizza crust they devoured as kids, leaving crumbs in his sheets for him to sleep in. Her hair, a soft pillow for him to rest his face, a sponge to soak his tears.

Some people hated the rain, hated how cold it was, how it

leaked through coats and sneakers, through the sealant in the car door, into basements through the flower beds. Some people prayed for the sun, wanted only the lightness of life. But he'd always loved the rain, loved how it nourished everything it touched, loved how it only came when it wanted, how it could be forceful and direct, or as soft and playful as falling snow. And most of all, he loved how it forced her indoors, to take solace in his refuge, to sit beside him in the quiet dark and breathe and laugh and play and love, huddled together like two birds trying to keep warm.

"I'm a junkie," he said. "I think that's what I've always been."

A car honked at him to move out of the road. They both flipped off the driver until the car finally drove around.

"That's not true," Monti said.

"I promised that I wasn't the person you should've feared that summer. But you were right all along, not to trust me. I promised to take care of you and instead I became this."

She stepped off the curb and joined him in the street. The rain fell around them. She put a hand to his face. It was wet and warm, and all he wanted was to curl up inside and melt into her palm. But he kept going.

"I said I was protecting you by hiding those things about your mom, but really I just didn't want to lose you. I was selfish."

She shushed him and kissed his forehead. But he couldn't stop now.

"It made me feel safer when you were helpless, because then you couldn't leave me. I thought I could fix it all, I thought we could make it together. If I'd just spoken up, things could've been so different for both of us."

He let her hold him, stroking the back of his now soaked hair.

"And now all I want to do is pick up where we left off. But how can I ask you to love me like this?"

There was so much more to say, but he forgot it instantly. Because her hands were under his shirt, rubbing the skin and keeping him warm. He kissed her forehead and said *I'm sorry* for what felt like a hundred times. And each time she answered,

"We were just kids."

Sasha pulled back and wiped his eyes.

"But I'm not a kid anymore. This is what I'll always be. An addict. High or sober. I am an addict. And after everything that's happened to us, the least I can do is make sure you have better. Because what will you do when I mess up again?"

He turned his back on her and walked to the truck. His hands were cold and wet and he struggled with the keys. The keys jangled in his hands, because as she stood in the street, watching him go, she continued to shout, again and again and again until the engine turned over,

"I'd forgive you! I'd forgive you! I'd forgive you!"

CHAPTER THIRTY-NINE

RING RING RING! Ring Ring Ring!

There'd been nothing to do but stay home and wait by the telephone. Montgomery pulled the quilt she'd covered herself with up to her chin. Thunder rattled the window panes, and the hard tinker of new rain drummed against her roof. She watched the phone on the side table by the couch. The caller might be Victor, checking up on his partner. It might be her sergeant, wondering when she planned on coming back to work. It could be the neighbor asking if she'd be willing to feed her dog over the weekend. But her heart raced. She finished the rest of the beer she'd been drinking, and set the bottle on the coffee table. Something didn't feel right. She picked up the receiver.

"Hello?"

A rattle of words screeched through the earpiece, stinging her eardrum.

"Slow down! I can't understand you."

"Sasha died!" Penn sobbed into the phone.

"*What!* What happened?"

"Jay and I asked him to move out if he wasn't going to treatment. We left to give him some space, and when we came back we found him in his room. He shot a speedball. His heart wasn't beating and he wasn't breathing. We're at the hospital now. They brought him back in the ambulance, but the doctor said he's in critical condition. God, his face was so blue. What if we lost him?"

Montgomery coaxed Penn through his panic long enough to learn that Sasha had been taken to Harborview. She hung up on him mid-sentence and rushed to the kitchen to find her keys. Sasha couldn't die. She would not allow it.

She ran back into the living room, trying to force her sneakers on when she saw Richard standing in the doorway.

"I can't talk now!" she shouted. She tried to push him away from the door. "Move!"

He grabbed her shoulders and pushed her back onto the couch. She smelled alcohol on his clothes.

"Did you talk to the cops?" he asked.

"What?"

"I'm being followed. They're watching me, even though Clarke confessed. What's going on?"

"I don't have time for your bullshit right now!" she said.

"My bullshit?" His green eyes turned black, and Montgomery shrank back into the couch cushions. "After everything I did for you? I saved your life!"

Montgomery took a deep breath and forced herself to be calm.

"Let's get one thing straight. You rented to me. I worked twenty-five hours a week to stay in a pool house that was smaller than your living room. You were not my savior. You were my landlord."

"Did you know my mom once ran a clothes hanger down my back? Or that she drank away the money my grandfather set aside for my college?" He started pacing. Rambling. His eyes were bloodshot.

"Why the hell would I know any of that?"

"But you know what it's like. The guilt of having parents who love you but can't figure out how to take care of you? We're the same kind of people. Survivors."

Montgomery didn't answer.

"Just tell me if you told the police something that might reflect poorly on me. And then I'll go."

She clenched her fists. Sasha needed her. And she'd plow through a field of barbed wire to get to him. But she couldn't let Richard's sense of entitlement stand for one minute longer.

"Do you know what an alleybat is?" she asked.

He gave her a confused look.

"My mother called you that, when you and Clarke came to our doorstep eight years ago. *Alleybat*. It's a southern term used for white men, even die-hard segregationists, who secretly liked to visit black prostitutes."

Richard's mouth drew a hard line.

"The police have that photograph of my mother and you together on the last day she was alive. I don't think she would've asked a man who paid her for sex to help her troubled daughter."

"You don't know what you're talking about."

She shrugged, grabbing the beer bottle from the table and feigning a drink. "Maybe not. But Detective Rawlings said it best. All the evidence points to you. If Clarke didn't kill my mother, then who did?"

Richard rubbed his face with his hands. He gripped the ends of his hair, and let out a sigh until it seemed he deflated. "She tried to blackmail me."

"And you couldn't stand your reputation getting dragged through the mud. But that doesn't matter anymore. Your reputation doesn't mean shit now."

"Your mother was a junkie whore who would've ruined your life. You should be thanking me."

"My mother was an addict. But she would have survived. It may have been imperfect, but her life was valid. You took that from her."

Montgomery stood and moved towards the door, but Richard blocked her path.

"They can't prove anything."

"The jury was split fifty-fifty. The County Prosecutor is making a deal with Clarke. No death penalty if he's willing to testify against you. Plus, there's me and all those other women who know your secret. The motive will be clear to the jury this time around."

She knew her words were reckless. Goading. And Sasha needed her. But what good would she be to him, unless she was willing to fight for her family no matter the cost?

Richard got the upper-hand, moving from desperation to violence faster than she'd anticipated. He punched her hard in the face. Blood spilled from her nose. The bottle was still in her hand, and she smashed it against his head. He tackled her, and they fell against the coffee table, shattering its legs with their weight. She struggled against his hands, hands that seemed unsure of whether to fondle or maim. Eventually they decided to maim, and formed a collar around her neck. She saw tears in his eyes as her vision began to fade, saw the veins in his neck bulge as he squeezed harder and harder. Richard grabbed one of the broken legs from the coffee table. He hit Montgomery with such force she felt her teeth rattle. In her mind, the people who mattered most called out to her.

How can I ask you to love me like this?

Richard struck her in the head again. This time she knew it was hard enough to kill her.

Sometimes you make so much history with someone, the present just don't make sense.

She reached her hand along the floor and found the shattered mouthpiece of the beer bottle. She drove it into Richard's neck, and then everything went black.

Ballard, Seattle
Easter Sunday, 1990

MONTGOMERY'S HEAD dropped and hit the wall behind her bed. And with that subtle throb she remembered the safety of his bedroom, the warmth of his skinny arms wrapped tightly around her, his hands covering her ears to block the sound of Birdie's screams and Reggie's yelling. She lifted her head and let it hit again, a reset for the past and a promise to remember.

After the fight with Richard, she had come to on her living room floor. Victor was leaning over her, slapping her face and demanding she wake up. Her neighbors had heard the commotion and called the police. Richard was dead.

She'd been in the hospital for two weeks, and then spring came. She suffered a concussion, and multiple fractures in her face. There had been brain swelling, and she had reconstructive surgery that made her look like herself again.

She called David from her hospital bed for news of Sasha. And he had none to give her. After Sasha was stabilized, he checked himself out of the hospital and disappeared.

Montgomery had been given time off from work, time she'd need to recuperate. Time needed to deal with everything she'd been through. The death of her mother. And, what she was now coming to grips with, the unbearable loss of her best friend.

Though Victor had invited her to spend Easter with his family, Montgomery felt it was better to spend it with the memory of her own. She'd driven back to The Bridgewater, and went to her old apartment. A friendly resident named Linda let her inside because the place had been vacant for weeks.

"The landlord passed away days ago," Linda had said. "I offered to take charge of the place for awhile. I think the Coens are dealing with some things. Anyway, most people are moving out. I hear the building will be sold in the next few months."

Montgomery walked through each room and was reminded of Birdie. The living room, where she often lay on the couch, caught in a nightmare haze of intoxication. Or where she'd sit for hours braiding Monti's hair. The kitchen, where she sang Diana Ross songs and grilled hotlinks for dinner. Or forgot to stock the cupboards for weeks at a time. And then Montgomery walked to her bedroom, and the wall she'd shared with Sasha.

Once she'd healed enough, she tried to find him. But the hospital wouldn't release his information because she wasn't family and no crime had been involved. She scoured the obituaries, and was relieved she didn't find his name. Sasha's grandparents had moved away, having resigned themselves to his fate after the intervention. They knew nothing of his whereabouts. It seemed everyone who once knew Mikael Sasha Coen needed a break to mend their broken hearts. She called radio stations, went to punk shows, looking for any information about Fungus Reign's lead singer. And all she kept hearing was,

"I heard he OD'd."

She'd held on to hope, but too much time had passed. More than a month with no word. And now she tried to adjust to life again without Sasha Kent. She lifted her head, and let it fall. Hard. Loud. Whatever plain he'd found, she wanted him to hear.

And then two knocks sounded behind her, stopping her heart mid-beat. She heard it clearly. *I'm here.* Her shoulders slumped. His ghost would haunt her always.

She lifted her head again, and hit it against the wall. It was still sore, still hurt, and if she had to go on without him it was better this way.

But then two more knocks sent Montgomery from the floor to her feet and out the front door. She stopped on the stoop, and noted how different the courtyard looked. The cherry blossoms on the trees were in full bloom. The rhododendrons at the center of the courtyard were no longer dead, and had opened their fuchsia and purple buds. From where she stood, the blossoms blocked her view of the porch next door, but through the brush she saw an angel's yellow hair. There was a pair of Chucks on the welcome mat. She took a deep breath. She smelled burnt dandelions as a cloud of smoke wafted through the branches.

She stepped forward. There was Sasha, a sprightly grin on his face, so wide and big his nose nearly touched his lips.

"Hey Monti," he said.

"*Hey Monti?* I thought you were dead. I thought you OD'd in a back alley somewhere. Do you know how many morgues and medical examiners I called, looking for a John Doe who matched your description?"

He shrugged. "I'm sorry."

"I thought you were dead!"

"Technically I was when they found me. They revived me in the ambulance, but I died again. They shocked my heart at the hospital until I stabilized. And when I woke up, I knew what I had to do. I checked myself out of the hospital and went straight to rehab."

He stubbed out his cigarette and sat on his porch.

Her knees shook. She was afraid to look at him.

"It's been over a month," she said finally.

"It was a strict program. No calls in or out. To keep patients from contacting their dealers or trigger people. I left a note at the hospital to tell everyone, but they must have forgot or lost it."

Montgomery stared into the courtyard.

"Did you finish the program then?" she asked.

Sasha shook his head. "I saw my dad's obituary in the paper and left early. I wasn't ready to see my grandparents yet, so I went to his grave alone, to say goodbye. I tried calling you, but your numbers weren't working. And I didn't know where you live."

"Right," she said. "I had to change them." She explained that after her cover had been blown she didn't feel comfortable keeping the same pager and phone numbers, and was considering selling her house.

A moment passed.

"I'm sorry about your dad."

"Thanks. I should be dead too, you know?"

Finally her knees gave way to shock and she sank onto her stoop, pulling them to her chest.

"Were you going to find me?" she asked.

He walked to where she sat. He lifted her chin, forcing her gaze to meet his eyes, which were now an even brighter shade of blue.

"Of course."

"What about Carmine?"

"I wish her the best. But we were what we were. And that's over now."

"And what exactly are we?" she asked.

"There you go again," he said, rolling his eyes. He threw his cigarette on the ground. "We're best friends for life."

A white pigeon landed on the walkway by her feet and plucked between the cobblestones. Life teemed all around them. Montgomery wondered where Birdie's spirit was now, and hoped she could hear the radio waves that still played her music. And then she cried, in teardrops the size of rain.

He wiped the snot from her lip with his thumb.

"So damn beautiful," he said.

"So is the album any good?" she asked, wiping her face.

"Surprisingly yes. People seem to like it."

"I'm not surprised."

He laughed. "Who knows? Maybe this Grunge thing will take off. We might even make enough money to buy a cottage on Lake Union."

She cleared her throat.

"We?"

He wrapped his hands around hers and kissed each knuckle. "I want you to come on tour with me. I don't ever want to be apart from you again. Life won't be perfect. I won't be perfect, but I—"

"Yes." she said. "I'll come with you."

Sasha pulled her into his arms. There was more to say. More things to confess, more secrets to unearth. But now there was also time, and in his own way, she felt he must have always known. They would have their time. Either on this plain, or the next.

But one thing needed to be said, a secret she'd carried since the summer of 1981. So she nestled her face into his neck and whispered,

"I love you, Mikael Sasha Coen."

His hand went to the nape of her neck. He kissed her and grunted softly as he lifted her up to straddle his waist. As he carried her into that old apartment, the one she'd been so afraid to let him see, he grinned so wide that waves formed in the soft skin at the corners of his eyes. When he opened his mouth, she waited for him to say the same. But instead, all that came was a simple phrase, one that sealed forever their days to come.

"No shit, Monti."

THE END

ACKNOWLEDGMENTS

So many people helped make this book possible. First I'd like to thank my husband, who's been a solid rock of support and encouragement. It takes a special human to read a book five times, and you are that type of human. Thank you to my editor, Rowe Carenen of The Book Concierge, for pushing my writing to its best and calling out the places where I can improve. You helped me polish my voice and see the merit of my work. Thanks to my fellow writer, Alisa Weis, for multiple readings, notes and sharing the ins and outs of the process with me. Another thanks to a fellow writer, Courtney Carter, for pointing out the obvious that I was just too close to see. Thank you to Alyssa H., for your extensive notes and "criticisms." This book is better because of them. Thank you Rachel F., for helping me see that every character deserves to be humanized. I fell in love with more of my characters thanks to you. Madeline C. - you gave my ego a shot of confidence to share this story with the world, so thank you. Anna H., thank you for reading an early draft and giving your feedback - your enthusiasm was contagious. And finally, I'd like to thank my family, my mom, my dad, my brothers and sisters, for being who you are and for molding who I've become.